Summer on Blossom Street

**Center Point
Large Print**

Debbie Macomber's *Blossom Street* Series:

Summer on Blossom Street

DEBBIE MACOMBER

CENTER POINT PUBLISHING
THORNDIKE, MAINE

This Center Point Large Print edition
is published in the year 2009 by arrangement with
Harlequin Books S.A.

The text of this Large Print edition is unabridged.
In other aspects, this book may vary
from the original edition.
Printed in the United States of America.
Set in 16-point Times New Roman type.

ISBN: 978-1-60285-454-3

Library of Congress Cataloging-in-Publication Data

Macomber, Debbie.
    Summer on Blossom Street / Debbie Macomber. — Center Point large print ed.
        p. cm.
    Originally published: Don Mills, Ont., Canada : Harlequin, 2009.
    ISBN 978-1-60285-454-3 (library binding : alk. paper)
    1. Female friendship—Fiction. 2. Knitting—Fiction. 3. Large type books. I. Title.
    PS3563.A2364S86 2009
    813'.54—dc22
    2009008460

To Delilah

My God-given friend

CHAPTER 1

In knitting, as in life, we grow when we challenge ourselves. The concentration required to learn a new stitch or technique is good for both our hands and our brains.

—Bev Galeskas, Fiber Trends Patterns
and U.S. distributor of
Naturally New Zealand Yarns.
www.fibertrends.com

Lydia Goetz

Wednesday morning, a not-so-perfect June day, I turned over the Open sign at my yarn store on Blossom Street. Standing in the doorway I breathed in the sweet scent of day lilies, gladiolas, roses and lavender from Susannah's Garden, the flower shop next door.

It was the beginning of summer, and although the sky was overcast and rain threatened to fall at any moment, the sun shone brightly in my heart. (My husband, Brad, always laughs when I say things like that. But I don't care. As a woman who's survived cancer not once but twice, I feel entitled to the occasional sentimental remark. Especially today . . .)

I took a deep breath and exhaled slowly, enjoying

the early-morning peace. I just don't think there's anyplace more beautiful than Seattle in the summer. All the flowers spilling out of Susannah's Garden are one of the benefits. The array of colors, as well as the heady perfume drifting in my direction, makes me so glad A Good Yarn is located where it is.

Whiskers, my shop cat, as Brad calls him, ambled across the hardwood floor and leaped into the window display, nestling among the skeins of pastel yarns. He takes up residence there most days and has long been a neighborhood favorite. The apartment upstairs is an extra storeroom for yarn at the moment; perhaps one day I'll rent it out again but that isn't in the plans yet.

The French Café across the street was already busy, as it is every morning. The windows were filled with pastries, breads and croissants warm from the oven, and their delectable aroma added to the scents I associate with summer on Blossom Street. Alix Turner is usually there by five to bake many of these wonderful temptations. She's one of my dearest friends—and was among my first customers. I'm so proud of everything she's accomplished in the past few years. It's fair to say she reinvented her life—with a little help from her friends. She has an education and a career now, and she's married to a man who seems completely right for her.

Blossom Street Books down the street was ready for business, too. Anne Marie Roche and her staff often leave the front door open as a welcoming gesture, inviting those who wander past to come inside and browse. She and her daughter, Ellen, would be coming home from Paris later today.

Nearly every afternoon Ellen walks their Yorkie past the window so Whiskers and Baxter can stare fiercely at each other. Ellen insists it's all for show, that the cat and dog are actually good friends but don't want any of us to know that.

I grinned at Whiskers because I couldn't resist sharing my joy and excitement—even with the cat. In fact, I wanted to tell the whole world my news. Yesterday, we found out that we'd been approved for adoption. I hadn't yet shared this information with anyone, including my sister, Margaret. We've been through the interviews, the home test and fingerprinting. And last night we heard.

We're going to adopt a baby.

Because of my cancer, pregnancy is out of the question. While the ability to conceive has been taken from me, the desire for a baby hasn't. It's like an ache that never quite goes away. As much as possible I've tried to hide this from Brad. Whenever thoughts of what cancer has stolen from me enter my head, I try hard to counter them by remembering all the blessings I've received in my life. I want to celebrate every day, savor every minute, without resentment or regret.

I have so much for which to be grateful. I'm alive and cancer-free. I'm married to a man I adore. His son, Cody, now nine years old, has become my son, too. And I have a successful business, one that brings me great pleasure and satisfaction. When I first opened A Good Yarn, it was my way of shouting to the world that I refused to let cancer rob me of anything else. I was going to *live* and I was going to do it without the constant threat of illness and death. I was determined to bask in the sunshine. I still am.

So A Good Yarn was the start of my new life. Within a year of opening the store, I met Brad Goetz and we were married the following spring. Because of what I'd been through in my teens and again in my twenties, I didn't have a lot of experience with men or relationships. At first, Brad's love terrified me. Then I learned not to reject something good just because I was afraid of its loss. I learned that I could trust this man—and myself.

How blessed I am to be loved by him and Cody. Each and every day I thank God for the two men in my life.

Even with all I have, my arms ached to hold a baby. *Our* baby. Brad, who knows me so well, understood my need. After discussing the subject for weeks on end, after vacillating, weighing the pros and cons, we'd reached our decision.

Yes, we were going to adopt.

The catalyst for all this happened when Anne Marie Roche adopted eight-year-old Ellen.

I realized the wait for a newborn might be

lengthy but we were both prepared for that. Although we'd be thrilled with an infant of either sex, I secretly longed for a little girl.

I heard the back door close and turned to see my sister, Margaret. She's worked with me almost from the first day I opened the shop. Although we're as different as any two sisters could be, we've become close. Margaret is a good balance for me, ever practical and pragmatic, and I think I balance her, too, since I'm much more optimistic and given to occasional whimsy.

"Good morning!" I greeted her cheerfully, unable to disguise my happiness.

"It's going to pour," she muttered, taking off her raincoat and hanging it in the back storeroom.

My sister tends to see the negative. The glass would always be half-empty to Margaret. Or completely empty—if not shattered on the floor. Over the years I've grown accustomed to her attitude and simply ignore it.

When she'd finished removing her coat, Margaret stared at me, then frowned. "Why are *you* so happy?" she demanded. "Anybody can see we're about to have a downpour."

"Me? Happy?" There wasn't much point in trying to hold back my news, even though I knew Margaret was the one person who wouldn't understand my pleasure. She'd disapprove and would have no qualms about imparting her opinion. It's her pessimistic nature, I suppose, and the fact that she

11

worries about me, although she'd never admit that.

Margaret continued to glare. "You're grinning from ear to ear."

I made busy work at the cash register in order to avoid eye contact. I might as well tell her, although I dreaded her response. "Brad and I have applied for adoption," I blurted out, unable to stop myself. "And our application's been accepted."

A startled silence followed.

"I know you think we're making a mistake," I rushed to add.

"I didn't say that." Margaret walked slowly toward me.

"You didn't need to *say* anything," I told her. Just once I wanted Margaret to be happy for me, without doubts and objections and concerns. "Your silence said it all."

Margaret joined me at the counter next to the cash register. She seemed to sense that her reaction had hurt me. "I'm only wondering if adoption's a wise choice for you."

"Margaret," I began, sighing as I spoke. "Brad and I know what we're doing." Although Margaret hadn't said it openly, I could guess what concerned her most. She was afraid the cancer would return. I'm well aware of the possibility and have been ever since its recurrence ten years ago. It was a serious consideration and one that neither Brad nor I took lightly.

"Brad agrees?" My sister sounded skeptical.

"Of course he agrees! I'd never go against his wishes."

Margaret still didn't look convinced. "You're *sure* this is what you want?"

"Yes." I was adamant. Sometimes that's the only way to reach her. "Brad knows the risks as well as I do. You don't need to spell it out, Margaret. I understand why you're afraid for me, but I'm through with living in fear."

Margaret's eyes revealed her apprehensions. She studied me and after a moment asked, "What if the adoption agency doesn't find you a child?"

This was something Brad and I had discussed and it could certainly happen. I shrugged. "Nothing ventured, nothing gained. We'll take the chance."

"You want an infant?"

"Yes." I pictured a newborn, wrapped in a soft pink blanket, gently placed in my waiting arms. I held on to the image, allowing it to bring me comfort, to fill me with hope.

To my surprise Margaret didn't immediately voice another objection. After a thoughtful minute or two, she said in low tones, "You'd be a good mother . . . you already are."

I'm sure my jaw fell open. The shock of Margaret's endorsement was almost more than I could take in. This was as close as Margaret had ever come to bestowing her approval on anything regarding my personal life. No, that wasn't fair. She'd been partially responsible for Brad and me

13

getting back together when I'd pushed him away—a reconciliation that led directly to our marriage.

"Thank you," I whispered and touched her arm.

Margaret made some gruff, unintelligible reply and moved to the table at the back of the store. She pulled out a chair, sat down and took out her crocheting.

"I put up the poster you made for our new class," I told her, doing my best to conceal the emotion that crept into my voice. The last thing I'd expected from Margaret had been her blessing, and I was deeply touched by her words.

She acknowledged my comment with a nod.

The idea for our new knitting class had been Margaret's. "Knit to Quit," she called it, and I loved her suggestion. Since opening the yarn store five years earlier, I'd noticed how many different reasons my customers—mostly women but also a few men—had for learning to knit. Some came looking for a distraction or an escape, a focus to take their minds off some habit or preoccupation. Others were there because of a passion for the craft and still others hoped to express their love or cre-ativity—or both—with something handmade.

Four years ago, Courtney Pulanski, a high school girl, had signed up for my sock-knitting class, which contributed to her successful attempt to lose weight. Hard to believe Courtney was a college senior now and still a knitter. More importantly, she'd kept off the weight she lost that summer.

"I hope Alix takes the hint," Margaret said, cutting into my thoughts.

I missed the connection. "I beg your pardon?"

"Alix is smoking again."

It wasn't as if I'd missed that. She smelled of cigarettes every time she walked into the store. There was no disguising the way smoke clung to her clothes and her hair. And yet Alix seemed to think no one noticed, although of course everyone did.

"My guess is she'd like to quit."

"Then she should sign up for the class," Margaret said emphatically. "She could use it."

How typical of Margaret to feel she knew what was best for everyone. Currently, though, I was more amused than annoyed by her take-charge attitude.

My first customer of the morning—a woman I'd never met before—stepped into the shop and fifteen minutes later, I rang up a hundred-dollar yarn sale. A promising start to the day.

As soon as the door closed, Margaret set aside her project, an afghan for our mother who resides at a nearby assisted-living complex. "You know what's going to happen, don't you?"

"Happen with what?" I asked.

"This adoption thing."

I froze. I should've known Margaret wouldn't leave the subject alone. At least not until she'd cast a net of dire predictions. I understood that this impulse was one she couldn't resist, just as I under-

15

stood that it was motivated by her protectiveness toward me. But I didn't need to hear it right now.

"What's that?" I asked, hoping my irritation didn't show.

"Have you talked to a social worker yet?"

"Well, of course." I'd spoken to Anne Marie, and she'd recommended Evelyn Boyle, the social worker who'd been assigned to Ellen and had handled her adoption. Anne Marie and Ellen fit so perfectly together that their story had inspired me to look beyond my fears. So Brad and I had approached Evelyn.

Margaret shook her head, which annoyed me even more.

"Anne Marie gave me the phone number of the woman who helped her adopt Ellen," I said.

Margaret's brows came together in consternation and she tightened her lips.

"What now?" I asked, trying to remain calm.

"I wouldn't recommend that."

"Why not? It's too late anyway."

"This social worker deals with foster kids, right?"

"I guess so." I knew so, but didn't see how that was relevant. "Why should it matter?"

My sister rolled her eyes, as though it should be obvious. "Because she's got children in her case files," Margaret said with exaggerated patience. "She probably has lots of kids and nowhere to place them. Mark my words, she'll find a reason to leave some needy child with you. And not a baby, either."

"Margaret," I said pointedly, "Brad and I are going to adopt an infant. This social worker, Evelyn, is helping us through the process, nothing more."

Margaret didn't respond for several minutes. Just when it seemed she was prepared to drop the subject, she added, "Finding an infant might not be that easy."

"Perhaps not," I agreed, unwilling to argue. "We'll have to wait and see what the adoption agency has to say."

"It might be expensive, what with lawyers and everything."

"Brad and I will cross that bridge when we come to it."

Margaret looked away, frowning slightly, as if she needed to consider every negative aspect of this process. "There are private adoption agencies, too, you know."

I did know about them, but it made better financial sense to approach the state agency first.

"What about adopting from outside the country?"

Margaret was apparently trying to be helpful, but I wasn't convinced I should let down my guard.

"We're holding that in reserve," I said.

"I hear it's even more expensive than private adoptions."

"Yes, well, it's another option to investigate. . . ."

Margaret's shoulders rose in a deep sigh. "Are you going to tell Mom?"

With our mother's fragile health and declining mental condition it wasn't something I'd considered doing. "Probably not . . ."

Margaret nodded, her mouth a tight line.

"Mom has a hard enough time remembering that Cody's my stepson," I reminded her. On our last visit she'd asked copious questions about the "young man" I'd brought with me.

My sister swallowed visibly. "Mom didn't recognize Julia when we went to see her a few days ago."

I felt a jolt of pain—for Margaret, for her daughter, Julia, for Mom. This was the first time Margaret had mentioned it. Our mother's mental state had declined rapidly over the past two years and I suspected that in a little while she wouldn't recognize me anymore, either. Margaret and I shared responsibility for checking in on her and making sure she was well and contented. These days my sister and I had taken over the parental role, looking after our mother.

I could pinpoint exactly when that role reversal had taken place. It'd been the day Mom's neighbor found her unconscious in the garden. She'd collapsed while watering her flowers. Everything had changed from that moment on.

Our mother had ceased to be the woman we'd always known. Living in a care facility now, she was increasingly confused and uncertain. It broke my heart to see Mom struggling so hard to hide her bewilderment at what was happening to her.

"Mom will be happy for you," Margaret mumbled. "At some point her mind will clear and she'll realize you have an infant."

I smiled and hoped this was true, although I had my doubts . . . and I knew Margaret did, too.

The bell above the door chimed before we could discuss it further, and I glanced up at an attractive young woman who'd entered the shop. I hadn't seen her before.

"Hello," I said, welcoming her with an encouraging smile. "Can I help you?"

The woman nodded and toyed nervously with the cell phone in her hand. "Yes . . . I saw the notice in the window for the Knit to Quit class."

"Do you know how to knit?"

She shook her head. "No . . . well, some. I learned years ago but I've forgotten. Would this class be too advanced for someone like me?"

"Not at all. I'm sure you'll pick it up in no time. I'll be happy to help you refresh your skills." I went on to explain that there'd be seven sessions and told her the price of the class.

She nodded again. "You can sign up for the class no matter what you want to quit?" She stared down at the floor as she spoke.

"Of course," I assured her.

"Good." She set her bag and cell phone on the

counter. "I'd like to pay now." She handed me a credit card and I read her name—Phoebe Rylander.

"You're our very first class member," I told her.

"So the class starts next week?"

"Yes."

"The sign said Wednesdays from six to eight?"

"Yes. I'm keeping the store open late. It'll be my first night class."

I processed her payment and wrote her name on the sign-up sheet. "What are you trying to quit?" I asked in a friendly voice.

"Not what, who," she whispered.

"Oh . . ." Her answer took me by surprise.

"There's a man I need to get over," she said with tears in her eyes. "A man I . . . once loved."

CHAPTER
2

Phoebe Rylander

Clark made their breakup far more difficult than it needed to be. Phoebe had just stepped out of A Good Yarn when her cell phone chirped again. She didn't have to check Caller ID to know it was Clark Snowden, her fiancé. No . . . ex-fiancé.

The man she still loved, despite everything.

She'd had no choice except to end their engagement, no matter how much her heart ached. When she thought about what he'd done, she knew she couldn't allow him to dissuade her again. Not this time. It was final. She told herself that nothing he could say or do would change her mind. But soon she'd be walking into an empty condo and it would feel so lonely and isolated that she was afraid her resolve would weaken. This afternoon she'd felt stronger and more in control of her emotions. The knitting class would help, too.

Knowing what she had to do didn't make it easy. Clark's efforts to win her back turned the whole ordeal into an even bigger mess. He'd gone so far as to involve their families. But she couldn't, she simply couldn't, let herself give in.

Her cell phone continued to make its little chirping noises, announcing his call.

If Phoebe didn't answer, Clark would just leave a message and then try again. She flipped open her phone. "Don't call me anymore," she said emphatically, surprised at the conviction in her voice. "How many times do I have to tell you that?"

"Phoebe, please . . . don't. Let me—"

"This conversation is over." She started to hang up.

"Phoebe, please, the least you can do is hear me out."

"I already have." She hesitated. "There's nothing more to say."

"I'm begging you."

"Clark, I returned your engagement ring. It's over. We're through."

"You're angry and you have every right to be.

But if you'd give me five minutes, just five minutes, I could explain everything."

Oh, he was good—as plenty of juries had discovered. "No, Clark, I fell for that the first time. This is it. I'm done. As of a week ago we are officially unengaged."

"You don't mean that! You can't. You love me and I'm crazy about you. . . . You know that, Phoebe. You *have* to know that. I'd never, ever do anything to hurt you. I'd rather die."

"If that was the case, I'd be picking out a coffin for you because you *have* hurt me, Clark." Her voice faltered and she hated the fact that she'd shown even this small weakness. Rather than continue the conversation, she closed her cell.

Walking at a clipped pace, she hurried down Blossom Street, her vision blurred by tears. At the intersection, she swiped one hand across her cheek, sniffling despite herself. She'd gone for a walk on her lunch hour and ventured much farther than she normally did. In fact, she'd never set foot on Blossom Street before today. But by now she was late; she had to get back to work. Her boss at Madison Avenue Physical Therapy was understanding, but he wouldn't appreciate it if she kept a patient waiting.

When she got to the clinic, Phoebe was breathless. She hadn't eaten lunch and her stomach was already in knots. Well, there was nothing she could do about that.

Mrs. Dover was in the clinic's waiting room as Phoebe rushed in the front door. Her patient lowered the magazine and smiled at Phoebe, who did her best to smile back. Caroline Dover had undergone a complete knee replacement and she had a regularly scheduled appointment at one o'clock every Wednesday. She'd been seeing Phoebe for the past six weeks; they were making progress, although it was slow.

"Come on back," Phoebe told the older woman. She hurried ahead of her and drew in a deep breath. It would take a lot of resolve to get through the afternoon.

By concentrating strictly on her patients, she made it to the end of the day. At five-ten, she pulled on her jacket and grabbed her purse, eager to escape. Because she couldn't resist, she checked her cell phone. Clark had left three messages. Refusing to be swayed, she erased each one without listening.

She dared not let herself hear his voice; she was too susceptible. The problem was, she *wanted* to believe him. . . . She so badly wanted all of this to go away. That was why she'd impulsively signed up for the knitting class. Knit to Quit. The sign in the yarn shop window had been like a flashing neon light. If she was going to convince Clark that she was serious—and she was—she'd need a distraction to help her through the next few weeks.

Her hand tightened on her cell phone. Even as

her fingers pushed the buttons to erase Clark's messages, she yearned to talk to him. She wanted to be reassured of his love, wanted him to offer some plausible reason that would explain his need to seek out other women. However, there *were* no reasons. No excuses. Nothing he could say would change what he'd done.

"Did you and Clark have another spat?" Bill Boyington, her boss, asked as she started out the door.

The question caught her unawares.

"What makes you ask?" Phoebe had done her utmost to remain professional and therefore unemotional all week. She hadn't revealed to anyone at work that she'd ended her engagement.

"There were flowers delivered for you." He motioned to the receptionist's desk.

Sure enough, a huge floral arrangement sat on the corner. She wondered how she'd missed seeing it. Orchids, lilies and roses were interspersed among white hydrangeas; obviously Clark had spared no expense. It occurred to her that they were more fitting for a funeral than a reconciliation. But in many ways this *was* a funeral and Phoebe felt like weeping all over again.

Determined to be strong, she squared her shoulders. "I don't want them."

Bill looked at her oddly.

"Take them home to Louise," she suggested, knowing Bill's wife would enjoy them.

Her boss didn't seem convinced. "I'll bet he spent two hundred bucks on that."

For a second Phoebe was tempted to forgive him. Clark was so determined, so intent on overcoming her resistance. Still, she couldn't allow even a small crack in her defenses. She shook her head. "I . . . I don't want them. Either give them to Louise or throw them away."

"You're serious?" Bill asked, frowning as if this was some weird joke.

"It's over between Clark and me," she said bleakly.

"No patching it up this time?"

Phoebe blinked back tears. "No . . . I really don't have any choice."

Her boss patted her shoulder gently. "Do you want to talk about it with anyone? Me or . . ." He nodded at the receptionist's desk. Claudia was around the same age as Phoebe's mother.

"Thanks, but . . . I don't think so. I'm still feeling pretty raw."

Again Bill patted her shoulder. "I'm sorry. I know how much you loved him."

With a trembling hand, Phoebe reached into her purse for a tissue and blew her nose. Anger and indignation would only carry her so far and then the regrets would take over. Experience had taught her that she needed to be prepared, that she needed an action plan to combat the depression she knew would follow.

"Bill, would you do something for me?"

"Of course." His unquestioning allegiance and willingness to help made it harder to hold back the emotion.

"I'd appreciate it if you told Claudia to refuse anything else Clark Snowden has delivered here." Her voice broke just a bit when she said it. If she forgave Clark this time she'd lose all self-respect. Shunning him would take real effort. She'd have to work at it, just like Caroline Dover worked at making her knee function properly. But eventually Phoebe would learn to stop loving Clark. Eventually her heart would stop aching.

Bill hugged her as she left, and that brought fresh tears to her eyes. On her way to the parking garage her cell phone chirped again. She didn't bother to see who it was. A cheery jingle announced that she had a message.

As she walked, her feet slowed. Clark wouldn't give up easily. He would hound her, send her gifts, plead with her until she weakened. And she just might. She had before.

It was hard to turn away from the man you loved, hard to fight the desire to accept his excuses. This was familiar ground—territory she'd sworn she'd never travel again and yet . . . here she was.

No, she couldn't give in. She couldn't falter.

Walking by the phone shop, the same shop she passed five days a week, she really noticed it for the first time. After a short hesitation, Phoebe turned back. Staring in the window, she saw the latest cell phone accessories.

It went without saying that Clark would continue to call her until he made a dent in her resolve. She knew his plan and had fallen for it once before. If she was truly serious about avoiding Clark she had to send him the right signals.

Stepping inside the store, Phoebe looked around.

"You'll need to take a number," a harried saleswoman instructed her.

"I have a question."

"You'll still need to take a number."

"Okay." She got a ticket that read 57 and leaned casually against the wall. There was no reason to rush home. All that awaited her was an empty apartment—well, empty except for her cat, Princess.

The cat had more common sense than Phoebe did. Princess had never cared for Clark and the feeling was mutual. He'd said that when they were married, he wanted her to give Princess to her widowed mother. To her own disgust, Phoebe had tentatively agreed.

The saleswoman called out "Fifty-seven!" twice before Phoebe realized it was her turn. The process of changing her cell phone number was relatively easy, although it would be a nuisance to notify her family and friends.

Family.

One person she hadn't updated so far was her mother, who loved Clark and had championed him after the first . . . indiscretion. All Phoebe could do was pray that her mother would take her side this time around.

When she got home, she was feeling less vulnerable. Princess greeted her at the door of her condo, purring as she rubbed Phoebe's ankles.

Bending down and scooping Princess into her arms, Phoebe buried her face in the soft gray fur. "You were right all along," she whispered. "I should have trusted your character assessment. It would've saved me a lot of grief."

The light on her phone blinked madly; Phoebe could guess who'd made most of the calls. So she was surprised to discover that the first message was from her mother.

"Call me as soon as you're home," Leanne Rylander implored. "This is important, Phoebe. I *have* to speak to you."

Phoebe rested her forehead against the cupboard door. Sooner or later, she'd need to tell her mother, although from the tone of Leanne's voice, Phoebe suspected she'd already heard.

Taking a moment to gather her resolve, she reached for the phone.

"Is that you, Phoebe?" Leanne asked urgently.

"I assume Clark's contacted you?" Phoebe asked with resignation.

"He did. Oh, Phoebe, he's beside himself."

"He should be," she snapped. "Mother, *please* don't tell me you're on *his* side." It was difficult enough to withstand Clark's pleas—and nearly impossible to ignore them when her mother's voice joined his.

"Well, no . . . What he did was inexcusable."

"Thank you," she whispered.

"You have every right to be upset," her mother continued soothingly.

"Every right!" Phoebe thought fleetingly that Clark had used the same words. She wondered if Leanne knew the full story. "Mom, do you realize Clark was arrested for solicitation?"

"Yes, he told me. It's no excuse but he said he just didn't think being with a prostitute was really cheating."

The fact that Clark had told her mother the truth, or part of it, anyway, shocked her. "But . . . he tried to hire a hooker!"

She heard sympathy in her mother's voice. "Yes, I know."

"This isn't his first arrest, either."

Her mother released a long sigh. "I can only imagine how upset you are."

"No, you can't!" she cried. "You can't *begin* to imagine how upset and humiliated I am."

"But, Phoebe, sweetheart, you don't understand. There are extenuating circumstances. Clark was set up. This is a clear case of entrapment. He assured me it'll never go to trial. In fact, Clark is considering a lawsuit against the Seattle Police Department for causing him this embarrassment."

Phoebe closed her eyes. "Mother. Please listen to what you're saying. It doesn't matter if this was entrapment. It doesn't matter that the girl he tried to hire was an undercover policewoman. It doesn't matter if this goes to court or not. What *does* matter is that the man I was going to marry has this . . . this weakness. This need for other women. Not even for a relationship. Just for sex. How humiliating is that? I don't know if he's excited by the danger of picking someone up on the street or what. All I know is that I can't and won't marry a man who's betrayed me like this."

Her mother sighed again. "Phoebe, listen to me. You're my daughter and I want you to be happy—but you should consider the circumstances."

The conversation was becoming painful. "The bottom line is that Clark was willing to pay another woman for sex. Can I say it any plainer than that?"

"Oh, Phoebe, enough of that kind of talk. There's no need to be crude."

"How would you like me to pretty it up?" she cried. "Clark wanted to sleep with another woman? A woman he *paid!* Does that make it any less offensive to you?"

"Oh, dear. You *are* angry, aren't you?"

"Angry? Angry?" Yes, she was angry, and at the moment outrage was good therapy. "I'm furious, Mom. I'm also hurt, disillusioned, humiliated, devastated and brokenhearted—and that only scratches the surface."

Her mother didn't immediately respond. "You should sleep on it before you do anything drastic," she finally said.

"Sleep on what? The fact that the man I love is a cheat? Mom, do you actually believe this behavior will stop once we're married?"

"Men—"

"Mom," she wailed, cutting her off. "Don't make excuses for Clark."

"But, honey, he explained it to me. I know it's bad but he really doesn't feel that being with a . . . you know, call girl is cheating."

"So that makes it all right? You can't be serious!"

Her mother paused. "It's just that Clark's so well-connected and his mother and I—"

"His mother invited you to the country club and you met all the people you read about in the paper." It was hard to even say the words, but it was the truth. Leanne enjoyed being affiliated with the Snowdens. They were a wealthy, well-known family.

"Don't you remember how excited I was when you mentioned your new patient?" her mother said, sounding as brokenhearted now as Phoebe felt.

Phoebe did. Her mother's favorite section of the paper had always been the society pages. When Clark damaged his knee in a skiing accident, she'd been his physical therapist. He'd asked her out after their very first session. Phoebe had declined; it was against company policy to date a patient.

Clark had courted her for weeks, sending her flowers, bringing her gifts, charming her. Despite his efforts, she resisted every attempt he made and refused to see him outside the clinic—until he'd finished his therapy. She should've learned her lesson then. Clark didn't take rejection well. *She'd* broken off the engagement, and that had injured his pride. He wasn't about to let her walk away. In his view of the world, he was in control; he did the leaving.

The minute her mother had heard Clark's name, she'd been ecstatic. Early on, Leanne hinted that it would be fine to bend the rules just a bit for someone of his stature. As soon as they'd started dating, Leanne had told all her friends that her daughter was seeing Max and Marlene Snowden's only son. Clark was part of his father's prestigious legal firm and destined to become a full partner within the next five years. As far as Leanne Rylander was concerned, Phoebe had struck gold.

And Clark had swept her off her feet. Just like a romantic hero. He'd escorted her to parties and concerts. He'd lavished gifts on her, flattered her— and asked her to marry him.

The first sign of trouble came when a woman from his office stopped by the clinic and asked to speak to Phoebe privately. Kellie Kramer warned her that Clark had a nasty habit of paying for sex. Phoebe hadn't believed it. Why should she? This woman obviously had a vendetta against Clark.

Then Kellie had provided proof, showing her a copy of the warrant issued when Clark was arrested—the first time. She'd risked her job removing it from the file because she felt Phoebe had a right to know. Kellie claimed, as well, that there'd been plenty of other occasions. Clark just hadn't been caught.

Stunned, Phoebe had confronted Clark, who seemed genuinely surprised that she was upset. According to her fiancé this was something practically all men did. Sex with a prostitute didn't mean anything, he said.

Phoebe had found it difficult to listen to these inadequate excuses. She'd wanted to break off the engagement immediately. Clark had begged for a second chance. He'd called her at all hours of the day and night. He'd sent flowers and left pleading messages, until she'd weakened enough to agree. But the person who'd really convinced her to give him a second chance had been her own mother.

Leanne felt Phoebe needed to let Clark prove himself. Now that he understood such behavior was unacceptable, she'd argued, it would stop.

Clark had said all the right things. He'd vowed with tears in his eyes that nothing like this would ever happen again. He loved her. If Phoebe walked out on him, his life would be ruined.

He'd also told her that Kellie Kramer had been fired. She'd overstepped her bounds, and her insubordination wouldn't be tolerated. Her motive had been to hurt Clark and his father. If Phoebe ended their engagement, Kellie would succeed. He'd begged for another chance and, with her mother's encouragement ringing in her ears, Phoebe had let him convince her.

"Phoebe? Phoebe, are you still there?" her mother asked plaintively.

"I'm here, Mom."

"Promise me you'll sleep on this," she said again. "Your entire future is at stake."

"I already told you, Mother. There's nothing to sleep on. Clark was with this other woman. He admitted it!"

"Yes, but she entrapped him."

"That doesn't matter. What does is that he broke his word."

"I'm so afraid you're going to do something you'll regret for the rest of your life."

You mean something *you're* going to regret, Phoebe thought but didn't say. She closed her eyes. "I . . . I can't talk about this anymore. Good night, Mom."

She had to persevere, not only against Clark but against her own mother, who'd rather see Phoebe sacrifice her happiness and integrity than end a socially advantageous—but emotionally corrupt—relationship.

She couldn't get to that knitting class fast enough, she told herself wryly. She had to banish Clark Snowden from her life and that meant she needed all the fortification she could get.

CHAPTER
3

Bryan "Hutch" Hutchinson

Hutch sat in Dr. Dave Wellington's office, waiting. His physician and former classmate wanted to speak to him and that couldn't be good. He'd gone in for his annual physical, except that it wasn't so annual, and following a series of tests, Dave's nurse had ushered him into his office.

Hutch and Dave had been friends for years; they'd gone to high school and college together, both star football players. Before Hutch took over the family business, they'd golfed together every Wednesday afternoon. Golf. Like so much else, he'd given it up after his father's sudden death. Hutch had assumed the position of CEO at Mount Rainier Chocolates, and his life hadn't been the same since.

There was no longer time for golf in the middle of the day. And now, with the pending lawsuit . . .

Hutch didn't want to think about that because whenever he did he grew irritated. He figured that was bad for his blood pressure, which the nurse had told him was elevated. Little wonder. So okay, he probably wasn't as fit as he'd been in college. He didn't have time to work out. The company's demands made it impossible.

"Am I going to live?" Hutch joked as his friend walked in. Dave strode to the other side of his desk and pulled out the chair.

"That depends."

The smiled died on Hutch's lips. "You're joking, right?"

Dave leaned toward him. "Your blood pressure is far too high."

"Yeah, but . . ." He frowned. These days his stress level was through the roof, thanks largely to a frivolous lawsuit recently filed against the company. Some woman claimed that eating Mount Rainier Chocolates had made her fat. Oh, the lawsuit dressed it up with fancy words about "psychological dependence" and "exploitive advertising" but the plaintiff's weight gain was the basis of her legal action. Talk about stupid! And yet it was just the kind of case he'd often read about, in which a jury awarded huge sums as punitive damages. The plaintiff shouldn't have stood a chance of winning, but she had a crackerjack attorney who'd charged Mount Rainier Chocolates with malicious and willful misconduct and obviously hoped to create a precedent that would make his name. Every time Hutch thought about it, he became more agitated. Whatever happened to personal responsibility? To common sense? To accountability?

Hutch didn't care what it cost; he wasn't caving in, not to blackmail, and that was what he considered this. Okay, so his blood pressure was high; he'd deal with it. "Fine, I'll take a pill."

Dave shook his head. "It's more than that. You're working too hard, not exercising enough and I'm well aware that your diet is atrocious. You have all the classic symptoms of a man headed for a heart attack."

"Hey, I'm only thirty-five."

"Unmarried. And you know what the statistics say about the benefits of marriage—especially for men."

The fact that he didn't have a wife was also an issue with his mother. "I don't have time to meet women," he grumbled.

Dave talked right over that. "You also have a family history of heart disease."

"Yes, but—"

"How old was your father when he died?"

Hutch exhaled. "Fifty-eight." He'd never forget the day he lost his father. He'd been twenty-five, carefree, selfish and a little arrogant. Back in those days, he had time for golf and dating and friends. That had all changed, literally overnight.

He'd always accepted that eventually he'd step into his father's shoes as head of the family enterprise. But he'd figured it would be years before Bryan Sr. retired and he hadn't concerned himself with details about the business. Although Hutch had showed up for work every day, he hadn't paid much attention. Certainly not enough to assume the company's leadership on such short notice.

It had taken him two years to learn everything he needed to know about the business and the CEO's role. He'd made mistakes and the company had floundered. Not only did he have responsibilities to their employees, his mother depended on the income. Mount Rainier Chocolates had lost market share, and those lessons had been hard, but Hutch had slowly found his way. Over the next few years, the company did marginally better and then, gradually, there'd been a turnaround. His confidence increased. Hutch had encouraged the development of new products, which he wanted to test. He'd switched distributors. He was involved in every aspect of the business, from research to hiring to advertising and everything in between. And because of all that, he worked twelve- and fourteen-hour days. This wasn't a good time to be sued, in other words. Then again, was there ever?

"I'll write you a prescription," Dave said sternly, "but what you really need is a change in lifestyle."

Hutch resisted the urge to groan aloud. He couldn't add one more thing to his already crowded schedule. "Like what?"

"Diet."

Now, that rankled—although he agreed that he skipped too many meals and ate too much junk food on the run. "I'm not overweight," he argued.

"True, but you're close to being anemic, your potassium is low and you're putting your immune system at risk. That's one of the reasons it's taking your thumb so long to heal."

More than a month ago Hutch had sliced open the flesh between his thumb and index finger while he was trying to cut a rubbery, two-day-old piece of pizza. The injury had required several stitches. To this day it continued to bother him. His improperly healed thumb was what had prompted him to make the appointment for his physical. It'd been a year and a half since he'd last seen Dave in a professional capacity. Or any capacity, really, except for a drink at Christmas.

"What about vitamins?" Hutch asked hopefully.

"I'm going to recommend one and put you on iron tablets, as well as blood pressure medication, but that isn't enough. You need to start taking better care of yourself." The unspoken words hung in the air between them. Otherwise Hutch would end up like his father—prematurely dead of a heart attack.

And this time, there wouldn't be anyone to take over the business.

"Okay, I'll sign up for a gym."

Dave shrugged as if this wasn't a big enough concession. "You've got to do more than sign up. You've got to work out at least three times a week."

"Okay, fine. I'll do it."

"You might also join a class or two."

There was more? "What kind of class?"

Dave leaned back, grinning as he studied Hutch. "Don't laugh," he said.

"Why should I laugh?"

"Because I'm going to suggest you take up knitting."

Hutch shook his head. "This *is* a joke, isn't it?"

"No, it's not. I had a male patient come in to my office with sky-high blood pressure. He decided to start knitting—I think his wife talked him into it. I have to tell you I was shocked at the difference in him. I'm not kidding. I saw the evidence myself."

What a ridiculous idea. "Like I have time for . . . crafts?"

"It's only a suggestion, but it'll help your thumb, too."

Hutch jerked his thumb back and forth and felt it tighten. It was especially stiff in the morning. But knitting? Him? The gym he could handle, but knitting? If any of his friends or employees heard about *that,* he'd be a laughingstock.

"How about you?" Hutch asked, suddenly suspicious. "Do you knit?"

"Yeah." Dave grinned again. "My wife taught me."

"Get outta here!"

"It works, Hutch. Give it a try." Dave reached for his pad, wrote out the prescriptions and handed it to him.

Hutch stared down at the small sheet of paper. He never would've believed he'd be on blood pressure medication in his thirties. Dave was right; this didn't bode well.

"I want to see you again in two months."

Hutch nodded. He stood and pulled a candy bar from his inside pocket. "I brought you something."

Dave accepted it and looked up expectantly.

"We're about to launch this nationwide. It's called the Mount Saint Helens bar."

Dave turned it over and read the description. "Coconut covered with dark chocolate and a liquid chocolate center. An explosion of flavor."

"That's what I've been working on for the last eighteen months. We finally have a national distributor willing to give us a shot." His friend couldn't appreciate how difficult it was to get into the bigger markets when he was up against the huge candy companies. Hutch believed in this new product and was prepared to gamble on the future of the business. So far, everything seemed positive—*if* he didn't end up forking out millions over a frivolous lawsuit.

Dave examined the packaging and Hutch could tell he was impressed. "Sugar's not too high," he murmured, "and 70 percent cocoa is good."

"Practically health food," Hutch said with a smile. He began to turn away.

Dave stopped him. "Two months, Hutch. Don't disappoint me."

"I won't." He walked out of the office and galloped down four flights of stairs instead of taking

41

the elevator. He couldn't disagree with Dave about getting more exercise. But there just weren't enough hours in the day. He delegated whatever he could but so much still demanded his personal attention.

By the time he returned to his office, Dave was fifteen minutes behind schedule. Gail Wendell, his personal assistant, relaxed her anxious face the moment he walked in the door. She stood as if expecting him to need something right away.

"Mr. Williams is waiting in your office," she told him.

Hutch glanced at his watch. It was past one and he'd skipped breakfast and was feeling light-headed. Hardly surprising, considering all the blood Dave had taken earlier. "Can you order me lunch?"

"Teriyaki chicken?" Gail asked.

It was one of his favorites. High sodium, though. "Could you get me a salad with a side of cottage cheese?"

She raised her eyebrows. "I thought you didn't like cottage cheese."

"I don't, but it's supposed to be good for you. Doc said I need a more balanced diet."

"Okay, cottage cheese it is. Anything else?"

Hutch nodded. "Find a gym close to my place and sign me up."

His assistant made a note on her pad.

"And . . ." He hesitated, feeling a bit embar-rassed. "I need a knitting class."

He watched, but Gail didn't bat an eye.

"See if you can find an evening class somewhere in the downtown Seattle area." His condo was in a central location and he didn't want to travel far for this craziness. Actually, he'd be astonished if Gail found such a class, which would be fine by him. He could tell Dave he'd tried and leave it at that.

"I'll look into it right away."

Dave reached inside his pocket for the prescription. "Would you please have this filled for me, too?"

"Of course."

"Thanks, Gail, you're the greatest."

She grinned. "Your father used to say the same thing."

She was a valuable asset to the company, and Hutch was grateful she'd stayed on through this lengthy transition period. He knew, however, that it wouldn't be long before she retired. He hadn't worked out what he'd do then. Thankfully, it wasn't a question he needed to answer that minute.

The remainder of his day was routine, with meetings stacked on meetings, and it was nearly seven o'clock when he left the office. Instead of driving to his condo, he stopped at his mother's house in Bellevue. She'd tried to call him earlier in the afternoon but he'd been tied up in a meeting with the ad agency.

Gloria Hutchinson's face brightened the instant Hutch walked in the door. "I'm so glad you came by."

He made an effort to visit and update her on what was happening at the office at least once a week.

"Have you eaten dinner yet?"

"No, but I had a late lunch."

"It doesn't matter. You should eat." Hutch enjoyed the way she fussed over him and knew his mother needed to be needed. She'd adjusted to widowhood with difficulty. Fortunately his sister, Jessie, spent a lot of time with her, for which Hutch was grateful. The three of them had always been close and still were.

"I called you this afternoon."

"I got the message," he said as he followed her into the kitchen.

Opening the refrigerator, his mother took out eggs and cheese and set them on the kitchen counter. "I called to see how your physical went."

"It was fine." No reason to worry her.

"How's your cholesterol?"

"Excellent." That was true, anyway.

"Oh, good." The rest of his health was far from excellent, but he didn't plan to mention that.

"You're too thin."

Hutch didn't think so but he didn't want to argue. "Yeah, I could put on a few pounds," he said mildly.

She added grated cheese to the eggs and whipped them together. Melting a pat of butter in the pan, she poured in the eggs and cheese and stirred.

Without asking, Hutch slid two slices of bread—

whole wheat, he told himself righteously—in the toaster.

"I can't tell you the number of nights I made your father eggs for dinner," his mother went on to say. "The two of you are so much alike." As if she suddenly realized what she'd said, Gloria paused. "Do take care of yourself, Hutch. You will, won't you?" She turned to cast him a pleading look.

"Don't worry, Mom," he said in a cheerful voice that took a bit of effort. "I'm fit as a fiddle."

Her eyes grew sad. "I thought your father was, too."

"I got a gym membership today."

"That's wonderful." She spooned the scrambled eggs onto a plate and set it on the breakfast bar.

Hutch pulled up a stool. "I start an exercise program first thing in the morning." He'd set his alarm an hour earlier and launch into his three-times-a-week regimen. The prospect of losing an hour's sleep left him feeling vaguely depressed. But that was nothing compared to how he felt about the knitting class. . . .

The toast popped up; his mother buttered it and brought it to him. Hutch stood to get some of his favorite homemade raspberry jelly from the refrigerator.

"What you really need is a wife."

This was a frequent topic of conversation initiated by his mother. The truth was, Hutch would've liked nothing better, but meeting the right woman wasn't easy. Not with his busy schedule. He'd tried the Internet but that hadn't worked out. It was too complicated, too time-consuming. Neither had the dating service he'd contacted. Whenever he'd met a woman, who, according to the professional matchmakers, was perfect for him, the spark just wasn't there. It'd happened repeatedly until he'd finally given up.

"Do you have a candidate in mind?" he asked.

From her returning smile, he knew she did.

"It's a school friend of Jessie's."

"Okay." His sister had impeccable taste—in everything. "Divorced?"

His mother nodded.

"Kids?"

"A boy and girl and they're both darling."

"So you've met her?"

His mother grinned sheepishly. "Yes, and I think she's delightful. Would you like her phone number?"

"Sure." He had no idea when he'd be able to meet this "delightful" woman, but that was a minor detail. The least he could do was try.

"Don't tell the whole world, but I'm taking a knitting class." He offered this tidbit because he thought it would please his mother—and to shift the conversation away from his marital status.

Her eyes widened. "You?"

"It's supposed to help me relax and Dave said it might be good therapy for my thumb."

"Really."

"Yeah. It's on Wednesday nights. First class is next week."

She blinked. "You aren't pulling my leg, are you?"

"Would I do that?"

She laughed, then placed her hands on both sides of his face and affectionately kissed his cheek. "I never guessed that my son would become a knitter." She laughed again. "Not me, not my daughter, but my son."

His own laughter was a little forced. However, he'd committed himself now. And how hard could knitting be, anyway?

CHAPTER
4

Alix Turner

Friday afternoon Alix Turner hung up her baker's apron in the kitchen of the French Café. Her shift had started at five that morning and now, at two-thirty, she was finished. Jordan, her husband, was a youth pastor. He wouldn't be done at the church until close to six, which gave her time to take care of a few personal matters.

Standing in the alley behind the café, Alix lit her cigarette and took a long drag. She was down to five a day now, and was gradually working herself up to quitting completely. All five were smoked during breaks at work. Nights were the hardest, but she knew Jordan wouldn't appreciate her lighting up at home. Jordan didn't want her smoking at all. He was worried about the effects of cigarettes on her health, and he was right to be concerned. She worried about it, too. But all the dire warnings hadn't been enough to successfully break her addiction to nicotine. She was careful not to smoke in front of the kids in Jordan's youth group, since it wouldn't be appropriate for the minister's wife to provide such a bad example.

Jordan was well aware that he wasn't getting any angel when he married her. But her past wasn't a problem between them, and she wanted to be sure the smoking wasn't, either—or didn't become one. She'd quit before, lots of times, and she could do it again.

Alix blamed the wedding for the fact that she was smoking now. Between her friend Jacqueline and Jordan's mother, the whole affair had turned into a circus. In the midst of all that pressure, Alix had to find something to settle her nerves. She'd bought a pack of cigarettes on impulse and that was that.

In the end, Alix and Jordan had a lovely wedding at Star Lake, on Grandma Turner's property. However, by then the habit of smoking had insinuated itself into her life and now, a year later, she was struggling to break it.

Although Alix had never told her husband or her

friends about the cigarettes, they all knew. She couldn't hide the smell on her clothes, and the smoke clung to her hair, her hands. No one said anything. Jordan never chastised her or demanded she stop, but he wished she would, especially now that they were talking about starting a family.

Alix *wanted* to quit. It was important to give it up before she got pregnant. Jordan was due for a new job title and pay increase, and they'd decided it was the right time to become parents.

While she longed for a baby, her fears nearly overwhelmed her. She had so many concerns. So many doubts. It wasn't as if Alix had grown up with a good model of what a family ought to be. Her own mother was incarcerated at the women's prison in Purdy. This wasn't her first stint in jail, either.

The mere thought of having a child thrilled her and terrified her in equal parts. Alix had no idea what kind of mother she'd be. Her own parents had been drunk most of the time. And when they drank, they fought.

As a child, Alix had often hidden in a closet where she lived with an imaginary family. In her make-believe world, she had a mother and father who loved each other and cherished her. She'd held on to that dream for years, escaping to a fictional world because the real one had become increasingly violent.

She was still in grade school when the state

removed both Alix and her older brother from the family home. Between then and age sixteen, she'd drifted from one foster home to the next. Some weren't so bad, but a few were dreadful. The only constant had been her brother. He'd died of a drug overdose while she was in her teens.

As much as possible, she tried to put those terrible years behind her.

Despite all her misgivings, the prospect of having Jordan's baby excited her. She decided she'd knit a special blanket for their yet-to-be conceived child. That would show Jordan she was serious about quitting, too.

As she crossed the street to A Good Yarn, Alix noticed a sign in the window for a new knitting class. *Knit to Quit.* Alix had taken two of Lydia's classes previously and enjoyed them both. More than that, she considered Lydia one of her dearest friends. Other than Jordan and her mentor, Jacqueline Donovan, Lydia was the person she confided in.

"Alix." Lydia's face lit up the instant Alix stepped inside. Whiskers, who'd been asleep in the window, extended his front paws and stretched his sleek back as he yawned, showing his pink gums and needle-sharp teeth.

"Hey, it's been a while, hasn't it?" Alix walked over and gently scratched his ears. She loved Whiskers.

Lydia immediately hugged her. For a long time

Alix hadn't been comfortable with other people touching her. It still made her a little uneasy. Lydia was different, though, and she briefly hugged her back.

"I hope you didn't bring us any croissants," Margaret said, joining them at the front of the store. "I'm watching my weight and those croissants are my weakness. Especially the almond ones."

"Not to fear. We sold out."

"Good." Margaret sighed with relief. "What makes them so yummy, anyway?"

Alix answered her with a single word. "Butter."

Margaret rolled her eyes. "I should've known."

"Actually I came for yarn," Alix said. She was automatically drawn toward the DK-weight yarn in soft pastel colors. Lydia had displayed them in bins close to the cash register.

"Do you have a project in mind?" Lydia asked, following Alix's gaze.

Alix felt funny telling others about the baby. But this was Lydia, so she figured that made it okay. "It's kind of a secret," she began, "but Jordan and I are talking seriously about getting pregnant and I thought I should knit something for the baby."

Margaret looked at Lydia. "I don't suppose she happened to see the sign in the window."

Lydia's face flooded with irritation. "Margaret!"

"Well, Alix is smoking, isn't she? All the evidence says it's not good for a pregnant woman to smoke."

51

"I know that," Alix said, more defensively than she'd intended. "You can talk directly to me, Margaret. I'm standing right here. Besides, I'm not pregnant yet—and I only smoke five cigarettes a day."

"That's five too many," Margaret said emphatically.

Margaret made overcoming an addiction sound simple. "Quitting isn't easy," Alix said. "It's not just a matter of willpower, you know."

"I've never smoked," Lydia returned in that calming way of hers. "But I've heard that cigarettes are as addictive as heroin. We'd love to have you in the class, Alix, if you'd care to join."

The thought tempted her; still, she hesitated. "When is it?"

Lydia told her.

Alix decided to consider it. "What's the project?"

Lydia's classes were always interesting, not only the projects but the people who signed up. It was through that first knitting class that she'd met Jacqueline, who'd become both mentor and friend.

"I was thinking of having everyone work on a sampler scarf with a variety of patterns," Lydia explained. "From what I can assess so far, everyone's at a different skill level. The scarf shouldn't be too difficult for a beginner but it'll offer a bit of a challenge for more experienced knitters, too. I think it's going to be a lot of fun."

A sampler scarf appealed to her. "How many people have signed up?"

"Just two so far, so there's plenty of room."

"What's everyone quitting? Anyone else giving up smoking?"

Lydia shrugged. "Not that they said. And guess what? A man joined the class. His personal assistant found my ad in the phone directory."

"A man?" That was intriguing. Apparently plenty of men were knitters, although they didn't usually take classes. But then what did she know? She'd never actually met any and they had to learn somehow. So, why not a class?

"According to his assistant, he doesn't currently knit."

"What's he quitting?"

Lydia looked uncertain. "She didn't say, and I didn't speak to him personally."

"The lady who stopped in on Wednesday seemed almost distraught," Margaret inserted. "She said something about a man, so I assume she's either just out of a relationship or trying to end one."

The group would certainly be varied, which made for a stimulating mix of ideas and personalities. "You know, it might not be a bad idea for me to do this. I'm going to need a scarf for this winter and I can work on the baby blanket when I'm finished."

Lydia smiled. "It would be wonderful to have you in one of my classes again."

"It sure can't hurt, especially if you're sincere about giving up smoking," Margaret put in.

Rather than take offense at Margaret's attitude, Alix let her remark pass. Lydia's sister didn't have the ease with people or the engaging manner Lydia did, but she was a kindhearted person. A little critical, true—not that she was wrong in this instance. No matter what it took, Alix was quitting cigarettes once and for all.

Alix lingered a while longer and purchased what she'd need for the class, then headed home to their cramped apartment. It was near the church, on a street off Blossom. They'd have to make other living arrangements before the baby arrived, since the apartment was barely big enough for two.

She made a Cobb salad for dinner, with grilled chicken strips, blue cheese, hard-boiled eggs and sliced pickled beets, one of her favorite vegetables. Jordan liked turkey bacon on his, but she'd added that to the grocery list because they were out of it. Just as she was putting the finishing touches on their dinner, Jordan walked in.

"Hi, sweetie," he said, kissing her cheek. "How'd your day go?"

"Good."

"Mine, too," he told her. He sat down at their dining table. "Have you got a moment to chat?" he asked.

A formal request like that wasn't typical, so this must be important. "Of course," she said.

Jordan studied her as Alix left what she referred

to as her alcove kitchen and sat down at the small table with the two chairs.

"Something wrong?" she inquired, feeling slightly nervous.

"Not really . . . It's just that I got a call from my dad this afternoon. I must've spent an hour on the phone with him."

Jordan and his father kept in close contact and spoke often, so the call in itself wasn't unusual. "And?" she prodded.

"The family's been trying to sell Grandma Turner's house on the lake."

That wasn't new. After the funeral, the house had gone up for sale. The housing market was weak, and even lakefront properties weren't selling. Grandma's house was older, too. Alix felt the family was making a big mistake; she feared that in years to come they'd regret ever letting go of that wonderful home where Grandma Turner had spent her entire married life.

Alix loved the old house with its expansive front yard and wide flower beds. Grandma Turner had worked in her yard until the day before she died. She and Alix had developed a special friendship. Much of their time together was spent gardening, and the smell, the feel, of sun-warmed earth was something Alix would always associate with Sarah Turner. The older woman was everything she hoped to be one day: generous, gracious, accepting and loving.

Not only had Jordan's grandmother welcomed her into their family, but when Alix had been uncertain about going through with the wedding, Sarah had taken her in and sheltered her.

"Did the house sell?" Alix asked.

"Not yet."

Her immediate reaction was a feeling of relief. The price had been lowered twice, but still no takers. What would've sold quickly as little as a year ago lingered on the market now.

"Dad doesn't think it's a good idea to leave the house vacant for so long."

Alix agreed, but she was worried about renting it out. "Is he going to put it on the rental market?" she asked warily.

"Not exactly," Jordan told her. "Dad suggested you and I move there until a buyer's found."

Alix nearly squealed with delight. Not once had the thought occurred to her and yet it was the perfect solution. "Jordan, I'd love that!" Their apartment was so tiny they had virtually no storage space. Wedding gifts had to be kept at his parents' home because there was simply nowhere to put them.

No similar enthusiasm showed in her husband's eyes. "We need to think this through carefully, Alix. It sounds like a good idea now. I know you love the house, but there are complications."

Alix was aware of those, but she didn't care. Any inconvenience would be minimal compared to the benefits. "Well, sure, there are bound to be some changes," she said. "For one thing, we'll have to commute to the city every morning."

"It's more than that." Jordan shook his head. "There's no telling how soon it'll be before someone makes an offer and the deal closes. Then we'd have to pack up and move out."

"That's okay," Alix said eagerly. They didn't have much furniture so it wouldn't take long to move again. No matter how many—or how few—months they had in the house by the lake, it would be worth the inconvenience.

Jordan didn't seem to hear her. "In addition to that, there's no guarantee we'd find another apartment as reasonable as this one."

"Can't we trust the Lord to look after the details?" she asked. "Doesn't it feel as if this is meant to be?"

"Alix, do you know how much work is involved in moving?"

He had to be joking! She'd moved almost every six months her entire life. Her parents could never manage to pay the rent and still afford booze. Eviction never seemed to faze them; there were always other houses, other neighborhoods.

Later, as a foster child, Alix had never lasted long with any family. By sixteen she was essentially on her own.

"Jordan," she said, reaching out to take his hand. "I do know all the work involved in moving."

He frowned. "I can't believe you're serious about this."

"But I am! I think it's a great opportunity."

He squeezed her fingers. "I know you loved Grandma Turner and she loved you, but I didn't believe you'd actually be willing to move into her house. I mean, because of the distance and the fact that we'd have no guarantees . . ."

"What . . . what about rent?" Their budget was tight because they'd been saving every extra penny for a down payment on a house. Unfortunately, it couldn't be Sarah Turner's house with its extensive property. She'd seen the asking price and it was way beyond what they'd be able to afford.

Jordan shrugged. "The one advantage is that we'd be living rent-free."

Alix threw her arms in the air. "That's so generous! It's perfect, Jordan! Just perfect. We'll be able to save for our own house and when you get your raise, we can put that money aside, too." Another advantage was Sarah's furniture; much of it was still there. Whatever the family wanted had already been taken. The rest was left for whoever purchased the house.

"But you have to remember that utilities will be higher, and then there's the cost of the commute." He made these sound like monumental issues.

"I'll take the bus," Alix said happily. The house was on a bus route and she could always read or knit while traveling into the city, even if she had to leave extra-early in the morning. The afternoons wouldn't be so bad. She actually looked forward to riding the bus.

"I'll take public transportation, too, but there are certain days I'll need the car and with the price of gas—"

"Weren't you the one who just said we should leave the details to God?" she challenged.

"No, you did."

Alix giggled. "Then I heard it from you first."

"I never thought you'd go for this," he said in a wondering tone.

"Jordan, we were married at the lake house. Aren't you the romantic one in the family?"

"Yes, well . . ."

"There's another benefit you're forgetting," she whispered seductively.

"What's that?"

"We've been talking about me getting pregnant, right?"

"Right . . . when you're ready."

That was his subtle reminder that she had to quit smoking first.

"I should be soon. And Jordan, wouldn't it be wonderful if we conceived our baby in a home that's been in your family for generations?"

Jordan's gaze held hers. "That does sound like a wonderful idea. . . ."

Alix grinned. "I knew you'd think so."

CHAPER
5

Anne Marie Roche

Anne Marie and Ellen Roche hauled their suitcases up the stairs to the small apartment above Blossom Street Books. The flight from Paris had landed them back in Seattle midafternoon but it felt like the middle of the night to Anne Marie.

Nine-year-old Ellen had slept for most of the flight, but not Anne Marie. Instead, she'd cradled her daughter with one arm and reveled in each and every precious memory of their two-week vacation.

Even after nearly eight months it seemed unbelievable that she was now legally Ellen's mother. A few words in front of a judge had made it so. In truth, the judge's proclamation had been a mere formality. Anne Marie had become Ellen's mother in her mind, in her heart, long before anything was official.

Almost a year and a half earlier, on Valentine's Day, Anne Marie, together with three other widows, had made a list of twenty wishes. One of her wishes was to travel to Paris with someone she loved. That someone had turned out to be Ellen. A number of her wishes had come to pass, and some, like the Paris trip, had taken place in unexpected ways.

"Can we get Baxter now?" Ellen asked, racing out of her small bedroom, where she'd deposited her suitcase.

"In a little while."

Anne Marie missed her Yorkie, too. Her friend Elise Beaumont—one of the group of Valentine widows—had looked after Baxter these past two weeks. Anne Marie had predicted that by the time they got back, Elise would recognize the benefits of canine companionship.

"I want to teach Baxter French," Ellen said.

The girl had picked up phrases with surprising ease and was determined not to forget a single word.

"J'aime la France," Ellen said.

"Moi, aussi." Anne Marie remembered that much French, despite her exhaustion.

"S'il vous plaît, donne moi quelques bon-bons?" Ellen asked next.

"No, you can't have any candy!"

"Ah, Mom . . ."

Anne Marie returned to her unpacking. "Let me put in a load of wash and then we'll go get Baxter."

Ellen went back to her bedroom and finished unpacking her own suitcase. Then she stored it beneath her bed, which was littered with souvenirs she'd purchased in Paris for herself and special friends.

Anne Marie was touched by the girl's generosity. Ellen had spent all the money she'd saved from her allowance on trinkets for her school friends as well as Melissa, Anne Marie's stepdaughter, and her baby boy.

After dumping a load of clothes in the washer and setting the dial, Anne Marie called Elise and asked if it would be convenient to collect Baxter. She was told they could come anytime. While she was on the phone she decided to check her voice mail. With pen and pad in hand, she prepared to listen to two weeks' worth of messages. Among them, as she expected, were a number of calls from real estate agents.

The time had come to search for a home. The apartment above the bookstore had been fine when it was just her, but she had a daughter to consider now. Anne Marie had started looking and hoped to find a place this summer. With Ellen's circumstances so changed, she'd delayed the move, wanting the child to feel secure in her new life.

There were four or five calls regarding houses in the neighborhood Anne Marie had chosen. She wanted Ellen to be able to attend the same school. Unfortunately, the homes in that neighborhood were older, and many were badly in need of updating and repairs. Anne Marie would have to pay for the work, and that added extensively to the cost.

To her surprise there were a number of hang-ups, as well. She generally didn't get more than one or two a month, if that. After the third, she began counting and tallied seven. Someone seemed to be trying hard to get hold of her, although she had no idea who it might be.

Well, no point in worrying about it. Anyone this persistent was bound to try again. However, the fact that this person hadn't left a message was a bit disconcerting.

"Is anything wrong?" Ellen murmured as she entered the kitchen.

"No, of course not. Why do you ask?"

"You're frowning," Ellen said, studying her, sensitive as always to her moods.

It meant that Anne Marie had to be careful not to overdramatize her emotions. "Everything's fine. Now let's go pick up Baxter," she said, grabbing Ellen about the waist and tickling her.

The girl squealed delightedly.

Reaching for her purse, Anne Marie followed Ellen, who bounced down the stairs ahead of her.

Teresa, her full-time employee, looked up when Ellen burst into the bookstore. "I didn't expect you guys to go out so soon," she commented. She stood behind the cash register, opening the latest order from Ingram's, a distributor. Cartons of books were stacked behind her, a good indication that business hadn't slacked off while Anne Marie was away.

"We're going to get Baxter," Anne Marie explained. "We probably won't be long."

"Aren't you tired?"

"Exhausted," Anne Marie told her.

"Ellen seems raring to go."

That wasn't unusual. But Anne Marie suspected jet lag would catch up with her soon.

"Can we say hello to Susannah?" Ellen asked.

"Of course, but remember if she's with a customer we'll have to wait."

"Okay." Ellen held the shop door open for her.

Susannah had two customers, but when she saw Anne Marie and Ellen, she smiled and waved.

"Lydia and Margaret don't look busy," Ellen said as she peered into the front window of A Good Yarn. Her small hands framed her face and she stared at the sleeping cat. "Whiskers misses Baxter, too, don't you, Whiskers?" she asked. "Can we go in, Mom?"

"We can only visit for a few minutes," Anne Marie cautioned. "Elise is waiting and so is Baxter."

"Okay."

As soon as they walked in, Lydia leaped to her feet. "Anne Marie! Ellen! Welcome home. How was Paris?"

Anne Marie sighed luxuriously. "Wonderful! Everything I've ever imagined and more."

Lydia clasped her hands together and smiled warmly. "I knew it would be."

"How did the neighborhood survive without us?" Anne Marie teased.

"It was a lot quieter," Margaret called from the back of the shop where she sat crocheting. Then

64

she broke into a huge grin. "And a lot less inter-esting, too."

"I think Whiskers missed Baxter," Lydia said.

"We're going to get him right now," Ellen told her. "I missed Baxter more than anyone."

"I'd miss Whiskers, too." Lydia turned to Anne Marie, her eyes shining. "Listen, do you have a moment?" she asked.

"Sure," Anne Marie said. "What's up?"

Lydia's joy was contagious. "Brad and I are going to adopt. We've requested an infant."

Anne Marie clapped her hands excitedly. "That's *incredible* news."

"I heard this morning that Brad and I have been approved by the state."

"Did you speak with Evelyn Boyle?" She'd been Ellen's social worker and Anne Marie had come to treasure the other woman, who'd been so instrumental in facilitating the adoption. She'd given Lydia Evelyn's phone number weeks ago and had been wondering if anything had come of it.

Lydia nodded. "She's been so helpful. We really appreciate the referral."

"Any word on how long it'll be before you can adopt a baby?"

"Not yet. Brad and I are prepared to wait, though."

"Well, I hope it happens soon."

"Me, too." Lydia smiled happily. "We're celebrating tonight. Brad's taking Cody and me out to dinner."

"Can we come, too?" Ellen asked.

"Ellen! No, we can't," Anne Marie chastened. "It's not polite to invite yourself along."

"I know, but I have a gift for Cody from Paris and I want to give it to him."

"There'll be plenty of time for that later," Anne Marie reminded her and then, despite her best efforts, yawned. "I don't think anyone's mentioned jet lag to Ellen yet. I expect it'll hit her in a couple of hours." As for Anne Marie, her feet were dragging. Once they'd returned with Baxter, she was planning on taking a nap. Ellen would be tired by then, too—she hoped.

"I see you're starting a new class this week." The sign in the window had caught her notice and she found herself intrigued by the concept. Not that there was anything she needed to quit. She was satisfied with her life at the moment—more satisfied than she'd been since the early days of her marriage.

"Are you interested?" Lydia told her about the project she'd chosen. Anne Marie liked the sound of it, but a night class would be too difficult.

Maybe she could get the pattern from Lydia. She'd bought some beautiful yarn in Paris and a scarf would be the perfect thing to knit.

"Do you want to join the class?" Lydia asked. "Even if you're not trying to give up any bad habits. Alix already signed up because she wants to quit smoking—again."

"I'd love to—but I can't leave Ellen by herself. I want to make the scarf, though."

"I'll be happy to help with the pattern if you run into any problems."

"Thanks, Lydia, I'll keep that in mind."

As Anne Marie and Ellen left the shop, the little girl pointed across the street to the French Café. "Alix!" she cried. "I want to say hello to Alix."

"Ellen, we'll have to do that later. Besides, Alix is probably off work by now."

"Oh, yeah, I forgot. . . ."

"Are you ready for Baxter?"

"Yeah!"

Ellen ran ahead of her to where Anne Marie kept her car in the alley behind the bookstore. She wondered if she'd have any problems after leaving it for over two weeks unused, but the engine fired immediately to life. Anne Marie backed carefully out of her parking space and onto Blossom Street.

As they arrived at Elise's small condominium just north of downtown, Anne Marie called to let her know they'd be up in a minute. Elise and Baxter were waiting, and the instant Baxter caught sight of them he nearly did flips of joy. He barked and ran around, then leaped into Ellen's arms.

Ellen hugged him close as Baxter spread happy kisses across her face and yelped excitedly all over again.

"I think he missed us," Anne Marie laughed.

"Well, he certainly didn't lack for attention here," Elise said, smiling as she spoke. "I enjoyed his companionship so much I've decided to get a dog of my own."

Anne Marie had hoped this would happen. Elise had gone through a painful grieving period after her husband's death. It had been different, in some ways, from Anne Marie's experience, since Elise's husband—Maverick by name and maverick by nature, as he used to describe himself—had died of cancer. He'd lingered for several years, and Elise had said she was grateful for each extra day. Anne Marie's husband, Robert, however, had died suddenly, unexpectedly, of a massive heart attack.

"Do you want a Yorkie like Baxter?" Ellen asked.

"I'm not sure just yet," Elise said in a pensive tone. "I'll go down to the Humane Society and see what dogs they have available. It seems to me that Maverick would want me to adopt a rescue dog. He always believed in second chances. . . ."

Her gaze fell lovingly on the portrait of her late husband. He wore his cowboy hat and smiled directly into the camera. There was an irrepressible quality about him, Anne Marie thought. As though taking risks was all part of life—taking risks and accepting the consequences with a grin and a wink.

Anne Marie and Ellen left soon after. They'd brought Elise a gift of thanks for looking after the dog—a lovely blue silk scarf with a fleur-de-lis pattern. Ellen cradled Baxter in her arms, murmuring to him as they walked to the car. When they clambered into the backseat, Baxter curled up on Ellen's lap and promptly went to sleep.

By the time Anne Marie pulled in behind Blossom Street Books, both Ellen and Baxter were napping soundly. It seemed a shame to wake Ellen, who looked up at her with drooping eyes.

"We're home?" the little girl asked.

Anne Marie nodded. "Let's go upstairs and tuck you into bed, all right?"

"Okay."

Anne Marie helped her climb the stairs as the dog scrambled up ahead of them. Ellen fell asleep again within minutes. Anne Marie wanted to do a few chores before she took a nap herself. After transferring the wash to the dryer, she noticed the light blinking on her phone. Checking voice mail again, she discovered another hang-up.

Curious now, Anne Marie hurried down to the bookstore. Teresa glanced up from some new greeting cards she was arranging in the rack.

"Oh, Anne Marie, hi. I didn't expect to see you for the rest of the day."

"How are things?" she asked, looking around. She saw nothing out of the ordinary.

"Great. The summer releases are so good this year, I can hardly keep the new hardcovers on the shelves."

This was welcome news.

"Anything . . . unusual happen while I was away?" Anne Marie wasn't sure how to phrase the question.

Teresa bit her lip as if considering how to respond. "Not really . . . What makes you ask?"

"There were a number of hang-ups on my personal phone. I've never had that before. I just wondered if it was something to do with the bookstore."

Teresa shrugged. "I'm sorry. I have no idea."

"Okay, I was just curious. It's a bit odd, that's all." Anne Marie collected her mail and turned away.

"Wait a minute," Teresa said, stopping her.

Anne Marie turned back. "Yes?"

"There was someone here earlier in the week. A man. He asked to speak to you regarding a private matter."

A private matter? "Did he leave his name or number?"

"No. I asked, and he said he'd contact you later."

Again, this was all rather odd. "Did he say anything else?"

Teresa's eyes narrowed slightly. "No, not that I can recall."

"What did he look like?"

A smile wavered on her lips. "Actually, he was pretty hot."

Anne Marie grinned. "Define *hot.*"

"Tall—about six-one, maybe six-two. In good shape. He's nice-looking. *Very* nice-looking."

"Dark hair? Or blond?"

"Dark. And brown eyes. He seemed anxious to talk to you. Do you know who it might be?"

Anne Marie shook her head.

"What about your hang-ups? That might've been him. Is there a number on caller ID?"

Anne Marie exhaled loudly. "It came up No Data."

"Then I guess we'll have to wait and see if he comes by again."

That was her thought, too. Well, a tall, dark and handsome stranger apparently wanted to meet her. Things could be worse.

CHAPTER
6

Honey, knitting is so much more than just plain obsessive compulsive behavior . . . it's the healthiest addiction I know!

—Antje Gillingham,
owner of The Knitting Nest in Maryville, TN

Lydia Goetz

It's my habit to check each room before retiring for the night. Brad was already in bed, reading Michael Connelly's latest suspense novel. As I walked through the house, I checked the locks and turned off the lights in the kitchen. Then I looked in on Cody, who was fast asleep.

Chase, my stepson's golden retriever, slept on the braided rug next to Cody's bed. When I opened the bedroom door a crack, Chase—ever vigilant—raised his head. Seeing me, he lowered his head again.

All was well in the house and in my world. I had a new feeling of anticipation, a sense of excitement that stayed with me. It had begun the day I received a call from Evelyn Boyle regarding our approval as adoption candidates.

Just as I entered our bedroom, the phone rang.

"Good grief, who'd be calling after ten o'clock?" Brad asked as he set his book aside.

"I'll get it." I reached for the telephone on my bedstand, half expecting this had to do with my mother. "Hello," I said tentatively.

"Oh, Lydia, it's Evelyn Boyle. I apologize for contacting you this late."

"Evelyn?" My gaze automatically sought out Brad's. It didn't seem possible that they'd have an infant for us so soon. Nevertheless my heart raced. "What can I do for you?"

"Listen, I wouldn't ask if I had any alternative."

"Ask what?"

"I have a foster child—a girl. It's an emergency case and I need a home for Casey for two nights."

This was the very thing Margaret had said would happen, the very thing she'd warned me about. "Two nights," I repeated, the hesitation in my voice impossible to disguise.

"Casey is attending summer school and unless she finishes, she won't be able to go on to the eighth grade in September. Sending her back to seventh grade would be a disaster. She's only twelve and this is a difficult year for her."

"I thought summer school just started." A friend of Cody's had gotten behind in math and was now attending a summer program that had recently begun and would go through the month of July.

"Well, yes, but if Casey can spend tonight and possibly tomorrow night with you, that'll give me the necessary time to find her another long-term foster home."

"I see." I bit my lip, uncertain what to say.

"Two nights, Lydia. Just two nights. It would make a world of difference to Casey. She really can't miss a single class."

I looked at Brad. "I'll need to discuss this with my husband."

"Of course."

"Can I call you right back?"

"Ah . . . I could stay on the line."

"You're sure this is only for a couple of nights?"

"Positive."

"Okay, I'll ask." I held the receiver against my shoulder. "It's Evelyn Boyle. . . . She has a twelve-year-old girl who needs a bed for the next two nights."

"I take it she wants to bring the girl here?"

I nodded, ready to accept whatever Brad decided.

He seemed as hesitant as I felt. "I can't imagine Evelyn would ask if she had any other option," he said in a low voice.

"She told me Casey, that's the girl's name, is attending math classes at summer school and can't afford to miss any or she won't be able to advance to the eighth grade."

Brad made the connection right away. "In other words, she needs to keep Casey in the same school district."

"Exactly."

Brad met my eyes. "What do you think?"

I shrugged, torn between generosity and fear. I wanted to help Evelyn, but I wasn't the least bit prepared to deal with a twelve-year-old. Still, it would only be for a couple of nights. "I don't suppose it would hurt."

Brad nodded. "Tell her to bring Casey over." He squeezed my hand. "I hope we know what we're getting ourselves into," he muttered.

"So do I." I lifted the receiver to my ear. "Brad says we can take Casey for the next two nights." I made sure Evelyn understood that we were willing to fill in, but just for the limited time she'd requested.

The social worker's sigh of relief sounded over the phone. "I can't thank you enough. I'll be dropping Casey off in the next half hour."

"I'll wait up for her," I promised. Thirty minutes would give me a chance to straighten the spare room and remake the bed. I'd need to put a few things away, too. The sewing machine was out because I'd repaired Cody's jeans earlier that evening. In addition, there were plastic tubs of yarn and knitting projects I'd lost interest in for one reason or another. The closet was filled with clothes I planned to donate to charity and some items from before my marriage that I hadn't figured out what to do with. The room had become a catch-all, a storage area for anything that didn't have a firm place in our lives.

"Do you need any help?" Brad asked as I started toward the bedroom.

"I'm just going to put some stuff in the closet and move the sewing machine," I explained. "It's only for a couple of days," I said again.

"Right."

I could already hear Margaret's loud "I told you so" the moment she heard about this. Well, nothing I could do about that. I refused to allow my sister's ominous predictions to rule my life. I'd been asked to help out and I'd agreed. Nearly anyone would. It was part of the way we'd been raised, and I suspected that if Evelyn had called Margaret, my sister would've done exactly the same thing.

When I'd finished with the bed, I threw a robe over my nightgown, then joined Brad in the living room. The doorbell rang and he unlocked the front door with me right behind him. Chase immediately started scratching at Cody's bedroom door, ready to protect us against an intruder. Brad left to deal with the dog as I let Evelyn and Casey into the house. The first thing I noticed was how small Casey was for her age. Her backpack, hooked over one arm, was almost bigger than she was.

Brad returned, clutching the dog's collar as Chase whined eagerly, his nails scrabbling on the hardwood. "Chase, sit," he said calmly, and Chase did.

"Lydia and Brad, this is Casey Marshall."

The twelve-year-old refused to look at us. Instead she stared down at the floor.

"Hello, Casey," Brad said. "Welcome to our home."

"Welcome," I echoed. "I'll bet you're exhausted. I've got the bed made up for you."

Casey continued to stare at the floor.

"Casey," Evelyn murmured, her arm loosely around the girl's thin shoulders.

Reluctantly Casey looked up. Defiance flashed in her cool dark eyes. I wasn't sure what I'd expected. Gratitude? Appreciation? Relief? If so, all three were sadly lacking in Casey's expression and demeanor.

"Casey will walk to class in the morning," Evelyn said. "She's at Carver Middle School."

"I'll drive her," I volunteered. "It's on my way."

Casey's eyes darted toward Chase and softened perceptibly until she saw me watching her. Quickly she diverted her attention, glancing around the foyer and into the living room.

"I don't need a ride, I'll walk," Casey insisted.

"Whatever you want," I said. This wasn't going well. It was almost as if Brad and I were intruding on the girl's life, although we were making every effort to accommodate her.

"I'll leave you now," Evelyn said. She handed Brad her business card. "This has my office number and my cell. If you have any questions or problems, don't hesitate to phone anytime."

Brad accepted the card and studied it, although we already had Evelyn's contact information.

As Evelyn said her goodbyes, I stepped forward. She paused, a question in her eyes. I felt out of my depth here—what did I know about dealing with a troubled young girl? I was afraid this wasn't going to work, but Evelyn offered me a reassuring smile, then turned to leave.

Well, we'd agreed to do this, I reminded myself, and it was only for two days. We'd muddle through and so would Casey.

"I'll show you to your room," I said as soon as Evelyn left. I tried not to reveal how nervous I was.

Casey raised one shoulder, implying that she really didn't care. She was slender for her age, with straight, badly cut hair that fell below her ears. Her jeans were tattered but not fashionably and the wording on her T-shirt was long since washed out. It had once been bright pink, I thought, but was now an off-white with reddish splotches here and there.

I led the way down the hall. "This will be your room," I said. I turned the light on. The bed was made and everything had been put in the closet or stacked on the dresser. I'd brought in some fresh towels and extra hangers, which I'd laid on the quilt.

Casey looked around, then stepped into the room.

"Our son, Cody, is asleep next door. Chase is his dog. Cody named him that because he was always having to chase after him." She didn't smile. "Do you like dogs?"

Casey gave another one-sided shrug. "They're all right."

"Can we get you anything?" Brad asked, coming to stand behind me. He placed his hands on my shoulders.

Casey considered his question and shook her head.

"The bathroom's at the end of the hall."

She nodded.

"We'll see you in the morning," I said. I didn't want to leave the girl, but I didn't know what else to say or do. Casey obviously had no interest in conversation. She acted as though she couldn't be rid of us fast enough.

"Night," Brad said.

"Yes, good night," I added with what I hoped was an encouraging smile.

Casey nodded and closed the bedroom door. Brad and I were left standing out in the hallway.

"I hope we did the right thing," Brad whispered.

"Me, too."

I woke during the night and knew instantly that something was different. It took me a couple of minutes to realize what it was. Then I remembered—a girl was sleeping down the hall. A girl we didn't know. Casey clearly didn't want to be in our home and revealed no appreciation for our hospitality.

About seven, just before the alarm rang, Cody's voice boomed, "Mom, there's a girl in the house!"

Tossing aside the covers, I jumped out of bed. I grabbed my housecoat and hurried into the kitchen, where Casey sat at the table, eating a bowl of cereal. Cody stood in his pajamas with Chase at his side, tail wagging slowly. My son seemed to be in a state of shock.

"This is Casey," I said.

Cody's eyes narrowed. "Does she talk?"

"Casey, this is our son, Cody."

The girl went on eating her breakfast. "Uh-huh."

"He's not bad for a boy," I told her and was rewarded with the glimmer of a smile.

"Mom," Cody protested. "She's not *staying,* is she?"

Whatever slight enjoyment had shown in Casey's eyes immediately disappeared. "Don't worry. I'll be gone soon."

I swallowed the words to tell Casey she was welcome to stay as long as she needed. To be honest, I didn't know if that was true. We'd merely agreed to a short-term visit; I suspected that was all we could handle. This girl made me feel uncomfortable in my own home.

"I'll be late tonight—" I said, reaching for the coffeepot. Brad worked for UPS and had left an hour before my alarm went off. He'd made coffee, as usual—for which I was profoundly grateful.

"Can we go to the park?" Cody asked as I filled a mug and stirred in cream and sugar. "You said we could."

"I'll take you and Chase there this morning," I told him after my first restorative sip. With the shop open until eight that night, I wasn't due at work until twelve. Margaret would open and Elise would arrive later in the afternoon.

Casey mumbled something I couldn't decipher.

Cody bristled. "I'm not a baby."

"Babies go to the park with their mommies."

"Casey, that was uncalled for," I said disapprovingly. "You're a guest in our home, but I can't and won't put up with any form of disrespect. Is that understood?"

Casey didn't respond. Instead she stood and carried her bowl to the sink. "I need to leave for school now."

"It's too early, isn't it?"

"No," she said with such defiance that I was hard-pressed to question her.

Casey disappeared into her room and returned a minute later with a book in her hand.

"What time does school get out?" I asked.

"Noon."

"Oh." We hadn't discussed this aspect of Casey's stay. "Brad won't be home until after three."

Casey didn't seem concerned. "I'll hang out with my friends," she said.

Frankly I wasn't sure that was such a good idea. "Would you like to catch the bus and come on down to my yarn store? I'll talk to Ms. Boyle and see about getting you signed up for day camp if you like. Maybe you could start tomorrow."

"A *yarn* store?" Casey made it sound like the last place on earth she wanted to be.

"I can teach you to knit if you're interested."

Casey ignored me.

I wrote out instructions about which bus to take and which stop to get off at and gave her the fare. Casey stuffed the coins in her jeans pocket and left soon afterward.

As soon as the door closed, Cody whirled around to face me. "She's not staying, is she?"

"It's just for a couple of days," I promised him.

"I don't like her."

"We haven't had a chance to get to know her," I said. In every likelihood that wouldn't happen, either.

No sooner had I spoken than the phone rang. A quick glance at the call display screen told me it was Evelyn Boyle.

"Morning," I said as cheerfully as I could manage.

"How'd it go last night?"

Looking at the kitchen door, I wondered what to tell her. "Okay, I guess," I finally said. "Casey went to bed almost right away." I couldn't prevent a sigh. "Unfortunately, things didn't start off well this morning. I'm afraid Casey and Cody don't have a lot in common."

"Give them both time to adjust," Evelyn advised.

"Time?" I echoed. "Casey's leaving tomorrow, isn't she?"

Evelyn paused, and that short silence told me everything I needed to know.

"The problem is," Evelyn said with obvious reluctance, "the family that was going to foster Casey is on vacation. I can try to find another one, but that'll take a day or two, and we're always short of homes in the summer." She paused. "I hate to ask this, but to be on the safe side could she stay with you for a week? I should be able to find a suitable family in that time."

"A week," I repeated, a little shocked. "I'll need to check with Brad, of course."

Cody walked up and stood directly in front of me, hands on hips, his thin arms jutting out as he glared up at me. His thoughts on the matter were perfectly clear.

"And of course Cody will have a say, as well."

At this rate I'd need clearance from Chase, too.

"I'd appreciate it if you'd get back to me as soon as you can," Evelyn said.

"Of course." Slowly I replaced the receiver.

"Mom!" Cody wailed.

I looked down at him. "Can we be kind enough to let Casey stay with us an entire week?" I asked. "What do you think?"

My son shook his head. "No way!"

"Okay, then I'll call Ms. Boyle back and tell her it's impossible. Casey will have to pack her things and go."

Cody studied his bare feet and shifted his weight from one leg to the other. "Just a week, right?"

"That's what Evelyn said." I didn't mention that a few hours before, the social worker had promised that it would be two nights at the most.

Cody chewed his lip. "What do *you* think?"

I was of two minds, but compassion won out. It wouldn't be an easy adjustment for any of us. Casey wasn't going to make this pleasant. However, I'd seen that glimmer of a smile in the young girl's eyes. When I'd said Cody wasn't bad for a boy, Casey and I had connected for a few seconds.

"Mom?" Cody pressed.

"If your father agrees, I think it'd be fine for Casey to stay the week," I told him.

"Okay," Cody muttered. "But only one week and she can't call me a baby ever again." He nodded emphatically, as if that settled the point.

CHAPTER
7

Phoebe Rylander

At 5:20, forty minutes before her first knitting lesson, Phoebe left work. Clark didn't know about the class; her mother didn't, either. Phoebe couldn't explain why she preferred it that way; she just knew she did.

It was hard not to answer the constant phone calls and messages, although she realized the sanest approach was simply to ignore them. She should have changed her home number, too, but that was more complicated, or so she told herself. She hated to admit that maybe, with one small part of her, she *did* want to hear from him. Still, she wasn't even sure whether Clark was calling because he wanted her back or because he couldn't tolerate what he saw as her rejection. Winning was everything to him. If their engagement was broken *he* wanted to be the one to call it off. He hadn't let up since she'd returned his engagement ring.

Phoebe badly needed a reprieve. The knitting class offered that.

Although Leanne hadn't admitted it, Phoebe was fairly certain her mother had joined forces with Clark's parents and was doing everything in her power to repair the rift. What her mother, and more importantly, Clark, failed to understand was that Phoebe intended to keep the breakup permanent, no matter how much she wished it could be different.

Even now, knowing what he did, part of her yearned to believe that Clark didn't comprehend what he'd done or why she was upset. But she'd told him the first time—she couldn't have been any clearer—and this time she wouldn't give in. She *couldn't.* Phoebe knew his weakness for paid sex would continue after they were married. It was an addiction; it had to be. Otherwise he wouldn't go on taking these ridiculous risks. Twice he'd been arrested for solicitation, and heaven only knew how many other occasions there'd been, occasions when he'd been fortunate enough not to get caught. A woman off the streets, no less. If he was going to pay for sex, Phoebe would have assumed he'd want a higher-class prostitute. Unless it was the danger that thrilled him? She sighed. None of this made sense to her.

He'd promised it would never happen again and she'd reluctantly forgiven him that first time. She'd believed he was sincere—and yet he'd succumbed again. She needed a man who'd be completely committed to her and their relationship. Addiction, attraction to danger, whatever it was, Clark seemed either unwilling or unable to control it. She refused to put her emotional and physical health at risk because of his weakness.

So far she'd held out. Whenever she wavered, Clark seemed to sense that and bombarded her with notes and flowers and gifts, all of which she'd sent back. That didn't seem to bother him. If anything, he redoubled his efforts.

Rather than take her car out of the garage at work, Phoebe decided to walk the half mile or so to Blossom Street. She'd brought her brand-new knitting bag, filled with skeins of yarn in a restful sage-green color, her pattern and a pair of needles still in their clear plastic case. It was a lovely evening, but cool enough to require a sweater. Because she was early, she stopped at the French Café and purchased a half sandwich, pastrami on rye with mustard, and a cup of coffee.

Since the breakup, her appetite had suffered and she'd lost weight. This was the first hunger pang she'd experienced in two weeks, which was an encouraging sign. It felt like years since she'd been with Clark. That, too, was encouraging, and yet . . .

She struggled to hold back unexpected tears. The end of her engagement, the end of Clark's presence in her life, necessary though it was, had brought her such grief. This was so much harder than anyone else imagined, than anyone would ever know. To her friends and her mother she came across as determined and unshakable, but Clark lingered constantly in her mind. It would get better soon; she'd told herself this so often that she'd actually started to believe it.

It *had* to.

Eventually this ache in her heart would lessen. However, right then, sitting by herself outside a café on a perfect summer evening, watching couples wander past holding hands, made her feel ten times worse. Ten times as lonely . . .

She crossed the street to A Good Yarn at precisely six. While eating her meal, she'd seen two other people walking into the yarn store and wondered if they were part of the Knit to Quit class, too. It didn't seem likely. One was a man and the other apparently a street-savvy teenager.

The bell above the door jangled when she stepped inside, self-consciously clutching her supplies.

"Hi, Phoebe," Lydia said, hurrying forward to greet her. "Everyone else is already here. Come on back and join us."

Phoebe followed her to the rear of the store. The teenager and the man had both taken places at a large table and looked up as she approached. So she was wrong—these two were indeed part of the class. Well, it made for an interesting mix.

"This is Phoebe Rylander," Lydia said, slipping an arm around Phoebe's shoulders.

"Hi," she said, nervously wiggling her fingers.

The man stood and extended his hand. "I'm Bryan Hutchinson. Everyone calls me Hutch."

"Hi," she said. Normally Phoebe wasn't shy, but for some reason she felt awkward and unsure of herself. Maybe because this was a whole new venture for her, one that required skills she lacked. Although she'd done a bit of knitting as a girl, she'd never been very interested in any of the domestic crafts. Maybe that was about to change.

"I'm Alix, spelled with an *I*," the girl said. Her hair was black, probably dyed, and she wore it in a short, spiky fashion that suited her. She had on a leather jacket and jeans. When she'd first noticed Alix-with-an-*I*, Phoebe had assumed she was a teenager, but on closer inspection she decided Alix had to be in her early twenties. The leather jacket was unzipped and revealed a cotton shirt with a lace collar in stark contrast to the rest of her appearance. She was obviously a bit unorthodox but that seemed rather charming to Phoebe. Smiling at Alix, who smiled back, Phoebe pulled out the chair next to her.

Lydia moved closer to the table. "Since this is a Knit to Quit class, I thought it might be helpful if we each shared the reason we joined and what we're hoping to achieve by knitting." She looked at Alix. "Would you mind starting us off, Alix?"

The young woman shrugged. "Sure, why not. As you know by now, my name is Alix."

"With an *I*," Hutch inserted, grinning.

"Right." Alix gave him a cocky thumbs up. "I assume Lydia asked me to begin because I've taken classes here before. I learned to knit almost five years ago, when Lydia opened the shop."

"Alix was in my original class and has become one of my dearest friends," Lydia told them.

"I've changed a lot since that first class," Alix went on to say. "Back then, I was pretty angry at the world. I'd gotten a bum rap on a drug possession charge. I think the judge must've realized that because he sentenced me to community service rather than jail."

Hutch leaned closer to the table. "And you took up knitting as your community service? How did that work?"

"It was knitting for charity. I got approval from the court to knit a baby blanket for Project Linus. I figured it wouldn't hurt to learn something constructive for once in my life."

"Good idea," Phoebe said, nodding. Alix certainly wasn't typical of other young women her age. But then again, maybe she was. . . .

"The reason I signed up for this class is that I started smoking before Jordan and I were married. All the stuff going on before the wedding turned out to be pretty stressful and I decided I needed a cigarette. I told myself I'd only smoke the one pack. As you might've guessed it ended up being a lot more than that and now I'm trying to quit."

"I can't believe you're married," Phoebe blurted out, then felt like a fool. "I mean, you seem so young."

"I'm older than I look." She laughed softly. "I

89

hope it's my appearance and not my behavior that made you think I was younger."

"Of course!" Phoebe said.

"Definitely," Hutch mumbled.

"Anyway, Jordan and I want to start a family. Before I get pregnant, I have to quit smoking. Knitting's helped me through other things and . . . here I am."

"And we're glad you are," Lydia told her. She turned to Hutch next. "What about you, Hutch?"

He was a nice-looking man, Phoebe thought, studying him across the table. It was difficult to tell how old he was. Midthirties, she guessed—although she'd just proven she wasn't very good at judging age. He had pleasant, regular features and light-brown hair. Although she hated to admit it, he didn't possess the strong masculine appeal of Clark. He seemed like a regular guy, not that there was anything wrong with that. What Phoebe did like was how interested he was in what everyone had to say. Other than her boss, she didn't know many men who were good listeners.

Hutch sat back in his chair. "Actually, my doctor's the one who suggested I try knitting. He's a college classmate of mine. I was in for my annual checkup recently and Dave lectured me about working too hard and not getting enough exercise. I'm on medication for high blood pressure and, with a history of heart disease in the family, he felt I should find a method of relaxation. In fact,"

Hutch said, "he told me he knits himself. I suppose that convinced me."

"Your doctor's very wise." Lydia picked up the conversation. "Various studies have shown the health benefits of knitting as a form of relaxation. And from personal experience, I'd say that while our hands are at work on a project, we're able to quiet our thoughts."

Hutch nodded slowly. "Makes sense."

"I think you've made an excellent choice. Obviously," she added with a quick grin.

"Dave also said knitting would aid the healing process with my thumb." He held up his right hand and showed where he'd cut himself. The scar was red and ugly.

"Another good point," Lydia commented.

"So I'm here, but I have to tell you I've never held a pair of knitting needles in my life."

"That's not a problem," Lydia said. "I've taught people how to knit since I was a teenager. I'm sure you'll learn it easily."

Hutch grinned. "Your confidence is reassuring."

Lydia turned to Phoebe and gestured toward her. "Phoebe, can you tell us what prompted you to join Knit to Quit?"

She hesitated. Spilling her grief to strangers was more than she was ready to do. She stared up at Lydia. "I was engaged and . . ." What came out next was a complete surprise. She certainly hadn't intended to lie, although the truth embarrassed and humiliated her. "My fiancé died."

Lydia's eyes softened with sympathy. "Oh, Phoebe, I had no idea. I . . . I thought—" She stopped abruptly. "It doesn't matter what I thought. I'm so very sorry."

"I need to get over him," she said and swallowed hard. Tears clogged her throat and she struggled to hide the fact that she was close to weeping.

Thankfully no one asked for the details of Clark's supposed demise.

"I'm sorry," Alix said. Leaning across the table, she gently squeezed her hand. "I can't begin to imagine what it would be like if I lost Jordan."

Phoebe avoided their eyes. It was bad enough that she'd lied, but now she'd be obliged to continue with the charade. Everyone's sympathy only added to her guilt. Although Hutch hadn't spoken, his gaze was caring, concerned.

Blindly Phoebe unwrapped her knitting needles, indicating she was ready for class to begin.

Responding to her cue, Lydia held out the scarf pattern. "I chose this Bev Galeskas pattern because I feel everyone can knit this, no matter what level they are. It starts with the basic stitch." She reached into a bag behind her and brought out a scarf in soft gray wool. "I knit this up so everyone could see the finished project."

"I could knit *that?*" Hutch asked, sounding shocked.

"We all will."

"You're *sure* I can do that?"

Alix laughed. "I felt the same way in my first class when Lydia showed me the baby blanket. I guarantee you'll be impressed with yourself."

"It'll impress my sister, anyway." He smiled at Lydia. "If mine turns out even half as good as yours, I thought I'd give it to her for her birthday."

His sister? If he'd mentioned his sister rather than his wife, that probably meant he wasn't married. Phoebe wasn't in any mood to get romantically involved, but she felt increasingly curious about Hutch. His personality seemed the opposite of Clark's. He didn't need to be the center of attention and, instead, listened carefully to everyone else. As far as Phoebe was concerned, that was a rare quality. He might look ordinary but even on short acquaintance she could see that he was anything but.

Before they cast on stitches, Lydia described the pattern and explained that reading it over first prevented mistakes later. She also offered to photocopy their patterns to use as "working copies."

"That way the copied sheet can be marked up and carried with the project. Then if it's lost, the original is always available."

After that, Lydia demonstrated how to cast on stitches. The skill came back to Phoebe faster than she'd thought it would.

Sitting beside Hutch, Lydia reviewed the technique with him repeatedly. He followed her instructions carefully and although he found it difficult to hold the needles and yarn and cast on at the same time, he never once lost patience. Phoebe couldn't picture Clark not throwing the needles and yarn down in disgust.

Clark.

How easily he'd slipped into her mind, despite her resolve. Forcing herself to concentrate, she knit methodically to the end of the row. Then the next one . . .

About an hour into the class, the phone rang. Lydia excused herself and moved to the front counter.

From what Phoebe could hear, this call was of a personal nature.

"Water balloons in the house?" Lydia gasped at one point, covering her eyes with her free hand.

When she returned a few minutes later, she looked troubled.

Alix was the one who broached the subject. "Is everything all right with Cody and Brad?"

"I . . . I'm not sure. We have a houseguest, and it appears that she's managed to ruffle a few feathers."

"How long is your guest staying?" Hutch asked.

"A week." She frowned but didn't volunteer any further information.

It was still light out when the class was officially over. As Phoebe gathered up her knitting bag and her purse, the shop door opened and a clean-cut young man walked in.

"Jordan," Alix said, her voice elevated. "Hi!"

The man went over to Alix and slid his arm around her waist. "I thought I'd stop by and pick you up."

Alix smiled at Hutch and Phoebe. "This is my husband, Jordan Turner."

Jordan exchanged handshakes with both of them. "Pleased to meet you."

Seeing the love between Alix and her husband brought an unexpected twinge of pain.

Phoebe averted her eyes. She remembered when Clark—She immediately halted her thoughts.

No, she wasn't going to think about him. While it had been an outright lie to say he was dead, it was, in a manner of speaking, the truth. He was dead to her. The sooner that message went from her head to her heart, the sooner she'd get over him. The sooner this agony would stop.

Phoebe wished everyone a good evening and hurried out the door. Hutch was right behind her. A couple of times in the past two hours she'd tried to include him in the conversation. Hutch, however, had been so focused on learning the basic knit and purl stitches that he hadn't looked up even once. Phoebe admired his persistence.

"It was nice to meet you, Phoebe," he said now, clutching the briefcase that held his yarn and needles.

They stood on the sidewalk facing each other. "You, too," she told him.

"I'm sorry about your fiancé."

"I know . . . I am, too." She glanced away, uncomfortable about perpetuating the lie.

"Are you parked close by?" he asked.

"Relatively close. I left my car at the parking garage where I work."

"Can I give you a ride there?"

It was a kind offer, but Phoebe refused. "Thanks. I'll enjoy the walk."

"Sure. See you next week."

"See you then."

Phoebe did enjoy the stroll. It'd been an interesting class and she'd look forward to spending time with Alix, Hutch and Lydia next week. This was the first night in a long while that she hadn't been consumed by the loneliness that haunted her evenings. Her one regret was the lie. Still, it had saved her from difficult explanations that she preferred not to share.

Phoebe entered the condo lobby and headed for the elevator, wondering about Lydia and her situation at home. She'd obviously been disturbed by that phone call and—

"Where were you?"

She whirled around to find Clark standing directly behind her. "What are you doing here?" she demanded. No way was she answering his questions.

"What do you think I'm doing here? I've been waiting for you for the last two hours. Phoebe, this can't go on. I'm miserable without you. I need you."

"Clark . . ."

"Hear me out. Please."

She had to close her eyes for fear of being influenced by the expression on his face, the pleading in his voice. "Don't do this." To her great relief, the elevator arrived and she dashed inside. "Just go!"

Clark stuck his arm between the doors, effectively keeping them open. "Answer me one thing and then I'll leave." His gaze beseeched hers. "Tell me that while I sat here for two hours, you weren't out with another man. I couldn't bear that, Phoebe. I could take anything but that."

What he couldn't take was losing, she thought. After a moment's hesitation, she decided it was best to tell him the truth. "I . . . I'm not seeing anyone else."

He nodded and whispered "Thank you." Then he stepped back as the elevator doors slid closed.

CHAPTER
8

Anne Marie Roche

They'd been home for a week, but Anne Marie was only now rediscovering the routine of her life. She sat in her small office at the store and paid the bills that had accumulated in her absence, although her mind drifted frequently from the task at hand. Memories of Paris were still with her.

Sainte-Chapelle had taken her breath away. A visit to the magnificent Nôtre Dame had humbled her and the ride up the Eiffel Tower had thrilled her. Boat trips on the Seine, the Louvre, meals at charming little bistros . . . The trip had been everything Anne Marie had dreamed and more.

Ellen had barely been able to absorb it all, and Anne Marie felt the same mixture of awe and wonder. Now that she'd had the experience, all she could think about was returning.

Anne Marie was delighted by Ellen's ability to learn French. She picked it up with ease, hearing words once or twice and remembering them. Anne Marie wanted her to retain as much as possible and Ellen practiced every chance she got, especially on Baxter. Because of their special communication, the dog seemed to understand her, no matter what language Ellen spoke. It was the modulation in the child's voice that cued the dog, or so Anne Marie assumed. In any case, Baxter had quickly learned *assis* for "sit" and *parle* for "speak."

During the remainder of the summer Ellen would be going to the day camp associated with the Free Methodist church around the corner. The program was reasonably priced and Ellen seemed to like it. Cody Goetz attended, too. So did Casey, Lydia and Brad's foster girl, although that was only supposed to be for just a few more days. The church camp sponsored frequent field trips, plus craft classes and sports activities. Jordan Turner, Alix's husband, headed the program, with the assistance of several young staffers.

Shortly after the adoption, Anne Marie and Ellen had started going to Sunday school and morning worship services. As a new mother, even if her baby was almost nine at the time, Anne Marie felt it was the right thing to do.

She'd fallen out of the habit of church attendance after she'd separated from Robert. Later, when the husband she loved had died—as they were on the verge of reconciling—Anne Marie had been angry with God. So angry . . .

However, she knew that a strong religious upbringing was something Ellen's grandmother had wanted for her only grandchild. Dolores Falk had loved her granddaughter deeply, and Anne Marie felt a responsibility to do as Dolores had requested.

Anne Marie understood that Dolores's love had protected the girl. Fortunately Ellen's birth mother, Dolores's daughter, who'd fallen into a life of drugs and crime, had surrendered all parental rights. This had made it possible for Anne Marie to adopt the child.

Teresa stuck her head in the office. "He's back."

Lost in her thoughts, Anne Marie glanced up. "Who's back?"

"The man."

"What man?"

"The one who came by when you and Ellen were

in Paris," Teresa said, sounding a little impatient.

"Oh." Anne Marie hadn't actually forgotten but she'd relegated the matter to the bottom of her list. "Has he asked to speak to me?"

"Not yet, but I guarantee that's what he's here to do."

"Okay." Anne Marie pushed away from her desk and rose to her feet.

Teresa remained standing in the doorway. She winked outrageously at Anne Marie, then lowered her voice. "He's still hot."

"Teresa! You're a married woman."

Her friend grinned from ear to ear. "True, but I'm not blind."

Anne Marie came around her desk and stepped quietly out of the office. Sure enough, a man stood at the counter, a man whose gaze went instantly to her face. Over the course of her life, men had often looked at her. She knew she was reasonably attractive and yet the look this man gave her expressed more than casual interest, more than mere appreciation. His gaze was intent, meaningful, even expectant. Anne Marie felt confused by it.

She moved behind the counter by the cash register. "Can I help you?" she asked, keeping her voice cool and yet polite.

"Are you Anne Marie Roche?" he asked.

"I am." She wondered again why this strikingly handsome man was seeking her out. Most likely he was here to sell her insurance or to show her a new gift line. She'd never seen him before, so it couldn't be anything personal. Which was just as well; attractive though he was, Anne Marie could only respond to him in an abstract way. Since Robert's death, she hadn't been interested in dating. And once Ellen entered her life, her entire world had begun to revolve around her daughter.

His demeanor changed. His eyes narrowed ever so slightly. "I'm Tim Carlsen."

What was that about? If he was a salesman, he hadn't bothered with a friendly approach. "Hello, Tim," she said, refusing to allow him to intimidate her. "Can I help you with something?"

He looked at Teresa, who'd busied herself organizing a display of new children's books. She did her best to pretend she wasn't listening in on the conversation, although she couldn't avoid hearing it.

"Can I ask what this is about?" Anne Marie asked, trying again.

"Perhaps it would be better if we spoke privately," Tim said.

"About?"

He stiffened his shoulders. "Ellen," he said quietly. "This is in regard to the child you've recently adopted."

Anne Marie felt the oxygen rush from her lungs. But rather than reveal her surprise, she gestured calmly toward her office. She felt paralyzed as she tried to figure out what possible connection this man could have to her daughter. The birth certificate hadn't named a father, and yet . . .

Inside the office, she took her seat behind the desk. Tim pulled up a chair across from her, not waiting for an invitation.

"You know *my* daughter?" she asked, wanting to make sure he understood that no one else had any legal right to the child.

Her visitor shook his head. "I'm sorry to say that I do not."

For some reason, this information reassured Anne Marie. "How do you know about Ellen, then?"

"I've only heard of her." Tim stared at the floor. "I'm a recovering alcoholic with eight years' sobriety."

Heard of her how? was the first thing she wanted to ask. But she had no idea how to respond to his confession, nor did she understand why he felt it was necessary to tell her such a personal fact.

"Congratulations," she said tentatively, "but what's that got to do with Ellen or me?"

"I met Candy Falk at probably the lowest point in my life," he continued, ignoring her question.

No one needed to remind Anne Marie that Candy Falk was Ellen's birth mother and a known drug addict.

"Back then Candy and I were both using."

"Drugs?"

Tim nodded. "Drugs, all kinds of drugs, you name

102

it. But also alcohol. It wasn't a good time. . . . Like I said, it was a low point for me."

A tingling spread down Anne Marie's neck. Her suspicion had been correct. She was starting to connect the dots and she didn't like the picture that was taking shape in her mind.

"You still haven't told me what any of this has to do with my daughter," she said curtly. Ellen was part of Anne Marie's life now. A very precious part, and she wasn't about to let some man—some stranger—step in and make a claim.

Again Tim ignored her question. "Candy and I broke up, and my family arranged for me to enter rehab. I've been clean and sober ever since."

"And?"

"I follow the twelve steps and traditions of AA. With my sponsor's support, I've begun making amends wherever possible."

"That's good of you, but I don't see what any of this has to do with Ellen or me." As far as Anne Marie was concerned, this conversation was over. She stood and motioned toward the door.

"Please sit down, Ms. Roche."

Her resolve melted under the force of his gaze and Anne Marie slowly sank back into her chair.

"As part of my attempt to make amends, I tried to locate Candy," Tim said. "I couldn't find her but I remembered where her mother used to live." He looked away. "I needed her forgiveness, too."

"Dolores?"

He spoke in a clear, even voice. "Candy and I stole money from her mother and I wanted to return it."

Anne Marie swallowed. This was only a fraction, a tiny fraction, of the pain Candy Falk had brought into her mother's life.

"I remembered the house where Candy had taken me, but it was empty."

"Yes, I know."

He didn't seem to hear. "The neighbor was watering her rosebushes and we got to talking. She said Dolores had passed away some time ago and that her grandchild had been adopted."

Anne Marie didn't comment.

"I asked where Candy was, but the neighbor didn't know."

This was information Anne Marie was willing to pass along. "I don't know, either. Someplace in California, I think. I understand she's still an addict."

"I suspected as much," he said with a grimace.

"It's sad. . . ." In case Tim hadn't heard, she added, "Ellen's aunt, Clarisse, is in prison."

He shook his head, and there was a brief silence. "I asked the neighbor a few more questions," he said a moment later, "and found out that Dolores had custody of a little girl—Candy's daughter. When I inquired about the child, the neighbor told me Ellen was eight when her grandmother died."

"She's nine now."

Tim looked directly into her eyes. "It was almost ten years ago that Candy and I lived together. We . . . didn't use any form of birth control. It hit me that there's a possibility Ellen might be my daughter."

This was what Anne Marie had feared he was about to say. She was ending his visit right now.

"You're mistaken, Mr. Carlsen. Ellen couldn't possibly be your daughter," Anne Marie insisted.

"Ellen is *my* child, and I have the paperwork to prove it." Bolting to her feet once again, she planted her hands on the edge of her desk. "I think you should leave."

"No." Tim didn't move and his dark eyes burned into hers. "I understand this comes as a shock and I apologize for that. All I'm asking for is the truth. I want to know if I'm Ellen's father. I don't feel that's an unreasonable request."

"Unfortunately, it *is* unreasonable. Ellen has been adopted by me. As I just explained, Ellen is my child."

"When you adopted her did you receive parental consent?"

Anne Marie felt she owed him nothing more than the bare facts. "Your name isn't on the birth certificate and the state had no way of contacting you, even if it does turn out that you're Ellen's biological father."

Tim's features tightened. "I haven't stopped thinking about her from the moment I heard Candy had a baby." He ran his hand through his hair. "What you don't know is that after we split and I was in rehab, Candy twice attempted to contact me."

"Yes, but—"

"I never read her letter or returned her phone call," he said, interrupting her. "As far as I was concerned, she was bad news and involved in a life I no longer wanted to live. It's stupid of me, I guess, but it never occurred to me that she might be pregnant."

Anne Marie spoke slowly, trying to ensure that everything was clear. "Candy Falk rescinded all parental rights. Nothing can be done to change this. It's over and done with."

"I realize that."

"Good. Then you also realize that you have no rights whatsoever with regard to Ellen."

"I do have rights." He obviously wasn't willing to back down and glared at her unflinchingly. "If Ellen's my child, and I have every reason to believe she is, then I want to know her. She has a right to know me, too."

Anne Marie shook her head. "Whether Ellen is your biological daughter or not isn't the issue. Ellen has another family now."

"Another father?"

Anne Marie hesitated.

"Are you married?"

"That's none of your business."

"I disagree. It's very much my business. Perhaps I should speak with your husband," Tim said. He seemed to think he was calling her bluff or, worse, that he'd be able to reason with another man. Either way, his suggestion infuriated her.

Anne Marie paused, unwilling to admit that she was widowed. She saw that he'd noticed her silence and hurriedly added, "I'm sorry, that's impossible just now."

"I have no intention of taking Ellen away from you."

She nearly laughed out loud. "I'd like to see you try. As I keep telling you, Ellen is my child now, my daughter. Whether or not she's related to you is beside the point."

"Perhaps it is to you. However, to me, it's vital. If I'm Ellen's biological father, I should at least have the opportunity to meet my own daughter."

"It's too late for that," Anne Marie said, refusing to bend.

"I never knew Candy was pregnant," he told her again. "I might've been a lot of things over the years, but at no time would I have abandoned my own flesh and blood."

"That's very noble of you, Mr. Carlsen, but as I said, it's too late. I'm sure there's something in the AA rules that will help you sort it all out. My advice is to let go of this. Ellen's happy. She has a good life with me."

"Not with your husband?" he pressed.

"My husband . . ."

Tim's eyes narrowed and she could tell he already knew she was widowed. His earlier remarks had been a bluff of his own. Continuing the pretense would be senseless.

"I'm Ellen's family now," Anne Marie said, sidestepping the question. She was finished with this conversation. "I believe it's time you left, Mr. Carlsen, otherwise I'll have to call the authorities."

Tim slowly stood. "I didn't want to get an attorney involved, but I will if I have to."

"You do that."

Tim waited a moment, as if undecided what to do next. After several seconds, he said, "Thank you for seeing me."

Arms folded, Anne Marie nodded abruptly.

Tim walked out of the office, and Anne Marie sat down again, so shaken that she started to tremble.

A few minutes later, Teresa stepped into the office. "Is everything okay?" she asked.

Anne Marie managed a wobbly smile. "Not really . . ."

"Oh?" Teresa watched her carefully. "Is there anything I can do to help?"

Anne Marie braced her elbows on the desk and covered her eyes. "I'm not sure. . . . I need time to think."

"If I can help in any way, just let me know," Teresa urged.

Anne Marie murmured a thank-you. It would take a while to figure out what to do about this difficult conversation—including the fact that Tim had threatened legal action. Fine, she'd fight him with every resource she possessed. First, however, she needed to find out what her own rights were.

Her hand shook as she flipped through the Rolodex on the corner of her desk until she came to Evelyn Boyle's name. Evelyn, as a social worker, knew adoption law. Evelyn would be able to tell Anne Marie her rights.

Her heart felt as though it might implode. She'd already lost her husband, becoming a widow at the age of thirty-eight. Then life had taken a wonderful and unexpected turn and brought her Ellen. Anne Marie wasn't going to give the child up. Not for anyone.

CHAPTER
9

We don't knit to make *things*. There are cheaper, faster and easier ways to obtain a sweater than to knit it. We knit to make ourselves *happy*. *We* are in charge of getting the most joy out of our yarn and stitches.
—Annie Modesitt, author of
Confessions of a Knitting Heretic and
Knit with Courage, Live with Hope.
www.anniemodesitt.com

Lydia Goetz

Tuesday evening my stomach was in knots as I pulled into the driveway after work. Casey had been with us for almost a week. Before I left the shop, I'd gotten no less than three phone calls from Cody and had talked with Brad an equal number of times. Each and every one of those calls had been about Casey. The girl had created a complete upheaval in our peaceful family life. As Evelyn had said, there were a few adjustment problems. She'd also predicted that the kids would accept each other in a day or two; it hadn't happened. Brad felt inadequate to deal with the conflict between Cody and Casey on his own. He seemed to think I'd handle it better, but I wasn't really sure what to do, either.

"I'm home," I called as I entered the kitchen through the door that led from the garage. I realized an announcement had been unnecessary. Both Cody and Brad were waiting for me. The relief on their faces was comical and they released a collective sigh at my arrival.

I kissed my husband on the cheek. As he usually did, Brad had started dinner—chicken and Spanish rice. Casey sat at the kitchen table with her head bent over one of my cookbooks, open to the section on baking. I found that interesting but knew better than to comment.

Cody scowled at her from the other side of the room. "I need to talk to you," he said, then added "privately" in a whisper.

"Okay," I agreed. I went over and hugged him, but he remained stiff and angry.

It took me a moment to divest myself of my purse and bag and to change shoes. "How was school?" I asked Casey, coming back into the kitchen.

She shrugged.

"What can I get you?" I decided to ask a question that required an actual response.

"I don't need anything." The words, as well as her body language, were defiant.

"Okay, but let me know if you do."

"Can I talk to you and Dad *now?*" Cody asked.

"Okay by me," Brad told him. He turned down the burner under the pan of rice. The chicken was in the oven, and it would be about half an hour before the evening meal was ready.

"Would you excuse us for a few minutes?" I asked Casey.

Once again she didn't bother to respond. Brad and I left the kitchen. Cody led us into his bedroom with Chase a step or two behind. He waited until we were inside, then firmly closed the door. Brad and I sat next to each other on Cody's sloppily made bed and my husband reached for my hand.

Before Brad could even ask what this was all about, Cody whirled around, frowning at us. "I don't like her."

"Cody . . ."

"She's rude and mean and she said I'm spoiled and called me a baby—right to my face!"

"Cody—" Brad tried again, but our son was in no mood to be reasonable.

"The three of us talked about adopting, remember?" Cody asked. "And I said okay, and you said you'd listen to what *I* wanted."

"Of course we'll listen! But Casey will only be with us a couple more days—at the most," I reminded him. It wasn't as though the girl was about to become part of our family.

"She was supposed to stay two nights and now she's here for a whole week." Cody's eyes flashed with indignation. "Seeing that you let her stay longer than you said, I have a list of demands."

"A *list?*" I repeated.

"Demands?" Brad arched his eyebrows.

"Go ahead and read us your list," I said. I felt we owed Cody that much. He was right; the situation had changed without warning and without real discussion. Granted, he was nine years old; he wouldn't be making decisions for the family. But this did affect him and we needed to acknowledge his feelings—and accommodate them where we could.

The fact that Cody had actually been thinking about the possibility of adoption pleased me. I wanted open communication among all of us, especially when it came to something as important as bringing a baby into our family.

"Okay, I will." Cody marched to the end of his bed, slipped his hand under the mattress and took out a folded piece of paper. Chase hovered near the door, watching him.

Brad and I exchanged a look of surprise and made an effort to hide our amusement. Apparently Cody was upset enough to reveal his secret hiding place without even realizing it.

Chase settled on the braided rug beside the bed and rested his chin on his paws as his dark eyes followed Cody. He seemed a little uneasy, no doubt because he was so sensitive to our son's moods.

Standing directly in front of us, Cody unfolded the single sheet of paper, then cleared his throat. "Demand number one. If you're going to adopt another kid, I want a brother, not a sister."

Brad sighed. "We won't necessarily have a say in the matter, Cody. It would be the same as if Lydia were to get pregnant. We wouldn't know until much later if it was a boy or a girl."

"I want a *brother*," Cody insisted.

"We'll do our best to get you a brother," I said.

"What else is on your, uh, list of demands?" Brad asked in a serious voice.

"I get to be the oldest kid in the family." He looked directly at us, his mouth a straight, angry line. "I was here first, right? If you bring in some other kid, then that kid can't be the boss of me."

"Sounds fair," Brad assured our son. I nodded.

He seemed shocked by our agreement. "You promise?"

"I can't make it a real promise," Brad said, "because we won't know the age until we decide on the child our family would like to adopt. But we're asking for a baby, so it's probably not an issue."

Cody seemed somewhat mollified.

"Anything else?" I asked.

"Yes." Cody looked at us again and his face tightened with determination. "I'm not giving in on this," he said, sounding as though he was engaged in some high-level diplomatic negotiation. Well, I guess from his point of view, he was. "And if you don't say yes, then I don't want anything to do with our family getting another kid."

"Let's hear it," Brad said.

"I want full approval." He spoke with such fervor

his voice trembled. "I get to say which kid we adopt. If I don't like 'em, they can't live here."

"Like your dad said, we're hoping for a baby, so I think that should meet your demand. We'll request a boy . . . although it might take a while." I was discouraged by how long the list of potential parents already was.

Mildly appeased, Cody glanced down at the dog. "Chase gets approval, too."

I almost started to giggle, but Brad frowned. "Son, listen, I know you're upset because Casey—".

"I just want to make sure you aren't going to adopt *her*," he cried.

"No," Brad said evenly. "As Lydia's explained, Casey's stay with us is temporary."

I heard a noise outside the door and I suspected Casey had been standing on the other side, listening to our conversation. When I returned to the kitchen, however, she was sitting at the table, exactly as we'd left her.

I prepared the salad and asked Casey to clear the table so we could set it for dinner. Silently she removed the cookbook, returning it to the shelf. I wondered how she was doing in her math class, but she never volunteered any information and evaded my questions. She hadn't asked for help, so I assumed all was well. Casey took the plates down from the cupboard and added glasses and silverware. Although I tried to make conversation, she remained uncommunicative, even stoic.

"Casey," I said gently. I placed my hand on her shoulder, hoping to reassure her. She shrugged it off as if she found my touch repulsive. I forged ahead, feeling I needed to say something just in case she'd heard part of our conversation with Cody. "I know being here is uncomfortable for you and I apologize. I feel we've been exceedingly rude. You are most welcome in our home."

She snickered. "Yeah, right."

She looked at me and for an instant, for the briefest flicker of time, I saw pain in her eyes. It was quickly gone, replaced by anger and defiance.

Dinner was a miserable affair. Casey didn't utter a single word, nor did she bother to eat more than a couple of bites. Cody didn't do much better. Although Spanish rice was one of his favorites, his plate was practically untouched. A war of wills seemed to be taking place between Cody and Casey and they glared openly at each other across the table.

Brad and I made several attempts to find a safe topic of conversation, but apparently there was none. Neither child responded to our comments about movies or my cat's clever antics or anything else, and by the time they left the table, I felt exhausted.

As soon as they were excused, both kids disappeared into their bedrooms. Brad sighed and I shook my head, hardly knowing what to say.

"That was an unqualified disaster," he said, keeping his voice low.

I could only agree.

"Is there any chance Evelyn could find another foster home for Casey?" he asked.

"I . . . don't know. I suppose I can call her." I hated the thought, but one more meal like this and we'd be at each other's throats.

Brad looked as discouraged as I did. "I guess we should let her stay until the end of the week."

We'd briefly discussed keeping her until classes were finished, but that was out of the question now. The current situation wasn't working. I'd had no idea that two children could take such an immediate and uncompromising dislike to each other.

Cody, I could understand. Casey had been thrust upon him without warning. If there'd been time to talk to him beforehand, I was sure he would've welcomed—or at least accepted—her. And I suppose Casey's attitude sprang from a natural defensiveness, given her background.

Cody was in bed by nine and while Brad went in to say goodnight and hear his prayers, I decided to check on Casey. I hadn't heard a peep out of her since she'd gone into her room and closed the door.

I knocked quietly, waited a moment and when there was no response, I let myself in. "Casey?" I whispered.

I could see that she was already in bed, facing the wall. Either she was asleep or pretending to be; I assumed it was the latter. Coming all the way into the room, I bent over and laid my hand lightly on her back.

She jerked away from me. I stood there for several minutes, wondering what I should say. A dozen possible remarks swirled around in my head. I felt terribly inadequate to console her, and yet I knew I had to try.

"How many foster homes have you been in?" I asked her.

She didn't answer.

"More than five?"

Casey nodded.

"I want you to meet my friend Alix. She was a foster kid, too."

"Who?"

The question brought me up short. I hadn't really expected her to respond. "Alix," I repeated. "She took a knitting class from me soon after I opened my yarn store. She knit a baby blanket in order to satisfy some community service hours she was assigned by the court." I'd offered to teach Casey, too, but she'd declined, claiming she wasn't interested.

I waited for a comment or another question, and when none came, I said, "Alix works at the French Café across the street from me now."

Silence.

Apparently that one-word question a few minutes earlier was all the response I was going to get. "You'll be with a new family soon and you can settle in there."

Again nothing.

"Remember, if you want to learn to knit, I'll be happy to teach you."

Casey scrambled closer to the wall as if the very idea of me teaching her anything disgusted her. After a few more minutes, I tiptoed out of the room, feeling frustrated and depressed.

Brad met me in the hallway outside the bedrooms. "How'd it go?" he asked.

"Badly. What about Cody?"

"He wants her gone."

I nodded. "I feel terrible for her," I said. "I just wish there was something I could say or do that would help. She's upset about being removed from her last foster home and the fact that she has to be with us." The home where she'd been earlier had been closed by the state because of some code violations. Evelyn hadn't provided more than the scantiest details. I didn't know what the circumstances had been, and I couldn't ask Casey.

"I don't think she's a bad kid," Brad murmured as he headed for our bedroom. "Unfortunately, she just isn't a good fit for us."

"It's only a couple more days," I reminded him, not for the first time.

While Brad showered, I slipped into my nightclothes and climbed into bed. I'd been looking forward to teaching Casey to knit. I suppose it was naive of me to think I could initiate some sort of communication with her through knitting. I'd seen it work so well with others that I'd been hopeful, despite her unambiguous refusal.

I picked up the book I was reading—a biography of C. S. Lewis—which I thought was laudably ambitious. I generally read every night before I fall asleep; Brad does, too. I find it comforting to lie beside my husband, each of us with a book in our hands. I see it as a period of calm and intimacy, and as the perfect metaphor—together, yet individual—for our marriage.

It wasn't long before Brad joined me, his hair still wet from the shower. I smiled at him and began to speak, then paused when I heard a noise.

"Did you hear that?" I asked in a low voice.

He glanced up from his book. "Hear what?"

I listened hard, then shook my head.

A moment later I heard it again. "Brad?"

"It's nothing."

I wasn't so sure and was just about to go and investigate when Chase started to bark.

"There's someone in the house," I said in a hoarse whisper, trying to hide my panic. There'd been a rash of home invasions in the news lately and an intruder was the first thought that came to me.

"I locked all the doors," Brad said.

"I know," I told him, but he was already out of bed, reaching for his pants. "Stay here," he instructed me.

"Should I call 9-1-1?" I asked, surprised by how tightly my throat muscles had constricted.

"Not yet." He creaked open our bedroom door and turned on the hallway light.

Unable to remain passively behind, I followed him and quickly discovered the same thing he had. Casey's bedroom door was open.

"Casey!"

Brad called her name, hurrying down the narrow hallway. I rounded the corner into the foyer and saw that my husband had taken hold of the girl's arm, his face flushed with anger. "I caught her walking out the front door," he said accusingly.

"Casey?" I said. "Were you running away?"

She gazed down at the living room carpet. "You don't want me here and I don't want to be here."

"Where would you go?"

She looked up at me then, her eyes flashing with anger. "What do you care?"

"We do," I insisted, stretching out one arm but careful not to touch her. "Running away never solved anything. Listen, we're all going to try harder. It would help if you gave us a chance, too, you know."

Cody was up now, standing blurry-eyed with Chase beside him, watching us. Casey stared at him and he stared back.

"It's only until Friday," Brad promised, and it was as much a promise to her as it was to us. "Can you last that long, Casey?" he asked.

She gave him the same silent treatment she had me.

"You should stay," Cody said.

I wanted to hug my son for his generous heart. I knew it had taken a great deal for him to say those words. I'd never loved him more.

"Friday—another two days. If you can stick it out, so can we," Brad said, trying again. "Can you do that?"

Reluctantly Casey nodded.

"Okay, agreed." Brad sounded relieved. So was I.

"No more of this, right?" I said.

Casey met my eyes, then Cody's. "I'll stay, but I won't like it."

"Thank you," I whispered.

With that Casey went down the hall, past Cody and Chase, and into her bedroom, closing the door hard. After she was gone, Cody returned to his own room, holding Chase by the collar.

Brad slid one arm around my waist and I leaned against him as I tried to absorb what had just happened. I'd noticed that Casey had made enough noise to alert us to her escape plans. That told me she didn't really want to go. She wanted us to stop her.

For the first time since her arrival, I started to think I might actually understand this rejected child. I prayed we could prove to her that we did care.

All of us, even Cody.

CHAPTER
10

"Hutch" Hutchinson

Gritting his teeth, Hutch hung up the phone after speaking with his attorney, John Custer. He could feel his blood pressure rising. John, who'd been a longtime friend and confidant of his father's, had suggested a settlement offer to the nuisance lawsuit. The woman who'd filed was in her forties. Her ridiculous claim was that Mount Rainier Chocolates had caused her to gain weight; furthermore, because she was overweight, she was viewed in a prejudicial light by prospective employers.

But Hutch hadn't *forced* her to consume his candy. She was the one who'd chosen to overeat.

What had happened to self-discipline? Hutch wondered as he often did these days. It wasn't as if he'd added an addictive element to his chocolate or crammed them into her mouth. As far as Hutch was concerned, if he gave in to this lawsuit he was making himself—and every other candy manufacturer—vulnerable to a thousand more. This lawsuit was an opportunistic attempt to repeat what had happened with the tobacco companies years earlier.

What he really wanted, he decided as he leaned

back in his office chair, was for this woman to withdraw her suit. But there was no chance of that, since the plaintiff—no doubt encouraged by her attorney—saw the suit as an opportunity for easy cash.

Gail tapped politely at his door.

"What is it?" he asked, far more waspishly than he'd meant to.

His assistant came into his office. "I thought you'd want to know your mother just pulled into the parking lot."

"Thanks." Hutch nodded and didn't hesitate to apologize. "I didn't mean to snap at you."

"I know." She forgave him with a faint smile. "That was John Custer on the phone, right?"

"Right."

"Is everything okay?"

He shook his head. "It looks like this lawsuit's going all the way to court." His wasn't the only company that had been faced with nuisance suits, many of which were settled out of court, as John was quick to remind him. A settlement was easier than suffering through the ordeal of taking the matter to a jury. According to John, juries were fickle and there were no guarantees. Hutch wished he knew what his father would've done. Perhaps he was foolish not to listen to his attorney's advice.

"Oh, Hutch, I'm sorry," Gail was saying.

"Yeah, me, too."

If this lawsuit did end up in the courtroom, the

media would inevitably come into play. They might not show him in a sympathetic light, either. His father had once told him there was no such thing as bad publicity, but Hutch wasn't convinced. And he could do without the stress of this ludicrous situation.

"Should I send your mother in?" Gail asked on her way out the door.

Hutch nodded. He felt protective toward his mother and, as much as possible, tried to spare her any worry. In return, she felt it was her duty to look after him, to enquire about his diet and whether he got enough sleep and had enough of a social life. In most instances Hutch didn't mind. Lately, however, she'd been on this marriage kick. She said it was because she didn't want him to repeat his father's mistakes and bury himself in work.

Bury, in his father's case, had been the literal truth. The company had killed him, and after his latest medical checkup, Hutch could see that he was headed in the same direction.

Well aware of his tendency to work too hard and too long, he was taking measures to prevent that. The knitting class was a good example, along with his gym membership. He cringed, remembering that he'd only been there once, the day he'd plunked down his membership fee. He resolved to start exercising that very afternoon—no more excuses or delays.

A few minutes later, Gail opened his door and his

mother stepped inside, a frown on her usually serene face. She was dressed for a day on the town, in a crisp lavender pantsuit with a matching purse and shoes. "I haven't heard from you all week," she said.

Had it actually been that long? "Sorry, Mom, I guess the time got away from me."

"You haven't been sick, have you?"

"No, no." He glanced at his assistant. "Would you bring us each a cup of green tea?" he asked.

"I'd be happy to," Gail assured him with a knowing smile. He'd asked as a way of distracting his mother and Gail knew it.

His mother waited until Gail had left the room. "Green tea?" she asked, sounding surprised.

"I've turned over a new leaf," he told her. Realizing what he'd said, he added, "No pun intended."

His mother smiled. In her eyes, there was little he could do wrong.

"I did mention I've joined a gym, didn't I?" There was no need to tell her he'd only been once.

"Oh, yes, and knitting classes, too."

As if to prove he was taking his physician's advice seriously, he reached behind his desk where he kept his knitting, although he hadn't picked it up since that initial class. "I learned how to cast on last week," he announced proudly, waving the needle with its clumped stitches to show her. He'd managed to knit three or four rows, although for every stitch he made he'd had to unravel two. But, he reasoned, he was learning.

Gloria clapped her hands in delight as he shoved the needle, trailing its skein of white yarn, back in his briefcase. She made him feel there wasn't anything he couldn't tackle. Everyone needed a mother like his and in that sense Hutch considered himself one of the fortunate people of this world.

"Did you make that phone call yet?" she asked, looking expectantly at him as she took her place on the leather sofa.

Phone call? Hutch was supposed to have made a phone call? He wracked his brain, but for the life of him he couldn't remember.

"Bryan, you *promised.*"

She was Bryan to him when he'd disappointed her. Apparently his blank expression gave him away. "Remind me again who you wanted me to phone."

Thankfully Gail's timing was impeccable and she chose just that moment to return with a small tray. The teapot was covered with a white cozy and she'd arranged two cups, together with a small pitcher of milk and packets of sugar. She set it on the corner of his desk and quietly left.

"I'll pour." His mother stood and moved toward him.

"I take mine black . . . or green as the case may be," he said, thinking himself rather clever.

"Jessie's friend," Gloria said, handing him the first mug.

His sister had lots of friends—and then it hit him. "Oh, that friend." His mother had mentioned *something* about a woman, but it'd been early last week and had completely slipped his mind.

"Her name's Mia Northfield." With her own tea in hand, she sat on the sofa and sipped delicately.

The fact was, Hutch didn't remember much of their conversation. Nor did he recall promising his mother that he'd contact this Mia.

"She's divorced."

He nodded. That sounded vaguely familiar.

His mother's eyes brightened. "I don't mean to nag, I really don't. All I want is for you to find some nice woman and settle down and have two or three children . . . or ten."

Hutch nearly choked on his tea. *"Ten?"*

"I'd spoil every one of them, you know."

"I do know." The image of his mother with young children gathered around her was strangely appealing. The problem was, he hadn't dated anyone in quite a long time. He was embarrassed to admit just how long it'd been. There didn't seem to be enough hours in the day for an active social life, not like the one he'd had before his father's death.

All of a sudden Phoebe Rylander's face flashed before him. A warm feeling came over him as he pictured her fragile smile and dark, lively eyes. "As it happens," he murmured, holding his cup with both hands, "I have met someone."

His mother sat up straighter. "When?" she asked

speculatively, almost as if she didn't believe him.

"Last week in my knitting class." He grinned and knew instantly that his mother had noticed.

"Tell me about her."

There wasn't really that much to say. "The class is called Knit to Quit," he began.

Gloria looked worried. "She's not a smoker, is she?" Then before he could respond, she asked, "Does this girl have a weight issue?" She seemed to regret that question. "Actually, that doesn't concern me nearly as much as the smoking."

"This *woman* doesn't smoke—" he hoped that was true "—and she's certainly not overweight."

"Then tell me about her. Why is she in the class?"

Hutch reviewed the introductions Lydia had asked each of them to make. "To be honest, I don't remember exactly what Phoebe's hoping to quit." What he did recall was a rather sad story. "Apparently she was engaged and her fiancé died shortly before the wedding." He raised one shoulder in a shrug. "I guess she's trying to get over him."

"Phoebe. What a lovely name." His mother's eyes clouded with sympathy. "The poor girl."

"She's as lovely as her name." Hutch didn't realize he'd spoken the words aloud until he saw his mother's reaction.

Gloria sipped her tea, sending him a thoughtful look over the rim of her cup. "She'll need time to heal, of course. Did she say when this happened?"

Phoebe hadn't given the group many details. In fact, she seemed reluctant to talk about her fiancé's death at all, which told him she was still dealing with the loss.

Hutch could understand that. He would never forget how he'd felt when he'd learned about his father's heart attack. That kind of trauma wasn't quickly laid to rest.

"Be patient with her," his mother advised.

Hutch simply agreed. He'd hoped Gloria would be satisfied with a few remarks about Phoebe, but he could tell that wasn't going to be the case.

"What does she look like?" His mother pressed and then laughed. "Outward appearance doesn't mean much, but she's obviously captured your fancy and that makes me wonder. She must be beautiful."

"She is." At least in his eyes, Phoebe was strikingly attractive. "She has big, dark eyes." In them he read her pain and determination to survive this and whatever else life threw at her. The woman had courage, and that appealed to him even more than her beauty. As for describing her features, all he could come up with was that she looked *pretty.*

"She's about your height," he said, turning to his mother. The fact that Phoebe had slipped so easily into his mind was actually surprising. He hadn't thought about her since last week's knitting class.

"Short, then."

"No-o-o." Hutch didn't view her that way.

"Petite." Not a word he normally used, but it seemed to describe Phoebe.

"How does she wear her hair?"

"Her hair," he repeated. "It's . . . it's . . ." He made several futile attempts to depict it with his hands and finally gave up. "She wears it sort of . . . long. To her shoulders, I guess. It's uh, wavy." That was the best he could do.

His mother laughed, apparently finding his antics amusing. Finally Hutch shook his head. "You'll meet her soon enough, so all your questions will be answered."

His mother fairly beamed with excitement. "You've already asked her out?"

"Well . . ."

"Move slowly with her, Hutch. She's suffered a tremendous loss and the last thing she needs is to be rushed into a new relationship."

"Yes, Mother."

The way he said it made his mother smile. "I know, I know, you don't need dating advice from me."

She was right, but he wasn't willing to say so.

His mother finished her tea and left soon afterward. Hutch walked her to her car as she chatted about meeting his younger sister for lunch and the shopping trip the two of them had planned.

As he returned to the office, Phoebe Rylander's image came to mind again. He thought of her sitting across the table from him, working quietly on her project while he struggled to learn the craft. He suddenly felt unnerved as he recognized how much attention he'd paid to her. Until his mother's visit, he hadn't even realized it. That said a lot. He'd been out of the dating world for so many years, he found it hard to remember what it was like to have a relationship.

Offering to walk Phoebe to her car after class had been a matter of courtesy. Only now did he acknowledge his disappointment when she'd refused. He was completely out of his element with women these days—that was an unavoidable conclusion—but he was going to pursue Phoebe. In the gentlest possible way, of course. He'd follow his mother's suggestion and take things slowly. For all he knew, Phoebe might already be in another relationship. Somehow he didn't think so.

The phone on Gail's desk rang as Hutch stepped into the office. He heard her answer, then say, "Just a minute, Mr. Custer. I'll see if he's available."

He paused.

Holding her hand over the receiver, Gail said, "It's John—want to talk to him again?"

Hutch had been half expecting the attorney to call back. "I'll take it at my desk." He hurried into his office, closing the door.

"Hutch," John said excitedly. "Listen, these people are ready to deal. They don't want to go to court any more than we do."

"Good." Naturally he hoped the plaintiff in this

case could drop it entirely. That, however, was unlikely.

"Her attorney said he'd make everything go away for half a million dollars."

Hutch nearly laughed out loud. "There is absolutely no way!"

"Hutch, be reasonable," John said in a persuasive voice. "Getting rid of the aggravation factor is worth half a mil in itself. Be done with this once and for all."

Hutch hesitated, then decided to go with his gut. "In my opinion, this is blackmail, plain and simple."

"True, but it can also turn around and bite you if you don't settle now. It's a take it or leave it proposition. They're insisting on an answer by this afternoon."

Hutch had to admit he was tempted. He'd like nothing more than to put an end to this whole mess. "If we pay them off, what's to prevent someone else from filing the same suit two months down the road?"

John didn't respond for a moment. "That's unlikely. Let's deal with what's in front of us right now," he urged. "This can all be resolved today if we pay up. Don't you feel that's worth it?"

Hutch desperately wanted this lawsuit to disappear. However, writing a cheque for half a million dollars meant he'd be *buying* peace, and a tentative one at that. If he settled now, he was convinced he'd be opening the door for other such lawsuits and he refused to let that happen.

"I can't do it, John."

His father's old friend sighed loudly. "I figured you wouldn't take it."

"Do you seriously think I should?"

"I won't say. The decision is yours, and you went with your instincts. It's what your father would've done."

Hutch replaced the receiver, pleased with the comparison—until he remembered that his father had died at the age of fifty-eight.

CHAPTER
11

Phoebe Rylander

Phoebe hurried through the rain to the waterfront restaurant where she'd agreed to meet her mother for lunch. She wasn't foolish enough to believe the invitation had been prompted by any desire for her company. In every likelihood, Clark would be the main topic of conversation.

Her first instinct had been to beg off. Several convenient excuses readily presented themselves. For one thing, Phoebe only had an hour's lunch break and there was no guarantee she'd get back on time. Second, she'd seen her mother recently, although she'd cut their visit short because of

Leanne's insistence on discussing Clark.

Yet, even though her mother would pressure her to forgive Clark and forget the entire unsavory mess, Phoebe had agreed to this lunch. She didn't know why.

Then again, she did.

A part of her, the part that missed Clark so much, that missed his kisses and larger-than-life energy, hungered for any word of him. If she couldn't have Clark—and she *couldn't*—then, fool that she was, Phoebe wanted to hear about him. Her mother would be more than willing to give her the details she secretly longed for.

The outrage had faded now, replaced with a burning sadness. She loved Clark. He'd been a very important part of her life for nearly two years. It felt as if a giant hole had opened up in her everyday existence, a hole that seemed to grow deeper and wider every single day. Phoebe wavered between wishing Clark could be wiped from her memory and pathetically craving any scrap of information about him.

Breaking off the relationship would've been so much easier if she could just turn off her feelings. Or ignore them. But despite everything, she still wanted Clark. Although she had a job that meant a lot to her, the days seemed empty. Her evenings were listless as she looked for ways to fill the time she would otherwise have spent with Clark.

The waterfront restaurant, close to Pike Place

Market, was one of the places often frequented by tourists. The hostess was busy seating patrons when Phoebe arrived. She removed the scarf that had protected her hair from the drizzle and glanced over at the bank of windows with their view of the murky green waters of Puget Sound. To her surprise, her mother was already seated. Leanne waved; Phoebe waved back, then made her way through the maze of tables.

"You're early." That was a rarity. Phoebe took off her raincoat, hanging it on a hook outside the circular booth, and slid in next to her mother.

"I wanted to get us a good seat." Leanne set aside the menu. "I see you're right on time, as usual."

Phoebe didn't comment. Her mother spoke as if being prompt was a character flaw.

"The special of the day is a squash risotto and the soup is tomato basil."

"They both sound nice," Phoebe said, although she didn't have much of an appetite.

"I'm ordering the barbecued shrimp," her mother declared. "It's supposed to be excellent. Marlene Snowden recommended it the last time we ate here." She paused, apparently wondering if she'd done the wrong thing in mentioning Clark's mother.

Phoebe let the remark slide. "I'll just have the soup."

Leanne continued, a bit cautiously. "Speaking of Clark's mother . . ."

"Must we?" Phoebe asked pointedly.

"Oh, Phoebe, I don't think you realize how upset everyone is. Marlene phoned me in tears. She can't believe you'd do something like this."

"Me?" Phoebe cried, arousing curious looks from the people seated close by. "Why does all the blame fall on me?" she asked, lowering her voice. "Clark's the one who can't keep his pants zipped."

Her mother blanched. "Phoebe, please . . ."

"I didn't come here to discuss Clark, his family or anything to do with them," she said, although that wasn't strictly true. "If you feel you have to bring his name into the conversation, it might be best if I left now."

"Oh, sweetie, don't do that. I'm sorry. It's just that this is painful for me, too. Marlene and I have become such good friends."

"Even if Clark and I are no longer engaged, there's no reason you can't still be friends with his mother," Phoebe whispered, although she already knew the relationship was doomed. Her mother and Marlene had little in common. Leanne had loved being included in the Snowdens' social circle, but with the engagement over, it was unlikely that Marlene would continue to invite Phoebe's mother to the exclusive events she'd enjoyed so much.

The waiter came for their drink order and to Phoebe's astonishment her mother ordered an expensive glass of white wine. Phoebe asked for coffee. The weather seemed to suggest a hot drink; besides, she had to work this afternoon.

Minutes later, their server was back with their drinks and wrote down their lunch choices.

"My first knitting class went well," Phoebe said, trying to steer the conversation away from the Snowdens.

Her mother's eyes widened. "I didn't know you were learning to knit."

"Well, relearning . . ." Phoebe had forgotten that she'd decided to keep it a secret. "I needed something . . ." She left the rest unsaid. Her mother had to know how lost and lonely she must feel without Clark in her life.

Leanne sipped her wine. "Max recommended this Sauvignon Blanc. It's from New Zealand and it has a nice, crisp citrus flavor. You really must try it sometime."

Phoebe sighed. She genuinely liked Clark's father. He had a wonderful wit and charm. After Clark's first "indiscretion," Max was the one who'd come to talk to her, to plead his son's case. Although he was as disgusted and shocked as Phoebe had been, he'd asked her to give Clark one last chance. To his credit, Max hadn't contacted her since she'd returned Clark's engagement ring. She suspected he wouldn't.

"Is Clark's family going to be part of every conversation?" Phoebe asked, struggling to keep her voice even.

"Oh, my, I did it again, didn't I?" Her mother at least looked regretful.

How sincere her apology was, Phoebe couldn't tell. "Mom, you don't need to tell me how hard this is on you. I know, because it's even more difficult for me." Her mother seemed to conveniently forget that.

"Of course it is. Forgive me for being so thoughtless, sweetie."

Phoebe stared out the window and tried to force her thoughts away from Clark. It was practically impossible with Leanne dragging his parents' names into every topic imaginable. She'd known that, but she'd still come to lunch. As much as she despised her own weakness, Phoebe was eager for news. And yet she had to stop this, stop giving in to—

"Leanne, Phoebe, how delightful to see you here."

As if the mere thought of her ex-fiancé was enough to conjure him up, Clark appeared out of nowhere. Before she could object, he slid into the booth beside Phoebe, trapping her there.

Phoebe stiffened and refused to glance in his direction.

"Clark!" Her mother feigned surprise and frankly did a poor job of it. "What are *you* doing here?"

"I was meeting a client for lunch, but he cancelled at the last minute. I was about to leave when I saw the two of you sitting here. I hope you don't mind if I join you?"

How smoothly he lied, how easily the words rolled off his tongue, but Phoebe wasn't fooled. She knew this was a setup.

"As a matter of fact, I do," she said flatly.

"Phoebe, please, what will it hurt to have lunch with me?" he asked. He sounded so calm and reasonable that for a moment she was tempted to agree.

"It'll hurt a great deal, I'm afraid. Please go."

"Where are your manners?" her mother chastised.

Phoebe turned to face Leanne and didn't bother to disguise the betrayal she felt. "You arranged this. My own mother! I can't believe it."

"Don't get upset with your mother. This is my fault," Clark said softly. "I'm the one who put her up to it. I was desperate to talk to you and this seemed the only way."

"All I ask," her mother pleaded, "is that you hear Clark out. If you'd listen, you might understand that the whole thing was police entrapment."

As far as Phoebe was concerned, how it happened was of no relevance. *That* it happened was everything. Still, she knew arguing would do no good. Clark was a master manipulator. He could turn the tables so quickly that it made her head spin. It was pointless to argue with him—a losing proposition.

Clark reached for her hand and while she wanted to resist, she didn't.

"I've missed you, baby," he said, his voice low and seductive.

Phoebe could almost feel her resolve melting. For her own peace of mind, she refused to look at him, refused to make eye contact. Once she did, she'd be lost. . . .

The waiter scurried over with a menu, which he handed Clark, who gave it a perfunctory glance and quickly placed his order for a rare sirloin steak. Leave it to Clark to order steak in one of the finest seafood restaurants on the west coast. He always seemed to take the contrary view, always stood apart.

He waited until the server was gone before he returned his attention to Phoebe. His thumb gently rubbed the top of her hand in a manner that was almost sexual. Phoebe jerked it away, staring at the dark, swirling waters of Puget Sound.

"I've been doing a lot of thinking," Clark told her, with Leanne listening avidly. "You have every right to be angry. If our situations were reversed, I can imagine how I'd feel."

"Really?" she couldn't resist asking. "If I were to pay for sex, that would bother you?"

He blinked as if he found the thought completely discordant.

"But why should it?" she went on. "It doesn't mean anything, does it? It's just . . . something people do and it really doesn't affect our relationship. Isn't that what you said?"

"I did, but I was wrong."

"You were wrong twice—that I know of."

He exhaled slowly. "Some of us are slow learners. But it'll never happen again. I swear by everything I hold dear."

"What you had with these women wasn't an emotional connection, remember? Only a physical one." This was another rationale of his. Presumably it was supposed to appease her.

Clark closed his eyes. "I was wrong," he said again.

"What excuse do you have for the same thing happening a second time?"

At first she didn't think he was going to answer; when he did his voice was strained. It seemed to vibrate with pain, whether real or fabricated, she wasn't sure.

"I was drunk. Drunk out of my mind. I had no idea what I was doing. If it makes any difference, you should know I didn't even find her attractive."

"It doesn't," Phoebe snapped. "That's completely irrelevant."

Clark lowered his head. "I'm sorry."

She so badly wanted to believe him, and yet she knew she couldn't. "Being drunk doesn't excuse that kind of behavior."

"You're right, it doesn't, but maybe it'll help you understand why it happened. I was weak and—"

"What guarantee do I have that you won't be . . . weak again?" Phoebe asked.

"Because it would kill me to hurt you this way. It won't happen. I give you my word."

"He means it, sweetie," her mother said imploringly. "Listen to Clark. Every word is sincere. He couldn't be more repentant. Let him have one more chance. That's all he wants, all any of us want."

Phoebe turned to Clark, meeting his eyes for the first time. He wore a woebegone look that would've softened the hardest heart. Despite everything, Phoebe found herself on the verge of surrender. She was about to capitulate when the waiter arrived with their meals. The relief she felt at being interrupted, at not agreeing to yet another chance, nearly overwhelmed her. Winning was vital to Clark; she couldn't know whether he meant what he said or just needed to remain in control by persuading her to take him back.

Clark seemed to sense that her determination was flagging because he reached for her hand, intertwining their fingers. He held on to her while the waiter served them.

"Shall I order champagne?" he asked her. "Tell me we have something to celebrate."

"Not yet," she whispered.

Her mother leaned forward. "Phoebe, please. It would mean the world to Marlene and me if you and Clark were engaged again."

As if on cue, Clark took the solitaire diamond engagement ring from his suit pocket and set it on the table next to her bowl. "I've carried it with me from the moment you dropped it off," he confessed brokenly. "I can't tell you the number of times I've looked at this diamond. I can't lose you, Phoebe. I can't. You're everything to me."

"Unless you're drunk," she added. She knew she sounded bitter and angry, but didn't care.

"If it'll help, I'll quit drinking. You say the word and I swear I won't touch another drop."

Phoebe pulled her hand away. "Why would you do that?" Clark enjoyed his drinks. To the best of her knowledge he rarely overindulged.

"If that's the only way I can have you back, then I'll give up alcohol for good."

"Why are you trying so hard?" she demanded. She needed proof that this was more than his pride talking, more than his desire to be in control of their relationship.

He blinked as though he didn't understand the question. "You don't know?" he asked softly. "You honestly don't know?"

"Tell her," Leanne urged. "Tell her what you told me."

"I love you," Clark stated emphatically. "It's as simple as that. I want to spend the rest of my life with you. I want us to raise our family together and when we're old and gray, you're the one I want at my side."

A lump filled her throat. No woman could listen to those words and not be affected. "I . . . I have to think."

Clark's gaze held hers, filled with triumph at the first crack in her defenses. She suddenly realized it was what he needed, what he'd been hoping to achieve.

"I'm going to the ladies' room," she said.

"You'll be right back?" her mother asked. "Do you want me to go with you?"

"Don't be ridiculous."

Reluctantly Clark slid out of the booth and she followed, leaving her raincoat behind. Taking her purse, she hurried across the restaurant to the restroom and quickly went in.

Locking herself inside a stall, she leaned against the door and closed her eyes.

The fleeting look on Clark's face just then. She'd seen it—that small display of satisfaction that he could manipulate her. He assumed he'd won her back . . . and he almost had. He'd almost done it, but now that she was away from his influence, away from her mother, cool reason returned.

Without questioning her own actions, Phoebe left the stall and hurried out of the restaurant. Thankfully there was a taxi parked at the curb. With rain beating down on her, she climbed in the backseat and gave the driver her work address.

Not until she was several blocks away could she breathe easily again. She felt like someone who'd taken a wrong step, who'd lost her footing and faltered. Only now, safe from Clark, did she feel secure.

CHAPTER
12

Alix Turner

During her fifteen-minute morning break Alix lit up a cigarette in the alley behind the café. Closing her eyes, she took her first drag. She held the smoke in her lungs an extra-long moment, savoring the instant sense of relief before exhaling. When she opened her eyes again, she could imagine—all too clearly—her husband's pained look of disappointment.

Good boy that he was, Jordan Turner had never smoked. He couldn't begin to understand how difficult it was to quit. What he understood even less was why Alix had started again after four years of not smoking.

She *wanted* to quit. Except that she couldn't seem to do it, although they both agreed that she needed to be one hundred percent free of nicotine before she got pregnant.

A baby.

Tension skittered down her spine. Alix hoped to get pregnant soon and Jordan wanted that, too. They'd moved into his grandma Turner's house on Star Lake and it was ideal, certainly for her, but perhaps even more for him. So many of his childhood memories were associated with the lake house. Only last night Jordan had said it was the perfect place to start their family. Which, of course, she'd been saying all along. . . .

It'd be nice, Alix mused, really nice—until her gaze fell on the cigarette. In a fit of frustration and anger she tossed it on the asphalt and crushed it with the toe of her work shoe. And then she immediately regretted wasting most of a cigarette.

Besides being a nasty habit that made her hair smell and stained her fingers, it was an expensive one. At least she was down to a maximum of five cigarettes a day—less than two packs a week. The daily total varied, depending on the sort of day she'd had, but she never exceeded five. That was her limit, and she was proud of her discipline, proud she'd whittled the number down from twice that many just a few months ago. She knew it wasn't sufficient. But still . . .

Jordan had been kind enough not to say anything about the cost, but it had to be on his mind. It bothered Alix, too. But she recognized that her inability to give up cigarettes was about more than the addiction. As much as she wanted Jordan's baby, she was afraid.

She didn't think of herself as a fearful person. A few years back she'd stood up to an armed drug dealer without even flinching. But back then she didn't much care if she lived or died.

The truth was, becoming a mother terrified her. She'd tried to describe her fears to Jordan. He was better at listening these days, but after only a few words she realized her feelings on this subject were simply beyond his experience.

His family had nothing, absolutely nothing, in common with hers.

Jordan's father was a pastor; Jordan was following in his footsteps and would one day have his own church.

Jordan's parents were good people—loving, compassionate, down to earth. His mom was the *Brady Bunch* kind of mother who baked cookies and still owned an ironing board.

Parents like hers didn't fall within Jordan's frame of reference. He couldn't possibly comprehend what it was to hide in a closet to drown out the noise of her parents' drunken brawls. He knew things like that happened because he'd worked with troubled teens in the past. But he knew it in a theoretical, indirect way. It wasn't part of him, a memory always hovering, always *there*.

Okay, so motherhood was scary. Alix admitted it and suspected the cigarettes were an avoidance technique. If she smoked, she could put off dealing with her doubts. She could defer finding out whether she was capable of being a mother. After all, crying babies upset her. She thought messy diapers were disgusting. As for breast-feeding an infant, which Jordan seemed to think came naturally to women, the idea filled her with trepidation. Other women might have strong maternal instincts, but not Alix. And after her mother's example, who could blame her?

"Alix."

Becky Major, the middle-aged prep cook, stuck her head out the door.

"Winter's looking for you." Winter Adams was the woman who owned the French Café.

"Hey, I've got another ten minutes." Alix intended to take her full allotment of time. After a week of dismal rain, the sun was shining and she wanted to enjoy it as long as she could.

"Lydia's here, too. She'd like to talk to you."

Alix didn't hesitate. She'd return to her motherhood worries later. A visit with Lydia was always a treat. On her way through the kitchen Alix poured herself a cup of coffee. If she couldn't have nicotine, she'd settle for caffeine.

Lydia was waiting for her at the counter with a cup of her own. "Have you got a few minutes?"

Alix noticed her friend's anxious look. "Of course. What do you need? Shall we go outside?" she asked, and Lydia nodded. They'd have more privacy there.

The sidewalk tables were set up with the umbrellas open and Alix chose a shady one close to the café. Lydia sat across from her.

"I hope you don't mind me interrupting your morning."

"Not at all," Alix assured her. Actually, she was grateful for a reprieve from her scattered thoughts.

"It's about Casey."

"Who?" As soon as Alix asked the question, she remembered. "Oh, yeah. The foster kid."

"Right." Lydia held her coffee mug with both hands, resting them on the table.

"Wasn't Casey only supposed to be with you for a week?" She knew that because of a comment Margaret had made during last week's class.

"She was." Lydia sighed. "Now it might be longer."

Alix didn't ask her why. Lydia would explain if she wanted to. But Alix didn't have any difficulty figuring out that the social worker hadn't found another home for Casey. Alix wasn't surprised, either; she'd been shuffled around enough to know what that was like.

"So, how's it going with Casey?" she asked, although she had a fairly clear idea.

"About all I can say is that we've tolerated one another. When Casey comes home from day camp, she goes straight to her room and closes the door." Lydia paused. "It's the craziest thing . . ."

"What?"

"She hoards stuff."

"Like what?"

Lydia looked mildly embarrassed. "Toilet paper. I came across six rolls in her bedroom. Last Monday I got groceries and then later couldn't find the crackers. They were in Casey's room, hidden under the bed. The end of the box was sticking out and when I knelt down to pick it up, I found a box of cereal, some cookies and the toilet paper. When I asked her about it, she said she might need them."

"Did you take the stuff away from her?" Alix asked.

Lydia shook her head. "I decided that if she felt more secure keeping those things in her room, it was okay with me."

Alix suspected there'd been a time and a place when necessities like crackers, cereal and toilet paper had been withheld from Casey. During her years in foster care, Alix had developed some idiosyncrasies of her own.

"Dinners are the worst," Lydia went on to say.

"How do you mean?"

Lydia's expression was strained. "At least she eats, but she barely talks. I've done everything I can to draw her out. Nothing I say or do seems to reach her. From the looks she gives me, it's as if she resents my showing any interest in her. Cody's been great lately and Brad, too, but there just doesn't seem to be any way to connect with her."

Alix had been in enough foster homes to recognize the behavior. "She knows she's going to be leaving soon, so she's trying not to care about any of you."

"But why? Brad and I have bent over backward to make her feel welcome."

This was so hard for others to understand.

"Listen," Alix said, leaning toward her friend. "Let me put it like this. You've got a piece of tape and you stick it to something and it stays put. Okay?"

Lydia blinked. "Okay. Yes."

"Peel it off and stick it again and what happens?"

"It still sticks," she answered.

"Right. But what happens when you peel it away for the third or fourth time?"

Lydia shrugged. "Most of the stickiness is gone."

"Well, it's the same with kids. Casey's protecting whatever stickiness she has left for the family who'll keep her and care for her and love her. She can't risk her heart on a family that'll be part of her life for a couple of weeks."

Lydia shook her head again as if she wanted to argue. "Brad and I *do* care about her."

"Sure you do." Alix didn't mean to sound flippant or cynical but she couldn't help it. "You care about her now. Casey knows that six months down the road you'll have trouble remembering her name, especially if you take in other foster kids in emergency situations."

"Oh." Lydia appeared to mull that over. "Would it be better if we didn't care?"

"No. Give her all the attention and love you can. It'll fill her up. And that's a good thing, especially when it comes time for her to change homes."

Looking down, Lydia clasped and unclasped her hands. "She's been with us for nine days now."

"It seems longer than that, doesn't it?"

"Oh, yeah." Lydia grinned. "She's already tried to run away once."

"Did she make it obvious?"

Her question surprised Lydia, who nodded.

"Typical." Alix had tried it more than once herself. If Casey had really wanted to slip away unnoticed she would've managed to do so. It was a ploy to see if Lydia and Brad would stop her.

"What do you know about her family background?"

"Next to nothing," Lydia told her. "Evelyn didn't think it was necessary to tell us much, seeing that Casey was supposed to be with us for such a short while."

"So now what?"

"Evelyn phoned yesterday afternoon and asked if there was any way Brad and I could keep Casey for another couple of weeks—until her classes are finished. Apparently the state will have to place her in a home in a different school district. Evelyn said there's a real shortage of foster homes this summer."

"What are you going to do?" Alix asked without emotion.

"I talked to Brad and Cody, and the three of us decided we'd be okay with having Casey stay longer. Only . . . only we don't believe she *wants* to stay with us."

"She does," Alix told her confidently. "The

problem is, she's been moved around so much she's afraid to let anyone know what she wants for fear it'll be taken away from her."

Lydia's frown showed her dismay. "You mean . . . love? Security?"

"Yes . . . and even toilet paper," Alix said with a small laugh.

This was a whole different world to her friend. Lydia couldn't understand the mind of a child like Casey, not the way Alix did. Alix, too, had been a case number, a name on a file. Evelyn Boyd did her best; she was a good woman with a huge heart but she carried a heavy load.

"You talked about the tape and stickiness," Lydia reminded her.

"Yes."

"How can I give Casey some of her glue back?"

Good question. Alix leaned forward, resting an elbow on the table, and thought about it, recalling that time in her own life. When she was in the eighth grade, she'd lived in three different foster homes and attended three different schools. It'd been a bad year for her, and she suspected that once Casey left Lydia and Brad's, her year would follow the same downward spiral.

"Does Casey have any family? A grandmother? Aunt? Cousins? Does—" She stopped when Lydia started to nod.

"She mentioned a brother," she said eagerly, then paused. "Actually, I think it was Evelyn who told me that Casey has an older brother. Apparently he's at the Kent Juvenile Facility."

Alix had briefly been incarcerated there herself. Kent was a south Seattle community with the largest juvenile facility in the area, possibly the state.

"It would help if you could arrange for Casey to visit her brother."

"But how?" Lydia sounded perplexed.

"Get Evelyn involved. I can guarantee that Casey will feel a whole lot better if she can spend even a small amount of time with him."

Alix had loved her brother, too. She didn't talk about Tom and very few people knew about him. Tom's death had been the turning point in Alix's life. Up until then, she'd experimented with drugs, hung out with losers and generally got herself into trouble.

Then Tom had been found dead. He'd choked to death on his own vomit after shooting up heroin. As long as she lived, Alix would never forget the day she'd learned that the only person who'd ever truly loved her was gone. Forever. She'd wanted to die herself.

Giving herself a mental shake, Alix returned her attention to Lydia.

"I'll call Evelyn as soon as I get back to the store," Lydia said. "I appreciate the advice."

"I'm glad I could help."

"Anything else you can suggest?"

"Well . . . you're going to need lots of patience."

"You mean more than Brad and I have already given her?" Lydia asked wryly.

Remembering her own youth, Alix nodded. "*Lots* more."

"I was afraid of that." Lydia laughed a little.

Alix laughed, too. She wondered whether Lydia's sister had any opinions on this latest development—and was sure she did. "What does Margaret have to say about the situation with Casey?"

"You don't want to hear." Lydia's smile wavered and she shook her head. "Margaret means well. It's just that she's so used to looking after me. Even now Margaret's always positive that she knows best."

Alix glanced at her watch and realized her break had ended five minutes earlier. She'd better find out why Winter had asked to see her.

"I need to get back to work," she said and stood, collecting their empty cups.

"Thanks again," Lydia murmured.

"Let me know if there's anything else I can do. Or if you ever need to talk," Alix said, and she meant it.

CHAPTER
13

"Hutch" Hutchinson

Hutch sat at the table in the back of A Good Yarn and tried to concentrate on his knitting. The sampler scarf was progressing well as far as he could see, at least the first and second sections were. He'd learned to knit and purl, which seemed to impress everyone, from his mother to his assistant, Gail. This was the third class and Lydia was showing them how to make cable stitches, which was bound to *really* impress Gloria and Gail.

Lydia was teaching them in stages, and he suspected the stitches would become progressively more difficult with every week. He felt a little hesitant about this, since knitting didn't come naturally to him. He'd hoped for relaxation, not another challenge—despite the bragging rights conferred by his new skill. He might have considered dropping out if not for an even more interesting challenge.

Phoebe Rylander.

She was already there when he arrived, and he'd been distracted from the moment he sat down. He hoped his fascination with her wasn't obvious; he was afraid of embarrassing himself and frightening her off.

He couldn't believe how romantically inept he was, although he told himself there were extenuating circumstances. Phoebe was still grieving the death of her fiancé, and he didn't want to appear insensitive to her pain. At the same time . . . well, he'd like to get to know her.

He was trying to heed his mother's advice—to go slow—but if he went any more slowly, the next ice age might overtake the world before he'd managed to ask her out on an actual date.

This was the third week he'd sat across from her. He felt as if he was still in junior high—and he didn't like the feeling. He'd offered to escort her to her car that first class. Phoebe had declined, so during the second class he didn't mention it again. They'd spoken a few times, about inconsequential things. She'd laughed at his jokes. That was a good sign, but then Alix and Lydia had laughed, too.

"I've really come to enjoy these classes," Phoebe had said at the end of class as she packed her knitting bag.

Hutch continued to keep his supplies in his briefcase. It wasn't so much that he didn't want anyone to know he was knitting. He just preferred not to walk around carrying an oversize purse, especially one of those quilted ones that looked like a diaper bag.

At the end of the second class Phoebe had started to leave first. Hutch had hurried forward to open the door for her and she'd smiled her appreciation.

Hutch had smiled back, then stood there like a dope as she'd moved down the sidewalk.

Phoebe had been a half a block away when he'd instinctively begun to follow her. He'd stopped abruptly midstep, uncertain what to say or do next. After that initial statement during the first class, she'd said nothing more about her fiancé. Hutch had assumed the other man's death was recent but couldn't be sure.

He was definitely interested in getting to know Phoebe, but he didn't want to start a conversation by opening a half-healed wound. He had no idea whether it would be appropriate to refer to her fiancé, yet it seemed heartless to completely ignore this man she'd so obviously loved.

The way he figured it, he needed to make a move soon or forget it entirely. And forgetting Phoebe was definitely something he didn't want to do. But if he waited too long, didn't make his interest clear, the whole thing would become awkward. For both of them. He'd tried to work out the best approach.

Unfortunately he'd come up blank. He'd never had trouble starting conversations with women while he was in college and in his twenties. Of course, he'd never encountered a situation like this one, either. It didn't help that he hadn't dated anyone in so long his skills had rusted away.

"Would you like me to check your stitches?" Lydia asked, breaking into his thoughts. He'd reviewed what he had—and hadn't—said to

Phoebe a dozen times. In the end, he hadn't approached her, and regretted it for the rest of the week. This third class was it, he decided. If he didn't act now he was afraid he never would.

Hutch glanced up at Lydia and found her regarding him expectantly. Thinking he might have missed part of the conversation, he handed her his knitting.

She took it from him and frowned.

"Did I do something wrong?" he asked. Although his attention had been on Phoebe, he'd carefully tried to follow Lydia's instructions.

Lydia gave him a reassuring smile. "The pattern's perfect."

Hutch had thought so, too, but it felt good to have Lydia confirm it.

"The problem is your tension, Hutch. See how tight these stitches are?"

It was true that he had difficulty moving the yarn on the needles, but it'd been like that from the moment he cast on his first stitches.

"It's almost as if you're knitting armor," she teased.

"I've done it like this from the start."

"Relax," Lydia said. "That's the reason you signed up for this class, isn't it? To relax?"

Hutch nodded.

He looked quickly at Phoebe. Lydia was right; he'd enrolled in this class to help lower his blood pressure and learn new techniques for dealing with stress. However . . . he'd met Phoebe, and she'd inadvertently *increased* his stress. At least his thumb was improving. The knitting had benefitted him there.

"I have just the opposite problem," Phoebe volunteered after Lydia had left the table. "My stitches are too loose. At the rate I'm going, this scarf is going to be ten feet long."

"And mine will be ten inches."

She laughed at his rather lame joke, which encouraged him. "Are you enjoying the class?" he asked, then wanted to groan. If his joke was lame, this effort at conversation was even worse.

Phoebe smiled at him. "Very much. What about you?"

"A lot." Hutch didn't mention that she was responsible for about ninety-nine percent of his pleasure. He'd been looking forward to this evening and dreading it at the same time. His thoughts had been on Phoebe all week and now here she was—yet he felt as much hesitation as he had before. He was even more reluctant to take a risk with her for fear of offending her so soon after a major loss . . . and perhaps a fear of being rejected, too, although he hated to admit that. He paused, hoping for further encouraging signs. None came but, determined now, he forged ahead. "I don't suppose . . . I mean, after class . . . but if you've got other plans, I understand . . ." That sounded *so* pathetic, it was all he could do not to get up and walk away. He closed his mouth, deciding he wouldn't say another word. What was wrong with him? He was a competent businessman who headed a family-owned enterprise and commanded the respect of over a hundred employees. Yet around Phoebe he acted like a kid in junior high.

"Other plans for what?" she asked curiously.

Well, he'd bungled that, despite his attempt to sound casual. "Would you like to have coffee?" he asked, his voice gruff now, almost angry. This was going from bad to dismal.

To his utter astonishment, Phoebe nodded. "I'd like that."

He clamped his mouth shut before he could talk her out of it.

"There's the French Café across the street." Alix looked up from her knitting. "They're open until ten tonight."

"Great idea," Phoebe said. "You work there, right?"

"Sure do. I'm part of the morning staff. I do the baking."

"So you're the one responsible for those wonderful pastries," Phoebe commented. "I stopped by the other day and picked up a half-dozen for the clinic. They were fabulous."

"I can't take all the credit," Alix said.

"Yes, you can," Lydia cut in. "I've seen and tasted Alix's handiwork."

"Me, too," Margaret agreed. "You see this extra fat on my hips? Blame Alix."

"Hey, you're the one who chose to eat those Danishes and croissants," Alix reminded her.

"I second that," Hutch added, remembering the lawsuit hanging over his head. It wasn't just the candy business that could be jeopardized by this lawsuit. If he lost, bakeries would be prime candidates, too. And restaurants. No telling where this craziness would end.

"All right, all right." Margaret sighed. "I deserve every ounce of this extra weight."

Hutch grinned, then caught Phoebe watching him. She smiled back. He felt a sensation of warmth. Of happiness—and comfort. Maybe he hadn't seemed as big an idiot as he'd thought.

"Shall we walk over to the French Café after class?" she asked.

"Sure." If she'd suggested they have coffee in Costa Rica, he would've found a way to get there. Walking across the street was no problem—if he didn't do something stupid like throw himself in front of a bus.

The Knit to Quit class ended a few minutes before eight. Alix had been especially quiet most of the evening. Hutch liked her and her husband, too, who came to pick her up again. Apparently Jordan worked late the evenings Alix was at A Good Yarn, which meant they could drive home together.

Phoebe stood and gathered her things. Hutch did, too.

"Good night, you two," Lydia said as they walked toward the front door.

"Night," Hutch echoed.

"See you next week," Phoebe said, looking over her shoulder.

Lydia waved them off. As they closed the door, Hutch happened to hear Margaret speculating on a romance between him and Phoebe. For an instant he was tempted to stop and listen, wondering how they viewed his chances.

Once outside, Hutch threw his briefcase into his car. He'd been lucky enough to find a parking place almost directly in front of A Good Yarn— maybe that was a sign. Phoebe waited and then they hurried across the street.

The French Café was brightly lit and there were a number of couples scattered around the restaurant, eating a late dinner or sipping coffee.

"What would you like?" Hutch asked as they approached the counter.

"Just black coffee," she replied.

"Why don't you choose a table and I'll go get our coffees."

She nodded and he watched as she selected a quiet place in the back of the restaurant. After ordering and paying for their drinks, he carried both mugs to the table.

Now that he was alone with Phoebe, he found

himself at a loss. He tried to recall his college days, but everything had been so easy back then. So natural and effortless. He used to see himself as witty and social—something he could hardly believe now.

"So," he began. "Tell me about yourself."

Phoebe brushed the hair from her face, which he'd noticed was a habit of hers. More than once he'd been tempted to reach out and do it for her, which would've been inappropriate to put it mildly. He clasped his hands in his lap.

"Well . . . I think I already mentioned I'm a physical therapist."

He nodded. "You told us that during our first class."

"What about you?" she asked.

Obviously what he'd said about himself wasn't memorable. "I work for a family-owned business," he told her.

"Oh, yes. I remember that now."

He'd made a point of not referring to Mount Rainier Chocolates by name. The company was well-known in the area, and the moment people learned about his connection, they bombarded him with questions—always the same ones. He was tired of answering them, tired of all the silly jokes and sly remarks. Besides, there was more to him than his job.

"You took the class to relax, isn't that what you said? And because of your thumb."

"Yeah." He raised his hand and waggled his thumb, feeling a twinge of pain.

"Have you had physical therapy?" she asked.

He shook his head. Physical therapy took time he couldn't spare; not only that, his injury wasn't serious, despite its slowness in healing.

"There are various exercises you can do to regain dexterity," she said.

"You mean other than knitting armor?" he joked.

Phoebe smiled again and it seemed the entire room grew a little brighter.

The conversation went well from that point forward. Phoebe was easy to talk to, her own comments interesting and animated. If the conversation lagged she picked it up. Still, Hutch felt he needed to say something about her fiancé. He might as well do it now. Get it over with, if that wasn't too crass a description.

"I know how difficult this time is for you," he said solemnly when a discussion of recent movies had run its course.

Her gaze shot to his. "You do?"

"Losing your fiancé . . ."

"Yes, well . . . these things happen." He could tell that talking about the man she'd loved flustered and upset her. Hutch felt bad about bringing up such a painful subject, but he wanted to be sure Phoebe knew he sympathized.

He decided to take his cue from her and move on. He said the first thing that came to mind. "I've enjoyed being in the class with you."

Her eyes softened as she cast her eyes down. "I feel the same way."

"I'd . . . like to see you again, outside class." He didn't give her a chance to respond. "But only if you're ready. If it's too soon, I understand. All I ask is that you let me know when you feel ready to date again."

"I . . . I . . ." She hesitated.

His heart sank.

"I believe I'm ready now," she said, meeting his eyes.

A sense of exhilaration filled him. "That's wonderful." Then, because he felt he had to clarify what he'd said, he added quickly, "Wonderful that you're willing to see me again. Not wonderful that your fiancé died." The instant the words left his tongue, Hutch wanted to yank them back. He couldn't have said anything stupider or more insensitive. "That didn't come out right."

"Don't worry. I knew what you meant."

He exhaled a sigh of relief. "The Fourth of July is this weekend," he said.

"So I noticed."

"Would you like to go on a picnic?" he asked. It was a traditional Fourth of July activity, he figured. "I have a couple of bicycles," he said on the spur of the moment.

"That sounds like fun. Anyplace special you'd like to ride?"

Hutch hadn't taken out his bicycle in years. "I biked through the Skagit Valley once and really enjoyed that." The landscape was flat. He didn't want to huff and puff his way up a hill; he'd prefer to play it safe.

Phoebe's eyes brightened. "I love the Skagit Valley."

He felt like standing up and cheering. "Then it's a date."

"I look forward to it."

They parted outside the café and Hutch experienced an unfamiliar feeling of satisfaction—with the conversation, with her and even with himself.

The next morning Hutch arrived at the office in an exceptionally good mood.

"You're *whistling*," Gail said.

"I was? When?"

"Just now." She seemed to approve, however, because she sent him a contented smile.

"I didn't realize it," he said, feeling vaguely puzzled. "Listen, I need you to do a couple of things for me."

"Sure."

"Order me two fully assembled mountain bikes. One blue and one red, complete with helmets. Have them delivered to my house."

"Right away."

That morning he'd checked out the bikes in his garage and they were old and not in the best condition. Rather than spend the time getting them updated and repaired, it would be simpler to purchase new ones.

"Anything else?"

"Yes." He felt a bit self-conscious about this. "Go online and order me a book, if you would."

"Of course. Do you have the title or the author's name?"

"I don't know the author, but the title should be along the lines of *Dating for Dummies* or *Relationships for Idiots.*"

Gail couldn't disguise her amusement, which Hutch chose to overlook. He couldn't blame her. However, he was willing to start his romantic education from scratch, as long as he could spend time with Phoebe Rylander.

CHAPTER
14

Anne Marie Roche

Blossom Street Books." Anne Marie answered the phone in her usual pleasant tone, assuming the caller would be asking about her hours or whether a particular title had come in.

"Anne Marie, this is Tim Carlsen."

Anne Marie froze and drew in a deep breath. She'd known it was too much to hope that she'd never hear from him again. Fortunately she was alone in the bookstore. "What can I do for you, Mr. Carlsen?" she asked stiffly.

He ignored the lack of welcome in her voice. "Have you given any more thought to our conversation last week?" he asked.

It'd been ten days since she'd heard from Tim Carlsen. Ten days since the Monday afternoon he'd told her he might be Ellen's biological father. From that moment until now, Anne Marie had been waiting, wondering if he planned to follow through with his threat to take legal action.

"I assumed the next move was yours," she said, hoping her bluntness would tell him she had no intention of allowing him into *her* daughter's life. It was too late—and besides, the law was on her side.

"Listen," Tim said, "I'm not going to get an attorney. You're right. Ellen's your family now. Whether I'm her biological father or not isn't relevant."

Anne Marie was prepared to battle him all the way to the Supreme Court. That he'd capitulated so readily took her by surprise. "Thank you," she whispered, hardly knowing what else to say.

"If you ever decide you'd be willing to have Ellen tested . . ."

"I won't."

Undaunted, he continued. "Or if one day Ellen asks about her father, I hope you'll contact me."

Anne Marie wasn't sure if this was a ploy. "I doubt that'll be necessary."

"At some point there might be a medical issue," he countered.

"What do you mean?" she asked anxiously. "Is there something you're not telling me?"

"No, not at all. I just want you to realize you can call me if anything like that ever surfaces."

"Oh."

"Don't worry, I won't contact you again. I'd like to leave my phone numbers with you, though. If at any time, for any reason, you have a change of heart, I'd appreciate it if you'd call me."

He slowly recited three numbers: his home, office and cell, which she dutifully copied down and repeated, although she didn't plan to use any of them except in the direst of circumstances.

A silence followed before he said, "I guess there's nothing more to say." There was no denying the misery in his voice.

"No, there isn't," Anne Marie agreed. As far as she was concerned, the conversation was over.

"If Ellen—" He didn't finish what he'd started to say.

"What about Ellen?"

"If she ever needs anything or if you'd ever consider letting me into her life . . ."

"We've already discussed this, Mr. Carlsen. You have my answer."

"Yes," he said. He sounded utterly defeated. "Thank you, Ms. Roche."

Anne Marie replaced the telephone, although

her hand lingered on the receiver. She was grateful Tim Carlsen wasn't going to fight her on this, and the tension in her chest slowly dissipated. She hoped, for Ellen's sake, that she'd made the right decision.

That very evening, Anne Marie had reason to doubt she had.

Ellen returned from day camp full of enthusiasm, chattering about the games she'd played and the song she'd learned. She collected Baxter and took him for a walk along Blossom Street, skipping down the sidewalk with boundless energy, greeting her friends along the way.

Standing in the doorway of the bookstore, Anne Marie watched her daughter. Ellen was a happy child now. She remembered how reticent and quiet Ellen had been when they first met. Where was Tim Carlsen *then?* Where was Ellen's father when she'd needed him most?

Anne Marie recognized immediately how unfair she was being to Tim. He'd had no idea Candy Falk had given birth to a child. Even with the little she knew about Candy's history, Anne Marie was well aware that any one of a number of men could have fathered Ellen.

That night, when Anne Marie went to check on her daughter, she found Ellen sitting cross-legged on her bed holding a pencil and pad. Baxter lay curled on the bed beside her. Ellen appeared to be deep in thought.

"What have you got there?" Anne Marie asked, sitting beside her.

"My list of twenty wishes."

"Are you adding to it?"

Ellen chewed on the end of her pencil. "No. I'm looking at all the wishes I already wrote down."

"A lot of them have come true, haven't they?" Anne Marie asked. The girl had wanted to learn how to knit, which she'd done. She had her own bedroom furniture now and a friend from school had recently spent the night.

"Not *every* wish has come true," Ellen said. "Not this one."

"Which one is that?"

"The one about finding my father."

What was going on? It was almost as if Ellen had heard her phone conversation with Tim Carlsen earlier that day.

"What do you think my father looks like?" Ellen asked.

To hide her discomfort, Anne Marie grimaced. "I bet he has warts."

"Warts?"

"Yup, big ones. All over his face."

Setting aside her pad and pen, Ellen giggled and got up on her knees.

"And really big feet. Size thirty-six shoes," Anne Marie added. "As big as those shoes clowns wear."

Ellen giggled again.

173

"I bet his arms are really long and drag on the ground." Anne Marie stood up and walked around the bed, hunching her shoulders, apelike, and letting her arms dangle so they brushed against the carpeted floor.

Her antics got Baxter's attention and he started barking frantically until Anne Marie stopped, sat down again and petted him. Mollified, Baxter returned to his nap.

Ellen petted him, too. "No, he doesn't," she said. "Not my father."

"Well, what do you suppose he looks like?" Anne Marie asked.

Ellen's eyes shone with excitement. "I bet he's *really* handsome."

Her daughter wasn't far off the mark there, Anne Marie mused. Tim Carlsen was attractive. Of course, there was always the possibility that he wasn't Ellen's father, but that was likely wishful thinking on her part.

"I wonder if he has hair like mine."

That, he did. Anne Marie realized how much Ellen resembled him. She had Tim's coloring, his dark, straight hair and the same deep, brown eyes. This conversation was becoming more difficult by the minute.

"I bet he likes animals, too."

Anne Marie couldn't venture a guess about that.

"My first mom didn't. She said she'd get me a dog but she never did."

"You certainly love animals," Anne Marie commented.

Ellen stroked the Yorkie's side. "Especially Baxter."

"Especially Baxter," Anne Marie agreed. She looked at the clock. "It's past your bedtime, young lady," she said with mock severity.

Ellen didn't protest. "Can I read before I go to sleep?" she pleaded.

Anne Marie nodded. As was her habit, she knelt next to the bed and listened to Ellen's prayers. The girl yawned loudly halfway through the list of friends she prayed for every night and ended with a sweet, heartfelt request that God say hello to her Grandma Dolores.

"Are you sure you want to read tonight?" Anne Marie asked as she bent to kiss Ellen's forehead.

Her daughter's eyes were half closed. "Maybe . . . not," she whispered.

Anne Marie smiled, then turned off the light and tiptoed from the room.

For a long time afterward, she sat in the living room, deliberating about Tim Carlsen. At first she was convinced she'd made the decision that was best for Ellen. After all, Carlsen had no legal rights.

She wasn't fooled. There was a very good reason he'd decided not to pursue this through the courts. He'd discovered what Evelyn Boyle had already confirmed; because the birth certificate hadn't acknowledged him as Ellen's father, the courts had no means of contacting him before the adoption. Which meant Tim wasn't part of this scenario and had no place in Ellen's life. Even if he could prove he was Ellen's biological father, it was too late.

The only way Tim would be able to know Ellen was if Anne Marie allowed it. She wasn't about to do that. The man had been a drunk and a drug addict. It didn't matter that he was clean and sober now—or claimed to be. There were consequences when you'd lived that kind of life. Besides, what guarantee was there that he wouldn't backslide? Anne Marie wasn't willing to risk that. No, it was better that Ellen never find out about this.

Having justified her decision yet again, Anne Marie was determined to stand by it. She got ready for bed and, unlike her daughter, managed to sit up and read for at least thirty minutes. But despite her most strenuous efforts, her thoughts repeatedly returned to Tim and their telephone conversation.

After she'd read the same paragraph three times and still missed its meaning, she slammed the book shut and set it on her nightstand.

"This is ridiculous," she muttered, switching off the lamp. She slid down in bed, arranged her pillows and nestled against them, then closed her eyes.

Instantly Tim Carlsen's image rose before her. "Go away," she groaned out loud. "Leave me alone."

She turned onto her side and tried to force herself to sleep.

An hour later she was still awake.

After Robert's death, Anne Marie had difficulty sleeping. For a while she'd taken coated aspirins that were supposed to aid sleep without upsetting her stomach. They almost always worked.

Retrieving a tablet from the bathroom, she swallowed it, then sat in the living room for another thirty minutes, knitting while she waited to feel sleepy. But even knitting didn't quiet her thoughts. Anne Marie sighed, feeling confusion, guilt, frustration. If Ellen hadn't mentioned her father, she would've dropped the whole matter and the two of them would've gone peacefully about their lives.

What was it with kids? Ellen seemed to have built-in radar, zeroing in on the very topic Anne Marie wanted to avoid.

Finally Anne Marie yawned and went back to bed. She crawled under the covers and closed her eyes with renewed determination to cast out all thoughts of Tim Carlsen and his unreasonable request.

She still couldn't sleep.

Her mind whirled with a thousand different subjects. She'd talked to two real estate agents that day and had an appointment to look at a house after the holiday weekend. But regardless of what entered her mind, her thoughts always came back to one subject.

Tim Carlsen.

She couldn't stand it any longer. Throwing on her

bathrobe, Anne Marie marched down the stairs to the bookstore. She switched off the alarm and turned on the lights as she went into her office, where she'd left the phone numbers Tim had given her.

She punched out his home number, her jaw tight and her teeth clenched.

His phone rang four times. She half expected a greeting to come on, inviting her to leave a message.

It didn't.

Instead, a groggy Tim answered. "This better be good," he said hoarsely.

"Tim?"

A short pause followed. "Anne Marie?"

"Yes," she snapped.

"What time is it?"

Anne Marie hadn't even checked. "Midnight," she said, glancing at the store clock. She wasn't about to apologize for phoning so late. *He* was the one who'd kept her up.

"Is Ellen all right?"

"Yes."

"And you phoned because . . ."

"Because I've decided you can have Ellen's DNA tested, but only under one condition."

He didn't hesitate. "Name it."

"She can't know." That was Anne Marie's stipulation and if Tim balked at that, it was over right then and there.

"Okay."

She hadn't expected him to agree so fast.

"When?" he asked.

"I . . ." Anne Marie hadn't thought that far ahead. "Could we meet this weekend?"

"That's the Fourth of July. We have plans." It was the truth; she and Ellen would be with Melissa and her family for a barbecue.

"Okay," he said. "Listen, anytime is fine. You say when and where, and I'll be there."

Without any deliberation, Anne Marie mentioned a nearby park and suggested they meet late Wednesday afternoon.

"I'll be there," he said again.

"What should I tell Ellen?" she asked, wondering how she'd introduce him.

"Tell her I'm your date," he said after a moment.

"My date?" So he knew she was a widow. He'd implied as much when he'd asked about Ellen's adoptive father and she'd refused to answer him.

"Have you got a better idea?"

"No . . . I guess not."

"It's settled, then?"

"Yes." She wished she felt more comfortable with this, but she was committed now, whatever the outcome. "Not a word about the two of you possibly being related," she warned.

"Not a word. You have my promise."

Whether he kept his promises remained to be seen.

CHAPTER
15

When I was nine years old my mother gave me a pair of shiny silver aluminum knitting needles and a ball of bright purple yarn and showed me how to cast on for a pair of mittens. I can still remember my excitement as the yarn came alive in my fingers and turned itself magically from string into a lumpy mitten. I never dreamed then that knitting would become my friend, my refuge, my psychiatrist, sometimes my enemy, and ultimately lead to my career.

—Jean Leinhauser,
Author, Designer, Publisher, Teacher

Lydia Goetz

My yarn store is closed on Mondays, which I reserve for appointments, meetings and housework. Margaret usually visits Mom on Mondays and I try to stop by on Wednesdays. We include her in weekend activities whenever possible.

That Monday morning began with the three of us at the breakfast table—Cody, Casey and me. They seemed to be getting along, I'd noticed, exchanging occasional comments with each other, often about Chase. Animals had a way of breaching people's defenses, allowing them to connect. I'd seen that with Whiskers, too.

Cody was dressed for day camp and Casey had her books set out for her remedial math class. She never asked for help with homework, although both Brad and I had offered. Her streak of independence was as wide as the Columbia River. Most days I felt she simply tolerated us. Meanwhile, I was working hard to find common ground with her.

She made that difficult with her mood swings and generally negative attitude. My hope was that today's visit with her brother—which she didn't know about yet—would somehow make a difference.

"I'll pick you up after class this morning," I told her casually.

Casey looked up from her cereal bowl. "Why are you doing that?"

"I thought we'd go to lunch," I said. I wanted to surprise her with the visit—but I didn't want to disappoint her if it all fell through.

Casey frowned, as though she wasn't pleased with the idea of joining me for lunch.

I'd discovered that her brother's name was Lee Marshall and he'd recently turned eighteen.

For a minute I thought Casey was going to say something. I half expected her to insist she didn't need any favors but she didn't, which was a relief. I didn't feel like arguing with her.

"Casey fixed my backpack," Cody piped up. "The zipper was stuck and she got it to work."

The girl shrugged, dismissing his appreciation. "No big deal."

"Well, Cody's grateful and so am I."

"You could've done it just as well," she said.

Cody had the same problem earlier and I'd had real difficulty getting the zipper unstuck. "Maybe I could have, and maybe not. But I didn't have to worry about it because you already fixed it. Thank you, Casey."

"Mom isn't very strong," Cody was quick to explain. "She had cancer, you know, and it's hard for her to do some stuff."

I bit my tongue to avoid contradicting Cody. My having had cancer had nothing to do with my ability to slide a zipper up or down.

"You had cancer?" Casey frowned as she looked at me.

"Twice," Cody said importantly. "In her head."

I made a feeble gesture with my hand, hoping to change the subject. So much of my life had revolved around my illness that I didn't speak of it all that often these days. But since Casey was obviously curious, I felt I should explain. "I was first diagnosed as a teenager and then later as a young adult."

"Are you going to die?"

This wasn't a question most people asked, even if they wondered about it. Anyone who did persist couched the enquiry in more subtle terms, referring to my "prognosis" or "remission."

"Everyone eventually dies, Casey. It's part of the human condition." I felt that was too philosophical, so I smiled. "But I'm hoping to live a good, long time and become a problem to my children." I made that plural because of our hopes for adoption. Her concern touched me; I hadn't expected it of her.

Casey nodded and returned to her cereal.

Casey and Cody left the house together and I tore into my weekly routine of housekeeping and laundry. I didn't have any appointments other than the one at the juvenile facility in south Seattle early that afternoon.

The morning sped by and soon it was almost twelve and time to pick up Casey. She slid sullenly into the passenger seat and slammed the door, sitting there without a word for several minutes.

Then out of the blue she asked, "Do you want me to get my things first?"

"What things?" I glanced at her as I drove.

"My clothes and stuff."

The question confused me. "For lunch?"

She looked directly at me, her eyes narrowed. "What about *after* lunch? You aren't taking me back to Mrs. Boyle?"

"No." I shook my head as I waited for a light.

A hint of a smile came to her, so fleeting that I thought I might have misread it.

"Did you think that's what was happening?" I asked, shocked by her assumption. I probably should've mentioned my plan earlier and regretted that I hadn't.

She didn't answer.

"Actually, I wanted this to be a surprise, but I might as well tell you now," I said.

I saw her stiffen, as though surprises of any kind were bad and something to be avoided.

"We're on our way to the Kent Juvenile Facility so you can visit your brother."

"Lee?" She jerked her neck to look at me with such speed I actually wondered if she'd dislocated it. "I get to see *Lee?*"

"I certainly hope so. I called Evelyn Boyle and she set it up for us." Not without pulling a few strings, I suspected.

From that moment forward, Casey couldn't sit still. Once I'd parked the car in the garage outside the facility, she nearly leaped out the passenger door.

Thankfully, everything went smoothly when I introduced Casey and myself. While the receptionist led her back to visit with her brother, I sat in the waiting area and took out my knitting. Because my little shop on Blossom Street had grown so busy, I found less and less time for my own projects. I knew I'd have a full hour to work on a sweater I was making for Cody. He'd chosen the colors himself—a dark green and brown that looked almost like camouflage when they were knit together. I'd have it finished before he started school.

I'd offered to knit a poncho for Casey but she'd rejected the idea. It'd hurt my feelings but I didn't let her know that. I had a pattern that several teenage girls had made, and I'd been so sure she'd like one.

The hour passed quickly. I spent it knitting—making substantial progress—thinking over some plans for the store and daydreaming about a baby. When Casey reappeared, her eyes were shining and she hurried over to me.

I tucked my knitting in my bag and stood. "How'd it go?" I asked.

"Great! Just great."

"Are you ready for lunch?"

"Yeah." She seemed delighted that I'd remembered. "I'm starved."

Since she was in such a good mood, I took a chance and placed my arm lightly around her shoulders. To my private satisfaction she didn't shake it off.

We chose a small Mexican restaurant in downtown Kent and decided to eat outside on the patio. We both ordered cheese enchiladas with rice and beans, which happened to be the luncheon special.

"Lee's doing really well," Casey said, volunteering the information between bites of chips and salsa.

"Will he be out soon?" I was curious to learn why he'd been incarcerated but Evelyn hadn't told me. Reading between the lines, I guessed it was for vandalism—probably not a first offense, either.

Casey scooped up more salsa. "He'll be released this fall. There's a new program through the state that helps foster kids with college expenses. Lee got his GED while he's been here and he's applied to take classes at Highline Community College this September. Oh, and he was really on my case about staying in school. I promised I would—and I will."

"That's wonderful." I nodded vigorously. I wanted her to know how much I approved. "Does Lee have a place to live and a job for when he gets out?"

"That's the best part. He's going into a group home and they'll help him find a job. Lee really wants to make it, you know? And I want him to, 'cause when he's got a real address and everything, I can go live with him."

"I'm so glad."

"Only . . . only that might take a while." She lowered her head. "I don't think he wants to be stuck with his little sister too soon." Her eyes dimmed slightly. "I can always hope it works out, though. Right?"

"Right," I said. I hoped Lee managed to stay on the straight and narrow so Casey could join him in a home of their own.

"He might go in the army. I don't know if that's

a good idea, but he said he's considering it."

In that case, she wouldn't be able to live with him.

"When's the last time you saw your brother?" I asked.

Casey paused, a chip half buried in the salsa. "I don't remember. Two years ago, I think. He almost didn't recognize me."

"Two *years?*"

"We talk on the phone and stuff, but it's hard. . . ."

"The state couldn't keep you together?"

She snickered. "They have enough trouble finding a home for one kid."

I was completely naive about the foster care program. All I knew was that there was a desperate need for families willing to take in kids.

Our meals arrived, and we dug into our lunch with enthusiasm. To my astonishment Casey spoke nearly nonstop. Alix had been so right; reconnecting her with her brother had broken down a barrier between us. It was as if I'd suddenly become trustworthy in her eyes. For the first time since she'd come to stay with us, I heard about her parents.

"My mom and dad divorced when I was too young to remember my dad," she said.

"What happened to your mom?" I asked when she didn't immediately continue. I know I'd do whatever it took to make sure I kept Cody with me. My instincts toward our son were no less maternal than if I'd given birth to him myself. His mother, Brad's ex-wife, drifted in and out of his life whenever the impulse struck her. Janice seemed to undergo periods of guilt, and then she'd want to spend time with Cody every week; after that, a month, sometimes two, would go by and we wouldn't hear from her. Cody accepted whatever time Janice gave him, and never asked either Brad or me when he'd see his mother again.

"Did she die, Casey?" I asked, since Casey hadn't replied. "Forgive me for bringing it up if the subject's too painful."

"No," she said softly, slowly. "It's okay. She died, but it was . . . later."

She put aside her fork. "Mom got involved with this guy who used to slap her around. Lee tried to step in, but he beat Lee up, too." She stared down at her plate as she spoke. "Then Martin started hitting me, and my teacher noticed the bruises and called Child Protective Services."

"And they took you and your brother out of the home?"

Casey nodded. "The state said if Mom wanted to keep her children, Martin had to leave. But Mom loved Martin—and the things he bought her."

I could hardly believe what I was hearing. "You mean your mother chose a man who abused her and her kids?" It was appalling to me—beyond appalling—that any mother would abandon her own children.

"Mom said we should go live with our dad, only no one knew where he was. When the state couldn't find him, Lee and I were put in foster homes."

"Oh, Casey, I'm so sorry." I reached across the table and clasped her arm.

"Hey, it's no big deal."

She began eating again, but I could tell it was more to get me to move my hand than from any interest in her meal.

"What happened to your mother after you and Lee were out of the house?"

She went rigid, the fork still in her hand. "I don't know. She died about three years ago. I think it was from drugs. Martin was her supplier."

"Oh, Casey."

She shrugged as if it hadn't affected her one way or the other, but no child could remain untouched by that kind of betrayal.

After lunch we drove back home. To my pleasure and surprise Casey wanted to bake cookies. After assembling all the ingredients, I let her work by herself while I folded laundry. Despite a small mishap, in which she set a kitchen towel on fire taking the cookie sheet out of the oven, she did a good job. As she dealt with the dishes I went into the other room to call Evelyn Boyle.

I told her that Brad, Cody and I had talked, and we'd arrived at a consensus—to let Casey stay with us until she'd finished her summer school program. I could hear the relief in Evelyn's voice.

"Oh, thank you," she breathed. "Casey's doing so well with you and Brad." Evelyn phoned Casey at least once a week. I wasn't privy to the conversations and assumed the case worker knew better than I did how Casey was adjusting to our family.

The first real sign of improvement I'd seen had come that afternoon. Apparently we'd made an impact on the girl's life, and that thrilled me.

While I had Evelyn on the phone, I asked her about Casey's parents. It wasn't that I didn't believe what the girl had said, but I suspected parts of her story were exaggerated. I was shocked to learn that everything Casey had told me was the truth.

"How'd the meeting between Casey and her brother go?" Evelyn asked.

"Very well. She seemed like a different person afterward."

"That's wonderful." Evelyn's voice rang with satisfaction. "You've made my day—no, make that my whole week."

I figured she had plenty of weeks when nothing at all went right, so I felt especially pleased that I'd contributed to one of her better days.

"Does Casey know she'll be with you until summer school is out?"

"Not yet." Brad and I planned to tell her at dinner that night, when the whole family was together.

"I can't thank you enough," Evelyn said fervently. I knew she'd been under tremendous pressure and that by volunteering, Brad and I had taken a load off her shoulders. The fact that Casey and Cody were now getting along made the decision easy.

That evening, as we sat around the dinner table, I gave Brad a meaningful look. He winked at me, understanding my signal that he should break the news to Casey.

"So, Casey," he said as he passed the macaroni salad to Cody. "I hear you had an exciting afternoon."

She nodded. "I saw my brother."

Cody grinned from ear to ear. "Tell her, Dad."

Casey glanced from one to the other. "Tell me what?"

"Mrs. Boyle asked if you could stay with us until you finished summer school. Your new foster home is in north Seattle, and rather than move you to another place so far from the school, we thought it'd be best if you stayed here."

We all waited for Casey's reaction.

"Okay," she said.

Okay. That was it?

"Would you like to do that?" Brad asked. Like me, he'd anticipated some sort of reaction—something other than the bland response she'd given us.

"I guess so," she said. I thought she sounded almost indifferent, and that stung a bit.

Somehow Brad and I managed to hide our disappointment until we climbed into bed that night. We both sat up, leaning against a pile of pillows, our books in our hands.

"I thought she'd act a little happier than that," Brad said.

He didn't need to clarify what—or rather, whom—he was talking about.

"I know, but I think we're making headway." Improvement came in small doses. I'd noticed a few days ago that she'd replaced the toilet paper in the hall closet. I wasn't sure if she still had the soda crackers and the other food. Regardless, Casey was beginning to trust us.

"How do you mean?"

Needless to say, Brad wasn't around her as much as I was. "Well, for one thing, she baked cookies this afternoon." I'd never mentioned the hoarding to him.

"And nearly burned down the house."

"Brad, be fair. That could've happened to anyone."

He grinned. "I suppose you're right."

"She's not a bad kid, you know."

"I agree with you. I see glimmers every now and then of the kid she *could* be."

I set my book on the nightstand and reached for the lamp beside my bed. As I turned off the light, I whispered, "You've been very patient, husband of mine."

"Patient enough to earn a reward?" he whispered back.

"I'd say so," I said, raising my eyebrows.

Brad put down his own book and turned off his light. A moment later, I was in my husband's arms, feeling loved and cherished.

Ah, yes, this had been a good day indeed.

CHAPTER
16

Phoebe Rylander

Another flower delivery for you," Claudia said when Phoebe returned from her lunchtime walk. These short outings had become part of her everyday routine; they helped revive her and refresh her.

Claudia pointed to a huge floral arrangement made up entirely of roses. They were stunning, exquisite. Red and white, surrounded by ferns and other delicate greenery in a crystal vase. Phoebe had to hand it to Clark. He never seemed to quit.

"Either take them home yourself or give them away." She was not letting Clark Snowden back in her life. He could send her a dozen roses every day for the next fifty years and it wouldn't shake her determination. Especially after the wonderful time she'd had with Hutch over the Fourth of July weekend.

She smiled thinking about their biking adventure in the Skagit Valley. The tulip fields were long past blooming but the countryside was still beautiful. Phoebe couldn't remember ever having that much fun with anyone. She'd laughed at his silly comments—he didn't worry about looking foolish—and exchanged views on all kinds of issues, from politics to household ecology. Hutch was completely unpretentious. Unassuming. And honest.

"Before you toss these roses," Claudia was saying, "you'd better read the card."

Phoebe shook her head. "Nothing Clark has to say is going to change my mind."

Claudia waved her index finger at Phoebe. "Maybe they aren't from Clark."

Phoebe stared at her. "They aren't?"

Claudia grinned and held up the card, sighing loudly. "I don't know how you managed to get two handsome men sending you flowers when I haven't found even one."

"Give me that!" Phoebe pretended to be annoyed with the receptionist. "Did Hutch send the flowers?"

Claudia smiled and handed her the card. Unlike Clark's notes, which were always romantic, Hutch's card read simply THANK YOU. HUTCH. Straightforward and unpretentious.

Unlike Clark, Hutch hadn't tried to impress her, hadn't taken her to a fancy restaurant with a celebrity chef. Instead, he'd brought a picnic, including a bottle of local wine. And to her surprise hc hadn't attcmptcd to kiss hcr, although Phocbc would've welcomed it.

She waited until three that afternoon, when she had a break and called Hutch at his office. She was put directly through by his assistant.

"This is Bryan Hutchinson," he said.

"Are you sure it isn't Lance Armstrong?" she teased.

"Oh, sorry. Lance speaking."

Phoebe laughed. "Thank you for the roses."

"I wanted you to have them on Monday, but Susannah said she preferred to wait until she had a fresh supply."

"Susannah from Susannah's Garden?" The shop was next to the yarn store and had the most gorgeous display of arrangements and bouquets. Phoebe found herself mesmerized every Wednesday as she gazed into the flower shop window before class.

"I hadn't heard of Susannah's Garden until I signed up for the Knit to Quit class," Hutch said. "Her flowers are exceptional."

"I think so, too. Thank you again."

Hutch hesitated. "I wanted you to know how much I enjoyed being with you last weekend."

"I had an absolutely fabulous time."

A short silence followed. Hutch wasn't good at small talk, and it always seemed to take him a while to feel comfortable with her. That didn't bother Phoebe. Actually, she liked the contrast with her ex-fiancé. Hutch wasn't smooth like Clark, who could talk his way into or out of anything.

"We have class tomorrow night," she said. She felt a pleasant sense of anticipation about seeing him again.

"Oh, yes, class. Have you done your homework yet?" Their weekly assignment was to finish the current section of the sampler scarf so they'd be ready for the next lesson.

"Yes. What about you?"

"I'm knitting furiously as we speak."

Phoebe laughed. She seemed to do that a lot with Hutch.

"How would you feel . . . I mean, I know it'd be early, unless you wanted to wait until after. Would that be too late?" He paused as if expecting a response.

"Are you asking me to meet you for dinner?" she speculated. "If so, the answer is yes."

Again that short pause. "Really?" he said. "Great!"

Hearing the pleasure in his voice made her smile. "Why did you sound so shocked when I agreed?"

"Did I? Tell me, what woman in her right mind would turn down an invitation from Lance Armstrong?"

"Not me, that's for sure, especially when he's sent me roses."

"That's what I thought. I'll see you tomorrow then?"

"What time?"

"I guess that depends on you. Would you rather eat early or late?"

"Early."

"I was hoping you'd say that."

"Any particular reason you prefer an early meal?" she asked.

"That way I won't have to wait so long to see you again."

Coming from anyone else, that would have sounded phony. But when Hutch said it, she knew he meant every word.

"That's very romantic," she murmured. She could practically see him blush.

"What about . . ." He stumbled on the question. "Are you busy, um, tonight?"

Phoebe wondered why that hadn't occurred to her. "No, as a matter of fact I'm not."

"Would you like to meet this evening instead? No, not instead because I'd be disappointed if you didn't show up for class tomorrow night, but—"

"I'll be at class."

"Good. At dinner with me tonight, too?"

"Of course."

"Really? I mean, that's terrific." His voice was exuberant, like that of a child who'd been granted an unexpected gift.

"No, I was just saying that," she teased. "Hutch, I'd love to meet you tonight. I hated the thought of rushing through our dinner and hurrying to class and afterward . . . Well, we both have to work in the morning, right?"

"Right. This is much better." They set a time, then Phoebe ended the conversation; she had a client at three-fifteen. "Bye, Hutch," she said quickly. "See you at six."

"Goodbye, Phoebe, and thanks."

She wasn't sure why he was thanking her. She felt *she* was the one who owed him thanks—for the weekend, the roses, tonight. And for making her laugh.

As she hung up the phone, it occurred to Phoebe that she didn't even know what Hutch's business was. Their conversations had been interesting but not personal. She hadn't spoken much about her job, either—or her ex-fiancé. The fiancé Hutch believed was dead. . . .

She supposed it didn't really matter what his family's company manufactured or what service they provided, as long as it wasn't immoral or unethical. Which it couldn't possibly be, knowing Hutch. She amused herself by guessing—shoelaces? Tractor parts? Toilets? The subject hadn't really arisen, but it wasn't as if he'd deliberately hidden anything from her. The number he'd given her was a direct line and his assistant had answered the phone, "Bryan Hutchinson's office." Nevertheless it was slightly mysterious. She'd ask him over dinner.

Phoebe dressed carefully that evening because

she wanted to look attractive, not because she was worried about impressing Hutch with her wardrobe or sense of style. He was a comfortable person, conscious of others' needs. While biking he'd stopped to help a couple who'd been lost and needed directions. Later he'd purchased a sandwich and a coffee for a homeless man. He hadn't done it for show; he was a genuinely caring person.

Hutch arrived a few minutes early as she was still brushing her hair. Phoebe thought she heard someone outside her condo door and when she went to look through the peephole, she saw him pacing the hallway, checking his watch.

"Hutch," she said, opening the door. "Why didn't you knock?"

He shrugged, his expression embarrassed, as he stepped inside her apartment. "The book said I wasn't supposed to appear too eager."

"What book?"

He came in, sat down on her sofa and exhaled noisily. Right away, Princess, her cat, jumped onto his lap.

Phoebe stared in wonder. Princess had detested Clark and hissed at him the very first time he entered her condo. After that Princess had consistently avoided him. Apparently her cat was a better judge of character than she was.

Hutch gently stroked Princess, who purred contentedly. "In case you hadn't guessed, I've been out of the dating scene for a while." He grinned wryly.

"I got a book about dating. It said I shouldn't arrive too early or I'd seem overeager and that, according to the book, is something women find off-putting."

"Seriously?" Phoebe nearly laughed. "*That's* why you were waiting outside my door?"

He frowned. "I probably shouldn't have told you."

"Probably not," she said with a smile, "but I love it that you did."

Her comment seemed to surprise him.

She sat beside Hutch, and Princess leaped effortlessly from his lap to hers. "What else did the book have to say?"

"Plenty. I've read it three times in the last six days."

Phoebe laughed outright. "Oh, Hutch, you're so sweet and funny."

His brows drew together. "I'm glad you find me amusing."

"And refreshing. And just plain wonderful."

That brought up a question. "When you say I'm *sweet,* do you mean sweet as in delightful and charming? Or sweet the way young people use it—as in cool, intriguing and *very* satisfactory?" He did a more-than-passable imitation of Bogart.

Phoebe's eyes widened. "Bogart's my hero. *The African Queen* is my all-time favorite movie."

Hutch went still for a moment. "Mine, too."

Phoebe knew he hadn't just invented that to flatter her; it wasn't the sort of thing he did. She got up to feed Princess, then collected her purse. Hutch had made a reservation for six-thirty at a Thai restaurant; Phoebe had immediately agreed when he suggested it. She hadn't eaten Thai in years. Clark felt that Asian restaurants didn't attract the "upscale" clientele he wanted to be seen with. He would never have patronized a place like Basil, which Hutch had chosen for their dinner.

It was obvious that he was acquainted with the owners, who insisted on making the menu selections for them. Phoebe could barely restrain herself from asking Hutch about his background. She waited until they'd been served glasses of icy cold beer.

"I realized after we hung up this afternoon that I don't know very much about you," she began.

"You mean other than my superior biking skills?"

"Yes," she said, smiling. "Other than that and your movie preferences and political views and—"

"What would you like to know?"

"Well . . . You're an executive with your family's business, but what exactly is it?"

He hesitated. "Ever heard of Mount Rainier Chocolates?"

Phoebe nearly choked on her beer. "You've got to be kidding! I *love* those chocolates."

"Thank you. My grandfather started the company shortly after the Second World War. He used a recipe passed down from his mother."

"I like the caramels best."

"Almost everyone does."

"How come you're only mentioning this now?"

"We were talking about other things," he said with a shrug. "I enjoyed our discussions and I saw no reason to bore you with details about my job."

She didn't doubt the sincerity of his answer. "Aren't you a bit young to be at the company helm?" she asked next.

Pain showed briefly in his face. "My father died of a heart attack. He was fifty-eight."

"I'm sorry."

"Yes, we all were. The company was everything to Dad. I felt a responsibility to follow in his footsteps. Unfortunately I wasn't ready to assume the role of CEO, so I had a lot to learn in a short amount of time." He went on to tell her about the new candy bar the company was introducing, which sounded tempting to Phoebe. "I'll bring a few to class soon," he promised.

Their food came in several courses and dinner couldn't have been more delicious. At nine o'clock, after coffee and a dessert of fresh fruit and coconut ice cream, they left with profuse thanks to the owners and staff.

They'd walked to the restaurant, and when they stepped outside, they noticed the evening had cooled considerably. Phoebe had brought a sweater; Hutch held it politely as she slipped her arms into the sleeves.

"That was a divine dinner."

"It always is," Hutch said. "That's why I chose this restaurant."

They walked side by side in silence, and then Hutch reached for her hand. "The book said hand-holding is acceptable after the second date," he told her.

"I see," she said with a nod.

"There's quite a list of rules, you know."

"I guess I didn't," she said. "What other rules are there?"

"For one thing . . ." He paused. "Hey, I'm not giving away *all* my secrets."

Phoebe laughed.

"Why do you want to know?" he asked.

"Just curious," she said.

They strolled down the well-lit street, holding hands, swinging them slightly.

"Anything in particular that's arousing your curiosity?"

"Actually, yes," she replied.

Hutch stopped walking and looked down at her. They'd come to a side street where traffic was light.

"I wondered what the book had to say about kissing."

"Kissing," he repeated. "According to the rules, it would be within the scope of respectable behavior to . . ."

"To do what?"

"To kiss you on the third date."

"The *third* date? When was this book published?"

"1952. I picked it up at a secondhand book-store—after reading *Dating for Dummies*. I happen to love old books and I found the advice in the older one more to my liking."

They had so many of the same likes and dislikes, and she kept discovering new similarities between them. "I love old books, too. I've collected them for years."

He shook his head, as if nothing she said would surprise him. "Me, too. I like old sci-fi novels."

"Old biographies for me," she said.

They continued walking, and Hutch escorted Phoebe to her door. "I had a great time," she told him, turning to smile up at him.

"I did, too."

He hesitated, so Phoebe took matters into her own hands. Rising onto the tips of her toes, she slid her arms around his neck and kissed him. Hutch placed his own arms around her waist, then tightened his embrace.

The kiss was magical. Romantic. Sexy. Clark always had to be in charge; Hutch simply let their kiss happen. It felt like something *shared*, as though it belonged to her as much as him.

When he lifted his head, he kept his eyes closed for several seconds. Then he cleared his throat. "That was very . . . nice."

"Yes." Phoebe pressed her hand to his heart, feeling the heavy thudding against her palm. "Yes, it was."

He kissed her again. She wouldn't have believed it was possible, but the second kiss was even better than the first.

"Good night, Phoebe."

"Good night, Hutch." She felt weak with longing as she fumbled with the key and opened the door.

Smiling, she set her purse down and immediately noticed the light on her phone. She checked caller ID. No surprise there—the call had come from Clark.

CHAPTER
17

Anne Marie Roche

"Where are we going again?" Ellen asked, skipping at Anne Marie's side as she held Baxter's leash.

"To the park." Anne Marie hadn't told her much about their meeting with Tim Carlsen. She still wasn't sure what to say or how much to explain. She'd mentioned only that they'd be seeing a "friend."

"Can I have some ice cream?" Ellen asked.

Anne Marie smiled at her. "I think that can be arranged."

"Goody."

Ellen was so easily pleased, her trust complete. Anne Marie prayed she was doing the right thing by introducing her daughter to Tim. Ever since her late-night phone call, she'd been racked with indecision. More times than she could count, she'd picked up the phone, determined to cancel. And then, overcome with doubt, she'd replace the phone, deciding to let this play out.

As recently as an hour ago, she'd been convinced it was a terrible mistake. But now she'd finally made up her mind—she'd grant Tim the privilege of getting to know Ellen.

Tim had suggested meeting at the fountain in the center of the park. Sure enough, there he was, sitting on the circular stone edge. Children raced around the park, their glee and excitement infectious in the afternoon sun.

He stood as they approached, and Anne Marie's heart felt lodged in her throat.

"Hello," Tim greeted them, his gaze focused on Ellen.

Not understanding, the girl looked up at Anne Marie.

"Hello, Tim," she managed to croak out.

When she didn't say anything further or make any effort to introduce him, Tim bent down and thrust out his hand. "You must be Ellen. My name is Tim."

Ellen edged closer to Anne Marie. "This is Baxter," she said, motioning toward the Yorkie, who stared curiously at Tim.

To Anne Marie's frequent annoyance, Baxter

barked up a mighty storm with just about everyone he encountered for the first time. Not with Tim, though. The small dog quietly and without reservation accepted him as a friend.

"Mom said she'd buy me an ice cream," Ellen announced.

Tim's smile was gentle. "What a great idea. I'll get ice cream for all of us. Why don't you two sit here and I'll be right back."

"Okay."

He started walking toward the nearby ice-cream vendor's cart, glancing back to send them another reassuring smile.

Anne Marie lowered herself to the stone bench, half listening to the melodic splashing of water behind her. Her mouth had gone dry and it felt as if her tongue was glued to her teeth. Normal conversation seemed impossible. She didn't know how she was going to get through this ordeal without Ellen sensing that something was very wrong.

"Who's Tim?" Ellen asked, sitting next to her. She brought Baxter onto her lap and waited for Anne Marie's explanation. If only there *was* an easy explanation!

"A friend," Anne Marie said again, surprised she was able to answer at all.

Ellen didn't speak for a moment. "Is he your . . . boyfriend?"

Because she hadn't come up with anything better, Anne Marie nodded. "Sort of."

That appeared to satisfy Ellen. "I like him."

"You'd like anyone who bought you ice cream," Anne Marie teased, hoping to make light of the girl's immediate acceptance of Tim.

Ellen giggled. "No, I wouldn't." She petted the Yorkie, who'd curled up in her lap. "Baxter likes him, too."

The little traitor, Anne Marie mused. "I saw that."

As promised, Tim was back within minutes, carrying three ice-cream bars. Ellen placed Baxter on the ground as he doled them out. "Thank you," she said, polite as always.

Unwrapping the bar, Ellen looked at Tim, her head slightly tilted. "Mom says you're her boyfriend."

Tim's eyes met hers.

"Sort-of boyfriend," Anne Marie corrected.

"Would you like that?" Tim asked Ellen, then took the first bite of his ice cream.

Ellen nodded. "You're okay."

"Just *okay?*" he said, pretending to be insulted. He grinned at Anne Marie, who smiled back stiffly.

Ellen laughed. "Baxter thinks you are, too."

"A dog with infinite good sense." Tim continued to eat his ice cream and had it half-consumed before Anne Marie had even removed her wrapper.

"Is there anything you want to ask me?" Tim directed the question to Ellen. "Since I might be dating your mother," he added.

She nodded again. "Do you have a job?"

"I do," he told her. "I work at an insurance agency with my father. Dad's retiring next year and I'll be taking over the business once he does."

Ellen looked at Anne Marie for clarification. "He's got a good job," she explained simply. "He works in an office."

Ellen's attention returned to Tim. "Do you drink?"

Anne Marie was shocked by that question. Surely Ellen couldn't recall her own mother's drinking—could she? She'd never indicated that in any way.

"I used to a long time ago but I don't anymore," he said in a solemn voice.

Ellen licked her ice cream while she thought about his response. "That's good."

"It is for me," he agreed.

"Do you love Jesus?"

"Ellen," Anne Marie whispered, worried that the questions were getting too personal.

"I do," Tim answered. "But I don't always go to church like I should."

Ellen accepted that. "Do you like animals?" she asked without a pause.

Tim nodded. "I had a dog as a kid."

"Like Baxter?"

"Not exactly. He was a big black Lab named Caesar."

"Do you have any pets now?"

Tim took her rapid-fire questions in stride. "A cat named Bozo."

Ellen giggled delightedly. "That's a funny name for a cat."

"Bozo's a funny cat." Tim crossed his legs at the ankles. He seemed relaxed, at ease, comfortable with the girl's interrogation.

Thankfully, Ellen's questions had distracted him—and Ellen herself—from the fact that Anne Marie had hardly said a word. She couldn't. If either of them so much as looked at her, Anne Marie was afraid she might just grab her daughter and take off running.

"Do you like kids?" Ellen asked next, studying Tim intently.

"I like them a lot."

"Little girls, too?"

"Little girls, too, especially pretty ones like you."

His answer made her smile, revealing front teeth that were still a bit too big for her mouth. Anne Marie couldn't help noticing that Ellen's dark hair and eyes were nearly a reflection of Tim's.

"Have you ever thought about having a father in your life, Ellen?" he asked.

Anne Marie shot him a warning frown.

"That's on my list!" She set the stick from her ice-cream bar carefully on the fountain's edge. "Mom and I have a list of twenty wishes," she said. "Do you know about it?"

Tim shook his head. "Do you want to tell me?"

"Okay." Ellen was always eager to talk about her wishes, almost as though she was trying to convert everyone she met. "Mom and her friends made these lists of twenty wishes. I made my own list and a bunch of my wishes already came true. I wanted to learn to knit and I did. Mom showed me how and I made a lap robe for my Grandma Dolores. She died."

"I know, and I'm sorry."

"She's up in heaven with Jesus now. She loved Him, too. Just like us."

"I bet she's watching over you from up there," Tim said sympathetically.

"That's what Mom said."

"Anything else on your list?"

"Lots! We went to Paris. We were supposed to go last Christmas, but then there was a problem with our airline, remember? It was on the TV news and everything, so we had to wait until this summer, but that was even better. I have a new wish now."

Anne Marie couldn't remember her daughter ever being this open with someone who was virtually a stranger.

"What's your new wish?" Tim asked her.

"To learn French. I say a new word every day. Baxter knows that *Viens ici* means *come here*." The dog raised his head and she laughed. "See? The *chien* understands."

"Good for you. Both of you."

"I've signed her up with a French tutor," Anne

211

Marie said. She'd found one through Teresa, who seemed acquainted with just about every teacher in the school district. "I'm going to be taking lessons, too."

Tim's eyes softened as he glanced at Anne Marie. "You're a terrific mother," he said in a low voice.

"I try."

"Do *you* have a list of wishes?" Ellen demanded.

"Not yet, but I already know what I'm going to wish for."

Anne Marie looked at him suspiciously as Ellen chattered blithely on. "Barbie and Lillie and Elise have wish lists, too," she was saying.

"Friends of yours?" Tim asked, turning to Anne Marie.

She nodded.

"Barbie met Mark," Ellen continued. "He's in a wheelchair and they're in love. And Lillie met Hector."

"Does she love him, too?"

"Yes!" Ellen said loudly. "They hold hands in *public*."

Tim tried to restrain a smile. "Tell me more about your wishes."

"Okay." Ellen's expression was solemn. "I signed up for karate classes. That was one of my wishes."

"How'd it go?"

Ellen wrinkled her nose. "Too many boys. They can be mean, you know."

Tim nodded gravely. "I heard that."

"Do you have kids?" she asked.

His eyes darted to Annc Marie. "Not yet, but I'd really like to be a daddy one day."

"A man needs children," Ellen said with all the wisdom of her nine years.

"Oh? Why's that?"

"Children are *important*."

Once again Tim glanced at Anne Marie. "I couldn't agree with you more."

"Oh, there's something else on my list. I nearly forgot. Only . . . only this wish hasn't come true yet."

"And what would that be?"

"I want to meet my dad."

Anne Marie placed a protective hand on Ellen's shoulder.

"Your dad?" he repeated slowly.

Ellen bent down to scoop up the dog and held him close. "Everybody has one, you know."

"I know," Tim said quietly. "Did anyone ever tell you anything about him?"

Ellen shook her head sadly. "I don't even have his picture."

That was a blessing as far as Anne Marie was concerned.

"I'm sure he wonders about you, too," Tim said. "I bet if he knew he had such a lovely little girl, he'd be very happy."

"Do you really think so?"

"I'm positive."

Before this could go any further, Anne Marie said, "Ellen, why don't you play on the swing set while Tim and I visit?"

"Okay. Can Baxter come with me?"

"He should probably stay here for now. You can take him on the merry-go-round later, okay?"

"Okay," she agreed readily enough, then dashed off to play with the other children.

"Enough about the father business," Anne Marie said with barely restrained anger.

Tim raised both hands in a gesture of surrender. "I didn't bring it up. She did."

"You led her on."

"I don't want to argue, Anne Marie. It's clear to me that Ellen is curious about her father. That's the reason you called me in the middle of the night, isn't it? Ellen asked you questions you couldn't answer."

Anne Marie ignored him.

"She's a delightful child," Tim said, his gaze resting fondly on Ellen.

No one needed to tell Anne Marie that. Reluctantly she handed over the baggie of hair she'd collected from Ellen's brush. That was all he required, Tim had said, to establish paternity.

He slipped it inside his pocket. "You've done a wonderful job with her."

"Her grandmother deserves most of the credit. Ellen's only been with me for a year or so."

"Nevertheless, she seems happy and well-adjusted."

If he thought he could flatter his way into their lives, he was mistaken. "Thank you," she said coolly.

"I appreciate that you allowed me to meet Ellen." He hesitated. "With your permission I'd like to meet again."

She held herself rigid. "When?"

"Whenever it's agreeable with you."

She looked at him narrowly. "Don't be so accommodating. It confuses me."

He grinned and his smile emphasized the laugh lines around his mouth and beside his eyes. Under any other circumstances she would've found him charming and attractive. She couldn't lower her guard with him, though. Not yet, and maybe not ever.

"Anne Marie," he said, his expression serious. "I hope you'll let me take you both out on another . . . date."

"I'll consider it." Anne Marie wasn't willing to make any promises beyond that.

"I *am* your boyfriend, remember? Your sort-of boyfriend, anyway."

She scowled at him.

Ellen had waited her turn for a swing and then joined the other kids, kicking her feet in the air as she soared higher and higher. Children's laughter rang through the park, and Anne Marie recognized the distinctive sound of her daughter's high-pitched giggle. After several minutes, Ellen raced back to the fountain. Baxter barked when he saw her, his tail wagging madly.

Tim got up as she approached. "It was very nice to meet you, Ellen. And I hope all your wishes come true."

"Me, too. Especially the one about my father." She wrinkled her forehead.

"What's the matter? You don't want to meet him?" Tim asked, obviously bewildered.

"I do, but I asked Mom what she thought he looked like and she said he probably had big warts on his face." She giggled again.

Tim slid a look toward Anne Marie. "Did she, now? What else did she have to say?"

"It was a joke," Anne Marie rushed to add.

"That he had really big feet." Ellen raised her leg. "Feet as big as a clown's."

"Personally, I doubt that's true," Tim said, squatting so the two of them were at eye level. "My guess is that your father's a handsome prince who'd like nothing better than to sweep you and your mom off to a magic kingdom."

Ellen's dark eyes rounded with pleasure. "Do you really think so?"

"Yes, I do."

"That would be so cool!"

"Yes, it would," Tim agreed and, straightening, he looked at Anne Marie. "Don't you agree?" he asked. And then he winked at her.

CHAPTER
18

Large or small, all types of women's bodies are beautiful and I want to give knitters permission to express their beauty through what they make and wear.

—Joan McGowan-Michael,
www.whiteliesdesigns.com and author of
Knitting Lingerie Style (2007)

Lydia Goetz

I'd noticed subtle changes in Casey since I'd taken her to see her brother, Lee, last Monday. A week had passed, and she'd begun spending more time with the family, instead of hiding in her bedroom with the door closed.

Without being asked, she'd set the dining-room table one night. I was pleased—and surprised—but I didn't dare comment. She started doing her homework at the kitchen table, too. All this had taken place since seeing her brother. His encouragement, and his talk about going to college and getting a job so he could send for her, had given her hope. I prayed everything would work out for Lee and consequently for Casey.

Monday night, I served my special meat loaf, from a recipe Margaret had shared with me. She hadn't gotten it via any of the usual methods today—cookbook, magazine or the Food Channel. Instead, my sister had heard about it at her hairdresser's. Like Margaret, I've discovered that some of the best recipes come by word of mouth. It had certainly proved true in this instance. Her meat loaf had become a family favorite.

It was a cool and rainy afternoon and because I was home all day doing housework, I didn't mind having the oven on, even if it was almost the middle of July.

I'd been to see my mother earlier that morning, having switched days with Margaret, and then after summer school, Casey had hung around me most of the afternoon instead of attending day camp. I thought she might want to make cookies again, but she declined. She asked if she could bake a cake instead. I agreed, and we found a recipe for an apple upside-down cake in my cherished old *Joy of Cooking*. It turned out really well, too.

Again without being asked, she set the table for dinner and called Brad and Cody once everything was ready.

"Janice phoned me this afternoon," Brad said as he loaded his plate with a helping of peas and mashed potatoes, followed by a thick slice of meat loaf.

Cody's mother hadn't contacted them since school was dismissed for the summer. I'd been figuring we'd hear from her sooner or later.

"She wants to see Cody tomorrow afternoon." Brad turned to me and then our son.

"That's nice," I said in what I hoped was an encouraging voice.

"What do you think about seeing your mother, buddy?" Brad asked, ladling gravy over everything on his plate.

Cody shrugged. "Do I have to spend the night?"

"Not unless you want to."

Cody seemed torn. "She doesn't have any computer games and she doesn't like Chase. Can I see her and hug her and go home again?"

I hid a smile. Cody was more concerned about being away from his Xbox and his dog than spending time with his mother. And I couldn't really blame him. Although he was only ten, he knew what Janice was like. He showed her the same level of interest she'd given him.

Casey frowned as she listened to the exchange. "I thought Lydia was your mother."

"She is," Cody said, smashing peas with his fork and mixing them into his potatoes. "I have two moms."

"I married Brad when Cody was eight," I explained to Casey.

"Why don't you have more kids?" she asked.

I set my fork beside my plate. "As a result of the chemo and radiation used to treat my cancer, I can't have children."

"That's why you applied for adoption?"

I nodded. The subject of my infertility wasn't as painful to me as it'd once been. For years I'd been convinced that even if I found a man willing to live with the uncertainty I faced as a two-time cancer survivor, my inability to bear a child would kill any hope of marriage. And then I'd met Brad Goetz. . . . I counted my blessings every day. My feelings of inadequacy had diminished because of his unstinting love and support. And since we'd set our adoption plans in motion, I'd been feeling almost serene.

Casey was quiet after that, as though the conversation distressed her.

"Cody's going to be with his mother tomorrow afternoon. Would you like to come by the yarn store after school?" I asked her as we finished our meal.

At first Casey didn't realize I'd spoken to her. "Me?" she asked as she looked around the table.

"Yes, you," I said, laughing. "If you like, I'll teach you to knit," I offered yet again.

She gave me her usual shrug. "I guess so."

"It's not hard," Cody piped up after he'd carried his plate to the sink. "Mom taught my whole class to knit last winter. Everyone made patches for Warm Up America, even the boys. Then Aunt Margaret crocheted them all together and we donated the blanket to a veterans' home in West Seattle."

For the first time since I'd mentioned knitting, Casey actually seemed interested.

"Knitting helps with math, too," Cody told her as if he were an expert.

"Speaking of math," Brad inserted, looking at Casey. "How's your class?"

Casey replied in the same indifferent way she typically did. "All right, I guess. Math is stupid."

"Unfortunately it's a necessary part of everyday life."

"I know," she said a bit defensively.

"If you want, I'll check over your homework," Brad suggested. He'd made the offer before, but Casey had always turned him down flat.

"If you want," she said after a moment.

Brad and I exchanged a private smile.

While Cody cleared the serving dishes, Brad and Casey sat in the living room as he reviewed her homework. I couldn't hear everything he said but they certainly had a lively discussion.

Afterward, Casey moved to the kitchen table and exhaled loudly as she threw herself into a chair. "I have to do this assignment over," she muttered.

I patted her shoulder encouragingly and stacked the dishes in the dishwasher.

Tuesday afternoon, shortly before one, Casey showed up at A Good Yarn, backpack slung over her shoulder. She'd taken the bus by herself. I was nervous about her coping with the different transit schedules, but Casey assured me it wasn't a problem. Apparently she was more skilled at finding her way around than I'd assumed, for which I was grateful.

"Hi," I said, waiting until Mrs. Sinclair, a repeat customer, had paid for her purchase. "I ordered lunch from across the street."

"Oh, thanks." Casey went to the back of the shop, to the table where I taught classes.

My sister had been unusually quiet about Casey. They'd met a couple of times, but just briefly. I'd only recently told her that Casey would be with us until she'd finished summer school. Margaret's reaction was to roll her eyes.

"I ordered us a Reuben," I said to Casey, sitting down with her. "As you can see, they're huge. I figured we could split one."

I'd left a knitting instruction book, a pair of size ten needles and a bright variegated skein of worsted weight yarn on the table for her, as well. It's been my experience that it's easier to pick up knitting basics when you're using larger needles and a thicker yarn.

"What's in a Reuben?" Casey asked, eyeing the sandwich suspiciously.

I set her half on a paper plate and slid it across the table.

"Corned beef and mustard, Swiss cheese and sauerkraut," I answered.

Casey studied it; her nose wrinkled as if she wasn't sure she was going to like this. "How do they get the corn in the beef?"

"There isn't any corn as far as I know." Funny, I'd never stopped to wonder where the name had come from.

"And who's this Reuben guy?"

"That I don't know, either," I told her. "But whoever he is, he invented a wonderful sandwich." I reached for my half and took the first bite. It was just as tasty as I remembered. I opened the bag of potato chips and emptied them out on a spare plate, then poured a large bottle of iced tea into two glasses.

"Go ahead and give it a try," I urged Casey, who seemed to do nothing more than stare at it.

She picked up her sandwich and tentatively took one small bite. Her eyes brightened. "Hey, this is good."

"Told you so."

By this time I'd eaten nearly half of mine. Still, Casey was finished before me.

"That was *really* good."

"I'm glad you enjoyed it."

I collected our paper plates and stuffed them in the recycling bin. "Ready for your first knitting lesson?"

Casey nodded.

I pushed yarn and needles toward her and sat in the adjoining chair. "How'd school go today?" I asked, making conversation as I delved into the center of the skein, searching for the beginning strand.

"I got an A on my homework."

I paused to say, "Casey, that's fantastic!" I'd located the strand I wanted and tugged it free.

Predictably, she shrugged at my compliment, but I knew she was pleased. Once Brad heard the news, he would be, too. I was proud of them both. Proud of Brad because he'd offered his help, been repeatedly rejected and yet tried again. And proud of Casey, too, because she'd been willing to admit she needed help.

I had to show her how to cast on two or three times. She couldn't seem to grasp the technique. In the end I simply did it for her.

Unfortunately, things didn't go any more smoothly when it came to learning the basic knit stitch. To her credit, Casey did try. I could see she was becoming frustrated, so I told her about other people I'd taught to knit.

"Does everyone have as much trouble as I'm having?" she asked. She bit her lip as she clutched the two needles. At one stage she held one needle under her arm as she wove the yarn around the tip of the other.

"Some do," I said.

Margaret wandered by and threw me a look I recognized from our childhood. It said I should have my sanity checked. Maybe so, but I wasn't willing to abandon hope yet.

Soon my nerves were frayed to the breaking point. Unfortunately, Casey's were, too. When the needle slipped out of her grasp and clattered onto the floor, Casey bolted upright and threw down the entire project.

"I can't do this!" she yelled.

"Casey."

"I *hate* knitting. I don't want to do it."

I longed to reassure her, to remind her that knitting came more quickly to some than it did to others. I didn't want her to give up so easily. Apparently I hadn't relayed that message effectively enough.

"You don't have to learn to knit if you don't want," I finally said.

"I don't. It's stupid."

I opened my mouth to argue, but realized there was no point. Picking up the yarn and needles, I set them back on the table. I was disappointed, although I made an effort not to show it.

"Would you like to read?" I asked, thinking I'd send Casey down to Blossom Street Books and let her choose a novel. Otherwise, I didn't know how I'd keep her entertained for the rest of the afternoon.

"No," she said flatly.

"So what *would* you like to do?"

Casey looked bored. "Do you have a TV?"

"Sorry, no."

The bell above the door chimed and Jacqueline Donovan, a good friend of mine, walked in. Jacqueline and Reese, her architect husband, had taken a cruise to Hawaii and they'd just returned. I was eager to see her, so I left Casey to her own devices for a few minutes.

"Jacqueline!" I said, hurrying toward her with my hands out. "You're back. Did you have a fabulous trip?"

"It was incredible. You and Brad should take a cruise sometime."

I'd love that; unfortunately I couldn't see it happening in the near future, especially if we were adding a baby to our family.

As she headed toward the yarn displays, Jacqueline burbled with all kinds of stories. She'd read a knitting magazine on the plane and decided she *had* to knit this wonderfully intricate vest for Reese. She examined an expensive hand-dyed alpaca yarn, choosing a lovely deep brown shade. I rang up her purchase.

When we'd said goodbye, with promises to see each other soon, I walked back to the table. To my astonishment, Margaret was sitting with Casey.

The two of them were crocheting.

Not knitting, *crocheting*.

Casey glanced up at me and broke into a smile. "This is fun," she said.

"Fun," I repeated, struck nearly speechless.

"I can *do* this."

"She's crocheting a washcloth." Righteousness rang in my sister's tone. "Look at her work, Lydia. The girl's a natural."

I wanted to wipe that grin off Margaret's face, which wasn't very generous of me. The thing is, she'd succeeded where I'd failed. Casey was relaxed, confident and actually enjoying herself.

"At the rate she's going," Margaret said, "she'll have it done before we close up shop."

"I'm impressed," I told them both. I meant it.

The bell above the door chimed again, and I left to greet my customer. As I turned away, an unexpected feeling of happiness came over me. Who would've guessed that my sister, not me, would be the one to reach Casey?

My first instinct had been a twinge of jealousy; however, that quickly passed. Margaret, so judgmental and disapproving of Casey, had been patient enough to teach the girl crocheting. I was grateful for her kindness.

Maybe there was hope for all of us—Casey, Margaret and me.

CHAPTER
19

"Hutch" Hutchinson

Hutch was already at the table with Alix, Margaret and Lydia when Phoebe arrived. He'd come ten minutes early, and it wasn't the thrill of learning a new pattern that had enticed him to leave his office ahead of schedule.

It was the thrill of falling for Phoebe Rylander.

At quarter past six, Hutch discovered that he'd checked his watch no fewer than ten times when Phoebe burst through the door, breathless and flushed.

"Sorry I'm late," she said, hurrying to the back of the store.

The spot next to him was empty. Hutch had arranged it by placing his briefcase on the chair until she showed up. Then, and only then, did he conveniently remove it.

Phoebe pulled out the chair and sent him a fleeting grin as she sat down, breathing hard. He wondered if something had happened and hoped she'd tell him. They'd planned to go for coffee after class.

"Don't worry, you didn't miss anything," Lydia assured her. "We've just started."

"Oh, good." Phoebe removed her knitting from the bag she carried, still a little out of breath.

Phoebe must've run the entire way from the clinic to Blossom Street, a distance of several blocks. He should know; after the past two classes, he'd walked her to the garage where she parked her car.

"So, how's everyone doing?" Lydia asked.

Hutch held up his scarf. In his own opinion he'd made exceptional progress, especially considering where he'd started.

"Oh, sorry," Lydia said, "I mean with the quitting

aspect of the class. I can see how the knitting's going, and you're all doing an excellent job."

"Well . . . I'm no longer knitting armor," Hutch told them. His tension had loosened considerably. He'd become more comfortable with the needles, and he credited Lydia for that. But he credited Phoebe for several other changes in his life.

When no one else responded, Hutch felt obliged to fill the silence. "The knitting's definitely helped me relax and it seems to have improved my blood pressure."

"Very good." Lydia smiled in his direction.

His mental attitude had improved, too. He'd stopped obsessing about the lawsuit, leaving it in the hands of his attorney. Nothing he did now would affect the outcome, anyway.

Knitting had changed his life, he thought with a grin. Through the class he'd met Phoebe and everything seemed different now. Because of her recent loss he didn't want to rush her, so he made a point of calling her no more than once every other day, counting the hours between calls and dates.

With Phoebe he felt witty, clever and downright fascinating. The prospect of seeing her excited him.

They shared many of the same interests. Her appreciation of old books was only one example of that. Over the weekend she'd shown him her collection, including a first edition of Mark Twain's *The Innocents Abroad* published in 1869 that, amazingly, she'd picked up at a garage sale for five dollars.

When he'd gone to her place on Saturday afternoon, he'd flipped through her stack of DVDs, which confirmed that they loved the same movies from Bogey to film noir to Indiana Jones. Afterward they'd walked to the theater and shared a bucket of buttered popcorn, watching a brand-new animated feature in the company of at least a hundred kids.

Hutch didn't think he'd ever enjoyed an afternoon as much. On his way home, he'd stopped at the office, out of pure habit. From the day he'd taken over as CEO, he'd spent every Saturday there. However, he stayed for less than an hour, his mind on everything but business.

"How's your thumb?" Lydia asked, bringing him out of his musings.

"Not bad, thanks," he said, bending his thumb to demonstrate his mobility.

Lydia nodded. "And Phoebe?" she asked next. "How are you doing?"

Phoebe glanced at Hutch. "Better. Much better."

"I know this is a painful time for you. . . ."

She lowered her eyes, and when she spoke, her voice was barely audible. "I was late for class because I ran into . . . an old friend of my fiancé's. I . . . I told him I'm seeing someone else now and he got terribly upset."

Under the table, Hutch clasped her hand. "Who you're seeing is none of his business," he insisted.

"I know, but he didn't want to hear that."

"Situations like this are difficult, especially when other people are still grieving, wanting to hold on to the past," Lydia said. "I hope you won't let that confrontation ruin your evening."

"I won't," Phoebe promised, squeezing Hutch's fingers, silently thanking him for his support. She exhaled slowly. "If you don't mind, I'd rather not discuss this right now. I'm still upset about it. But I'm trying to put it behind me."

Alix looked at them both as if seeing them with new eyes. Her gaze held his for an instant—and then she winked at him.

Hutch assumed that was her way of condoning the relationship. He winked back.

"I want everyone to know," Alix said. "I went twenty-four hours without a cigarette."

Lydia clapped her hands, and the rest of the group joined in. "Good for you, Alix!"

"Hey, congratulations," Hutch added.

Margaret nodded with dignified approval.

"It wasn't easy," Alix said. "I was so cranky that by dinnertime I wasn't fit company for man or beast. So I went outside and worked in the yard. I managed to weed the whole garden. My body was *screaming* for a cigarette."

"But you didn't give in to the craving." Lydia's tone praised her.

Alix shrugged. "No, but I think by then, Jordan was ready to beg me to smoke again."

"No, he wasn't." Margaret shook her head. "He wants you to quit as much as *you* want to quit. Maybe more."

"Have you tried any of the nicotine-withdrawal products?" Lydia asked.

"I've tried the gum. It does take the edge off."

"What about chocolate?" Hutch asked.

Alix groaned.

"I would, but with my addictive personality I'd weigh three hundred pounds in about three weeks."

Hutch grinned and reached into his briefcase, taking out a dozen of his company's new Mount Saint Helens candy bars. He figured Phoebe was right, and he should tell his fellow classmates about the family business.

"Hey, what's this?" Margaret was the first to comment, automatically picking up one of the bars. "I've never seen these before."

"They're our new product," he explained.

Phoebe smiled. "In case no one realized it, Hutch and his family own Mount Rainier Chocolates."

"Get out of here!" Alix said, eyes widening.

"Really?" This came from Margaret.

"How sweet," Lydia said next. "Pun intended."

"The company's been in the family for three generations. This is a new product we're about to launch nationally. Please take one. I'd appreciate your comments."

"You mean you're *giving* us these?" Margaret grabbed a second bar.

"You are kidding, aren't you?" Alix sounded shocked.

Hutch was amused by their reactions. He knew his chocolates were popular, but the members of his knitting class looked at him as if he were handing out hundred-dollar bills. "Take as many as you'd like. You'd be doing me a favor."

"How come this is our fifth class, but only now do you reveal who you are?" Margaret asked.

"Is it important?" Hutch returned.

"Not in the least," Lydia said, staring openly at her sister.

Margaret tore into one of the bars, and after the first bite, declared, "I hate to say it, but this is probably the best chocolate bar I've ever tasted."

Hutch raised his eyebrows. "Why do you hate to say that?"

"Because I love chocolate, and I could eat one— no, two or three—of these every day for the rest of my life. I'm struggling with my weight as it is." She slapped her legs. "I have the thighs that ate Seattle."

Margaret wasn't generally one to crack jokes, and Hutch laughed appreciatively at her unexpected remark.

Women were his target audience, although he didn't announce the fact. Research showed that women consumed far more chocolate than men; not only that, they were the primary purchasers within the family.

Once everyone had eaten a chocolate bar and murmured or groaned happily, they all resumed their knitting and that day's new stitch.

Class time sped by. All too soon it was eight o'clock, and they gathered up their things. Hutch and Phoebe crossed the street to the French Café.

Phoebe had said very little during class. Hutch waited until they were settled in their chairs and had taken their first sips of coffee.

"Do you feel like talking about what happened earlier this evening?" he asked. He didn't want to pry or prod her to talk if she felt uncomfortable. But confiding in someone could help, and he was a good listener.

Her shoulders slumped. "Oh, Hutch, it was awful."

"I'm sorry." He reached across the table and took her hand in a consoling gesture.

"His name—my fiancé's friend—is . . . oh, it doesn't matter. I thought, you know, that if I showed him I was getting on with my life that he'd . . . that he would, too."

Hutch waited a moment, then said, "Apparently he wasn't ready to hear that."

Shaking her head, she frowned. "He went ballistic."

Hutch felt that was excessive. The guy's friend was dead. It wasn't as though Phoebe could dedicate the rest of her life to the memory of the man she'd loved.

"Was he especially close to your fiancé?" he asked.

She didn't meet his gaze and simply nodded. "I'm still so upset that I don't really want to talk about it."

Hutch respected that. "Then we won't. Let's discuss something cheerful instead."

She grinned weakly. "Do you have any ideas?'

He'd considered this earlier. "What about a trip to the beach this weekend?" he asked. "My family owns a condo in Westport."

Hutch hadn't been there in years. His sister and her family were the only ones who really took advantage of the place. His mother made the trek once every summer with a few of her friends. Hutch figured he should have a turn, too.

Phoebe instantly brightened. "I'd love that."

He did want to clear up one thing. "Not to worry—there are three bedrooms. No pressure."

"I wasn't worried."

"Hey, my masculinity's suffering here. I was hoping you'd be so tempted by my wild sexuality that you wouldn't be able to keep your hands off me."

Phoebe laughed.

"I wasn't joking."

"Yes, you were."

He laughed, too. "Well, maybe, but not all *that* much." Hutch wanted to be far more than friends. Still, he'd never coerce her into a sexual relationship, although the subject was on his mind constantly.

"A weekend at the beach sounds like exactly what I need." She smiled at him gratefully. "It would be wonderful to get away for a couple of days."

"Then I'll make the arrangements. I'll pick you up Saturday morning at eight if that's not too early, and we'll drive back Sunday afternoon."

"That's perfect. I'll do the cooking."

"No need. There are wonderful restaurants in town."

"Please, I insist. I make a good seafood linguine."

"If you want to cook, fine, but it really isn't necessary."

"Yes, it is. And I'll make brunch on Sunday. My cheese omelet will melt in your mouth."

Hutch couldn't take his eyes off her. "Maybe we should leave tomorrow instead of waiting for the weekend."

For the first time all evening, Phoebe looked relaxed and carefree. "I'd love to," she told him, "but I have clients scheduled."

"And I have meetings."

"Then Saturday it is," she said.

"Saturday it is," he echoed. "And it can't come soon enough."

CHAPTER
20

Anne Marie Roche

Ellen packed her overnight bag as if she intended to spend a month with her new grandmother instead of overnight. "Should I take Thierry?" she asked Anne Marie, holding the stuffed teddy bear she'd purchased in France.

"I doubt he'll fit in your suitcase," Anne Marie told her, standing in the doorway of her daughter's room. "I think you'll be able to survive one night without him, don't you?"

"Okay," Ellen said, trying to zip up the small suitcase that bulged on both sides. Baxter slept on the bed, curled up tightly, snoozing away the Friday afternoon.

Anne Marie stepped inside the room. "Maybe I should help you close that."

"I can do it," Ellen insisted, and sure enough, she managed to pull the zipper all the way around, although it was a struggle. Turning, she smiled triumphantly at Anne Marie. "See?"

Anne Marie's mother had agreed to keep Ellen overnight. This wasn't the first night Ellen had spent with her Grandma Laura. Her mother's wholehearted support of the adoption meant a lot to Anne Marie, especially since their relationship had been a difficult one for some years.

"We're going to watch movies and have popcorn and then tomorrow Grandma Laura's taking me to the Pacific Science Center and she said I could ride on the monorail."

"You're going to have fun on Saturday."

"What are you doing?" Ellen asked. Apparently the thought had only now entered her mind.

"Well . . ." Anne Marie had a full schedule, too. "To start with, I'm seeing Tim again." She'd purposely made it sound like a date. Although they were meeting at a restaurant, this wasn't a social engagement. Tim had gotten the test results back and had asked to talk to her privately. "Then I'm—"

"I like him," Ellen said, interrupting her. "He's funny."

Anne Marie responded with a wobbly smile. "He is very nice," she agreed reluctantly. Intent on changing the subject, she quickly added, "Then on Saturday afternoon, when I'm finished at the bookstore, I'm going out with a real estate agent to look at a couple of houses."

Ellen's face fell. "I don't want to move. I like it here."

Anne Marie was well aware of her daughter's feelings, which was why she'd delayed leaving the neighborhood. Ellen loved their tiny apartment and the friends she'd made on Blossom Street. For most of her life, she'd been shuffled from foster home to foster home, and then to her Grandma Dolores's.

Understandably Ellen craved permanence and stability, and Anne Marie intended to provide that. Whenever they'd discussed moving from the apartment, Ellen had seemed apprehensive, so Anne Marie had waited. She was trying to handle this carefully to avoid undermining Ellen's still-fragile sense of security. She'd hoped to find a house this summer and move in by the time school started. Clearly, that wasn't going to happen.

"Once we're in our new house we'll never move again," Anne Marie promised.

She could tell that Ellen didn't want to talk about this anymore.

"What else are you doing?" the girl asked.

"Saturday afternoon I'll pick you up and we'll go see Melissa, Michael and the baby. Brandon's coming, too."

Ellen broke into a smile and clapped her hands. "Oh, goody!"

In the course of the past year, Anne Marie's relationship with her stepdaughter had gone from hostile, on Melissa's part, to one of mutual affection and shared confidences. Robert would be thrilled to know that the two women he'd loved were now close friends. His son, Brandon, had always been a supporter of Anne Marie's and that hadn't changed.

"You ready to head out?" Anne Marie asked.

Nodding, Ellen dragged the heavy bag off her bed.

On the drive over to her mother's house, Anne Marie reminded Ellen about her manners, although it wasn't really necessary, since Ellen was a well-behaved child. Anne Marie stayed only long enough to get her settled. They hugged goodbye and then Ellen stood in the front window, Grandma Laura behind her, waving wildly.

Nerves twisted Anne Marie's stomach as she got closer to her destination. She was meeting Tim Carlsen at a restaurant near his insurance agency—and as far from Blossom Street as possible.

Forty minutes later, she parked on the street Tim had mentioned. She saw him pacing in front of the old-fashioned diner, waiting for her. Glancing at her watch, she noted that she was right on time, almost to the minute.

Tim's eyes met hers as she crossed the street.

"Let's go inside," he said abruptly.

"Fine." She didn't know whether the DNA result was good news, or even what defined *good* in this situation. All she could tell was that Tim seemed uneasy. That could mean he'd learned he was Ellen's biological father—or that he wasn't.

They found a booth and slid inside, sitting opposite each other. The waitress brought over a coffeepot and Anne Marie righted her mug, as did Tim. He and the older woman exchanged fond greetings; he was obviously a regular and well-liked, which didn't surprise Anne Marie.

"So?" she asked anxiously. "What did you find out?"

Before he could answer, the waitress returned with menus and said, "The special today is chicken-fried steak. Cook uses a recipe he got from his grandmother who was from Texas," she announced proudly. "The soup's split pea."

After she left, Tim asked, "Are you hungry?"

She shook her head and then, as if to denounce her as a liar, her stomach growled loudly enough for him to hear.

He grinned. "The soup's homemade. I know, because I had it for lunch."

His smile intrigued Anne Marie. "All right, I'll have a bowl of the soup, but only if you eat something, too."

He agreed and when the waitress came back they placed their orders. A moment later, Anne Marie repeated the question that had been burning in her mind ever since his phone call. "So you got the results?"

Tim nodded, took an envelope out of his pocket and handed it to her. "Ellen's my daughter," he said without preamble.

Anne Marie went numb. She wasn't sure what she was supposed to feel, how she was supposed to react. The first emotion that struck her was fear.

"I'd like to remind you that Ellen's legally my daughter now," she finally managed. "You have no rights as far as the courts are concerned. You—"

Tim raised one hand to forestall her. "Don't worry. I have no intention of trying to take her away from you or proceeding with any form of legal action."

Anne Marie sighed with relief. "Thank you."

Staring down at the table, he unwrapped his silverware, setting it and the paper napkin aside. "I don't mind telling you the results shook me," he said in a low voice.

"I thought you already knew."

He glanced at her. "I suspected, but having that suspicion confirmed jolted me. All the emotions I felt—well, it was kind of a shock."

"How do you mean?"

He fidgeted with the fork, running his finger over the tines. "Well, for one thing, I felt tremendous guilt at having abandoned Candy."

"As I recall, you didn't even know she was pregnant." Because of that, he had no reason to feel guilty, in her view anyway.

"That's true," he said. "But Candy tried to let me know and that's been bothering me."

Anne Marie looked at him steadily but didn't speak.

"I had a long talk with my sponsor."

"Your sponsor?"

"Sorry. In Alcoholics Anonymous, part of the program includes having a sponsor, someone who's successfully stayed clean and sober. That person listens and encourages when needed."

"Of course." She should've known that was what he meant.

Tim set his fork aside and reached for the spoon. "Knowing I have a child threw me more than anything else since I entered rehab."

"I imagine the guilt and regret is only natural."

"I want to make it up to Ellen somehow and yet I know I can't," Tim said. "I have a beautiful, intelligent, delightful child I can't even acknowledge and it's killing me." He plowed his hand through his hair. Anne Marie recognized the agony in that gesture.

As if he suddenly realized what he'd said, his gaze shot to her. "Please don't misunderstand me. I don't blame you. Not in the slightest. If it wasn't for you in Ellen's life, I'm sure she wouldn't be as healthy and happy as she is now. After Dolores died, Ellen could've ended up who-knows-where. I can't even be sure I would've found my daughter if not for you or had the chance to confirm that Ellen's my child."

Despite everything, Anne Marie was beginning to feel sorry for him. "Did your sponsor help you sort through all these emotions?"

Tim responded with a nod. "What he said about acknowledging my feelings made sense. At the same time, the fact that Ellen's my own flesh and blood hasn't sunk in."

"Yes, well . . ."

"I've only seen Ellen once and I love her. I mean,

I *love* that little girl. There are years of my life that are more or less a blur. Years I squandered on stupid, destructive behavior. And yet out of that whole mess came Ellen. Precious, innocent, perfect Ellen."

"I guess that's why they say God works in mysterious ways."

Tim laughed. "That's for sure."

The waitress arrived with their meals, Anne Marie's soup and chicken-fried steak for Tim. They paused long enough to sample their food.

After taking a few bites, Tim put down his fork. "Would you allow me to see her again?"

Anne Marie hesitated, caught between contradictory impulses—compassion for Tim and fear for herself.

"Not alone or anything. You'd always be there."

Anne Marie knew that once this door was opened, there'd be no closing it. After a moment, she said—felt she *had* to say—"I think that would be fine."

For an instant she saw tears glistening in his eyes. "Thank you," he whispered. "You've been kind and generous when I haven't deserved either."

"We'll go about this very slowly," she warned.

"However you wish."

"Ellen believes you're my boyfriend, and I feel we should let her continue with that assumption."

"I agree," Tim said. "How soon before I can ask you two on another date?"

"When would you like?"

"Would this Sunday work for you?"

Anne Marie smiled. "That would work very well."

"I have a sailboat," Tim said eagerly. "Would you and Ellen enjoy going out on the water with me?"

Anne Marie wouldn't presume to speak for her daughter, but she knew she herself would love it. "Sounds great."

"It's docked at Lake Washington. I could meet you at the bookstore. Say one-thirty?"

"We'll be ready."

Tim ate with renewed vigor. When he'd almost finished his meal, he stopped and looked directly at Anne Marie. "Thank you," he said again. "For everything."

"Thank Ellen. She's the one with the list."

"Her twenty wishes."

"Yes. She wrote down that she wanted to meet her father."

"And she has." Tim picked up his coffee. "This can't be easy for you," he said. "I promise I'll never abuse your trust or break your rules."

"I believe you," she told him. "Besides, you're the one who reminded me that a child needs a father."

He smiled knowingly.

Anne Marie ate some of her soup and then answered questions about her history with Ellen. She wasn't sure why, but she told him about Robert and how she happened to meet shy, reticent Ellen. Like Ellen's finding her father, Anne Marie's connection with her daughter had started with her own list of twenty wishes.

"Ellen quiet?" Tim said. "You've got to be kidding."

"She's gradually come out of her shell."

"Tell me more about her. Tell me everything you can remember."

Anne Marie did, and before she knew it, almost two hours had passed. "Oh, my goodness, I've been talking up a storm." She laughed. "No, make that a hurricane."

"I've enjoyed every word," he said contentedly. His interest was genuine and his love for the daughter he'd never known had touched her heart.

"Do you want to go for a walk?" he asked.

Like her, he seemed reluctant to part.

"Okay."

"I'll take you by the agency where Dad and I work."

She nodded, curious about everything concerning her daughter's father.

Tim paid for their meals and they strolled down the street. When they came to the agency, he pointed to the names printed on the door. "I hope Ellen and my parents will get the opportunity to meet one day," he said casually. Then, as if he feared he'd said something he shouldn't, he added, "Only if you agree, of course."

"Eventually," she said, willing to consider it.

"They never lost faith in me," he said. "While I was using, they were tough. They didn't approve of the choices I was making and yet, when I hit bottom, my father was there for me. Mom, too. They're the ones who arranged for me to enter rehab." He hadn't told her much about what he referred to as his "wasted years."

"At the time I wasn't capable of doing anything for myself. I needed help and like I said, my parents were there."

"They sound like wonderful people."

"They are. I'm very fortunate. A lot of addicts and alcoholics don't have the family support I do. It's made all the difference to me."

"You've been clean and sober for eight years?"

"By the grace of God, nearly nine. For me, it's one day at a time and it always will be. I attend AA meetings at the rehab center every Thursday night. It's encouraging for people going through rehab to see someone who's successfully completed the program and stayed clean all these years."

They wandered back to where Anne Marie had parked her car. "Thank you for a good evening," she said. It had been, in more ways than he probably realized.

Tim opened her car door. "You're welcome. And . . . thank *you.*"

He stood on the curb, lifting one hand in a small wave as she pulled away.

Driving home, Anne Marie felt reassured, free of the worry and fear she'd experienced only a few hours ago. She hadn't been prepared to like Tim Carlsen, but she did.

She actually liked him quite a bit.

CHAPTER
21

Teaching a child to knit is one of the greatest joys a knitter can experience.
—Karen Thalacker, author of
Knitting with Gigi and
Gigi Knits . . . and Purls.
www.gigiknits.com

Lydia Goetz

I'd taken a rare Saturday off and wouldn't you know it, the day was gloomy and overcast. Brad and I had told the kids that if the weather was nice, we'd rent bikes so they could ride around Green Lake. Casey's eyes got big when we mentioned it, and I learned she'd never done anything like that. Brad and I generally walked; the three miles around the lake was good exercise and we enjoyed the scenery with its aura of peace and serenity.

When we woke to cloudy skies, everyone was disappointed, especially Cody. Casey didn't say much, but I knew she'd been looking forward to the adventure.

"It might not rain," Cody muttered with his nose pressed against the living-room window.

No sooner had he made his optimistic forecast than the downpour started. Unlike the usual drizzle we get in the Pacific Northwest, it rained buckets, the water hitting the sidewalk with such force it seemed to bounce.

"Put in a movie," I suggested.

Brad had decided to work in the garage, and I planned to use the opportunity to write my aunt Betty a letter. She was my father's sister and my godmother and we'd always had a special relationship. Betty didn't have a computer, so e-mail wasn't an option, but I liked writing her real letters on the stationery she got me for Christmas.

"Which movie?" Cody said listlessly. He inspected the DVDs we kept next to the television.

I could hear him and Casey discussing what to watch and noticed that Cody let Casey make the choice. She picked *School of Rock* with Jack Black. It was one he'd seen plenty of times and I knew he'd rather see something else. I was proud of him for putting someone else's desire above his own. Our son was growing up!

As the movie played, I checked in now and then. At one point I discovered that Cody had taken out a jigsaw puzzle Brad had completed last winter and then dismantled. It was a thousand-piece puzzle depicting a Civil War scene, far beyond our son's skill level. But I didn't want to discourage him, so I said nothing.

Cody had cleared off the dining-room table and set up the puzzle, just as Brad had months earlier. Then he propped up the box with the painting of Pickett's charge at Gettysburg and began turning all the pieces faceup, the way he'd seen his father do.

Casey sprawled on the sofa, staring at the screen. Chase lay on the floor nearby and Casey rested one bare foot on his soft back. I wondered why she wasn't crocheting. From the day Margaret had taught her, she'd had a crochet hook in her hand every spare minute. She'd crocheted five wash-cloths now and I'd given her some leftover yarn for granny squares, which she seemed to enjoy making.

Then I realized why she was gazing blankly at the TV. She was disappointed that our outing was cancelled because of the weather. I started to tell her we'd do it another day—and stopped. We would, but it might very well be after she'd left for her next foster home. I didn't want to remind either one of us of that.

When I finished my letter, I sealed the envelope and went in search of a stamp. I thought there might be one on the dining-room hutch. Entering the room to look for it, I saw that Casey had aban-doned the movie and was sitting next to Cody at the table.

"You need to find all the border pieces first," she was telling him. "Here, I'll help you."

"Okay."

Frankly, I'd never believed I'd ever see the two of them working together like this, with no squabbling and no complaining.

After a moment Cody triumphantly held up a corner piece. "Look!"

"Hey, that's great," Casey said. "We'll start building out from there." She set it on the far side of the table.

I located a stamp, then glanced over at the two of them. I noticed that Casey had allowed Cody to put several pieces in place.

"I want to do it," Cody said loudly when Casey added a small section she'd been working on.

"Hold on," Casey muttered.

Okay, so maybe I'd been a bit optimistic. But within a few minutes they'd settled back into their cooperative mood, and I heard nothing but occasional murmurs and yelps of satisfaction.

Around noon Brad came in for lunch. I'd heated tomato soup and made cheese sandwiches. "What's going on in there?" he asked, gesturing toward the dining room.

"Cody and Casey are putting together a jigsaw puzzle, the same one you did last winter."

He arched his brows but didn't comment.

"Lunch is ready, kids," I said, poking my head inside. When I saw that they'd already finished the entire border, I was impressed. "How'd you get so much done so quickly?"

Holding a single piece in his hand, Cody looked up. "Casey's really good at this."

"Hey, you are, too," she told him.

Cody couldn't stop grinning, he was so pleased. "Can I eat after?" he asked.

"You're not hungry?"

"I'd rather work on this."

I turned to Casey.

"I'll wait, too. We can reheat the soup later."

"No problem." The movie had long since ended, and the screen was black. I walked over and switched it off, then returned to the kitchen.

Brad and I ate alone, something that hardly ever happened anymore.

"That's not an easy puzzle, you know," he said.

I agreed. "They seem to be enjoying themselves, though."

Brad wolfed down the rest of his sandwich and carried his empty soup bowl to the sink. A moment later, he'd joined the two children, sitting in a chair between them.

When I'd put our few dishes in the dishwasher, I joined the family, too. We worked steadily on the puzzle, with a quick lunch break for the kids, and it must've been two hours before I realized the sun was shining through the dining-room window.

"Does anyone want to ride bikes around Green Lake?" I asked.

The three of them looked at me, their eyes blank until my comment registered.

"Hey!" Cody cried, pointing at the window. "The sun's out!"

Casey's smile lit up her face.

"Is everyone still game to go to the lake?" Brad asked.

He didn't need to repeat the question. Cody and Casey let their feelings be known with boisterous hollering.

After some discussion we decided to leave Chase behind. Cody protested loudly but I was afraid the dog would get loose. Chase was otherwise a reasonably well-behaved dog, but he had a bad habit of running ahead, forcing us to chase after him.

When we got to Green Lake, I was pleased to see that it wasn't nearly as crowded as usual. Like us, many families seemed to have abandoned their weekend plans because of the weather.

Now, just a couple of hours after the rainstorm, there wasn't a cloud in the sky. We reached the bicycle rental place and while Brad paid the fees and signed the paperwork, I helped Cody and Casey choose their bikes and put on their helmets. Brad and I thought that instead of walking today we'd cycle, too.

The path around the lake was well laid-out and Cody took off first, with Casey directly behind him. We circled the lake twice before we stopped for ice cream. Sitting on the bench along the pathway, the four of us licked chocolate-dipped cones, hurrying to eat the ice cream before it melted in the hot July sunshine.

"Did you hear about the surgical patient who woke up before the doctor was finished with the surgery?" Brad asked the children. He posed it as a serious question, like something he'd heard on the evening news.

Cody shook his head. "Not me."

"Me, neither," Casey said.

"Apparently, the man wanted to finish his own surgery. The surgeon explained that all that remained was the stitches."

I thought I knew what was coming.

"The man said he could do that, so the surgeon told him to suture himself."

Cody groaned.

"Good one," Casey said, grinning broadly. "Suture himself," she repeated, and burst out laughing.

Cody's laughter joined hers, while I was content to roll my eyes and lick my ice cream. Brad was obviously quite happy with himself.

Casey looked at me, her eyes brimming with joy. It was difficult to remember that this was the same angry, defiant girl who'd shown up on our doorstep a few weeks earlier.

"When do we have to return the bikes?" Cody wanted to know.

Brad checked his watch. "Fifteen minutes."

Cody roared to his feet. "That's long enough to ride around the lake one more time." He grabbed his helmet and slammed it on his head. "Last one back is a dead frog."

Well, I for one had no intention of being referred to as a dead frog, so I finished my cone and hopped on my bike. Cody and Casey were already way ahead of me. Brad took his time but it wasn't long before he sailed past.

I was the last to arrive at the bike rental shop—to no one's surprise. Cody leaned against the side of the building with his ankles crossed, as though he'd been waiting there for hours. Brad, who stood beside him, tapped his watch.

"Here comes Lydia, the dead frog," my husband announced.

Casey bent double with laughter as if this was the funniest thing she'd ever heard. Fortunately I'm a good sport.

"You three had better beware. You never know what might turn up in your stew tonight." I was planning to ask Brad to grill hamburgers, but I wasn't telling Cody and Casey that. "Frogs, anyone?"

Cody shifted toward Casey and said in a stage whisper, "Last Halloween Mom made monster eyeballs."

"Yuck." Casey pretended to be horrified.

"It was really meatballs with a green olive poking out," Cody explained.

"Don't forget the bat wings," I reminded him.

"They looked like chicken wings to me, but what do I know?" Brad said.

"Ghosts, too," Cody added. "Those were really just mashed potatoes."

Casey glanced at me. "You have a great imagination."

"I try," I said and looped my arm around her neck as we walked back to the car.

On the way home we stopped at the grocery store and picked up hamburger buns and fresh tomatoes, although Cody and Brad both hated them.

Casey and I liked tomatoes and cheese on our burgers, however, and I wasn't about to be cheated out of this small treat. While I picked out the best tomatoes, Brad and Cody went to the deli for potato salad and baked beans. We were going to have the perfect summer feast.

While Brad lit the barbecue, Casey and I got everything into serving dishes and set the picnic table in the backyard.

Chase and Cody raced around the grass. Cody tossed a Frisbee in the air and the dog caught it every time.

"You want to throw it?" Cody asked Casey when she'd finished helping me.

She shrugged. "I guess."

I could see that she was grateful, and again I wanted to hug Cody for his thoughtfulness. Our son was capable of real sensitivity and I was sure that was due, in part, to the difficult situation with his mother. He hadn't said much about his visit with Janice a week earlier, and I hadn't asked. Brad had stayed in the car, listening to the radio, while Cody was up in her condo.

Cody, like any little boy, loved his mother. He loved me, too, and I didn't want him to feel guilty about his feelings for Janice. I hurt for him that Janice showed so little interest in his life.

During dinner Brad told more of his silly jokes. I remembered a few old knock-knock jokes my father had told when I was a kid. We all laughed rowdily as if we were clever and funny when we were probably neither. We were just having fun as a family.

By the time we'd finished cleaning off the out-side table, we decided to work on the jigsaw puzzle again. With the four of us all finding pieces, it was coming together quickly. Eventually, we grew tired of that and gathered around the television to watch a movie Brad had rented while we were at the grocery store. When the final credits rolled, Cody was yawning. It'd been a full, full day.

"Church in the morning," Brad reminded the two children.

"Do we have to go?" Cody whined.

There were no Sunday School classes during the summer months, which meant Cody had to sit with Brad and me. It was his least favorite thing to do, but his father and I felt it was important.

Casey had accompanied us each week, without comment.

"We're all going," Brad informed Cody.

"You'll be glad you did," I told him.

"No, I won't," Cody said, pouting.

I had to laugh. He was such a typical kid.

"Come on, Chase," he muttered, starting down the hall toward his bedroom. He paused halfway, then started back.

I thought he might want to argue some more about church. Instead he hugged his father, then walked over to me and threw both arms around my waist.

"I had fun today."

"So did I," I said and hugged him back.

As Cody returned to his bedroom, I saw the look of pain in Casey's eyes.

"Hey, Casey," I said. "How about a hug from you, too?"

She seemed unsure.

But I didn't wait for her to come to me; I walked over and gave her a firm hug. "I'm glad you were with us today."

For a moment I thought she might let her arms dangle at her sides, but then she hugged me. "I had a good time, too."

"I'm glad."

"In fact," she whispered, "it was probably the very best day of my whole life."

CHAPTER
22

Phoebe Rylander

The weekend in Westport with Hutch was incredible and wonderful and exciting. Those were only a few of the words Phoebe could think of to describe their time together.

The condo overlooked the Pacific Ocean on one side and Gray's Harbor on the other. The community was filled with quaint shops, delectable seafood restaurants and antique stores and seemed completely unspoiled.

Holding hands, they'd walked barefoot along the beach and on Saturday afternoon, Hutch assembled huge, complicated kites for them to fly. Phoebe stood on the shore and laughed hysterically at Hutch's attempts to keep their strings from tangling. Later on Saturday, after a dinner of Phoebe's seafood linguine, they sat on the beach in front of a campfire that crackled and shot sparks in the air. Hutch slipped his arm around her shoulders and drew her close. They didn't talk; conversation seemed unnecessary. Instead, they'd looked into the mesmerizing flames as the driftwood burned and simply enjoyed being together.

Sunday morning, Phoebe insisted on making a cheese omelet, which Hutch praised as lavishly as he had her pasta the night before. They both grew subdued that afternoon, preparing to return to their respective lives. Phoebe regretted having to leave this idyllic place.

Hutch had kissed her several times, and Phoebe loved being in his arms. He didn't pressure her to sleep with him, which was a pleasant change from other men she'd dated—Clark in particular.

It was while she sat staring into the fire that she'd realized the biggest difference between the two men and the reason she'd always found an excuse to delay her wedding to Clark.

Hutch was sincere, genuine, kind, while Clark had shown little evidence of those qualities. Clark's entire world revolved around him—his career, his ambition, his needs. The more time she spent away from him, the more Phoebe saw how blind she'd been. His infidelity had been a blessing wrapped in pain and betrayal. How grateful she was now that she hadn't married him.

As she sat by the fire on the beach, thinking about Clark, Phoebe's eyes had welled with tears. She could only feel thankful that she'd recognized the truth before it was too late.

Hutch seemed to believe that her emotions were connected to the death of her fiancé. Phoebe wanted to tell him the truth and knew she needed to do it soon. She regretted the lie. When she'd first introduced herself to the class, it had just seemed easier than launching into a complicated explanation. This was the weekend she'd planned to tell him about Clark, but she'd been afraid. She hadn't wanted to ruin their time together, so she'd put it off yet again.

Hutch dropped Phoebe at her apartment around eight on Sunday evening. After giving Princess a few minutes' attention and refreshing her food and water, Phoebe checked her phone. The message light was blinking wildly. Caller ID informed her that the majority of calls had come from Clark.

Without listening to any of his attempts to contact her, Phoebe deleted each message until she got to her mother's.

"Phoebe, where are you? Why aren't you answering the phone?" Her mother's voice rang with urgency. "Clark's father suffered a massive heart attack. He's in the hospital. No one knows what's going to happen. Please call Clark as soon as you get this. I just pray it isn't too late."

Phoebe gasped. She'd always been fond of Clark's father, and the thought of losing Max shook her badly. Without thinking she grabbed the phone and dialed Clark's cell.

"Phoebe!" he said. "Thank God you called."

"How's your father?"

"He had emergency bypass surgery on Saturday morning. Where were you? No one seemed to have any idea."

"That isn't important," she told him. Phoebe didn't owe him any explanations and she certainly wasn't about to tell him she'd been in Westport with Hutch.

Her words had a sobering effect on him. "You're right, of course," he said. "Listen, Phoebe, Dad asked if you'd come and see him. Will you do that? You know how special you are to my father."

"Of course I'll visit him."

"Would it be possible for you to come now?" Clark asked softly.

"Now?"

"Please. It would mean the world to Dad."

"I . . . I suppose."

Clark gave her Max's room number at Swedish Hospital, which she wrote down on a pad near the phone. "I have one request," she said.

"Anything."

Clark was acting far too agreeable. Perhaps she was being cynical, but past experience had taught her he wasn't to be trusted.

"If I go to see your father now, you can't be there."

"But . . ." Clark hesitated.

"Agreed?"

"Phoebe, I—"

"That's my stipulation and either you agree or I'll arrange another time to come by the hospital." She'd visit Max during working hours because the one thing she could count on was that Clark wouldn't show up if it interfered with law-firm business.

Again he paused. "You've changed, Phoebe."

She wouldn't deny it. "Thanks to you, I'm not the same gullible woman I used to be. I refuse to play your games anymore."

His tone sobered. "My father's close to dying, Phoebe. This isn't a game."

"I'll come, Clark, but if you're anywhere in the vicinity, I guarantee you I'll walk right out the door."

Clark laughed.

"You think this is amusing?" she demanded irritably. She refused to let Clark manipulate her as he so often had in the past.

"I like the new you," he said, cajoling her. "I've seen that stubborn streak before, but there's a new determination in you that intrigues me. If this is how you want it, Phoebe, then so be it."

"I mean it, Clark."

"I don't doubt you for a moment. I won't be anywhere near the hospital. I promise."

She wasn't sure she could trust him and said nothing. If he did "just happen" to stop by, she'd keep her word. She'd simply leave.

As she hung up the phone, Phoebe closed her eyes. Why Max wanted to see her right now, she couldn't begin to guess. Was his condition really so dire that she had to rush to the hospital immediately?

Reaching for her sweater and purse, Phoebe hurried to the parking garage. All the way to the hospital, she resisted the urge to call Hutch and tell him about this unexpected turn of events.

But she couldn't discuss Clark with Hutch because he thought her fiancé was dead. That was the problem with a lie: it occasioned other lies and soon you'd created an ever-increasing spiral of them. And when it came to revealing the truth—well, that was difficult. She'd wanted to tell him; Hutch deserved to know about Clark. Yet she hadn't. She was afraid her deception would taint their relationship. And the longer she delayed, the more embarrassing and awkward the truth became.

Phoebe found a parking spot on a street that would be well lit once the sun went down and walked the short distance to Swedish Hospital. She wasn't all that far from Blossom Street.

Really, when she thought about it, she had a great deal for which to thank Clark. If not for him, she would never have met Alix, Lydia and Margaret, or for that matter, Hutch. Just thinking about him produced a sense of anticipation.

She had Max Snowden's room number, so Phoebe took the elevator directly to his floor and entered the surgical ward.

In the room, Phoebe found Marlene Snowden sitting by her husband's bedside, holding his hand. Thankfully, Clark was nowhere in sight.

When she saw Phoebe, Clark's mother released Max's hand and rose to her feet. "Phoebe! I'm so grateful you're here."

Max opened his eyes and smiled, stretching out his arm. "My dear."

"Oh, Max." He looked pale and weak, so unlike the robust man she'd known. "I'm so sorry this happened."

"He's going to get better soon. It's only a matter of time before he's back on the golf course and we're dancing at the country club again. Isn't that right, Max?" Marlene gazed down at her husband. "Of course, we'll be making some small lifestyle changes and—"

"Yes, Marlene," her husband said, cutting her off.

Marlene Snowden sighed. "I know Max wants to talk to you privately," she said, patting her husband's hand, "so I'll leave you to chat." She leaned forward and kissed Max on the brow. "I'll go get a cup of coffee."

Phoebe watched her go, then turned to Max. "What can I do for you?" she asked, frankly curious.

"You know I've always loved you," Max said hoarsely.

Phoebe nodded; the affection was mutual.

"I'm the one who talked you into taking Clark back the first time."

"Yes," she acknowledged. Pressure had come from all sides, including her own mother, but it was Max who'd convinced her to give Clark another chance. "You were so sure it would never happen

265

again. Only it did, Max, and frankly I don't think Clark will ever stop."

Max shook his head in disgust. "My son can be an idiot."

She squeezed his hand, echoing his sentiment.

"I would've enjoyed having you as my daughter-in-law—the daughter I never had."

It went without saying that she would've enjoyed being part of the Snowden family, too.

To her horror, Max's eyes filled with tears. "Is there any possibility that you'd be willing to forgive Clark and marry him?"

Phoebe hardly knew how to respond. "I—"

"You don't need to tell me that Clark deserves to lose you. If he hadn't done this before . . ." He let the rest fade and turned his head to stare out the hospital window. "In my heart I know Clark loves you. You're good for him, Phoebe. When he's with you, Clark is a better man."

"I'm not sure that's true. I—"

Again Max interrupted her. "Although Marlene insists I'm going to be as healthy as ever, I'm not convinced. As far as I can tell, I'm living on borrowed time."

"Oh, Max." Phoebe bit her lower lip. She had only vague memories of her own father, who'd played such a minor role in her life. From the first she'd felt a bond with Max, who was like a second father to her.

"I want to see my son married and settled down.

I'd be grateful to hold a grandchild in my arms one day, God willing. Now, I don't know if that'll ever happen."

"You've had a fright," she told him.

"It's more than that, Phoebe."

She swallowed hard. "Do you know something the doctors haven't told your family?"

Max didn't answer but he looked away, and she realized then that he did. She tightened her grip on his hand.

"I love my son," Max murmured. "I know his strengths and his weaknesses. I also know he regrets this mess and that he misses you terribly. He'd do anything to get you back."

"I don't think that's possible anymore," Phoebe whispered.

"If you'd be willing to reconsider, I could have a stipulation put in my will." Max's gaze implored her. "If Clark ever again commits any form of infidelity, I'd disinherit him."

"Max, I—"

"Hear me out," he pleaded. "You alone would inherit—not Clark. You and any children the two of you might have."

Aware of how much it must've hurt him to make such a suggestion, Phoebe pressed the back of his hand against her cheek. "Max, I'm sorry but I really don't think that's a solution."

"Consider it. That's all I ask." Max smiled up at her, although the effort seemed to drain him.

"You need to rest."

"I do," he said, "but I'd sleep a whole lot easier if I knew you'd reconsider marrying Clark." He paused as though gathering his strength in order to continue. "Clark might not admit it, but he needs you, Phoebe."

She didn't confirm or deny that. Knowing Clark so well, she believed he didn't need *her* as much as the evidence that he could manipulate her. What Clark craved above all was control, of everyone and everything around him.

"You're a good woman."

"Thank you, but . . ."

Max closed his eyes, his strength nearly gone. "Clark's learned his lesson."

"Does he know why you wanted to see me?" She had to find out whether Clark had a role in this before she could promise Max she'd reconsider.

"Yes," Max whispered. "He's desperate to have you back, on any terms, Phoebe, and asked me to help persuade you."

Oh, very clever of him, she mused skeptically. Being an attorney, a very skilled one, meant that his father's wishes wouldn't stand in his way. Clark would uncover a loophole. He certainly wouldn't allow her to take away his inheritance. None of that mattered, though.

Phoebe shook her head. "Max, I don't want a husband tied to me because of a stipulation in a will," she said softly. "If the bonds of love and commitment aren't enough, then there's nothing left to say."

"I agree . . ."

"Then why—"

"The fact that I'd even ask such a thing of you proves how badly I want to see my son settled. You're his equal in every way. Clark isn't an easy man to love—he's already proven that."

Despite herself Phoebe grinned.

"I wouldn't suggest this if I didn't believe he was truly sorry. He swore to me that it'll never happen again."

"He swore that to me, as well," Phoebe reminded him. "The first time."

Max frowned. "Like I said earlier, he doesn't deserve your forgiveness or your love."

Phoebe debated how much to tell Max, then decided she couldn't mislead him. "I've met someone else, Max."

Max's eyes dulled and it was several minutes before he spoke. "Clark doesn't know that, does he?"

Phoebe looked away. "I told him, but he didn't take it well. That's one of the reasons I insisted he not be here, otherwise I wouldn't be able to come."

Max sighed. "Forgive an old man for trying to make things right."

"There's nothing to forgive. You love your son."

"I love you, too, Phoebe. I wish this had worked out differently."

"So do I."

Max squeezed her hand. "Thank you for being honest with me."

"I'd appreciate it if you didn't mention our conversation to Clark."

"I won't," he assured her.

"Phoebe," Marlene Snowden said, startling her as she stepped into the room, holding a cup of coffee. "You're dating someone else now. It didn't take you long, did it?"

"Marlene," Max protested.

"Clark told me. He was in the cafeteria because you refused to see him. You were with that other man this weekend, weren't you?" Marlene Snowden demanded in a shrill voice. "No wonder we couldn't reach you."

Phoebe ignored the accusation.

"How dare you accuse my son of cheating!" Marlene continued. "Isn't that the pot calling the kettle black?"

"I think it's time I left," Phoebe said. She kissed the back of Max's hand and walked out of the room.

Thankfully, Clark's mother didn't follow her. She wished Max the very best, she'd miss him painfully, but she could never marry his son.

CHAPTER
23

Anne Marie Roche

Beach towels tucked under their arms, Ellen and her friend, Hallie Reynolds, paced anxiously in the apartment, waiting for Anne Marie.

"Hurry, Mom!" Ellen cried. "We'll be late."

"No, we won't," Anne Marie said as she grabbed the sunblock and threw it in her beach bag. She'd lathered each of the girls earlier. They were all headed to the water park, and even now, Anne Marie wasn't quite sure how she'd let Ellen and Tim talk her into this. She wore her swimsuit under her shorts and T-shirt, but she had no intention of going in the water. She'd leave that to Tim and the girls. Anne Marie planned to lie on the grass or the beach or whatever was there and laze away the afternoon reading.

"Mom!" Ellen cried again. "If you don't hurry up, everyone else will get the best spots."

"I'm almost ready." Anne Marie quickly put on lip gloss and paused to check her reflection in the bathroom mirror. She ran a brush through her hair, then plopped a brand-new straw hat on her head. This was about as good as it got.

She joined the girls, who'd linked arms around each other's necks. They'd met at the day camp

271

and become instant friends. For the last few weeks, they'd been inseparable.

After making sure Baxter had enough water, Anne Marie loaded the girls into her car. They squealed with delight at the prospect of spending the whole afternoon at the water park. When Tim had suggested the outing last weekend, Ellen had been so excited she could barely hold still. Anne Marie couldn't possibly have declined after that. So here she was, on her one free day of the week, wearing an old swimsuit, a cheap hat and sunglasses.

It'd been years since she'd worn this swimsuit. At least it fit, although she had to admit it wasn't even close to being fashionable. But that was fine, because she didn't intend for anyone other than Ellen to see it.

"Tim is my mom's boyfriend," Ellen told Hallie on the way to the water park. She was obviously pleased about imparting this information.

Anne Marie stopped herself from correcting her daughter just in time. Her relationship with Tim was far too complicated to explain. He'd dropped by the bookstore on Saturday and afterward they'd all gone to a movie. When it ended, he'd taken them to dinner at a pizza place, where he'd brought up this Wednesday outing.

Tim *wasn't* her boyfriend, of course, but Anne Marie had begun to enjoy his company. So had Ellen—who'd started asking a few too many questions about this purported romance.

However, except for that night at the diner, she'd only seen him in Ellen's presence. Nothing "romantic" could happen in those circumstances, and yet . . . Anne Marie wouldn't have minded if he'd tried to kiss her. Or wanted to see her on her own. Thinking of Tim in that way was the very last thing she would've expected. She suddenly recalled that at her stepdaughter, Melissa's, wedding, *she'd* caught the bouquet. Anne Marie had laughed at the time, telling everyone it was clearly a mistake. Then, all these months later, she'd met Tim, and now everything was falling into place. She was attracted to him, he was her daughter's father—it all seemed to fit. A picture of the three of them creating a family was so tempting, she had to force herself to be sensible. She'd started to build this fantasy and it had to stop.

When they arrived at their destination, Anne Marie had to drive to the farthest reaches of the parking lot before she located an empty space.

Ellen and Hallie were fidgeting, eager to get to the water. The second she turned off the engine, the girls unfastened their seat belts and leaped out of the car. Anne Marie was stuck hauling the beach bag with their inflatables, changes of clothing and everything else. As they neared the ticket stand, she saw Tim waiting there, as they'd agreed earlier.

When he saw them, he hurried over to Anne Marie and took the heavy bag from her arms.

"Thanks," she murmured.

He smiled at her, then asked the girls, "Are you two ready for some fun?"

In response, they gave high-pitched squeals.

Once inside the park, they chose a shady spot to arrange their towels and other paraphernalia. Tim helped Anne Marie spread out the blanket she'd brought, while the girls, unable to wait a moment longer, raced toward the wave pool.

"Go on, Tim," Anne Marie said. "I'll stay here."

"Aren't you coming in, too?" he asked, sounding disappointed.

"Maybe later," she said, kicking off her sandals and taking out a paperback novel she'd been looking forward to reading. "I'll hold down the fort," she told him, sitting cross-legged on the blanket. They'd been fortunate enough to secure a place on the grassy area in front of the water.

He jerked the T-shirt over his head, tossed it onto the blanket and ran to the wave pool. She couldn't help noticing that he had an impressive physique, with sculpted muscles and broad shoulders. He probably worked out, but he wasn't excessively muscular with that weight-lifter look she hated. He joined in the girls' antics as if he were nine years old all over again.

Anne Marie did make an effort to read. Soon, however, she abandoned all pretense of following the story and spent her time watching Tim and the girls.

"This is silly," she muttered and stripped off her

T-shirt and shorts. She waded into the pool. The shock of the cool water made her gasp, but after a minute or two she'd adjusted to the temperature. The wave machine, which was periodically turned off, wasn't on just then.

Ellen and Hallie rushed toward her, and Anne Marie instinctively held up her hands. "I'd like to keep my hair from getting—"

She didn't have a chance to finish before two teenage boys nearby decided to have a water fight. Caught between them, Anne Marie was drenched within seconds. Her hair hung in wet tendrils about her face. She wiped her eyes, blinking to clear them of water.

So much for that idea.

"You want me to splash them back?" Tim asked, making no effort to disguise his amusement. "I'll defend your honor."

Anne Marie played along, clasping her hands and batting her lashes outrageously. "My hero!"

"Mom, watch!" Ellen shouted and dove under-water. In a few seconds, she'd thrust her skinny legs into the air as she stood on her hands. She surfaced and shoved the wet hair out of her eyes. "Did you see? Did you see?"

"I didn't realize you were so agile," Anne Marie teased.

"What's *agile?*" Hallie asked.

"Limber," Tim explained.

Hallie exchanged a blank look with Ellen.

"It means I'm talented," Ellen said.

"So am I!" Hallie imitated the trick and a moment later both girls were upside down.

A bell rang, indicating that the waves were about to start again. When Anne Marie had watched earlier, she thought it looked tame enough—at least from the sidelines.

"Get back, Mom," Ellen warned.

"I'm fine," Anne Marie said.

Standing near the "shore" with both girls, Tim called out, "You might want to move to the shallow end."

"Would you two cut it out?" Anne Marie said as the first wave hit her. She was swept off her feet and went tumbling through the water. She came up choking and sputtering to the sounds of Tim, Ellen and Hallie roaring with laughter.

"Very funny," Anne Marie managed to say. Clutching her throat, she made a show of choking. Soon Ellen and Hallie were pounding her on the back.

Anne Marie's biggest concern was that the girls not get sunburned. Throughout the afternoon she repeatedly slathered them with sunblock. Returning the favor, Ellen rubbed the lotion on Anne Marie's back. At one point, Anne Marie caught Tim watching her—and suspected he would've enjoyed being the one to rub her back. It was a good feeling and she held on to it for several minutes.

They stayed at the park until after five and although the girls were bone-weary, they protested when Tim announced it was time to leave. In order to buy peace, Tim offered them dinner at McDonald's. They stopped at one close to the park, and Tim purchased cheeseburgers, fries and milk-shakes for everyone. Anne Marie couldn't remember having such a good appetite in years. She relished every bite of her burger and drank every drop of her milkshake.

When she'd finished her meal, Anne Marie felt completely relaxed, completely content. While the girls explored the playground, she and Tim sat in the booth, chatting.

"Thank you. That was a lot of fun," she said. "I didn't intend to go in the water but I'm glad I did."

His gaze held hers for an extra-long moment. "I'm glad you did, too."

Anne Marie smiled. "I didn't have much of a choice, did I?" The girls would eventually have dragged her into the water, one way or another.

Tim glanced at Ellen, who'd clambered to the top of a huge red slide. "She's terrific, isn't she? So confident and naturally charming . . ."

Anne Marie nodded, enjoying the opportunity to see her daughter through another person's eyes.

He sighed, and then looked tentatively at Anne Marie. "Would it be all right if just the two of us— just you and I—went out to dinner one night?"

Her heart skipped a beat. "Sure," she said, trying

to sound nonchalant. In reality she was excited about seeing Tim again. On their own. Without kids. It was her fantasy coming to life. . . .

"What about Friday?"

"Friday works for me," she replied. It wasn't as though she had to check her social calendar; she rarely had plans for Friday night.

"There's a wonderful Italian restaurant not far from Blossom Street," he was saying. "Their eggplant parmesan is out of this world."

"You like eggplant?" she asked, wrinkling her nose.

"Love it."

Anne Marie cringed.

"Would you rather eat somewhere else?"

"Oh, no, they'll have something other than eggplant on the menu. I'm a pasta girl myself."

Tim grinned. "Then Italian it is."

Apparently the girls were finished playing because they ran back to the booth, laughing as they did.

"You ready to go?" Anne Marie asked.

Ellen and Hallie both nodded.

As Tim slid out of the booth, Ellen turned to him, an odd look on her face. "You can kiss my mom if you want," she whispered loudly.

"Ellen!" Anne Marie said, shocked. She could see that Tim was trying to hide a grin.

"Actually, I've been thinking about doing exactly that," he announced. Leaning forward, he planted a loud kiss on Anne Marie's cheek.

Ellen frowned. "That's not a *real* kiss, not like in the movies."

"That's 'cause adults do it in the dark," Hallie said. "They don't like kids watching."

"Oh." Apparently this made everything clear to Ellen.

Anne Marie, Ellen and her friend parted company with Tim in the parking lot, although he insisted on following them back to Blossom Street. By the time she dropped Hallie off and drove home, it was almost seven-thirty. Ellen was struggling to keep her eyes open.

"Come on, sleepyhead," Anne Marie said.

Ellen trailed her sluggishly up the stairs, dragging her beach towel behind her. Baxter greeted them enthusiastically, no doubt ready for his supper, his walk and some intensive cuddling.

Anne Marie fed the dog, then threw their towels and swimsuits in the washing machine. Tim volunteered to take Baxter for a short walk and she accepted his offer. When he returned with the Yorkie, they found Ellen fast asleep on the sofa. Tim kissed her forehead, then lingered only a moment, declining coffee or tea. Anne Marie had to admit she was disappointed that he didn't take the opportunity to kiss *her.*

After seeing him out, she carried her daughter to the bedroom. Without bothering to change Ellen's clothes, Anne Marie put her to bed, tucked under a crisp, cool sheet. It'd been a long, exhausting day. An exhilarating day . . .

The phone rang as Anne Marie was putting their wet clothes in the dryer. The tiny laundry room adjoined the kitchen, and she dashed out, lunging for the phone on the second ring for fear it would wake Ellen.

"Hello," she said softly.

"Anne Marie?" her friend Barbie asked. "Is everything okay? It doesn't sound like you."

"I just spent an entire afternoon at a water park with Ellen and Tim. Ellen's asleep and I'm exhausted. Who would've guessed swimming could be so draining?"

Barbie laughed. "It can be a lot of fun, too."

Anne Marie knew how much Barbie and Mark enjoyed the hours they spent in her swimming pool. Mark was bound to a wheelchair and loved the freedom water afforded him.

"It was. We had a blast."

"So everything's going well with Tim?"

"Yes . . ." Anne Marie had been skeptical when Tim first approached her, but her reaction to him had moved into a whole new stage. The way she felt about his invitation proved that. It was time they got to know each other, she decided, time they tested this growing awareness between them.

"You're attracted to him, aren't you?"

"I am," Anne Marie admitted. "He's been wonderful with Ellen and he's respectful of my place in her life." Because she'd needed someone to confide in, Anne Marie had shared her concerns with Barbie when Tim made his initial overtures.

"There's more, right?"

Barbie seemed to have some kind of intuition when it came to relationships—romance radar, she called it. "Tim asked me out to dinner," she confessed.

"Just you?"

"Just me. On Friday night."

"Why don't you bring Ellen here?" Barbie said. "Actually, I was phoning to invite both of you to come over on Friday night for a pool party. Mom and Hector are coming."

"I wouldn't want Ellen to intrude."

"You're kidding, right? She wouldn't be any bother. Hector can bring one of his great-nieces and the two of them will entertain each other."

"Oh, Barbie, that would be great."

Never one to hold back, Barbie asked, "Has Tim kissed you yet?"

Anne Marie didn't think she could include that peck on her cheek.

"He has, hasn't he?" Barbie burst out.

"Technically, yes—but it was just for show."

Barbie laughed. "Don't kid yourself. This is ideal, you know."

"What is?" she asked, although she was beginning to feel the same way. She was falling for this guy, who happened to be her adopted daughter's biological father.

"It's a perfect scenario for Ellen," Barbie was saying.

"Maybe . . ." Anne Marie hated to seem so tentative. She'd begun to hope that a relationship between her and Tim was possible, but she wasn't quite ready to believe it. "Do you think so?"

"I do," Barbie insisted. "Ellen would have the mother who loves her *and* her biological father. This couldn't have worked out better if you'd planned it."

"But I didn't," Anne Marie said wryly.

"And that's why it's so perfect. Promise me one thing."

"Okay."

"Promise you'll tell me *everything* when you come to pick up Ellen on Friday night. Oh—and I want to meet him soon."

A few minutes later, Anne Marie put the phone down, wearing a huge grin. Despite Barbie's optimism, she hoped she wasn't counting on too much—and at the same time she felt encouraged by Tim's dinner invitation.

She sensed he was attracted to her, just as she was to him. In fact, she found herself thinking about him far too often, thinking about the two of them—and their daughter.

Her biggest fear was that she might be setting herself up for a major disappointment, one that would hurt Ellen, too.

CHAPTER 24

After thirty years in the courtroom telling yarns, I started to learn how to make it. The biggest revelation was that yarn, like society, is only held together by friction—and then only loosely.

—Cecil Miskin, owner, Buffalo Gold,
www.buffalogold.net

Lydia Goetz

"Casey!" Cody shouted at the top of his lungs. "Phone!"

Casey stuck her head out her bedroom door. "I got a phone call?" she asked, sounding more than a little surprised.

In the month and a half Casey had been living with us, she hadn't received a single call. When I'd asked her about this, she'd shrugged off the question, answering it with one of her own. "Why make friends when I'll be moving at the end of the summer anyway?"

That left me with another question, which I didn't ask. According to Evelyn Boyle, Casey had attended school in this neighborhood for most of the school year. Did Casey actually mean she hadn't made a single friend in that whole time? Of course it might just be that none of her school friends were part of the summer program. But then why didn't she keep in touch with them? It didn't seem natural to purposely avoid friends, even short-term ones. I'd made friends at summer camp while I was growing up and on vacation with my family. Some of those friendships had been brief, but they'd almost all left me with pleasant memories.

I'd noticed how reticent Casey was about opening up to others. That explained why it'd taken weeks for her to come outside her bedroom for anything other than meals. She liked the three of us, I could tell, and she enjoyed learning and doing new things. Brad and I had grown attached to her. In fact, we'd gone so far as to discuss taking her on as our foster daughter, but Evelyn had already made arrangements with a good family.

Twice now, Casey had come to the yarn store and worked for me. Well, maybe *worked* was a slight overstatement. She wanted to help, so I let her put price tags on skeins of yarn and restock the shelves. Despite a few mistakes, I paid her.

Within half an hour, she'd blown that first twenty dollars, buying a cover for an iPod she didn't have. She managed to hold on to the second twenty a bit longer. Two hours, I'd say.

Casey seemed to be doing better in her classes, too. I'm convinced that was due to Brad, who'd begun to check her homework every night. He showed limitless patience as he sat with her and explained fractions. The concept was hard for Casey to grasp.

She seemed reassured when I told her I'd had a difficult time with fractions, too. For her, the breakthrough came while she was baking a cake. I'd picked up a variety of mixes, which she made at least twice a week. We'd eaten more cake since her arrival than in the previous two years.

She was mixing a cake when Brad pointed out that she didn't need to pour in the water and oil separately if she could figure out how to add a cup and a quarter of water to a third of a cup of oil in the same measuring container. The two of them worked it out together. That practical lesson in fractions led to understanding, and for the first time she seemed to actually get it.

I was still waiting for Casey to come to the phone. "Who is it?" she called out.

"I don't know," Cody yelled. "It's a boy."

I smiled. Now, *this* was an intriguing development.

As if she had no interest in answering the phone, Casey came slowly out of her bedroom and shuffled down the hall.

I was knitting in the living room, while Brad read the paper—typical after-dinner activities, in other words. I didn't listen in on Casey's phone call, but I was relieved to know she was making friends.

The conversation ended after less than five minutes. I was jolted when she banged down the receiver and raced back to her bedroom. She slammed the door so hard I swear it shook the whole house.

Brad glanced up from the paper. "What was that all about?"

"I have no idea, but I think I should find out."

His nod told me he agreed.

I gave Casey ten minutes to cool down, then knocked politely on her bedroom door.

She ignored me.

"Casey?" I called. "What's wrong?" I knew better than to ask *if* anything was wrong. From experience I realized she'd deny it.

No answer.

Tentatively I opened the door and stepped inside to see her sprawled on the bed, face buried in her arms. She wasn't crying or showing any other sign of distress. But then, I'd never seen Casey cry.

I stood by the edge of the bed and gently stroked her hair. She shook off my hand.

"I . . . don't . . . need . . . anyone." Each word was said from between clenched teeth.

"Who was that on the phone?"

"No one."

"It would be kind of difficult for *no one* to make a telephone call."

She clearly didn't appreciate my weak attempt at humor. I stayed with her for a few more minutes. Everything about her body language told me she didn't want me there. The longer I stayed, the more she seemed to stiffen with resentment. She couldn't have made her feelings any plainer.

I hate to admit how discouraged I was. I'd been willing to listen and reassure Casey. I wanted her to confide in me. I yearned to hold her and show her how much I cared, to tell her that if her heart was broken, then so was mine. Instead, she rejected every overture of comfort.

Her dismissal hurt. I blinked back tears as I silently rose and left her alone. I sat in the living room not sure what to think.

After a while Brad lowered the paper. "You upset about something?" he asked. Sometimes men can be so obtuse. Obviously I was upset! All he had to do was look at me to know that.

"Yes," I snapped.

My husband has the most expressive eyebrows I've ever seen. They inched toward his hairline, conveying sympathy—and a bit of shock at my rudeness. "Do you want to talk about it?" he asked.

I crossed my arms and shook my head. I suppose I was acting like a rebellious child but at the moment I didn't care. Having Casey live with us hadn't been easy. This girl came complete with a matched set of emotional baggage.

"I take it this has to do with Casey?" Brad continued.

Cody dashed into the living room, Chase at his

heels. He halted abruptly when he saw us. "Are you guys fighting?"

"No," Brad answered. "Your mom's worried about Casey. Can you tell us anything about that phone call you took earlier?"

Cody sat down next to his father. "I heard him say his name was Lee."

"Lee," I repeated, dropping my arms. I leaned forward and looked at Brad. "That's her brother." And then all at once I knew. "When I took Casey to visit him, Lee told her he was going to college and would be getting a job."

"And he'd send for her," Brad murmured.

"She also said he was considering the army."

"If he does, she won't be moving in with him."

It was the only thing that would distress Casey this much. That short visit with her brother had given her hope—hope of getting out of the system, hope of being with him, hope of living a normal life.

"What should we do?"

Sometimes I worried that making an emotional investment in Casey was a big mistake. At the end of the summer she'd be leaving us and we had to accept that, just as she did. But how could we *not* care about her?

Brad frowned. "Should I see if she'll talk to me?" he asked.

Since I hadn't gotten anywhere, I didn't think he would either, but that was no reason not to try.

After all, Brad was the one who'd devoted hours to teaching her about fractions.

"Let me try," Cody piped up. "Me and Chase," he said in all seriousness.

Brad turned to me for my opinion and I gestured helplessly. "It can't hurt."

"Okay, son," Brad said. "See what you can do."

Cody nodded. "Come, Chase," he commanded. "Casey needs us."

The two of them trotted down the hallway to Casey's bedroom. Cody knocked, then opened the door and went inside.

Brad and I waited. My fear was that Casey would scream at him and hurt his feelings. Without realizing it, I sat on the edge of my cushion, ready to hurry to his rescue if the need arose.

Probably ten minutes passed, with each one feeling like a hundred. If Cody and Casey were talking, I couldn't hear their voices. I strained to listen and heard nothing.

"What do you suppose is happening in there?" Brad asked. He looked as tense as I felt.

"I don't have a clue."

Finally, just when I was about to investigate on my own, Casey's bedroom door opened. "Mom," Cody yelled, as if I was in the basement instead of one room away. "Do we have any ice cream?" He made it sound like a call to 9-1-1.

"I believe so," I said as calmly as I could.

"We need two bowls, okay?"

289

"Two bowls coming right up."

He closed the door, then jerked it open again. "What about chocolate syrup?"

"Ah . . . I'll check."

Brad was on his feet, too. "I'll make a quick run to the store if necessary."

I was already in the kitchen, investigating the cupboard where I knew I'd find chocolate syrup if we had any. "Got it," I called out triumphantly.

"Good." Cody's voice was relieved. "Hurry, okay?"

"In a minute," I promised him.

Working together, Brad and I quickly prepared two heaping bowls of vanilla ice cream covered with chocolate syrup. When I finished adding the chocolate, I asked, "Should I look for whipped topping?"

Brad shook his head. "I don't think so."

Each of us carrying a bowl, we approached the closed bedroom door.

Brad knocked and turned the knob. We stepped inside, holding out the ice cream as though we'd come bearing gifts of gold and precious jewels.

Casey sat on the bed with her back to the wall. Cody was sitting there, too, and Chase lay between them. Casey's hand was on his fur, which she stroked methodically, avoiding eye contact with either Brad or me.

"Thanks, Mom and Dad," Cody said.

We'd been dismissed.

We went back to the living room, where I picked up my knitting and Brad turned on the TV. We were halfway through an episode of *CSI: Miami* when the bedroom door opened and Cody came out, holding two empty bowls.

"Everything all right in there?" Brad asked.

Cody nodded. "Ice cream doesn't cure anything," he said sagely, "but it sure helps with the pain." He brought the bowls to the kitchen.

"Who told him that?" Brad wondered.

I ventured a guess. "Either Margaret or Alix."

"You hang around with wise women, my love," he said with a grin.

I had to agree. "You in the mood for ice cream?" I asked.

"Why not? It seems to work."

We smiled at each other. A crisis had been averted.

After a while Casey came out of her room with her crochet hook and a skein of yarn under one arm. "I need help with this," she said, as if the events of this evening had never occurred.

"Okay." I certainly wasn't an expert at crocheting but I could read the directions. If not, I could always contact my sister.

Casey sat on the sofa beside me. "I think I made a mistake here." She held it out for me to examine.

I studied the washcloth she'd started and didn't find anything wrong. "It looks fine to me, Casey."

"You're sure?"

I shrugged. "You might want to have Margaret check it tomorrow."

Her eyes flew up to meet mine. "Can I come to the shop again? You don't have to pay me."

"I've got a whole list of things that need your attention and of course I'll pay you."

I could see she was pleased, although she tried to hide it. "That would be okay, I guess." I realized she didn't want me to know how much she liked being at the yarn store.

That attitude always caught me unawares. This fear of losing what she valued most. Wasn't that exactly what Alix had warned me about?

She returned to her room, and I went to bed around ten, exhausted. All the melodrama of the evening had tired me out.

I still didn't know what Lee had said to Casey and most likely I never would. If she'd told Cody, he hadn't indicated in any way. Curious though I was, I didn't feel I could pry it out of him. That wasn't the example I wanted to set.

The phone rang just as Brad stepped out of the bathroom, dressed for bed. The sharp, unexpected sound startled us both. I reached for it quickly.

"Hello," I said in a hushed voice.

"Lydia," my sister boomed over the line. "It's Mom."

"What happened?" My mother's declining health had been a major concern for more than a year now.

"I'm at the E.R. Mom fell."

I gasped and reached out for Brad. He gripped my fingers. "Is she hurt?"

"It's her hip."

"No." Shivers raced down my spine.

"Thank God someone heard her."

More than a year earlier, Mom had been diagnosed with diabetes and had to have her blood sugars carefully monitored. That had been the beginning of her health problems. The decline had been rapid since then.

"Is it broken?" I asked, fearing the worst.

"No, just a hairline fracture. She also hit her head pretty hard, but that seems to be okay."

"I'll be there in twenty minutes," I said. Brad freed my hand and I tossed aside the covers. My feet were already on the ground when Margaret stopped me.

"There's no need. The tests are done. I didn't feel there was any reason to phone you until we knew something definite."

"You should've called me earlier," I cried, upset and relieved at the same time. I had a right to know about my own mother and yet . . . ignorance was bliss.

Guilt washed over me. I shouldn't be thinking that. I loved my mother and was grateful Margaret had been there to handle the situation.

"The doctor wants to keep Mom overnight for observation. She needs her sleep and frankly,"

Margaret said, sounding drained and emotionally depleted, "so do I."

"Go home," I advised. "Tell the hospital that if they need to contact anyone during the night, they should call me."

Margaret hesitated, then reluctantly agreed.

After she'd answered a few more questions, I replaced the receiver. Tears flowed unrestrained down my face, blurring my vision. I worried about my mother, but I had no idea how to help her.

Brad handed me a wad of tissues and I tried to explain what had happened.

"But she's fine, right?" Brad pressed.

I nodded. Mom was unaffected by this incident, as far as the physicians could tell, but I wasn't. It was all too obvious that I was going to lose my mother.

In many ways I already had. Margaret and I were her caregivers now. We'd assumed the role of adults, and she'd become almost a child— dependent, passive, at the mercy of others. I worried that I'd somehow failed her.

When I wiped my eyes, I saw Cody and Casey standing in the doorway to our bedroom, watching me.

"What's wrong?" Cody asked.

Before I could tell them, Casey offered me a tentative smile. "I think Lydia needs some ice cream," she said.

CHAPTER
25

Anne Marie Roche

Barbie's house rang with laughter when Anne Marie arrived to drop Ellen off. Lillie, Barbie's mother, answered the door, Hector at her side, and it was easy to see how much in love they were. How happy her friend was. Anne Marie felt only gratitude that Lillie had found love, but in some ways it was painful to watch, reminding her of what she'd lost. Still, she'd seen that falling in love again was possible—for Barbie and Mark, for Lillie and Hector. Maybe it was possible for her, too.

The big surprise in her own life had been meeting Tim. An even bigger surprise was the attraction she felt toward him. Life was filled with the unexpected, and some of those events were happy ones.

"Come in, come in," Lillie said, stepping aside to gesture them inside. They hugged, and Hector greeted her in his usual dignified manner.

"Maria, my grandniece, is with me," he told Ellen, "and she's eager to meet you. I hope you two can be friends."

Ellen followed shyly and stood next to Anne Marie. "My mom has a date with Tim," she announced. "It's just the two of them, so he can kiss her in the dark."

Anne Marie blushed, but before she could comment, Barbie bustled into the room.

"Oh, good. You're here." She wore an apron that suggested someone kiss the cook. Mark rolled out with her. He wasn't the type of man who openly showed affection, but Ellen had won him over from the moment they met and she moved instantly to his side to hug him.

"Next time bring your date to the party," Mark said as soon as he'd released Ellen.

"Will do," Anne Marie promised. She crouched down so she was eye-to-eye with Ellen. "Barbie has my cell number. If you need me for anything you can call, okay?"

Ellen nodded.

"I'll pick you up around ten."

"Okay." Ellen wrapped her thin arms around Anne Marie's neck and squeezed tight. Then she raised her head and whispered, "Kiss Tim for me."

Anne Marie smiled. "I will," she whispered back.

Lillie walked Anne Marie out to her car. "I'm so glad to see you dating again," she said. "My life changed when I met Hector. I look forward to each day, each minute, I have with him."

Anne Marie wondered if Tim would be her Hector. . . . Because, just like Lillie, just like

Barbie, she was ready to experience love again.

"I can't recommend being in love highly enough," Lillie said with a laugh. Hector stood in the doorway, waiting for her, and she stepped back as Anne Marie climbed into her car and started the engine. Pulling out of the driveway, she saw Hector join Lillie, sliding his arm around her waist and drawing her close.

Oh, yes, Anne Marie was ready for love. Ready to share her love for Ellen with someone who cared for the child as much as she did.

That thought stayed with her as she drove home and parked behind the bookstore.

One of the many things Anne Marie liked about Tim Carlsen was the fact that he didn't ignore social niceties and details. Although Monte's, the Italian restaurant he'd chosen, was within walking distance, he insisted on picking her up, despite her offer to meet him there.

When she opened the apartment door to let Tim in, Baxter yelped excitedly. Tim stooped down and paid him due attention, and when he straightened, his eyes widened with appreciation. "You look . . . wow," he said.

"Thank you." While Tim played with Baxter, Anne Marie went into her bedroom to get her purse. As she did, she noticed that her hand was trembling.

Although she'd tried to minimize this dinner date with her friends, she felt nervous. She could hardly remember the last time she'd been on an actual date. Before she'd married Robert, so that was . . . She decided not to do the math.

She'd dressed carefully in a white eyelet summer dress with a silky pink shawl and pink pumps.

"Are you ready?" Tim asked when Anne Marie met him in the living room.

She nodded. Because she felt flustered, she found herself chattering as they strolled to the restaurant. The evening was perfect, still sunny, with a light breeze scenting the air.

"I've been looking at houses," she said. "Ellen doesn't want to move, but the apartment's too small." She went on to tell him that she was considering houses in the same neighborhood as Hallie's, thinking that if Ellen had a friend close by, the move would be less traumatic.

By the time they reached the restaurant, Anne Marie realized she hadn't let Tim say a word. This behavior was so uncharacteristic for her, she felt she should explain.

"I generally don't talk this much," she said, embarrassed. "I guess I'm a little nervous."

Tim reassured her with a grin. "So am I," he admitted.

It was such a comforting thing to say that Anne Marie was instantly at ease.

The hostess seated them at a nice table near the window. When the waiter came to take their drink order, Tim said he'd stick to water but told Anne

Marie she should have a glass of wine. She ordered the house red.

"It doesn't bother you if other people drink?" she asked, feeling awkward.

"Not in the least. Other people can handle it. I can't."

Still, she felt guilty drinking in his presence. "I don't mind doing without wine," she said.

He held up his hand. "Please don't. Sobriety is up to me and me alone."

His attitude impressed her, and she sipped her wine, almost able to enjoy it.

When the waiter returned, they placed their dinner orders. Tim asked for the eggplant parmigiano and Anne Marie the clam spaghetti. The waiter left and Anne Marie smoothed her napkin repeatedly in her nervousness, waiting for Tim to speak. So far, she'd dominated the conversation.

"I'm hoping now that we've had a chance to get to know each other, you'll be comfortable with me," he said.

"I already feel that way." Anne Marie took a piece of bread and tore off a bite. "I can hardly believe how much." She dipped the bread in the small dish of olive oil in the center of the table, not looking at him as she spoke. "You've convinced me that you won't try to take Ellen away from me."

"I'd never do that. The two of you belong together. Dolores got that right. She knew you'd love and care for Ellen better than Candy—or anyone else, for that matter."

She flushed, feeling a surge of joy. The fact that he, of all people, had acknowledged this brought her not only gratitude but peace. "Thank you," she murmured.

They enjoyed their meal immensely, talking about a wide range of subjects from baseball to politics and everything in between.

Over spumoni and coffee, Tim grew quiet again. "If it's okay with you, Anne Marie, I'd like to tell my parents about Ellen."

It would be selfish to withhold a grandparent's love from her daughter, so Anne Marie agreed. "That would be fine."

His hand cradled the coffee cup, and he nodded solemnly. "Thank you."

"You told me Ellen's their only granddaughter."

"She is, and my mother's been dying to have a girl to spoil. My younger sister has two boys."

"She sounds just like my mother."

Tim stared down at his coffee. "Would you also be willing to let Ellen spend time with me alone?"

Anne Marie hadn't expected this subject to come up quite so soon, yet it was a reasonable request. "Are you asking about visitation?" she asked.

"Yes."

Still, she hesitated. "How often were you thinking?"

He shrugged. "I'll take whatever you're willing

to give me. I don't mean to pressure you, Anne Marie. If you'd rather wait, I understand."

"But you wanted to plant the thought in my mind."

"Yes, that's a good way of putting it."

"You're asking if you can tell Ellen that you're her father." This *was* the great unasked question, the one that underlay all the others.

"I would like to do that. Even before I got the test results I *felt* that Ellen was my child."

Now it was Anne Marie's turn to stare into her coffee. Her ice cream had started to melt, and she pushed it aside. Her first inclination, selfish though it might be, was to deny him. She glanced up and found him watching her intently, his eyes relaying a message of hope and expectancy.

"I want to be with Ellen when you tell her."

"Of course."

"We'll begin the visitations slowly. And you can't tell her until I feel she's ready."

"Like I said, you're the one setting the rules."

He was so agreeable, and that helped soothe her worries.

"Would it be all right if I took her one night next week? My parents' wedding anniversary is coming up and I'd like Ellen to meet them before the big party."

Before she could find an excuse to refuse him, Anne Marie nodded. "But they can't let her know who they are. What they are to her, I mean."

"I accept that." His gaze held hers. "Thank you."

301

This request probably explained why he'd asked her to dinner on her own, which was more than a little disappointing.

"I'm glad we got that settled," she said briskly.

"Actually," Tim said, "there's something else."

"Oh?"

He lowered his eyes. "I'm afraid I might have misled you in the past few weeks."

"Misled me? How?"

"I apologize. That was never my intention."

Anne Marie was even more confused. "What are you talking about?"

He inhaled deeply. "I guess the best way to tell you is just to tell you. I'm involved with someone else."

Anne Marie sat unmoving as the shock rippled through her. "You're . . . involved."

"Vanessa and I—"

"Her name's Vanessa?"

"Yes, and I have to tell you this whole situation has been very difficult for her."

Anne Marie bit off a sarcastic comment. She needed all the self-control she possessed not to reveal how shocked she was by his announcement.

"I didn't want you to—"

Anne Marie struggled to remain calm. "Don't you think you might've said something sooner?"

He opened his mouth, then closed it. "Yes, well . . . perhaps I should have, but there never seemed to be a good time."

"Really?" she muttered. Funny how he'd managed to get what he wanted before telling her this. She felt humiliated. Foolish. Naive. All these weeks she'd allowed the romantic daydream to grow, picturing the three of them as the perfect little family. No wonder he'd never kissed her. If she hadn't been walking around immersed in her stupid fantasies, she might have caught on earlier.

"I apologize if you think I was leading you on."

"Forget it," she said, focusing some distance beyond him, refusing to meet his eyes. She held herself stiff and couldn't wait to escape. This was what she got for risking her emotions. It wasn't worth it; deep down she knew she'd never fall in love again.

"I feel it's important that we remain friends for Ellen's sake," he was saying.

"We can certainly be cordial." What seemed most important at the moment, however, was getting away from Tim. She needed to think, to absorb what he'd told her.

She made a show of looking at her watch. "Do we have the check yet?"

In response he raised his hand to catch the waiter's attention.

"I'll want to meet Vanessa," Anne Marie said. No way was she letting her daughter go off with someone she'd never met. She didn't care if Vanessa was "involved" with Tim. That wasn't any kind of recommendation or guarantee.

He blinked, his expression wary.

"If she's going to be with you when you have Ellen . . ."

Tim relaxed. "I suppose she will. Some of the time, anyway."

"In that case, I need to meet her, don't you agree?" She did her best to keep the irritation out of her voice.

"Yes, of course. That's not a problem."

Another thought entered her mind, one that set off warning bells. "How did you and . . . Vanessa happen to meet?"

"I don't think that really matters," he said, bristling noticeably.

"She's in AA, too?" Anne Marie guessed.

Reluctantly Tim nodded.

"How much sobriety does she have?"

"She had three years."

"Had?"

"With everything that's been going on with you and me and Ellen, well . . . she slipped up."

"Just a minute here," Anne Marie said, her eyes narrowing. "Not more than an hour ago, you told me you were accountable for your own sobriety. Didn't I hear you say that?"

"Yes . . ."

"Are you now saying that you're taking responsibility for *Vanessa's* sobriety, too?" she asked.

The question appeared to shake him. "No."

Anne Marie held his gaze. "Ellen can meet

Vanessa, but I have to be there when she does. Otherwise the deal is off."

"Fine," he said curtly.

"Good. Then we understand each other."

All at once the room seemed unbearably stuffy. Oppressive. Anne Marie dropped her napkin on the table and stood. "I'll wait for you outside."

He stood, too. "I'll take care of the bill. I won't be long."

She needed breathing room. As the night air cooled her fevered skin, Anne Marie resisted the urge to cover her face with both hands. In all her life she'd never felt more embarrassed. How *stupid* she'd been. What a romantic *fool*.

And worse, Tim knew. He'd read the longing in her heart, saw it in her eyes. He knew. If she could've disappeared, simply vanished, she would gladly have done so.

CHAPTER
26

Phoebe Rylander

Night," Hutch said, lingering in the doorway of Phoebe's condo. He leaned close and kissed her gently. This wasn't the first time they'd kissed that evening. "I really have to leave now."

"Night," she whispered. She hated to see him go. They'd spent a wonderful evening, a memorable evening. They'd been together on Sunday, too, but even a day seemed too long to be apart. When he'd suggested they see each other tonight, she'd readily agreed.

It became more and more apparent that Hutch was nothing like Clark. In fact, he was the complete opposite of her former fiancé.

Hutch was thoughtful and caring and funny and *different*. He made her laugh and had lightened the load of pain she'd carried after her breakup with Clark. And yet she probably wouldn't have given him a second look if not for the knitting class. That class, which she'd enrolled in on impulse, had opened her eyes in so many ways.

Phoebe didn't want to think of herself as demanding or shallow when it came to the men she chose to date. Then again, perhaps she had been. Most of the men in her past had been like Clark— highly successful, established in their careers, urbane and handsome. Hutch was rather ordinary-looking but he possessed those other attributes, too. The ambition and the success. Only he was . . . better.

"I'll call you tomorrow," he said, moving slowly into the hall.

Meowing, Princess followed him out, apparently as unwilling to let him go as Phoebe was herself. She picked up her cat and held her close.

"Tomorrow," she said. Leaning against the door-jamb she waited until he was inside the elevator and had disappeared from sight. The time had gone by so quickly, she could hardly believe it was already after ten.

Hutch had met her at the clinic, after a meeting with his attorney. He'd refused to discuss the case, telling her he was leaving the whole mess to the professionals paid to deal with it. They'd rented a paddle boat on Lake Washington before eating at a hole-in-the-wall fish-and-chip place he'd gone to as a kid. It'd been a lazy summer's night, interspersed with laughter and a growing attraction. They'd sat under an umbrella table and made excuses to loiter in the early-evening sun.

When Hutch dropped her off after dinner, neither had wanted the evening to end. He'd gladly accepted her invitation for coffee, and they'd sat and talked for nearly an hour. But it was dark now, and they both had to work in the morning. Phoebe knew he got to the office by six, except for the days he visited the gym first.

The phone rang and Phoebe hurried to answer it, expecting to find it was Hutch. It would be just like him to call as soon as he was in the car. He often did that to say good-night a final time or discuss the next day's plans . . . or whisper that he missed her.

Instead, Caller ID showed that it was Clark.

Phoebe backed away from the phone. She didn't want to speak to him, didn't want anything to do with him. Her instinct was to let him leave a message. She did, and waited until her phone went to voice mail.

Unable to stop herself, she stood close to the phone and listened as he spoke.

"Phoebe, it's Clark." He sounded depressed. "I know you're there. I also know you don't want to talk to me. I wouldn't contact you if this wasn't important. Please call me back. You're at the condo, I know you are." He hesitated, then added in a broken voice, "Please."

Reluctantly Phoebe reached for the phone, but her hand hovered over the receiver. It was a week ago that she'd gone to the hospital to see his father and she wondered if Max had taken a turn for the worse. After all, he'd implied that he didn't think he'd live much longer.

Her pulse accelerated. Clark's father was such an extraordinary man. The family would fall apart without him.

She grabbed the phone.

Clark answered on the first ring. He didn't greet her; instead he whispered "Thank you" in a fervent voice.

"Is it your father?"

"I—"

"If this isn't something to do with Max, we have nothing to talk about." She started to disconnect when she heard him cry out.

"Don't hang up! There's no delicate way to say this . . . but my father's dying."

Phoebe gasped. "What happened?"

"He's got a high fever. They haven't been able to control it."

"Oh, Clark." There was no adequate response to that, no comfort she could offer. A lump formed in her throat.

"He's caught some sort of infection and that seems to be causing the fever. It's bad, Phoebe."

"Oh, no . . ."

"The doctors called Mother and me to the hospital."

"Are you there now?"

She heard Clark swallow hard. "Yes. Where else would I be?"

"I'm so sorry." She didn't know what she could do other than listen.

He spoke over her comment. "I was right, wasn't I? You were home but you didn't want to speak to me."

His question came at her more like an accusation, and she had no intention of answering.

"He was there, wasn't he?" Clark continued in the same aggressive tone. "This new man you're seeing. You're only doing it to hurt me, aren't you?"

"Who I'm seeing is none of your business."

"Isn't it?" he asked. "I wonder if you ever really loved me."

Phoebe felt dreadful but there was no reason for it. Clark was slinging guilt at her and she needed to step away, stop being his target. She couldn't, wouldn't, allow this conversation to revolve around *him* when his father might well be dying.

"Is he a good lover?"

"What?" Phoebe took a deep, shuddering breath. "This conversation is over."

"No, please," he begged. "Listen, just listen . . ."

Phoebe didn't want to hear any more. She considered hanging up, but Clark interrupted.

"Okay, okay, I'm sorry," he said quickly. "I don't have the right to ask you questions like that."

Phoebe desperately wanted to cut off this call; at the same time, she wanted to learn what she could about Max's condition.

Before she could decide, Clark said, "You can call me any name you like, Phoebe, and I'd probably deserve it, but one thing you have to admit is that I love my dad."

Phoebe knew that was true. Clark was close to both his parents—although his behavior certainly didn't resemble that of his father.

"Will you come sit with Mom and me?" he asked, his tone pleading. "The doctors said it would be a miracle if Dad lasts the night."

When she hesitated, Clark said, "Can't we put aside our differences for Dad's sake? Just for tonight?"

"You and Marlene are alone? What about the rest of the family?"

"The crisis appeared to be over. Everyone's gone—and now this. It's killing Mom and me."

Phoebe looked up at the ceiling, still unsure. Then, against her better judgment, she whispered, "All right. I'll be there as soon as I can."

His appreciation was almost palpable. "I can't thank you enough, Phoebe. This will mean the world to Mom."

Phoebe rather doubted *that*.

With her purse and car keys in hand, she'd reached the door, then came to an abrupt halt. It seemed to her that with all the connections the Snowdens had, Marlene and Clark shouldn't be alone. Why would he contact her when he had friends and relatives all over the city?

None of what he'd said really made sense. She hated to be so distrustful, but time had taught her some valuable lessons about Clark Snowden. He'd stop at nothing to get his own way. Now that he knew about Hutch, he'd be more intent than ever on winning her back. Then again, it wasn't as if he'd kidnap her. Despite her doubts, even Clark wouldn't go so far as to make up a story about his father's imminent death.

But just in case . . .

Phoebe decided not to take any chances. Turning back, she went to the phone and hit Speed Dial to call her mother.

Three rings later, Leanne answered sleepily. "Phoebe? Is everything all right?"

"Clark's father apparently isn't doing well."

"Oh, no." Her mother was instantly alert.

"Clark said he's contracted an infection. According to him, Max is fighting for his life. They aren't sure he'll last the night."

"What can we do?" her mother asked urgently. "Should I put his name on the church prayer chain?"

"That would be wonderful, Mom," Phoebe said.

"I'll do it first thing in the morning."

"Thank you." Phoebe felt guilty about using her mother like this, but she knew how eager Leanne was to ingratiate herself with the Snowdens. "Listen, Mom, Clark's holding vigil with his mother at the hospital. I gather they're alone. Why don't you go there with me? Marlene could use a friend at a time like this."

"Oh, Phoebe. I'm so glad you asked. We can't leave Marlene and Clark by themselves."

"Thanks, Mom." If Max *was* dying, Phoebe doubted she had the words to comfort Clark's mother; the relationship between them was already strained. Leanne would be a real help.

"I'll leave the house in fifteen minutes," Leanne said. "I'll just throw on some clothes and run a brush through my hair."

"I'll pick you up," Phoebe told her.

"You don't need to do that," her mother protested.

Oh, but she did. "I wouldn't want you driving in Seattle on your own this late, Mom."

"Oh," Leanne said as if she hadn't thought of

that. "Good idea. I'll be ready when you get here."

Phoebe waited a few minutes, then got her car from the condo parking garage and drove to her mother's home on Capitol Hill. During that brief time, Clark called not once, but twice.

"How did you get this number?" she demanded. She could only assume that her mother had given it to him, in one of her misguided attempts to influence Phoebe's decision.

He didn't answer. "I'd only use it in an emergency, which this is."

He was right about that, but his access to her cell number bothered her.

"I thought you were on your way," he complained. "You're still coming, aren't you?"

"I'll be there in a few minutes," she promised. "Has Max's condition changed?"

"No, nothing's changed. Hurry, please."

Pulling into the familiar neighborhood of her youth, Phoebe saw that her mother's porch light was on. As she stopped in the driveway, Leanne hurried out the front door and slid into the passenger side, fastening her seat belt.

"Poor Marlene, she must be beside herself." Leanne clasped her hands tightly together. "Have you heard anything new?"

"Not really." Clark's frantic call asking her to rush would only upset her mother, so Phoebe didn't mention it. Besides, he'd said Max's condition hadn't changed.

By the time they'd parked and reached the hospital's main entrance, Phoebe saw Clark pacing just inside. He seemed agitated and nervous, which was understandable. This had to be a tense night for him and his mother.

His face brightened the moment he saw her. But a frown formed as soon as he realized Leanne had accompanied her.

The glass doors slid open and Leanne ran toward Clark, hugging him hard. "Clark, this is such terrible news."

"Leanne," he said, hugging her back. Over her mother's shoulders, his eyes searched out Phoebe.

"Where's Marlene?" Leanne asked. "She must be frantic."

Clark dropped his arms and led the way into the hospital foyer. "She . . . she left."

Phoebe stared at him. "You don't know if your father's going to survive the night and your mother went *home?*"

"Yes, well . . . Dad seems to be doing better."

"Since when?" Phoebe asked, her suspicions building.

"A while ago," Clark said, meeting her gaze head-on.

"That's terrific," Leanne murmured, glancing from one to the other.

"Was Max ever desperately ill?" Phoebe asked, refusing to break eye contact with Clark. She wanted him to know he hadn't fooled her. When he'd first phoned, she'd hated being so mistrustful of his intentions; now it seemed she'd been right. Clark was willing to use anything to win her back, even an out-and-out lie. She shouldn't be surprised and yet she was. At the same time she was sickened that he'd sink to this level—that he'd exploit his father's condition in this way.

"Now that I'm here," she said, "I might as well check at the nurses' station to see for myself how Max is doing."

"They're very busy," Clark immediately countered.

"He's in ICU, isn't he?"

Clark exhaled. "Actually, he was moved earlier. . . ." He let the rest fade. "Why don't we all have a cup of coffee and I'll update you?"

"So your father made a miraculous recovery in the last thirty minutes." She didn't keep the sarcasm out of her voice.

"He's doing well enough for Mom to go home, but you have to understand he's still at serious risk."

Phoebe didn't believe it.

"I could do with a cup of coffee," Leanne said. "Decaf, of course. Anything with caffeine would keep me awake for hours."

"You two go ahead," Phoebe told them. "I'll meet you in a few minutes. I'm going to use the ladies' room."

Clark stared after her as she hurried down the

hall to the public restrooms. Once inside, she pulled out her cell phone, called directory assistance and had them connect her with the hospital's receptionist.

"Could you please tell me what room Max Snowden's in?" she began and silently asked God to forgive the lie. "I'd like to order flowers online and apparently they need a room number."

"Just a moment, please."

Before long the woman was back. "Our records show that Mr. Snowden was released from the hospital two days ago."

"I see," Phoebe said through gritted teeth. "Thank you for your trouble."

"It was my pleasure."

It would be Phoebe's pleasure to tell Clark what she thought of him. When she stepped out of the restroom, Clark and Leanne stood in the hallway waiting for her.

"Time to go, Mother," she said firmly.

Leanne cast her a confused glance. "But . . . what about coffee with Clark?"

Phoebe marched past him. "We aren't having coffee with Clark."

"Phoebe," her mother said, struggling to keep pace with her. "What's gotten into you? You're being rude. Clark's father is very ill. Like you, I'm disappointed that Marlene isn't here, but Clark told me she's been with Max for days and is emotionally and physically exhausted."

Phoebe stopped and turned to face her mother and Clark. "If that's the case, then she wasn't at the hospital."

"But of course she was," Leanne protested. "The entire family was gathered here. . . . Clark was just telling me about it."

"That's very interesting, Mom, since Max was released two days ago." She looked directly at Clark. "Did you think I couldn't call the hospital switchboard?"

He glared back at her and refused to answer.

"If anything like this ever happens again," she said slowly and distinctly, "I'm calling the police." She wanted to be sure he understood this wasn't an idle threat. "I'm serious, Clark. One more incident like this and I'll report you as a stalker."

Her mother whirled around and confronted Clark, an expression of shock and disbelief on her face. "Is that true?" she demanded.

"Clark Snowden is the last person you should be asking about the truth," Phoebe said in a withering voice as she turned and headed out the door, toward the parking garage.

Her mother scurried after her, half trotting in an effort to keep up. Angry as she was, Phoebe couldn't get away from Clark fast enough. If she'd ever had any doubts or second thoughts, this had sealed it. Thank goodness she'd followed her instincts and brought her mother along.

Leanne didn't say anything for several minutes. "I think you might be right about Clark," she finally said, breathless by the time they entered the parking garage. "That man isn't to be trusted."

CHAPTER
27

With my work as a designer, I feel like I am leaving a legacy to pass on to future generations. I can't imagine either of my children growing up without a relationship with knitting. I cannot wait until my kids are old enough to learn to knit, and we can sit and knit together. What other line of work allows you to create like this, alongside your family?
—Chrissy Gardiner, knit designer and teacher,
www.gardineryarnworks.com

Lydia Goetz

I couldn't help worrying about Casey. Ever since she'd received that phone call from Lee she'd been withdrawn and, frankly, difficult. Some days were definitely better than others, but this morning was apparently destined to be a bad one. When I called Casey for breakfast, I heard her slamming things around her bedroom and when she finally deigned to show up, she didn't so much as offer a greeting or even an acknowledgement.

Now, sitting at the kitchen table, she slouched over her cereal bowl almost as if she was afraid someone would jerk it away.

I tried talking to her and her responses, such as they were, came in the form of grunts and growls. My efforts were mostly ignored.

"Would you like to come to the yarn store with me?" I asked. Her classes were over, so her other option was day camp. "I'm going in early, even though I have class tonight." I don't know why I bothered to explain.

Her answer was a noncommittal shrug.

"Is that a yes or a no?" I asked, my patience growing thin.

She glared up at me. "I guess."

I wasn't sure what that meant, but I was willing to assume she wanted to go to work with me. "There's a new shipment of yarn that needs to be priced." One thing I could count on was Casey's interest in collecting a paycheck. Other than those mishaps early on, she'd done a fairly good job at every task I'd given her.

"Will Margaret be there?" she asked.

It was the first real sentence Casey had uttered all morning.

"Yes. And Brad will stop by after work to take you home."

She shrugged again, which appeared to be her universal response this morning.

It took me a moment to realize why she'd asked

about Margaret. "You can bring your crocheting if you want," I said, wanting her to know I'd paid attention.

She lifted one shoulder halfheartedly.

As far as breakfast-table conversation went, that was it. Unaware of the tension between Casey and me, Cody chattered away at astounding speed. I could hardly keep up with the rapid switching of subjects, but fortunately all he required was an occasional "Wow" or "Really?"

The three of us left the house and I dropped Cody off at the day camp. There was a field trip for his age group today—to the aquarium—and that was his very favorite activity.

Casey remained silent as I continued on to the store. I worked hard at remembering what Alix had told me about the years she herself had spent in foster care. She'd had varied experiences, some good, some bad. She'd said that Casey was prob-ably afraid to let anyone know what she enjoyed, as though she wasn't *allowed* to have any fun. At this point it was difficult to say that Casey took much pleasure in anything—with the one excep-tion of our day at Green Lake.

When I pulled up at the church, Cody leaped out of the car and ran toward his friends without a backward glance. He used to kiss my cheek, but that had changed this summer. He no longer con-sidered it "cool" to show me affection in front of his friends. I missed his goodbye hugs, but I understood. Cody was growing up.

I must have smiled because Casey gave me an odd look. "What's so funny?"

"Cody," I said, and explained why.

For just an instant I thought Casey might've been amused. I'd been waiting for her to lower her guard. For the past two days I'd been tiptoeing around the issue of her discontent and now I decided to confront it.

"Do you want to talk about what's bothering you?" I asked as gently as I could.

She turned to me as if to gauge the sincerity of my question.

"I'd thought—hoped, really—that you've enjoyed your time with our family."

The shrug was back, and Casey kept her gaze directly ahead of her. "It's okay."

"Okay!" I echoed in mock outrage.

Casey actually grinned. "If you must know, staying with you has been better than most summers."

Admitting that was quite a concession on her part. "That's more like it," I said.

Casey's mood seemed to improve once we got to the yarn store. I wanted to tell her that being there had the same effect on me. I could be angry or depressed or just plain tired. Yet the moment I entered my store, whatever was pressing on my heart instantly lifted.

The only other place I felt that same serenity was inside a church. But a yarn store? For reasons I can't even begin to explain, my shop on Blossom Street produced in me a contentment I'd rarely found since that first diagnosis of cancer back when I was a teenager.

As soon as I got there, so did three customers. It almost seemed as if they'd been waiting for me to turn over the Open sign, because a moment later, all three women walked in.

Margaret served the first woman and was busy with the other two when another customer came in with a knitting problem. I immediately saw what she'd done wrong and we sat together at the back table while I explained her mistake, which was relatively easy to fix. Using a crochet hook, I had to go down about fifteen rows. I'm always surprised by the number of knitters who can't bear to see someone unravel their work. This woman closed her eyes while I dropped the stitch.

After Casey had priced the new yarn and arranged it in the correct cubicles, she sat with Whiskers on her lap and stroked the cat for an hour straight. I was astonished that she could sit still for that long. Whiskers spent hours every day asleep in the front window, so this much attention was unusual. He purred with contentment; Casey's lap had obviously become one of his favorite places.

I grabbed lunch when I could between customers, bringing back a take-out container of salad for Casey.

"I'm going for a walk," Casey announced around two and headed out the door. She'd timed her declaration perfectly, waiting until I was busy figuring out yardage for a sweater project for Mary Kilborn, an experienced knitter. Because I was poring over a computer program that listed the brand name and skein yardage for every company, I barely had a chance to react to her statement.

"Brad will be here at—" I didn't get to finish as Casey was already gone and well out of earshot.

"Never mind," I said. Brad wouldn't appear for another two hours and Casey would surely be back by then.

As was so often the case with her, I was wrong. Brad showed up before Casey did.

"Where do you think she might be?" he asked, his brow furrowed with concern.

"I . . . I don't know. I never expected her to be gone this long." I started to rub my palms together, a nervous habit I'd developed over the summer— or more accurately, since Casey's arrival.

I could tell that Brad's day hadn't gone well, because it wasn't like him to be short-tempered. "Well, where did she *say* she was going?" he asked impatiently.

"That's just it. She didn't."

Brad frowned, even harder this time. "Do you suppose she's run away again?"

The thought hadn't even occurred to me. "No, why would she?"

"Why does she do anything?" he asked, throwing his hands in the air. "That kid's impossible to understand." He grinned, then added, "You'd think she was a teenager or something."

The "or something" was right. Casey wouldn't actually be a teenager until the following year, but she showed all the signs of being one now—especially the moodiness.

"She'll be back," Margaret assured us. She finished counting out change for a customer who'd come in to purchase an extra skein when she'd run out of yarn on a project.

"How can you be so sure?" Brad asked when the woman had gone.

"Two things." Margaret walked around the counter. "First, Casey didn't collect her pay for this morning and secondly—" Margaret pointed at the crocheting Casey had left on the lesson table "—she didn't take her work with her."

I nodded; my sister was right. "You might as well relax until she turns up," I advised my husband.

Brad muttered a comment under his breath, then accepted the inevitability of waiting. Sighing heavily, he sat down at the table.

Five minutes later, Casey strolled in as though she'd hardly been away at all.

Instantly Brad was on his feet. "Where were you?" he demanded.

"Out," Casey blurted, glaring at him defiantly.

In an effort to avoid an argument, I rested my hand on Brad's. "Everything's fine now. She's back and she's safe."

Casey pretended not to hear me as she walked over to the table and grabbed her crocheting, stuffing it inside the quilted bag I'd lent her. Then she straightened. "Are you ready?" she asked as if Brad had kept *her* waiting.

Brad glanced at me, eyebrows raised. I shook my head as the two of them left, giving each other the silent treatment.

Margaret watched them walk away and turned to me. "I bet you'll be glad when she's out of the house."

I didn't know exactly what I'd feel. What surprised me, though, was the sense of loss that came over me at that statement. Despite the difficulties we'd had with Casey, I'd become genuinely fond of the girl. I would miss her, and so would Brad and Cody.

In fact, Casey's stay with us had been good for our son. He'd learned the concept of sharing. Cody was the sole focus of our love and attention. Of course we hoped to add another child to our family, but as it was now, our lives revolved around his. He'd been a friend to Casey, and in the process had learned communication skills. Despite the moodiness she sometimes displayed, she seemed to like him.

"I'm going to miss her." I didn't realize I'd spoken out loud until my sister made a huffing sound. "What does *that* mean?" I asked, challenging Margaret to state her opinion.

She sent me that familiar disapproving look and simply shook her head.

That evening Alix was the first to arrive for class. As she walked into the store, I could smell cigarette smoke on her.

As if she could guess what I was thinking, she announced to both Margaret and me, "Okay, I'm smoking again. I went four days without a cigarette but I'm back to three a day, so don't give me any grief."

Obviously Alix and Casey were both in unsociable moods that day. "Three is better than ten or twenty or whatever you started out with." I wanted her to be aware that I wouldn't judge her.

"There is medical help, you know," Margaret said. "And if you weren't so stubborn you'd get it."

"No." Alix briefly shut her eyes. "I can do this. If I'm a little short-tempered it's because I just smoked my last cigarette for the day and I'm already craving another."

It was more than needing a cigarette. Alix was so rarely cross that I knew something else was troubling her. And my guess was that it had to do with Jordan. He wasn't with her, although he usually walked her to class and then either went over to the church or met with a men's group while Alix knitted.

"Jordan isn't with you tonight?" I ventured.

"No," she snapped.

I held up both hands as if to say *sorry I asked*—and I was.

Margaret, however, had never steered clear of a fight. "What is it with everyone today?" she said, arms akimbo. "First Casey and now you."

Alix's shoulders relaxed. "I didn't mean to be cranky. Jordan and I had a small argument."

"I'm sorry." I could sympathize. Whenever Brad and I were irritated with each other, I felt dreadful. I'm sure I wasn't much fun at times like that, either.

"It happens," Margaret said. "Get over it."

To my astonishment, Alix grinned. "Yeah, I guess I should. It's my own fault. We were supposed to meet at the café at five and I was late. He didn't feel he should hold on to a table, so he left."

"And when you did arrive, there wasn't one available," Margaret finished for her.

"Exactly." She exhaled slowly. "I didn't want to upset him and I'm usually on time, but there were extenuating circumstances."

I'd never known Alix to be intentionally late. In fact, she was generally the first to show up, as she had tonight. She needed structure, and since I knew what her life had been like as a child, I understood why.

"Casey wanted to talk. It wasn't like I could put

her off, and then I had to rush to finish up the menu plans for my boss. Winter's going on vacation and asked me to take over for her."

"Casey?" Alix had spent time with Casey? That afternoon? Suddenly it all made sense. I should've realized Casey would seek out Alix, but until that moment it hadn't occurred to me.

Alix nodded and looked from Margaret to me. "You mean you didn't know she was with me?"

"No," Margaret said flatly. "We didn't have a clue where she was, and she was gone for hours."

"I'm glad she could talk to you," I said, although it was difficult not to feel a twinge of jealousy. I so badly wanted Casey to feel safe enough, comfortable enough, to turn to me.

Instead she'd gone to Alix. Her reasons were completely logical—and, of course, I'd done the same thing. I'd gone to Alix, too, asking questions about her experience as a ward of the state so I could understand Casey's.

Alix seemed a bit confused. "She said you were the one who sent her to me."

I'd mentioned it, only that had been weeks ago. Naturally I was curious as to what Casey had said, especially since they'd talked for such a long time, but I didn't ask. I hoped Alix would volunteer the information; when she didn't, I left it at that.

"Is everything settled between you and Jordan?" I asked instead.

"Not really," Alix said, looking dejected. "He

was pretty upset with me. He said I should've called his cell, and he was right. Hopefully we'll grab some dinner after class." Then a smile twitched at the edges of her mouth, and the tension eased from her face. "I'll find a way to make it up to him later."

Margaret hooted with laughter. "I just bet you will," she said, winking at Alix.

CHAPTER
28

Phoebe Rylander

Phoebe wasn't a baseball fan. However, when Hutch invited her to attend Stitch and Pitch night at the Mariners' game, she was eager to accept. Everyone in the class had gotten tickets and it would be an enjoyable Thursday evening, quite different from her usual activities.

Hutch picked her up at work and had dressed in a Mariners' jersey, complete with baseball cap. She had to admit he looked athletic and rather charming in a boyish manner. She knew he'd started working out at a gym three mornings a week and it showed. In fact, she couldn't keep her eyes off him.

Judging by the way he kept stealing glances at her, the feeling was mutual. Ever since Monday night when Clark had tried to deceive her, Phoebe had a renewed appreciation of Hutch. He was honest and forthright, whereas anything Clark said simply couldn't be trusted. With him, the truth was all too flexible.

The crowds streamed into the stadium. As she and Hutch reached their seats, he left her to stand in a long line to purchase the ever-popular hot dogs.

Phoebe watched the pitcher warm up, and the excitement in the crowd was contagious. She saw Lydia, Brad, Casey and Cody filing into the row in front of her and Hutch, half a dozen seats to the right. Both kids had catcher's mitts, obviously hoping for foul balls. Lydia had her knitting; Phoebe had brought hers, too.

"Hello," she called out.

Grinning, Lydia turned around. "Hi! I don't suppose you've seen Margaret, have you?"

Phoebe nodded. "She was in line at the ladies' room."

"Oh, good. She made it."

"Elise Beaumont was there, too."

"I'm glad Margaret managed to talk her into coming," Lydia said.

"There's Anne Marie." Phoebe impulsively stood up to wave. Ellen was with her, as well as another couple she didn't recognize. Anne Marie waved back from several rows below.

Sitting down again, Phoebe leaned forward to ask Lydia, "Who's that couple with Anne Marie and Ellen?"

Lydia shaded her eyes, peering down at them, then shook her head. "I don't know." After a moment she twisted around to speak to Phoebe again. "Anne Marie's been dating this guy named Tim, but I don't think that's him."

"Why not?"

"Well, mainly because he's holding hands with the other woman."

"Oh."

She craned her neck to get a better view. "The thing is, it sort of looks like him."

"You've met him?"

"Once, when I dropped into the bookstore to pick something up and he was there."

Hutch returned, holding a cardboard container laden with two huge hot dogs slathered with condiments, including sauerkraut and mustard, plus two giant-size sodas and a bag of hot, roasted peanuts.

"I hope you're hungry," he warned, sitting down beside her.

"Starved."

"Did you bring me any chocolate, Mr. Mount Rainier?" Margaret asked, scooting past several other people in order to sit next to her sister. Elise trailed behind her, knitting in hand.

"Sorry, no."

"Don't apologize! I appreciate it."

Phoebe nudged him in the ribs. Ever since the knitting group had heard that he was the head of Mount Rainier Chocolates, Hutch had gotten into the habit of bringing chocolate to class. The Mount Saint Helens bar had launched nationally and, according to Hutch, had been well received. The sales reports were just coming back and he was thrilled with its success so far.

"Look!" Cody shouted, leaping to his feet. "We're on the big screen!"

Phoebe swiveled her head to the huge screen, and sure enough, the entire knitting section was on display. Cody, waving both arms, stood out prominently.

Phoebe laughed, and then everyone in the group held up their knitting. Unprepared, Hutch and Phoebe scrambled to flaunt their sampler scarves. She nearly dumped her hot dog on Margaret's head in the process, but saved it from catapulting forward in the nick of time.

Knitters sat on every side of them and the mood was jovial as they showed one another their current efforts. Several yarn stores had set up booths by the concession stands and Phoebe couldn't resist looking—and buying.

Until now, she'd resisted purchasing yarn for anything beyond her current project. She'd discovered that she enjoyed knitting; the problem was, she didn't have enough free time now that she was seeing Hutch almost every day. She'd taken to knitting during her lunch break, which was the only reason she'd been able to keep up with the class.

Next Wednesday, the first Wednesday of August, would be their last class. She'd be finished with her scarf, and she wanted to start something new. She chose sock yarn in the Mariners' colors, thinking she'd take another class—this one on sock-knitting taught by Elise—and give the finished product to Hutch.

"What did you buy?" Hutch asked when she rejoined him.

She opened the bag and proudly revealed her booty. "I'm going to learn to knit socks."

"Terrific."

"Do you like the colors?" she asked.

"You bet." He smiled down at her—and kept smiling.

For that matter so did Phoebe. Although they were surrounded by thousands of cheering fans, they were gazing only at each other.

"I thought I'd knit them for you," she whispered.

He didn't say anything, but reached for her hand and entwined their fingers, his grip hard. She squeezed back, wanting him to know she shared the intensity of his feelings.

"Excuse me, guys," Alix said, hurrying past.

"Oh, sorry," Hutch said, standing up so Alix and Jordan could get by.

"Where are they off to in such a hurry?" Phoebe asked no one in particular.

"No idea," Margaret answered, her fingers moving the crochet hook with speed and dexterity.

She seemed to be working on an afghan. Casey was crocheting, too, and Lydia was knitting. What most impressed Phoebe was that Lydia could knit without even looking at the needles. Phoebe, on the other hand, watched every single stitch for fear of making a mistake. The thought of having to rip out a row traumatized her, although she'd been forced to do so often enough.

A few minutes later, Alix was back, this time without Jordan. "Sorry," she mumbled as she stepped over Phoebe's feet. "All of a sudden I had to get to a restroom." She slipped past the couple sitting next to them.

Jordan followed soon after, apologizing as he did. He carried one hot dog and a soda, and when he sat down beside Alix, Phoebe noticed that the two of them were sharing the meal. Living on a youth pastor's salary probably made it difficult to splurge on dinner out two nights in a single week.

Phoebe knew from class yesterday that they'd squabbled, although she didn't know about what. Apparently that had happened before she'd arrived. At the end of class, Jordan had stopped by to pick up Alix as usual. He'd stood by the door, looking depressed, not at all his normal outgoing self.

As soon as Alix saw her husband, she'd set her knitting down and rushed to his side. For a long moment, all they did was stare at each other—and then Jordan had reached out and grabbed Alix with both arms, hugging her close.

Later that evening, just as she and Hutch had gone off in different directions, Phoebe caught sight of Alix and Jordan in a burger place, their heads together, eating and talking animatedly.

Obviously whatever strain had existed between them yesterday afternoon had passed.

Tonight's game ended with the Mariners winning at the bottom of the ninth. The crowd was jubilant as they poured out of Safeco Field. Walking hand in hand, Phoebe and Hutch made their way to the parking lot, where Hutch had left his vehicle.

For the first time that evening, he seemed somewhat withdrawn. She didn't need to ask what was troubling him—the lawsuit against Mount Rainier Chocolates. He'd occasionally mentioned it, never disclosing very much. She'd also seen an article about the lawsuit in the paper, but it hadn't provided any more information than she already had.

"How about a cup of coffee at my place?" she suggested.

He smiled at her and nodded, making a visible effort to resume his cheerful attitude.

She swallowed painfully. She was going to confess that she'd misled him—and everyone in the knitting class—about her fiancé. She should never have let the pretence go on for this long.

But when she was with Hutch there were so many other things to talk about. Still, he'd recently commented on the fact that she didn't have any pictures of her fiancé around the condo. For a moment his remark had jarred her, until she remembered that he thought Clark was dead.

She trusted that he'd forgive her this foolish deception, which had taken on a life, a momentum, of its own.

She also hoped that after tonight's confession, he'd feel free to share his worries over this lawsuit. In her opinion, the entire matter was frivolous, a waste of time. But whenever she'd asked him about it, Hutch had brushed aside her questions and said his attorney was handling it. He always added that he wasn't really worried. Only he was. That seemed very clear tonight.

Once they were at her condo, she put away her yarn purchase, ground fresh beans and made a small pot of coffee, just enough for two cups.

She joined Hutch in the living room and handed him his mug.

"There's something I need to tell you," she began softly.

Hutch stiffened, almost as if he knew what was coming—although he couldn't possibly. "Okay," he said. "Is it serious?"

She nodded. "I've been lying to you."

Hutch carefully set his mug on the low table beside him. "I'd rather deal with the truth now than later."

She took a sip of her coffee, then glanced down. "When I signed up for the knitting class, I told everyone I was engaged and that my fiancé died."

"So he's not dead?" Hutch frowned and anxiety flared in his eyes. "Please don't tell me you're married."

Despite her nervousness, she smiled. "No, he's not dead and I'm not married. It's nothing like that."

His shoulders slumped with relief.

"I was engaged and in love with a man who . . ." She paused, finding it difficult to continue. "I broke off the engagement two months ago, when I discovered he'd been arrested for solicitation."

Hutch pressed his hand over hers. He didn't say anything.

"It happened before this, too. I took him back the first time . . ."

"The first time you knew about," he commented.

"Exactly. I have to suspect there were other instances."

"Oh, Phoebe."

"He managed to convince me it would never happen again, and I believed him." She didn't mention the pressure she was under from both Clark's family and her own to forgive and forget.

"I'm sorry."

She licked her lips, which felt dry and cracked. "I did what I had to do, ended the engagement, and although it was painful I don't regret it, not for a second." Telling Hutch about Clark's most recent attempt to get her to take him back would only upset him. Phoebe decided to say nothing.

"So when you enrolled in the Knit to Quit class, it was because you were trying to stop loving your fiancé?"

Lowering her head, Phoebe nodded.

"Has it helped?"

She looked up at him and grinned. "More than you'll ever know. I was crushed, devastated, humiliated, angry. I realize now that while I did love Clark, his actions killed all the feelings I had for him."

Hutch brought her close and touched his forehead to hers. "Thank you for telling me."

"I couldn't lie to you any longer."

He kissed the tip of her nose, lightly, tenderly, in a way she'd come to adore. His gentleness stirred her more than a dozen passionate caresses. Slipping her arms around his neck, she raised her mouth to his and they kissed for a long time, each kiss connecting them on a deeper level. She leaned against his shoulder, her head spinning with desire. Hutch's breathing was ragged.

They sat like that, satiated and at peace, for a while.

"Tell me about the lawsuit," she finally said.

Hutch exhaled. "There isn't much to tell."

"You're worried, though."

"I am. My attorney's agreed to fight it but he'd prefer that I settled out of court. I refuse to do that. It would be like an admission of guilt. However, my attorney feels I'm taking a terrible risk letting this case go to trial." Hutch was silent for a moment. "The suit's raised a lot of interest nation-wide. If I lose, it opens the door for other people to sue the larger companies, claiming chocolate is addictive. And what about alcoholics suing wineries? Or prescription-drug abusers blaming the pharmaceuticals? You see what I mean. There's a lot more at stake than meets the eye."

"Is it worth all this angst?" she asked, siding with his attorney. In this particular instance it might be best to simply pay off this idiotic woman and be done with it.

"I don't know," he admitted with some reluc-tance. "I turned down their first settlement offer. I can't see handing over such a large chunk of cash just to make this go away. When my attorney suggested we might be willing to settle, the plaintiff came back with an even higher demand."

"Greed does nasty things to a person."

"No kidding. Besides, who's to say I won't be sued again next week, next month, next year? It's dangerous either way. I'd rather confront this head-on and have it dealt with once and for all."

Phoebe sighed. "I wish there was something I could do."

"There is."

"What?" she asked eagerly.

He folded her in his embrace. "Let me hold you

for a few more minutes," he whispered. "When you're in my arms I can't think of anything else."

Hutch might not be as eloquent as Clark had been, but his words were sincere. His emotions were real.

CHAPTER
29

Anne Marie Roche

This was going to be difficult; Anne Marie could see it already. As Tim had repeatedly reminded her, she was the one who'd insisted on being present when Ellen met Vanessa. That was certainly true, but Anne Marie didn't think meeting at the Mariners' game for Stitch and Pitch night—meeting "accidentally on purpose"—was such a brilliant idea. She'd agreed to do it his way, although it went against her instincts.

That had been her first mistake. They'd arrived at the game as planned and were headed toward their seats when Tim had called out to them. He'd made a pretense of just noticing them.

The evening had gone downhill from there.

Vanessa had been openly hostile to Anne Marie. To Ellen she'd been patronizing and saccharine sweet. The worst part, as far as Anne Marie was concerned, was that Tim didn't appear to perceive

anything amiss with Vanessa's behavior. To all outward appearances, he seemed to feel the meeting
couldn't have gone better.

In Anne Marie's opinion, the whole experience
had been a disaster. Now that they were home and
Ellen was preparing for bed, she had a chance to
mull over the events of the evening.

"Mom," Ellen called from her bedroom. "I'm
ready."

Time for their nightly ritual. Ellen climbed into
bed with Baxter cuddled next to her. Anne Marie
knelt on the floor so Ellen could say her prayers.

"Did you enjoy the baseball game?" Anne Marie
asked.

"It was all right."

It wasn't for Anne Marie, but she couldn't tell
Ellen that.

The girl looked guilelessly up at her. "I thought
you were Tim's girlfriend."

Doing her best to sound calm and serene, Anne
Marie smiled down at her daughter. "Tim and
Vanessa are a couple."

"Oh." Ellen frowned. "But he took you out to
dinner by yourself, remember?"

Anne Marie wasn't likely to forget. "Vanessa was
there," she half-lied. Perhaps not in the physical
sense but in every other way Tim's girlfriend had
been with them.

"You didn't tell me about her."

Anne Marie realized she didn't actually know

very much about the other woman. "I guess I should've told you earlier," she said.

In a short time Ellen had grown close to Tim. She admired him and talked about him incessantly. Along with Brad, Mark and Hector he was a positive male figure, and Anne Marie wouldn't say or do anything to jeopardize that special relationship.

"I know meeting Vanessa was a surprise." Tim had wanted to be the one to introduce Vanessa to Ellen, and Anne Marie had agreed. In retrospect it would've been a hundred times better if she'd been able to lead up to the subject of this other woman. She wished now that she'd suggested it and regretted that she hadn't.

"You like Tim, don't you?" Ellen asked.

For fear her voice would give her away, Anne Marie nodded instead.

"And he likes you?"

"Yes," she said, "just not in a girlfriend-boyfriend way."

"Oh." Clearly Ellen was disappointed as well as confused.

Who could blame her? "The person Tim really loves is you," Anne Marie murmured.

"Me?" Ellen's eyes flashed with delight. "I like him, too. He makes me laugh and takes us neat places."

"Yes, he does. Besides, Tim knew your grandmother and your other mom." Anne Marie didn't believe it was her place to inform the child that she was Tim's biological daughter. She'd leave that to him—at a mutually acceptable time and place. This evening had taught her a valuable lesson. She wasn't about to let Tim blurt out the news without first laying the groundwork.

Ellen's dark eyes widened. "He knew my Grandma Dolores? How come I never met him till now?"

Anne Marie wasn't prepared to answer that question. She'd already stretched the truth about as far as it would go. "You'll need to ask Tim the next time he stops by."

"Will Vanessa be there?"

"Probably. You like her, don't you?"

Ellen shrugged. "She's okay, but she talks to me like I'm a baby."

"She'll learn," Anne Marie assured her and prayed that was true. "Vanessa's a very nice person." She almost gritted her teeth as she said it.

Ellen seemed to consider that and then nodded. "She must be if Tim loves her."

Good point. Anne Marie hadn't thought of it in those terms. Out of the mouths of nine-year-olds . . .

"You're right." Anne Marie reached for Ellen's small hands and closed her eyes, prepared to listen while the child said her prayers. These sometimes went on for three or four minutes. She asked God to bless Anne Marie first, then listed all her friends from school and day camp, followed by her

Blossom Street friends and finally Tim. She hesitated and added Vanessa to the list.

"Amen," Ellen said, opening her eyes.

"Amen," Anne Marie echoed and kissed Ellen's cheek. She stroked Baxter's silky fur, then left the room, closing the door quietly behind her.

Restless and unsure, Anne Marie folded her arms and paced the kitchen, mulling over the conversation with her daughter. The truth was, she'd been hostile toward Vanessa. Well, maybe not hostile, but certainly not hospitable. She resented the other woman, who'd ruined the perfect scenario she'd created for Ellen, Tim and her.

Anne Marie was shocked to discover how strong her feelings for Tim were. She hadn't expected that in the beginning. But the transformation in her attitude had been gradual. He'd been so good, so natural, with Ellen. Anne Marie had watched him closely, initially unwilling to trust him, yet he'd earned her trust. Earned it to the point that she'd lowered her guard. She'd half convinced herself she was falling in love with him.

When he'd told her about Vanessa, she'd been angry and embarrassed, but in retrospect she understood that Tim had been in a difficult position. He'd already sprung the news that he was Ellen's biological father. He'd tried to be fair, giving Anne Marie a chance to get used to that reality before he introduced Vanessa into their lives, as well. Whether it was the best way to handle the situation didn't matter. What was done was done.

Unfortunately her relationship with Vanessa had started badly. They were both at fault, because both felt threatened. If it was ever going to be made right, Anne Marie would need to reach out to the other woman.

The next morning, she decided to get in touch with Vanessa as soon as possible. She'd have to ask Tim for her phone number; she'd call him later. After taking Ellen to day camp, she opened the bookstore. She was still counting cash into the till when she saw Tim standing at the door. He looked as if he hadn't slept all night.

"Good morning," she greeted him cheerfully.

He frowned.

"It isn't a good morning?" she teased, smiling at him.

Slowly he smiled back. "It is now," he said. "I didn't expect you to be in such a happy mood."

"Why not?"

He scratched his head. "Vanessa didn't feel things went well last night."

Anne Marie broke a roll of quarters and added them to the register drawer. "They didn't, but I take responsibility for that."

"You do?"

"I wasn't as . . . friendly as I might've been to Vanessa. I owe her—and you—an apology."

Tim just stared at her, as if he wasn't sure he should believe what she'd said. "You?"

"I should've taken Vanessa's feelings into account more. She felt I'd intruded on her territory, didn't she?"

"Well . . . yes, something like that."

This next part was the most difficult. "You were right—I'm afraid I read more into the situation between you and me than I should have. That probably caused a certain amount of animosity in our initial meeting." She was embarrassed to admit this, but he already knew. It wasn't as though she'd done a good job of hiding her feelings.

"I'm sorry about that."

"You have nothing to be sorry for," she said, eager to change the subject. "If you'll give me Vanessa's phone number, I'll call her and see if I can make amends. I'm sure she feels as awkward about what happened at the game as I do."

Tim stepped closer to the counter as he scribbled a number on the back of his business card. "Can you tell me exactly what *did* happen?"

Anne Marie shrugged. "It was nothing really. Just undercurrents between the two of us." Basically they'd stared daggers at each other. It had been a juvenile display that Anne Marie regretted.

"What did Ellen think of Vanessa?" Tim asked.

Anne Marie didn't answer immediately. "She told me that if you love Vanessa, she must be very special." No need to mention the comment about Vanessa speaking to her as if she were a baby.

Some of the tension seemed to leave Tim's shoulders. "She actually said that?"

"She did."

"You don't mind if I tell Vanessa, do you?"

"Not at all."

"Thank you," he said. "Thank you so much."

He was almost at the door when she stopped him. "It's time, you know."

He turned around. "Time?"

"For you to tell Ellen that you're her father. In her heart I think she already knows. The news isn't going to upset her."

Tim swallowed hard and nodded. "Would it be okay if I came by this evening?"

"That would be perfect. In the meantime, I'll contact Vanessa."

Anne Marie waited until midmorning to call Tim's friend. At first the conversation didn't go well.

"What do you want?" Vanessa demanded the instant she answered her cell phone.

Anne Marie had to bite her tongue to keep from responding in kind. "It seems to me that you and I should try to be friends," she said calmly.

"Yeah, like that's going to happen."

"It will if we both make the effort," Anne Marie told her. "The thing is, I behaved badly last evening and I want to apologize."

"Sure you do."

347

Anne Marie ignored that. "For Tim and Ellen's sake, I'd like to suggest we start over."

The phone went silent and for a moment Anne Marie thought the other woman had hung up.

"Vanessa, are you there?"

"I'm here."

Despite the inclination to give this up as useless, she tried again. "Would you be willing to accept my apology?"

Vanessa hesitated. In a lower voice, she answered, "All right."

"I mean it, Vanessa. I'm not a threat to your relationship with Tim. For him and for Ellen, it would help if you and I could come to some agreement."

"You agree to keep your hands off Tim, and we'll get along fine."

"No problem."

"Good."

Anne Marie smiled, relieved that she'd done what she needed to do. "Friends?" she asked.

After a short pause, Vanessa repeated the word, again with some hesitation. "Friends."

"Thank you."

"Stick to being Ellen's mother, and everything will work out just fine."

"I will," she promised. "It was a pleasure talking to you," she said. "Goodbye."

"Anne Marie," Vanessa said quickly. "This couldn't have been an easy call to make. I want you to know I appreciate it."

"You're welcome. I hope to see you soon."

"And you."

The truth was, Anne Marie would probably never be close friends with Vanessa but at least they understood each other now. Both were determined to make the best of an awkward situation.

The rest of the day, Anne Marie and Teresa were busy with customers. There was a run on the newest installment of a popular series, and Anne Marie found herself constantly occupied—for which she was grateful. About four-thirty, just before Ellen was due to return, Tim walked back into the store.

He looked, if anything, even worse than he had that morning. "Is Ellen here?" he asked.

"Not yet. I thought you were coming tonight."

He shook his head. "I don't think I can wait that long. Now that the decision's been made, I want to get this over with."

Anne Marie could understand. "I'd like to be in the room when you do," she said. "Are you okay with that?"

He nodded, hands buried in his pants pockets.

A few minutes later, Ellen ran into the store with her backpack bobbing on her shoulders. "Mom, Mom!" She stopped abruptly when she saw Tim, glancing from him back to Anne Marie.

"Hello again," Tim said in a deceptively casual voice.

"Hi. Vanessa's not with you?"

"Not this time."

"Tim has something he wants to tell you," Anne Marie said, reminding Tim that his visit had a purpose. She turned to Teresa, who'd been taking a phone order. "I'm going to the apartment for a few minutes. Would you cover for me?"

"Sure thing."

The three of them walked up the stairs, Ellen first, then Anne Marie and Tim. Having heard Ellen's voice, Baxter waited on the landing, eager to go out for his afternoon walk. He scurried into the bedroom and returned with the leash in his mouth. Ellen was proud of teaching him that trick.

"In a few minutes," Anne Marie told her Yorkie, bending to pick him up.

"Let's sit down," Tim said, motioning to the sofa.

Ellen did, and Anne Marie sat next to her with Baxter on her lap. She hooked her free arm around her daughter's shoulders.

Tim looked ashen as if he didn't know where to start or how.

Ellen sighed loudly enough for him to hear. He turned to her and opened his mouth but nothing came out.

"Are you my father?" she asked unexpectedly.

Tim nodded and sank to the carpet on his knees in front of her. His eyes were moist. "Yes, Ellen. I'm your father."

"I thought so." Smiling up at Anne Marie, she

said, "I wanted to meet my father, remember? It was one of my wishes. Then you told me that Tim knew Grandma Dolores and my other mom and I knew God had sent me my daddy."

With that she hurled her arms around Tim's neck and hugged him fiercely. "I'm so glad it's you."

Anne Marie felt tears in her own eyes.

They'd make this work, all of them. For Ellen.

CHAPTER
30

It is so important to allow yourself the time to be creative, because without creativity how can you imagine possibilities? For me, it's always been knitting and crochet and they have opened the door to limitless possibilities.

—Candi Jensen, author and producer of the Emmy-nominated PBS TV show, *Knit and Crochet Today*

Lydia Goetz

As I've mentioned, A Good Yarn is closed on Mondays; that's when I schedule my doctor, dentist and other appointments. I also catch up on paperwork and accounting.

I'd also started leaving part of every Monday open to visit my mother. Thankfully Mom was only in the hospital overnight. Ever since her fall she seemed so frail to me, and I noticed that her mind wandered more. Some days she seems lost in the past. A couple of weeks ago, I swear she didn't know who I was. Margaret and I both feel we won't have her much longer, so it's important to spend as much time with her as possible. Moving her into an assisted living complex had been a difficult decision, but more than ever, we realized it was the right one. Mom seemed to decline with every visit and she still missed her home, but we'd had no other choice, Margaret and I, since she couldn't live by herself anymore.

At least the situation with Casey had improved in the past week. The real change had come after the day she'd sought out Alix. Despite my tentative inquiries, neither one of them had divulged the topic of their conversation.

Whatever Alix said had helped Casey. I just wish she'd told me where she was going. I've hardly ever seen Brad so worried, fearful that she'd decided to run away again. My husband had come to care as deeply about Casey as I did.

"What are you doing today?" Casey asked as I finished packing lunches for her and Cody. She attended day camp with him unless she came to the shop with me.

"I'm getting groceries, and then I'm going to visit my mother," I said, adding a small bag of corn chips to Cody's lunch. Those were his favorites, and he'd eat them every day if I let him.

"Can I come with you?" She'd dressed in shorts and a T-shirt, her usual attire, with flip-flops.

The request surprised me—and it pleased me, too. "I'd like that."

"Cool."

Casey tried to sneak a cookie and I slapped her hand. "Not before breakfast."

She grabbed the cereal box instead. Before long Cody had joined her, and they sat side by side spooning up Rice Krispies and making exaggerated slurping sounds, which I chose to ignore.

I dropped Cody off, then Casey and I went to the grocery store.

She didn't have a lot to say while I steered the cart through the aisles and carefully followed my list. I noticed, however, that several items showed up at the check-out stand that I didn't remember putting in the cart. I allowed the cake mix and the cantaloupe to pass without comment, but removed the teen gossip magazine before it reached the cash register.

Holding it up, I looked at Casey, who shrugged as if she had no idea how that could possibly have landed in the cart. I replaced it in the magazine slot, poking her in the ribs. She laughed and so did I.

We brought the groceries home and made short work of putting everything away. Then we drove to the assisted living complex.

Casey had met my mother before but only briefly and only with the whole family present. Because this was her first real visit, I felt I needed to prepare her.

"Mom's mind is fading," I explained. "She's having some memory lapses."

"What's that mean?" she asked.

"She might forget your name."

"That's okay."

"And she's often confused." I didn't want to say too much—didn't want to frighten Casey or negatively influence her opinion.

"I get confused sometimes," she said.

I grinned. "Me, too," I admitted. It was probably best for Casey to form her own judgment.

I parked the car and exchanged hellos with the friendly staff as Casey and I passed through the wide foyer to the elevator, which would take us up to my mother's small apartment.

Tapping at her door, I let myself in. "Hi, Mom," I said cheerfully. Margaret and I had positioned her sofa in the living room, with the afghan Margaret had crocheted in lovely fall colors spread over the back. Across from the sofa were her favorite chair and the coffee and end tables that had been in the family home. There was no room for anything else.

The kitchen had a miniature refrigerator and a microwave, a sink and a few dishes, but that was about all. I cleaned out her fridge every week, tossing the open cans of tuna fish and the moldy cheese. Naturally I had to do that when Mom wasn't looking. She hated to discard anything.

Her bedroom was compact, too. There was just enough room for her bed, a nightstand and her beloved sewing machine. Mom didn't sew these days, but that machine had been a major part of her life for so many years, she'd never feel at home without it. Despite the restrictive quarters, Margaret and I had found a spot for it.

Mom glanced up from the television. When she saw it was me, she brightened. "Lydia. You brought Hailey with you."

Hailey was my sister's daughter. "No, Mom, this is Casey." I slipped an arm around the girl's shoulders. "She's spending the summer with Brad and me." I wasn't a hundred percent sure Mom would remember Brad. Some weeks she did; other weeks she looked blankly at me when I mentioned his name.

My mother tilted her head quizzically. "Have I met you before?" she asked Casey. "I'm so forgetful lately."

Casey slid her fingertips into the pockets of her jean shorts. "Not really."

I'd brought Mom to the house for dinner one Sunday afternoon shortly after Casey's arrival. Casey had spent most of the day in her room as if she felt she was intruding on family time. I'd tried to coax her out to no avail. There'd been a couple of similar occasions, including one at Margaret's, but as far as I knew, Casey hadn't exchanged more than a few words with my mother.

"You do look familiar, though," Mom said with a frown.

Casey sat on the sofa next to her chair and studied the TV screen. "What are you watching?"

I could've answered for her. My mother was enthralled by the cooking channel. Paula Deen was her favorite, and she watched her show faithfully, as well as four or five others. She used to write down the recipes, which she passed to Margaret and me, and she asked for cookbooks every Christmas. Mom didn't cook anymore, but that didn't alter her desire to create wonderful meals for her family. She'd given up writing out the recipes, and that concerned me. I was afraid she'd lost— what? Her sense of purpose? Her belief in a future? I suspected her ability to follow the instructions was already gone.

"Paula Deen's baking cookies this morning," Mom told Casey, who appeared interested in what was happening. That didn't surprise me, considering the cookies and cakes she'd baked herself.

I headed into the bedroom to gather up Mom's laundry, which I washed for her every week. The washer and dryer were down the hall and shared by the residents on the second floor.

"Lydia was a terrible cook as a child," I heard my mother say. "I couldn't trust her in the kitchen."

"Really?" Casey met my gaze, giggling delightedly.

I'd heard the story of how, at age eleven, I'd burned peanut butter cookies to a crisp countless times.

"I'll get the clothes into the washer and be right back," I said. Sometimes Mom had trouble remembering my name, but she recalled in vivid detail a long-ago incident from my youth. Maybe because it had been repeated so often over the years.

Judging by Casey's rapt attention, I doubted either of them heard me leave. After I'd loaded the washer I returned to find both Mom and Casey laughing, whether at something on the TV or a shared joke I didn't know.

Since Casey was keeping my mother entertained, I went back into the tiny bedroom to make her bed. Mom would be so embarrassed to realize she'd left it unmade. When I was a kid, my mother had been a real stickler about tucking in the sheets and smoothing out the blankets each and every morning. Having a properly made bed was right up there with brushing my teeth and saying my prayers, and it was a habit I'd never abandoned.

As I worked, I noticed that the laughter between Mom and Casey continued. It was so unusual to hear my mother laugh that I poked my head out the door to see what was so amusing.

The TV was actually off, and Casey sat on the floor at my mother's feet, doubled over with glee. When she caught sight of me, she pointed in my direction. "You read Margaret's diary?"

"Mom, are you telling tales on me?" I asked in mock outrage.

Mom nodded. "Your sister was so upset, she marched into the backyard and burned her diary. Your father said we were fortunate no one called the fire department."

Casey found that equally hilarious and laughed even harder. Mom did, too. Happy tears rolled down her weathered cheeks until she reached for the handkerchief she kept inside her sweater pocket and dabbed at her eyes.

It was true. At seventeen, I'd snuck into my sister's bedroom, searched for her diary and read page after page. As luck would have it, my sister had discovered me there, sitting on her bed, completely enthralled with what she'd written.

To say she was furious would be an understatement. Margaret had ripped the book from my hands and stormed out of the house, demanding that my parents "do something."

What Margaret didn't understand—or for that matter, my parents, either—was that I was starved for a normal life. In my view Margaret was a normal teenager and I wasn't because I had cancer. I craved my sister's life and the only way I could get a glimpse of *normal* was by reading her journal.

"She's forgiven me now," I said, then added, "I think."

Casey looked at me archly. "I wouldn't have."

"Thanks a lot, kid."

"Do you keep a diary?" Mom asked Casey.

She shook her head.

"Good thing." I said, hands on my hips. "I'd probably read yours, too."

Casey grinned and turned back to my mother, wanting to hear more tales of my sinful past.

We stayed until it was time for Mom to go to the dining room for lunch. She sat at the same table every day with three other widows. They all seemed to get along well and I was grateful she had at least this social interaction, since she rarely participated in events or day trips planned by the staff.

Casey escorted her to the dining room while I finished folding and putting away her clean laundry. Then I hurried downstairs, meeting the two of them as Casey helped Mom into her chair.

"Bring Hailey again," Mom said, smiling up at me.

Casey didn't seem upset that my mother thought she was my niece. "I'll do that." I gently hugged her goodbye. This was probably the best visit I'd had with her since the move. She was almost her old self again, and I had Casey to thank for that. The girl had been enthralled with my mother, even when Mom repeated the same stories over and over.

"I'm so glad you came with me," I said as we walked toward the visitor parking lot.

"Your mom's funny."

"I know."

"I don't have grandparents," she said a little sadly. "I mean, I never had one I actually remember."

I wasn't sure how to comment.

We were driving back to the house when Casey suddenly turned to me. "What was it like to have cancer?" she asked.

The question caught me unawares. My mother must have brought up the subject, although I couldn't guess how much or how little she'd said— or remembered.

"It wasn't a lot of fun, that's for sure." I thought it was preferable to keep the details to myself. I recalled how disturbed Mom and Margaret had been when I lost my hair during chemo. Good grief, that was the least of it! The drugs, the vomiting, the horrendous headaches that incapacitated me. Going bald was nothing.

Nearly a year of my life had been spent in the hospital. I'd be home for short periods of time, and then something else would happen that would force me to return. I didn't like to think about those years.

"How old were you?"

"Sixteen. I'd just gotten my driver's license." I kept my answers short and considered trying to change the subject. I didn't, because Casey obviously wanted to understand.

"What was the worst part, other than feeling sick all the time?"

"The worst part?" I echoed. "I think it was missing out on all the fun in high school." It was so much more than being unable to attend football games or dances. All my friends were dating and exploring their independence. Not me. Instead I'd been in the hospital for months on end, hooked up to IVs, in such physical and emotional pain that I didn't have the strength to open my eyes.

I'd desperately longed to be like everyone else. I was so sick of being sick.

"Did you ever go to a dance?"

I nodded. I'd gone with my girlfriends.

"Did you have a special dress?"

Unexpectedly a lump filled my throat. "Mom made me one, and it was beautiful."

"A date?"

I shook my head and managed a laugh. "The boys in my class tended to date girls who weren't bald." I'd generally worn a kerchief, since the wigs I had were so hot and uncomfortable.

"You lost your hair?" Casey asked in horror.

"Margaret has pictures. I think she took them as revenge for reading her diary."

Casey smiled, but then her expression grew serious again. "It was hard having cancer, wasn't it?"

I could make light of those years but decided on honesty instead. "Yes."

She was quiet for several minutes. "The cancer came back, didn't it?" she finally asked. "That's what Cody told me before."

"When I was in my early twenties. The fact is, it might still return. Life doesn't come with a guarantee that just because I'm a nice person the tumors won't grow again."

We pulled into the driveway and I turned off the engine. I climbed out of the car and waited, watching as Casey continued to sit there, apparently steeped in thought. A moment later, she joined me.

"You're a brave person," she said quietly.

I laughed because I certainly didn't think of myself in those terms. Looping my arm around her neck, I brought her head close to mine and kissed her hair. "Oh, yes. That's me, all right."

"You had cancer twice and you . . . you still let me live with you this summer."

That part, at least for this day, was pure joy.

CHAPTER
31

"Hutch" Hutchinson

Hutch was in love. Everyone around him recognized the signs and didn't have any qualms about pointing it out. Not that he was trying to hide it.

A little while ago—before Phoebe—his sister had attempted to set him up with a girlfriend of hers . . . Mia, Myra, something like that. He'd forgotten her name just as he was sure she'd forgotten his.

Meeting Phoebe had changed everything. The first time he'd seen her he'd felt the attraction. She was beautiful, and he wasn't reacting merely to her appearance. Phoebe was everything he'd ever hoped to find in a woman—and she loved *him*. He could hardly believe it.

Hutch was, however, somewhat disappointed that it'd taken Phoebe so long to admit that her fiancé wasn't dead. But although it troubled him, he could understand why she'd lied. In similar circumstances, he might have done the same thing in order to avoid embarrassment and lengthy explanations. It'd been simpler this way, and as she'd said to him, the minute her fiancé agreed to pay for sex with another woman he was dead to her.

Hutch wondered about this other man who'd once been a very important part of Phoebe's life. In the two months they'd been seeing each other Phoebe had never spoken of her engagement or offered up anything but the sketchiest details. All Hutch knew was that the man Phoebe had planned to marry had lied and cheated on her. When the truth came out—the second time—she'd severed the relationship for good. He realized how deeply hurt she'd been by what her ex-fiancé had done.

"I have your attorney on line one," Gail Wendell said, breaking into his thoughts.

Now that the trial date was approaching, he heard from John Custer nearly every day.

"Hutch speaking," he said, picking up the phone.

The conversation with John lasted only a few minutes. As soon as he'd finished, he tried to put the matter out of his mind. It was on days like this that he wanted, no, *needed,* to talk to Phoebe. As soon as he heard her voice, his blood pressure seemed to decrease.

Checking his watch, he reached for his phone again. Quarter to eleven. Phoebe was between clients. They spoke two and three times a day now, and even that wasn't enough.

"Hi," he said when she answered her cell.

"Hi, yourself," she said. "Did you talk to your attorney?"

"I did." Hutch closed his eyes. He loved hearing the sound of her voice. It flowed over him, easing his burdens, comforting him.

"And?"

Reality returned and his eyes flickered open. "We're scheduled to go to court next week. There doesn't seem to be any way around that."

"I'm sorry."

No sorrier than Hutch. "I was hoping, foolishly perhaps, that the other attorney would see reason. But from what I hear, Clark Snowden's confident he can win—and in the process make a name for himself."

"Snowden?" she repeated.

"Yes, that's the plaintiff's attorney."

"Oh."

Hutch looked down at a file on his desk that required his attention. One gratifying consequence of meeting Phoebe was that he'd learned to delegate. This evidence that he trusted his subordinates had improved his relationship with his department heads, as well. "What about dinner tonight?" he asked.

"I can't," she said quickly. "In fact, I'm tied up for the rest of the week."

Her rejection shocked him. Until now, she'd always been as eager to see him as he was her. Not wanting to sound possessive or unduly concerned, he murmured, "*All* week?"

"Yes . . . and next week, too."

Her voice had grown fragile. "I see." He didn't know what had changed, but clearly something had.

"Listen, Hutch," she said in a tight voice, "our relationship's happened very fast, don't you think? Maybe we should step back and analyze what's going on between us before we continue."

"It's been almost two months. I know what I feel."

"But do you know what you *want?*"

Hutch felt a distinct chill. He had the feeling that she was breaking up with him, but he had no idea why. "Yes," he countered sharply. "I want you in my life."

His words seemed to take her aback. After an

awkward moment, she said, "I don't . . . I need time—to think."

"About what?" he asked irritably. "Have I done anything to offend you?"

"No, never." Her voice softened perceptibly.

"Then what's this *needing time* all about? Isn't that rather sudden?"

"I . . . I need to think, I really do. I'm sorry, but it's for the best."

Maybe best for her but definitely not for him. Hutch wanted to argue with her, to figure out what had changed, but restrained himself. After all, it was up to her to accept or reject his love.

Phoebe said nothing, and he was shaken by the loss that tore through him.

If she wanted time, he'd give it to her. Pride wouldn't allow him to press his point or to plead.

"Tell you what," he said, his voice devoid of emotion. "When you're ready, you contact me."

"Okay."

"Bye, Phoebe."

She started to speak again but he couldn't bear to listen. Gently he replaced the receiver and sat staring into space, wondering what had just happened. In the course of a few minutes she'd ended the most promising relationship of his life.

Hutch stayed at his desk for the rest of the afternoon, attacking the paperwork in front of him.

At four-thirty, Gail stepped into his office. "Is everything all right?" she asked bluntly.

"Yup." Hutch glanced at her. "Never better. Why do you ask?"

Gail frowned, shaking her head. "For one thing, you've been very quiet ever since you got off the phone with John Custer."

Hutch made a show of studying his watch. "Isn't it quitting time?" he asked. In other words he had no intention of answering her question.

"Which brings me to something else," Gail said. "You're usually on the phone with Ms. Rylander about now."

"I won't be seeing Ms. Rylander again," he said starkly.

She didn't bother to hide her shock. "Why ever not? You're crazy about her and I know she feels the same way about you."

"Apparently you and I are both wrong about that."

The older woman clucked her tongue several times, sounding like an agitated hen. "And you're going to sit back and do *nothing?*"

"Yup."

"Oh, Hutch, for the love of Mary, don't be so stubborn."

"This wasn't my decision," he said.

"Did you at least find out why?"

"I tried."

"Try harder."

Hutch lifted his shoulders in a shrug. "As far as I'm concerned, the ball's in her court. If Phoebe wants to call me, fine, but I'm not holding my breath." He sounded resolute and sure of himself, although he didn't feel either of those things.

Gail hesitated and then, with a final shake of her head, left his office.

As soon as she shut the door, Hutch exhaled, letting go of the pretense, and his entire body sagged with defeat. For a moment he thought about confronting Phoebe and demanding she tell him what he'd done that was so terrible.

He couldn't think of a single thing to warrant this reaction and felt sick as he contemplated the new fact of his life—what had seemed so promising only hours earlier was now completely and utterly over.

He stayed at the office until nearly eight. Then, with a heavy heart, he drove home. Dinner was a frozen entrée he shoved in the microwave and ate in front of the television.

His phone rang twice but he didn't pick up. Whoever had called wasn't interested in leaving a message, which was fine because he wasn't interested in listening to one, either.

The late-night news flashed across the screen, and Hutch realized he'd been staring at the television for hours, but couldn't remember anything he'd seen. No matter how many times he went over his conversation with Phoebe, he couldn't explain her sudden decision—or *was* it sudden?—to end their relationship.

Needless to say, Hutch didn't sleep well that night or the next. He kept busy at work, met with his attorney and made every effort not to think about Phoebe. He didn't succeed but pretended he had. The lawsuit occupied his mind when he wasn't dwelling on Phoebe.

To her credit, Gail didn't mention Phoebe's name again, and neither did he. Every now and then he caught his assistant watching him, looking for any telltale sign. What she hoped to find, he didn't know. Perhaps Gail expected to uncover some crack in his resolve, some indication that he was weakening.

But if anything, Hutch grew more convinced that he simply wasn't cut out for love or marriage. He'd laid his heart on the line and Phoebe had ripped it to shreds without cause or provocation. If this was love, then he wanted no part of it.

He had a good life, albeit a lonely one, but he was used to that. As for children, he had his niece and nephew and God willing, eventually one of them, or both, would take over the family business. Otherwise he'd sell out, which he might have to do anyway, depending on the outcome of the court case.

Friday afternoon, five days after that last conversation with Phoebe, Hutch left the office even later than usual. It was mid-August now, and in his opinion no place on earth was more beautiful than the Pacific Northwest on a hot summer's day when the sky was blue and Mount Rainier glimmered like an apparition in the distance.

It was almost nine, but there was still plenty of sunshine. He was walking toward his parking space when he saw her.

Phoebe.

She stood next to his car, waiting for him.

Hutch stopped and instantly squelched the surge of joy he felt at seeing her. He wouldn't allow her to toy with his feelings. Not again. Apparently this was some game to her. A game he wasn't willing to play.

He strode decisively to his car, each step filled with purpose.

"Hello, Hutch," she said.

He didn't respond.

"I can't do it," she whispered brokenly. "I tried, but I can't do it."

He held his briefcase with both hands and just stared at her. He supposed she expected him to ask her questions or show how grateful he was to see her. He wouldn't do either.

She frowned. "Say something," she pleaded.

He shrugged. "What do you want me to say?"

She looked up at him, eyes brimming with tears. "You might tell me you . . . that you missed me."

He pressed his lips together, refusing to tell her any of that even if it was true.

She raised her hand as though to touch his face.

Hutch retreated a step.

She covered her mouth with one hand and began to sob.

His resolve finally faltered but he wouldn't let himself succumb to her tears, although it was impossible to remain stoic and indifferent to her pain.

"The thing is, I've discovered I *can* do it, Phoebe." He reached for his door handle. "I can live without you."

"There's something you don't know."

He stiffened, his back to her.

"Clark Snowden . . ."

At the mention of the plaintiff's attorney, he turned to face her. "What about him?"

"He was . . . he was my fiancé."

The words slammed into him with a force that was actually physical. He couldn't have spoken had his life depended on it.

"I knew if Clark found out you're the man I love, he'd do everything in his power to hurt you. I—I thought the only way to protect you was to break off our relationship . . . but I can't do it. I tried and I just can't. I'm too selfish and needy, Hutch, and I love you too much."

His briefcase fell to the pavement as he hauled her into his arms, holding on as if they'd both perish otherwise.

"You should have told me." His need for her was an ache that shot through him, that burned within him.

"I couldn't. . . . I was afraid."

Then they were kissing, straining against each other, trying to undo five days apart, five days of agony. Hutch tasted her salty tears and kissed them from her cheeks.

"What are we going to do?" she whispered, clinging to him. "Clark will try to destroy you . . . to ruin the business and discredit you. I can't stand by and let him."

"I know exactly what I'm going to do," he said. "It's simple. I'm going to win this lawsuit and then I'm going to marry you, if you'll agree."

He'd half lifted her from the pavement and with her arms around his neck, Phoebe sobbed her answer. "Yes, yes! Oh, Hutch, yes! I want to marry you more than anything in the world. I want to spend my life with you."

That was good to hear, because he wanted her with him for the rest of his, too. Nothing mattered but loving Phoebe. Snowden could do whatever he would; it made no difference to Hutch as long as he had Phoebe.

CHAPTER
32

Anne Marie Roche

Tim walked out to the curb to meet Anne Marie and Ellen as she parked her car outside his parents' house. Vanessa stood on the porch, waiting, making sure Anne Marie knew she was watching every move.

This had been Tim's idea, bringing Ellen over to meet his parents. The first time, it would be just his mother and father; later he planned to introduce her to his siblings.

Ellen needed to feel comfortable with Vanessa, too. Anne Marie hoped the air had been cleared, that there wouldn't be any problems between her and the other woman. Maybe Vanessa needed further reassurance that she had no designs on Tim.

Ever eager to see her father, Ellen unfastened her seat belt and hurtled out of the car and to his side. Without a pause, she threw her arms around his middle, then immediately asked, "Did you bring your motorcycle?"

"I said I would, didn't I?"

Ellen nodded enthusiastically.

Anne Marie climbed out of the car and waved to Vanessa, who halfheartedly returned the gesture.

Even from this distance, Anne Marie could see that the other woman didn't want her there.

Anne Marie hoped she'd have the opportunity to tell her that she wouldn't always be accompanying Ellen to Tim's family events. On this first occasion, however, she felt it was important to be there.

By the time she reached the porch steps, Tim and Ellen were in the garage examining Tim's Harley.

"Hello, Vanessa," Anne Marie gave the other woman an affable smile.

Vanessa had crossed her arms. "How come *you* have to be here?" she demanded. Any residual friendliness from their phone conversation had obviously evaporated.

"I felt Ellen needed to know I was close by in unfamiliar surroundings. It won't always be like this."

"I hope not." With that, Vanessa turned and walked into the house, letting the screen door slam behind her.

Not sure where to go, Anne Marie went in search of Ellen and Tim in the garage. Ellen sat on the Harley, the large black helmet on her head. She resembled one of those Roswell aliens, Anne Marie thought with amusement. Ellen saw her and waved frantically.

"Look, Mom! Look," she cried, her voice muffled by the helmet.

"Who's in there?" Anne Marie joked, peering through the visor.

"It's me! It's me!"

Laughing, she looked at Tim who smiled back. Their eyes held a fraction longer than necessary as they both shared in Ellen's delight.

Anne Marie had to force herself to glance away. Despite her reassurances to Vanessa, she still found Tim attractive, especially when she saw how happy Ellen was whenever the three of them were together.

Ellen talked incessantly about Tim. It was Dad this and Dad that. She'd taken to calling him Dad ever since he'd announced he was her father. That same night she'd marked the wish off her list. Anne Marie and Ellen had begun putting pictures of father and daughter in the girl's Twenty Wishes scrapbook.

After a few minutes, Tim helped Ellen remove the helmet and led the two of them inside. "Mom and Dad are eager to meet you," he said.

His parents—and Vanessa—were waiting in the living room. Tim held Ellen's hand, tugging her forward. Not wanting to intrude, Anne Marie hung back.

Vanessa sat on the sofa, arms still crossed as she glared suspiciously at Anne Marie—as if to ask what she'd been doing in the garage with Tim all that time.

"Hello," Tim's mother said softly. "You must be Ellen."

"Mom, Dad, meet your granddaughter."

Ellen sidled close to Tim, looking small and uncertain.

"My name is Mary," Tim's mother said, "but I hope you'll call me Grandma."

Ellen gave an almost imperceptible nod.

"I'm Thomas, and I'm your grandfather," Tim's father told her next.

"I didn't know I could have three grandmas," Ellen said in a tentative voice.

Anne Marie felt she needed to explain. "Ellen was living with her Grandma Dolores when we first met. After I adopted Ellen, my mother wanted to be called Grandma, too."

"Would you rather call me Mary?" his mother asked, glancing from Ellen to Anne Marie.

Anne Marie decided to let her daughter answer that herself.

"I'll call you Grandma," Ellen said after a bit.

"That would be very nice." Mary straightened. "I hope you like fried chicken because that's what we're having for dinner."

Ellen nodded.

"When your daddy was a little boy, he loved my southern fried chicken."

Relieved, Anne Marie exhaled slowly. Tim's parents were good people and it was clear that they loved Ellen already. Thomas stepped forward and thrust out his hand. "I'm Tim's dad, and you're Ellen's adoptive mother?"

She accepted it and returned his smile. "Anne Marie Roche."

"We appreciate your allowing us into Ellen's life."

It hadn't been an easy decision, but Anne Marie didn't tell him that.

"Ellen seems to be doing just fine, don't you think?" Vanessa said sharply. This was her way of telling Anne Marie that her job was done and it was time to move along now.

Taking her cue, she started to back away. "I'll leave you all to become better acquainted. When would you like me to come for Ellen?" she asked.

Tim narrowed his eyes. "You're not going, are you?"

"Please join us for dinner," Thomas said. "We'd like to get to know you, too, seeing that you're the one raising our granddaughter."

"Yes, well . . ." Anne Marie turned to Vanessa, unsure how to respond. She wanted the other woman to understand that she knew her place and had no intention of encroaching on her relationship with Tim.

"Thomas," Mary called from the kitchen. "I need you and Tim to move the picnic table out of the sun."

The two men promptly left and Anne Marie found herself alone with Vanessa, wondering what, if anything, she should say.

Vanessa released a long breath. "I shouldn't have said anything."

"Pardon?" Anne Marie felt awkward standing in the middle of the room, yet wasn't relaxed enough to sit.

"Just now," Vanessa elaborated. "When you first arrived. I shouldn't have said what I did."

"Oh, that," Anne Marie said, pretending to have forgotten the complete lack of welcome. "Trust me, I understand. You're in a difficult situation. We both are. The only thing we can do is deal with it, right?"

Vanessa didn't seem persuaded. "I guess, but it's kind of hard."

"Yes, it is," Anne Marie said. "Listen, I'll stay a little longer, then make my excuses and leave. You and Tim can bring Ellen home later, or if it's easier I can come back and pick her up. Whichever suits you best."

Vanessa nodded. "I'll ask Tim."

"We can make this work," Anne Marie told her, "but we need to keep the lines of communication open. I don't want you to feel uncomfortable."

"Why should I?" Vanessa said aggressively. "Tim and I are going to be married."

"You *shouldn't* be uncomfortable," Anne Marie agreed. "And by the same token, I want Ellen to feel at ease with you."

"She already does." Vanessa scowled, as though she expected Anne Marie to dispute that statement.

"I appreciate how readily you've accepted Ellen." Anne Marie wasn't convinced that was true, but didn't want to challenge the other woman.

Vanessa gave the same exasperated sigh she had

earlier. "You have no idea how difficult it is, sharing Tim with this child. What'll happen when we have our own children?"

Anne Marie didn't have an answer for her. "The two of you will figure that out when the time comes," she said. It was the best she could do.

"Right," Vanessa mumbled. "We will."

The two men returned, and Tim immediately went to Vanessa's side.

Rather than feel like an outsider, Anne Marie made her way to the kitchen, where Mary and Ellen were chatting amicably.

"Is there anything I can do?" she asked.

"Thanks, but I have everything under control. We'll be eating in a few minutes."

Ellen sat on a bar stool at the counter. "Look, Mom," she said excitedly. "Grandma Mary has a crooked little finger, the same as me." She held her two little fingers together and displayed how they veered off, forming the shape of a V.

"My father once told me they're a sign of high intelligence," Mary said.

"Does Dad have those, too?"

"He does." Mary sent Ellen a smile. She took the chicken from the oven and arranged the pieces on a large platter.

"I can carry that outside if you'd like," Anne Marie volunteered. She wished now that she'd declined the dinner invitation. It was too awkward for both her and Vanessa.

"Thanks. Ellen, why don't you tell everyone dinner's ready," Mary suggested.

"Okay, but can I show Grandpa something first?"

"Sure," Mary said.

Ellen dashed into the living room while Anne Marie carried the platter of fried chicken outside and set it on the table. She'd just come back into the house when she heard Ellen scream.

Anne Marie froze. She'd never heard her daughter scream like that. It was a cry of intense pain. In her rush to find Ellen, she nearly stumbled. Heart-wrenching sobs came from the garage.

Anne Marie saw Ellen on the cement floor with Tim bending over her. Thomas stood in the background, his face pale.

"What happened?" she cried, falling to her knees beside Ellen. The girl cradled her arm against her side and was in such pain she seemed to have trouble breathing. Sobs racked her thin body and she shook uncontrollably.

"She fell off the motorcycle," Tim said. "It was so fast I couldn't reach her in time to catch her." He was pale and shaken, too. "I think she broke her arm."

Anne Marie brought Ellen carefully into her embrace. "Call 9-1-1," she shouted.

Tim rushed into the other room.

Anne Marie didn't have a lot of medical experience, but it seemed to her that Ellen was going into shock. That was when she lost it, too. "What's taking so long?" she yelled, fighting to hold back the panic.

Thomas rushed into the house and returned with a blanket, which he wrapped around Ellen's shoulders. Ellen's sobs tore at Anne Marie's heart and soon her own face was streaked with tears. She rocked Ellen, whispering words of comfort and reassurance as they waited for the paramedics.

An eternity passed before she finally heard the siren. As soon as the medical personnel arrived, they took over, and within minutes Ellen was loaded into the aid car. Anne Marie rode with her; Tim followed in his vehicle.

Thankfully the emergency room wasn't crowded. Ellen was given something to relieve the pain, then sent to have an X-ray of her arm.

The second her daughter had been wheeled out, Anne Marie whirled on Tim. "How could you let this happen?" she cried.

He shook his head hopelessly. "It was all so fast . . ." he said again.

Covering her face with both hands, she fought for composure. There was no point in blaming Tim; Ellen could just as easily have fallen at home with Anne Marie.

"I'm sorry," she whispered.

He slid his arm around her shoulders. "So am I," he said, pressing his head to hers. "I knew the instant she landed that she'd broken a bone."

At just that moment Vanessa walked into the

cubicle. When she saw Tim with his arm around Anne Marie and their heads together, she exploded. "I knew it! I knew it! The minute I'm out of the picture you go after Tim. . . . So much for all that crap about not being interested in him. You've been after Tim from the day you met."

Anne Marie couldn't believe what she was hearing. She blinked in confusion. "What?" she asked.

"You want Tim."

"Vanessa!" he warned. "Stop it."

"I won't stop. Do you think I'm blind?" she demanded. "I saw how the two of you were looking at each other."

"Don't be ridiculous."

A nurse stepped into the cubicle. "You need to keep your voices down," she said. "If there's a problem here, I advise you to take it outside."

Reluctantly Tim stood up. "Come on," he said to Vanessa. "Let's talk about this without half the hospital listening in."

They left and Anne Marie relaxed a little. She'd had enough of Vanessa's hysterics for one day. Brushing her disheveled hair out of her face, she closed her eyes and wondered if she'd made a big mistake letting Tim into their lives. Just then, it seemed she had.

Before she could brood any more on the situation, the technician was back with Ellen and a copy of the X-ray. "Looks like you're going to get a cast," he said to Ellen.

Her daughter's face was dry of tears now but her eyes were wide and curious. "Can I have a pink one?"

"I'll see what Dr. Sawyer has to say about that."

It took another hour before the arm was set and the cast in place. Ellen looked admiringly down at her arm, which was encased in a hot-pink cast, and smiled up at Anne Marie. "It still hurts really bad."

"I know it does, sweetheart."

Ellen scooted out of the chair. "Where's Dad?"

"With Vanessa."

Ellen said nothing, just stared at the floor.

The assistant brought in paperwork for Anne Marie to sign. Once she did, they were free to go. Tim sat out in the waiting area and stood up when they appeared.

Ellen showed no delight at seeing him.

Tim knelt in front of her. "How's my girl?" he asked.

"Okay. I have a cast."

"So I see."

"If you'd take me back to my car, I'd appreciate it," Anne Marie said wearily.

"Of course. My dad lent me his. All I had at the house was the Harley."

Anne Marie didn't *care* who the car belonged to as long as she got where she needed to go. On the drive back to the family home, she didn't inquire about Vanessa. Frankly, she didn't care where the other woman was; she was just grateful not to be dealing with her anymore.

Anne Marie sat in the backseat with Ellen and got out as soon as he'd parked. All she wanted to do was escape, to get her daughter home.

"Apologize to your parents for me," she said, unfastening Ellen's seat belt. "I'm sure they'll understand."

Hands in his pockets, Tim stood helplessly by as Anne Marie led Ellen to her car. "If there's anything I can do . . ." he offered.

"There isn't," she said stiffly.

"Can I phone you later and see how Ellen's doing?"

She didn't mean to be rude but she couldn't face him again that night. "I'd rather you didn't. Tomorrow would be fine."

"Okay." He accepted that without argument. "Remember to call if there's anything I can do."

She nodded, but as far as Anne Marie was concerned Tim had done quite enough.

CHAPTER
33

Alix Turner

A lix, we need to talk."
Alix tensed. She recognized her
employer's tone of voice and it was ominous. Alix
had already had a heart-to-heart with Winter Adams,
owner of the French Café, a few days earlier.

Alix had made a costly mistake this morning, her
second that week. In both instances the entire batch
of dough had to be dumped, wasting the ingredients and the time. Alix knew she was in the wrong,
and she knew the mistakes had occurred because
she was so agitated, mentally and physically.

Although she'd gone several days without a cigarette, her body still screamed for nicotine. It was
supposed to get easier, but it hadn't. She knew why,
too, but that didn't help.

"Are you going to fire me?" Alix demanded. She
stepped into the office and held herself rigid,
expecting the worst. It was what she deserved. If
having to toss two different batches wasn't bad
enough, Alix had been irritable all week. She was
afraid her employer had grown tired of her short
temper, and what had happened this morning was
the final straw. Winter obviously intended to let her
go.

She looked at Alix and sighed loudly. "It's not what I want to do. If you recall, I asked you to take over as manager next week when I'm on vacation."

"But you're doing it anyway, right?" Alix didn't know why she felt the need to ask. Losing her job now would be disastrous. She and Jordan were living at the lake house, so with saving for a place of their own, increased transportation costs and much higher utilities, their budget was stretched to the limit. She'd had to give up cigarettes out of necessity as much as desire. She simply couldn't afford to smoke.

"No," Winter returned thoughtfully. "You've been a wonderful employee until just recently. I'm hoping you can resolve whatever's bothering you." She looked directly at Alix. "Do you think that's possible?"

Alix swallowed hard and nodded. It was easy to blame her bad mood on her need for a smoke; however, the reason was more than her craving for nicotine.

The cigarettes were a convenient excuse, but the underlying problem was her fear of motherhood. She yearned for a child; at the same time the prospect still terrified her. Jordan did his best to reassure her but Alix couldn't help worrying about her abilities as a mother. Her husband was willing to take the risk, willing to believe they'd be good parents. Alix was the one who doubted.

"I'll work on a better attitude," Alix promised as she left the office.

"Giving up smoking isn't easy," Winter said sympathetically. "It causes mood swings and concentration problems—but with you I sense it's more than that."

"It is," Alix agreed.

"Do you need some time to clear your head?" Winter asked.

"Could I have an hour?"

"Absolutely."

Removing her apron, Alix decided she'd take a walk. She set out for the small park close to Blossom Street, her strides brisk, her thoughts no less so.

The day was overcast, dark skies threatening rain, but the weather suited her mood. The play section of the park was deserted. Alix sat on a swing and placed both hands on the chain, gently swaying back and forth.

"Hi."

Alix glanced up to see Casey Marshall standing off to one side, looking morose. They'd talked a couple of times and understood each other, since they shared a similar background, with all the insecurities it engendered.

"Hey, what's got you down?" Alix asked, putting aside her own troubles.

"I came to say goodbye."

"Goodbye?"

"I'm going to my new foster home next week."

"So soon?"

Casey bit her lip. "It's a good place. Evelyn told me. The best, she said."

"I hated moving, too," Alix told her. She remembered stuffing everything she possessed in a small suitcase, leaving behind friends, pets and life as she'd known it for those months or years. Settling in with a new family was always difficult. She'd hated starting over.

"It's just that . . ." Casey left the rest unsaid. She sat in the swing next to Alix and kicked at the ground with the toe of her tennis shoes.

Alix didn't need her to finish the thought. "It's hard to leave Lydia and Brad, isn't it?"

Casey nodded. "They . . . they're great. I know I sort of got pushed on them," she murmured. "They want to adopt a baby . . . Everyone does, right?"

"Right." Alix couldn't argue with the facts. Infants were quickly adopted and older children were often shuffled from home to home, family to family, never having the opportunity to put down roots in any one community.

"When I first came to them, I . . . I didn't want to be there. It was only supposed to be a couple of days. Lydia and Brad opened their home to me and . . . and their hearts, too. I didn't want to like them, but I did. I do." Sadness seemed to emanate from her as she stared down at the ground.

"I know." And Alix did. In the beginning she'd tried to blend in with her foster families, too, trying to prove she could be one of them, that she was worthy of love.

"It didn't work," Casey continued. "Everything I did was a disaster."

"I'm sure that's not true." Alix was well aware of how hard Lydia had tried to make Casey feel welcome and part of their family.

"It *is!*" Casey cried. "Last night I tried to surprise Lydia and make dinner and then the casserole boiled over and smoke was pouring out of the oven and the fire alarm started beeping and dinner was ruined." She said this in one giant breath.

"Did Brad or Lydia get upset?"

Casey shook her head. "Brad made a big joke of it. He said the fire alarm should be called the dinner bell."

Despite the seriousness of the conversation, Alix smiled.

"And Cody thought it was cool 'cause we had to order pizza."

"And Lydia?"

Casey glanced away. "Lydia . . . put her arm around me and said I shouldn't worry about it. Then she showed me where she keeps the bigger casserole dish so if I wanted to try again I'd know which one to use."

"So no one was upset with you."

Casey jerked her head up. "*I* was upset with me,"

she countered. "This was my way of thanking them and the whole dinner backfired."

The girl still looked upset; Alix understood that. Casey had wanted to do something nice and instead she'd revealed her incompetence. She was being unnecessarily hard on herself, which was a tendency Alix shared. She exaggerated every little thing that went wrong. At the moment Alix was sure Casey felt her whole life had been one mistake after another and everything she attempted was a disaster.

"That's not all, either," Casey said. "Lydia hired me to do small jobs at the store and she even paid me. She didn't need to do that, but she did and then I goofed up really bad."

"How?"

It didn't seem possible that Casey's shoulders could droop any lower, but they did. "Lydia asked me to put price stickers on a shipment of yarn. There were two different kinds of yarn and I accidentally switched the prices, so the expensive yarn was priced really low. As soon as I got it on the shelf, a lady came in and bought every skein and said Lydia had to give her the price I put on."

"Did Lydia do it?"

Casey nodded.

Alix would bet Margaret had something to say about *that*.

"I told Lydia I'd pay her back but she said it

wasn't that big a deal. It was, though, and she lost a lot of money because I was careless."

"Casey," Alix said, "everyone makes mistakes. I made a big one this morning at the café and my employer had an excellent excuse to let me go."

"What did you do that was so bad?" she asked as though it couldn't possibly have been as bad as what she'd done.

Alix wasn't keen on proclaiming her stupidity. "I forgot the sugar in the cinnamon rolls. I bake them practically every morning and today I just left it out and the whole batch was ruined."

"Did everyone get mad?"

"No, but those ingredients cost money, and then there's also the time involved. Ms. Adams could've fired me, with good reason."

"She didn't though, right?"

"No, she didn't, and I'm grateful."

Casey sat up a little straighter. "So, like you said, everyone makes mistakes?"

"Yeah. What's important is the lessons we learn from them. You were telling me Lydia showed you where she kept the larger casserole dish so you'd know which one to use next time."

"Yeah."

"So when you decide to cook again, you'll use the bigger dish."

"Of course."

"See? Lesson learned."

Casey gave her a wry smile and shrugged.

"Besides, I don't like cleaning ovens. It's hard work, even if the oven's supposed to be self-cleaning."

"Which is precisely my point," Alix said. "Jordan always says that failure offers us an opportunity to learn and to grow." She grinned. "The trick is not to make the same mistake twice." From experience, including that week's baking calamities, Alix knew it was a lot easier said than done.

Casey brightened. "If I ever put price stickers on yarn again, I'll double-check to make sure the right price is on the right skein."

Alix patted the other girl's shoulder. "Exactly. See what I mean?"

"Cody makes mistakes, too. Only they aren't as big as mine." Casey said with a half smile.

"That's because he's younger than you. The mistakes get bigger as we get older."

"That makes sense," Casey agreed. "Breaking a glass when he's setting the table isn't as bad as ruining a whole dinner."

"You're pretty smart for a kid," Alix teased.

Gripping the chain with both hands, Casey started to swing higher. "I feel better."

"Good." For that matter, so did Alix.

"I bet you'll make a great mom."

Great mom. Great mom. The words repeated themselves in Alix's mind like a chant—or a prayer. "You think so?" she asked, unable to disguise her uncertainty.

"Yeah." Casey pushed herself higher on the swing. "Lydia told me you're quitting cigarettes so you and Jordan can get pregnant."

Unable to respond because of the lump clogging her throat, Alix simply nodded.

"Thank you," she whispered when she could speak again. *A great mom.* Casey couldn't have known how profoundly those words had affected her.

Their short conversation was the turning point in Alix's day. When she returned to work, she went to see Winter immediately.

"Yes?" her employer asked, looking up from her computer.

"I wanted to thank you for letting me keep my job," Alix said. "I love working here and I'm grateful that you're willing to forgive my crappy mood."

Winter smiled. "You're welcome, Alix. Except for this week, you've been a wonderful employee."

"That's not going to change," Alix told her fervently.

That afternoon, Alix could hardly wait to get home. On the bus ride, she tapped her foot nervously, the events of the afternoon tumbling through her mind.

Once she got to the lake house, she picked fresh lettuce from their small garden patch and made a Cobb salad, a favorite of Jordan's. When she'd finished preparing the salad, she put it in the refrigerator, then set the table outside. After that, she lay in the hammock with a book and fell asleep in the late-afternoon sunshine, waiting for Jordan.

The sound of the front door opening woke her. For a moment she was disoriented and then she knew—her husband was home.

"Alix?" Jordan called out.

"Jordan!" Alix rushed into the house toward him, catapulting herself into his arms. Before he could say a word, she spread eager kisses across his face, her lips moving from his eyes and cheeks and nose before settling on his lips.

Jordan grabbed her by the waist and staggered backward until he was leaning against the kitchen wall.

Alix wrapped her legs around his and hungrily kissed him again.

She lifted her head and smiled at him.

"What's this all about?" Jordan asked, his voice rough with longing. "Not that I'm complaining . . ."

"I'm going to be a good mother. A great one."

"Yes, I know," he said without hesitation. He supported the back of her head and returned her mouth to his for another series of deep, soul-filled kisses.

She gasped when the last kiss ended. Her lips remained close to his, so that she breathed his breath and he breathed hers.

He kissed her again, then asked, "What happened to convince you?"

Alix pressed her head to his shoulder. "Do you want to talk all night or do you want to make a baby?"

Jordan chuckled and scooped her up, Alix's arms around his neck. As he started toward their bedroom, he said, "That's a ridiculous question if I ever heard one," and her laughter joined his.

CHAPTER
34

Anne Marie Roche

Ellen's cast had been on for nearly a week and Tim had come by every afternoon to check on her. Vanessa hadn't accompanied him even once, which was just as well, considering the scene at the hospital. Anne Marie avoided mentioning the other woman's name and so did Tim.

Ellen's arm had stopped hurting and she thrived on the extra attention. Anne Marie had to ask Tim to stop bringing gifts. Ellen had so many stuffed animals now, there was no space in her bedroom for more.

"What time will my dad be here?" Ellen asked, bounding down the stairs with Baxter at her heels. She swung the leash in one hand.

"Soon."

"Does he know you have a hot date?"

The urge to roll her eyes was nearly overwhelming. Barbie and Mark had arranged for her to meet a friend of Mark's; Barbie had made the mistake of referring to the evening as a "hot date" in Ellen's presence. Ellen, of course, had picked up on the term and used it ever since.

"I didn't tell him where I was going, no," Anne Marie said. When she'd told him she had an appointment Friday evening, Tim had quickly offered to stay with Ellen. Foolishly, perhaps, Anne Marie had accepted. Her mother would gladly have had Ellen over for the night, but that would've entailed driving. It was simpler this way.

Tim genuinely loved Ellen. If Anne Marie had ever doubted that, he'd proved his feelings for the child the day Ellen broke her arm. He'd been as pale as a bleached sheet when he realized what had happened and he'd blamed himself. He'd been vigilant, almost excessively so, ever since.

"Can I tell him?" Ellen asked.

"Ah . . ." Anne Marie hesitated, preferring he not be told where she was going. It wasn't any of his business.

"Tell who what?" Barbie asked as she stepped into the bookstore. Mark followed in his wheelchair.

"My dad," Ellen said.

"Tim's staying with Ellen while I'm out this evening," Anne Marie explained.

"On a hot date," her daughter added with emphasis on the *hot*. She attached the leash to

Baxter's collar and after hugging both Barbie and Mark, shot out the door, taking Baxter for his afternoon stroll down Blossom Street.

"Hot date, huh?" Mark said once Ellen was halfway down the block.

Anne Marie pretended to be upset with him. "That's what she calls it, thanks to you two."

"Just wait till you meet Mel," Barbie said with a wink. "He's wonderful—smart, funny and sexy as hell."

Mark glared up at Barbie. "He's not *that* sexy."

Barbie's smile lit up her eyes. "Mark, don't tell me you're jealous?"

"Should I be?"

At that Barbie laughed outright. "You tell me."

They gazed at each other, exchanging some private message, and slowly a grin slid into place. "Maybe not," he murmured in a low, husky voice.

Barbie bent and kissed his cheek. "I don't have any reason for complaint, sir—and I don't think you do, either."

Now it was Mark who winked. "Your point is well taken, madam."

Anne Marie laughed. She loved the banter between these two. Barbie and Mark somehow brought out the best in each other. According to what she'd heard, he'd been surly and downright rude when he and Barbie originally met—at the movies, of all places. The first time Anne Marie had met him was in a fast-food restaurant and it was plain, at least to her, that Mark was in love with Barbie. She suspected he'd fought the attraction as long as he could, then simply surrendered to the sheer force of Barbie's personality.

"We've come to give you a few tips," Barbie announced.

Mark, however, seemed more interested in studying a selection of mysteries, which were displayed on a table close to the front of the store.

"What kind of tips?" Anne Marie asked.

"Dating tips, of course!"

Mark set aside Sue Grafton's *T is for Trespass* and glanced up. "This is all Barbie's idea."

Fortunately the bookstore was empty. Anne Marie would hate having customers privy to this conversation.

"It's been a while since you dated, hasn't it?"

Her last supposed date had been with Tim, when he'd dropped the bombshell about Vanessa. The memory of their evening together still embarrassed her.

In retrospect, she should've noticed the signs; she'd made the mistake of assuming Tim was interested in her just because she was enthralled with *him*. To her, it'd been like linking two pieces of puzzle and finding they fit perfectly. No, not two pieces, three. Tim and Ellen and her . . . the fantasy of a family.

"It has been a while," Anne Marie agreed.

"The rules have changed," Barbie said with authority.

Anne Marie turned to Mark for guidance. He, however, was back to exploring the mystery and thriller titles. He held Brad Meltzer's latest and was studying the cover. Seeing that he wasn't going to be any help, she sighed. "What do you mean?" she asked.

"Forget what those dating books tell you. Just be yourself," Barbie advised.

"I know Mel's a widower, but does he have children?" That was a subject she felt she could discuss. Knowing they shared common ground would be a great starting point.

"They're grown and married."

"How old is this guy, anyway?"

"Age is a matter of attitude," Barbie insisted.

Anne Marie groaned. "Oh, come on, Barbie."

Barbie relented. "He's not that old. In his fifties."

Robert's age, Anne Marie mused. Her husband had died of a heart attack far too young; he'd been in his fifties, too. Even now, it was hard to believe he was dead.

Out of the corner of her eye Anne Marie saw that Louis, her new part-time employee, had come in. He was a student at UW and worked evenings.

"I'm sure Mel and I won't have a problem finding things to talk about," Anne Marie told her friend. He'd lost his wife a year ago and Robert had been gone more than two.

"I'm sure you won't," Barbie said, taking a *Vogue* magazine from the rack and leafing through it.

"Listen, I wish I could chat longer, but I need to go and change."

"Wear something bright and cheerful," Barbie told her.

"Okay." Anne Marie didn't bother to say she'd already planned to.

"You're meeting at the restaurant, correct?"

"Correct," Anne Marie confirmed. She wanted it that way, despite Barbie and Mark's assurances that Mel would be happy to pick her up.

She hugged Barbie and pecked Mark on the cheek, then headed upstairs to change clothes for her "hot date."

By the time she'd finished, Ellen and Baxter had returned. Ellen stared at her. "You look really pretty."

That comment pleased Anne Marie, and she glanced at the hallway mirror. She wanted to make a positive first impression and had chosen her outfit carefully. She wore white linen pants with a pale yellow shell under a white blazer. Even to her own critical eye, she looked good.

She'd taken as long to decide on the jewelry—an antique cameo on a gold chain—as the clothes themselves. She'd had her hair done earlier in the day; she'd needed a haircut, anyway, so she'd timed it to coincide with her date.

A knock at the back door told her Tim had arrived. Ellen let him in. "What did you bring me, what did you bring me?" she asked, jumping up and down.

This was exactly the behavior Anne Marie wanted to put a stop to. Ellen had become a little too accustomed to his frequent gifts.

"Dinner." Tim set a white bag on the kitchen table. He did a double-take when he saw Anne Marie. "You look fabulous. What's the occasion?"

"Thanks." She ignored the question and drank in the appreciation shining in his eyes.

Ellen gladly supplied the news. "Mom's got a hot date."

Tim's smile faded. "You're going out? I thought you had an appointment."

"I do. It's an appointment for dinner." She didn't feel it was necessary to explain any more than she already had. Tim didn't keep *her* updated on his relationship with Vanessa.

"I see," he murmured, but he didn't ask any further questions.

"I won't be late . . . I don't think," she said as she retrieved her purse and her car keys.

"Ten?"

"Maybe, but to be on the safe side let's say eleven. If I'm going to be any later, I'll phone." She probably would anyway, just to check up on Ellen, whose arm still hurt at night.

"Take as long as you want," Tim said.

"You don't need to be home at any particular time?"

Tim shook his head. "None." He opened the door. "Have a nice evening." His gaze held hers and his words seemed sincere.

"Thank you." Anne Marie kissed Ellen, gave her final instructions, then left the apartment.

Mel turned out to be everything Barbie and Mark had promised. To begin with, he was distinguished-looking, dressed in a classy suit and tie, and sexy in that Sean Connery way she found so attractive. Like Mark, he was an architect. Their dinner conversation didn't lag even once; they discovered in short order that they shared the same political views, enjoyed many of the same movies and authors, and were both Placido Domingo fans. The evening passed so quickly that Anne Marie was startled to see it was after ten.

"Oh, my goodness," she said as she reached for her purse. "I need to check on my daughter." She paused, not wanting to appear rude.

Mel gestured with his hand. "Go ahead, by all means."

Tim answered on the second ring and immediately reassured Anne Marie. "Everything went great. Ellen's been asleep for over an hour."

"Did she say her prayers?"

Tim chuckled. "Oh, yes. Does it generally go on as long as it did this evening?"

"Five minutes?" The child took her prayers seriously.

"Longer."

"I figured as much." No doubt Ellen had been hoping to impress her father.

"She prayed for you," Tim informed her. "She seems to think you're going to marry your, uh, hot date."

"That's interesting. And how did she feel about it?"

"She seemed okay with it."

Anne Marie smiled across the table at Mel.

"When do you think you'll be back?" Tim was asking.

"In about half an hour." She didn't want to continue a conversation with Tim while she was with her date, so she ended the call. "See you then." She dropped the cell back in her bag.

They finished the last of their coffee, and then Anne Marie regretfully said she'd have to go. Mel walked her to her car, one hand lightly clasping her elbow. It was a gesture both protective and respectful, and it reminded her suddenly of Robert.

"Thank you for a lovely evening," she said. "I really enjoyed meeting you."

"Would it be possible to see you again?" Mel asked.

"I'd like that."

He leaned forward to kiss her cheek. "I haven't dated since Laura died, and . . . well, meeting you has been a *very* pleasant surprise."

It had been for Anne Marie, as well.

As she drove home, a relaxed, comfortable feeling stole over her. She'd agreed to this date because of Tim. Her attraction to him had shown her that she'd healed enough to enter into a new relationship. It'd led to an embarrassing situation but she'd recovered from that. One thing was certain: She wasn't going to make any assumptions about Mel. Like her, he still carried the pain of having lost a spouse. That loss would never entirely leave either of them.

Tim was flipping through a copy of *The New Yorker* when she walked into the apartment. As soon as he saw her, he threw down the magazine.

"Well," he said, standing, "how did it go?"

"Fine," she told him, then amended her statement. "Actually, it went really well. I like Mel."

Tim nodded, sliding his hands into his back jean pockets.

"Thank you for staying with Ellen. My mother said she'd watch her, but I hated to drag Ellen over there. She still wakes up once or twice a night because her arm aches."

"You're welcome," he said, but he seemed reluctant to leave.

"Anything I can get you?" she asked, taking off her linen jacket.

"A cup of coffee?"

"Sure." She moved into the kitchen and brewed a small pot, filling two cups. "How do you take it?"

404

"Black." She recalled that but didn't want to seem presumptuous—or interested enough to notice.

Tim was already sitting at the kitchen table, his elbows propped on a place mat. Anne Marie handed him the coffee, then sat across from him, waiting for him to speak.

Eventually he did. "I thought you should know I'm no longer seeing Vanessa."

"I'm . . . sorry to hear that."

"She recently had a second slip. She got drunk."

Anne Marie nodded; she remembered he'd mentioned the first time this had happened.

"Once I could forgive, but when I found out she'd been drinking again, I told her it was over. I can't expose Ellen to that, and Vanessa's behavior the afternoon Ellen broke her arm was inexcusable."

"I'm sorry if I played a role in this," Anne Marie felt obliged to say.

Tim ignored that. "Vanessa has to accept responsibility for her own actions, the same way we all do."

Anne Marie reached across the table and touched his arm. "I know this must be hard on you."

He gave her a sad smile. "I'd planned to tell you this earlier in the evening, about Vanessa and me." He hesitated.

"Yes?" Clearly there was more.

"And suggest the two of us start dating," he said.

"I never did have a good sense of timing," he added with a rueful laugh.

He couldn't have shocked her more. "The two of . . . us?" She'd put the matter so completely out of her mind, she hardly knew how to react.

"Would you consider it?" he asked.

"I . . . yes, I'll think about it," she said, still in a daze.

Tim took a single sip of his coffee, then got to his feet.

Anne Marie walked him to the door.

As they reached it, he turned back. "Maybe this will help," he said and before she realized what he was going to do, he pressed his mouth to hers. The kiss was tender and persuasive, so persuasive that her knees felt as if they might buckle.

"Good night, Anne Marie," he whispered in a voice that didn't sound like his.

He left, and Anne Marie leaned against the door, eyes wide with shock . . . and pleasure. This was a *most* unexpected turn of events.

CHAPTER 35

Watching a complex stitch pattern grow as I knit silences the voice in my head that tells me to sweep the floor. I imagine dust bunnies are knitting themselves together under my chair.
—Katherine Misegades, designer.
www.atimetoknit.com

Lydia Goetz

Casey was so quiet lately and standoffish, too. I'd tried to reach her, but the harder I tried the more she withdrew. This frustrated me to no end.

I had Saturday free, my first since the day we'd rented bikes at Green Lake. After looking through the newspaper ads, I decided to do some school shopping for Cody and for Casey, too. I assumed . . . I hoped Casey might enjoy going shopping with me.

Brad, Cody and I had already had breakfast by the time Casey emerged from her bedroom.

"Morning, beautiful," Brad said, smiling. He sat at the kitchen table, lingering over his coffee before he headed out to mow the lawn. During the summer he'd started calling Casey *beautiful* and *princess*.

At first Casey had scowled and claimed she

wasn't beautiful nor was she anyone's princess. Brad ignored those comments and continued— until she either accepted his affection or got tired of arguing with him.

"Morning," came her less-than-friendly reply.

"I'm glad you're up," I said, forcing some enthusiasm into my voice. "How about a trip to the mall? Just you and me."

Casey opened the cupboard and took out a box of cereal. "What for?"

Her wariness surprised me. I'd figured this would be one invitation she'd jump at. What twelve-year-old girl *didn't* want to visit the mall?

"Do you need a reason to shop?" I asked.

She shrugged, but I could see that, despite herself, her interest was piqued.

"I need to get Cody some jeans for school and a new winter coat. He hates shopping."

"So do I," Brad inserted.

"Like father, like son," I said blithely.

As Casey shook cereal into her bowl and poured milk over top, she offered me a quick smile.

"You can help me pick out the things he needs," I coaxed. "Wanna come?"

"I guess." This was said as if she was doing me a tremendous favor by keeping me company.

"While we're out we should get a few things for you, too." I waited in vain for a reaction, although I'd felt confident she'd be excited at the prospect.

As though the very idea bored her, she said, "I usually get my clothes from Goodwill."

"Then it'll be fun to have something new," I countered.

She shrugged again. "Can we see Grandma Hoffman today?"

I smiled, touched by the affection she felt for my mother. Their unlikely friendship was a gift for both of them. And for me. Casey had visited only that one time and I'd been hoping to arrange a second trip. "Sure," I said. "We'll do that."

"Okay." She ate her breakfast, disappeared for ten minutes, then returned dressed and ready to go.

"I still need to put on my makeup," I told her. It takes me longer to reach the beautiful stage, although I didn't point that out. "By the way, Margaret and her family will be over later this evening, so we'll pick up dessert on the way home."

"Are they coming for dinner?" Brad asked.

"No, Julia's got a softball game but they're stopping by for dessert afterward."

"What kind of dessert?" Cody asked, coming into the kitchen to get Chase a dog biscuit.

"I ordered an ice cream cake."

He grinned, nodding in approval. "Good idea, Mom."

I thought so, too. I always felt a bit guilty buying a cake when it was so easy to bake one, but ice cream was the perfect summertime dessert.

Casey sat in the living room waiting for me. She held a small paper bag and although I was curious, I didn't ask what it contained. Nor did she tell me.

"Can we see Grandma Hoffman first?" she asked when I'd backed the car out of the garage and onto the street.

"That's fine." The assisted living complex wasn't far from the mall.

We parked, and Casey was out of the car before I could even unfasten my seat belt. I hurried to catch up with her. Casey's eagerness was quite a contrast to Cody's discomfort. He'd been to visit my mother any number of times, but he quickly grew bored. After ten or fifteen minutes he was ready to leave.

I hadn't phoned ahead and hoped we wouldn't be interrupting anything. I found Mom sitting in front of the television, watching the Food Channel as usual. She had a pen and pad in hand and seemed to be trying to write down the instructions. I hadn't seen her do that in some time. Over the past few years, she'd filled several spiral-bound notebooks with carefully detailed recipes, but she hadn't done it recently. Often, when we spoke on the phone, it was about these wonderful cooks and the recipes they'd demonstrated on television. Mom had always enjoyed making family dinners, and it hurt me that this small joy had been taken away from her.

When Casey and I entered the apartment, Mom's eyes brightened, then immediately dimmed. I realized she'd forgotten Casey's name, although she obviously recognized her face.

"Casey and I thought we'd stop by for a quick visit," I said, mentioning her name so Mom wouldn't need to ask.

"Casey," Mom repeated, stretching out her hand.

Casey plopped down on the floor, sitting cross-legged next to Mom's chair. She took her hand. "I brought you a gift," she said.

"Me?"

"Yes." Casey bobbed her head. "We made them at day camp this summer and I want you to have it so you'll remember me."

Mom's pleasure was undeniable as she reached for the bag. "What could it be?" she asked pensively.

Casey knelt in front of her as she opened the plain brown sack. Inside was a photograph of Casey wearing a baseball cap, with her arm around Cody's neck. They were smiling into the camera. The picture was set inside a plastic canvas frame into which Casey had woven blue and teal yarn.

To my utter amazement my mother blinked back tears. "How nice," she whispered.

"It's got a magnet on the back so you can stick it on your fridge," Casey explained, turning it over so Mom could see.

I don't think she noticed how emotional my mother had become or, if she did, Casey chose to pretend otherwise. "Would you like me to put it on the fridge for you?"

411

Mom nodded. When Casey moved into the kitchen, Mom dabbed at her eyes with the handkerchief she always tucked in her sweater pocket.

"That was a lovely thing to do," I said, joining Casey in the kitchen. I put my arm around her shoulders but I could tell she didn't want me touching her, so I quickly let go.

"You don't mind that I gave it to Grandma Hoffman rather than you?" she asked a little anxiously.

I assured her I didn't. "It's a lovely photo and you can see how much it means to my mother."

For the first time in what seemed like weeks Casey gave me a genuine smile. "I'm going to miss everyone . . . I think your mom's so nice. And she's funny. I never had a grandma before, and well . . . I wanted her to have something to remember me by."

We didn't stay much longer; it was getting close to Mom's lunch and after that she'd nap for an hour or two.

Once we got to the mall, our first stop was the Sears store, where I traditionally purchased Cody's school clothes. I'd read their two-page advertisement that morning and noticed that all boys' jeans were on sale.

"You should buy him this shirt, too," Casey said, holding up an olive-green T-shirt with some monster character printed on the front.

Cody had been wearing mostly shirts in primary colors. He was long past the stage where he wanted to wear anything with Disney characters, but I wasn't really familiar with any appropriate alternatives.

"He'd like that?" I asked.

"He'd love it," Casey said confidently.

"All right, then. Put it on the stack."

Casey did and then glanced at another one.

"Do you see anything else he might like?"

She nodded. "Lots."

"Are they on sale, too?"

Casey pointed at the sign. *Fifty percent off.* Together we chose three other shirts and one good pair of pants and a button-down shirt for church. She picked out a winter coat, although it wasn't anything I would've selected.

Cody was growing like a well-watered plant and I suspected that by Christmas he'd need a size larger in jeans. Yet with so many sales and such reasonable prices, it was hard not to go overboard now.

We paid for our purchases, and I suggested we go to the teen department to buy something for Casey.

Casey didn't seem to like the idea. "Why?"

"You're going to need new clothes for school, too," I said.

"I'll get my stuff later. Don't worry about it."

The attitude was back and I didn't know why. "Casey, you don't have to buy your clothes second-hand."

Bored, she glanced away. "Whatever."

"Let's at least find you a pair of jeans, okay?"

Anyone looking at her disgruntled expression would think I was punishing her, and yet I knew she enjoyed shopping. While picking out clothes for Cody she'd been interested, even excited. She was good at it, too.

Despite her protests I managed to buy her one new pair of jeans. She rejected everything else. I didn't understand it.

As we ate at the food court I talked about how pleased my mother had been with her gift and gradually Casey's mood started to improve. On the way back to the house we went to the local ice cream parlor, where I'd ordered the cake.

By the time we returned home, the lawn had been mowed. Through my open window I breathed in the distinctive, pungent scent of fresh grass, which brought back immediate memories of childhood summers. When I'd parked, Casey carried in our purchases and I put the cake inside the garage freezer.

Brad and Cody had gathered around the table as Casey proudly showed off our bargains. "Wow, this is cool," Cody said, holding up the olive green T-shirt.

"Casey chose that for you," I said, and we exchanged a smile.

"Take her shopping with you all the time, Mom." Cody pulled off his old shirt and immediately slipped the new one over his head, muffling his last few words.

Casey looked down at the floor. "I won't be here," she said.

Brad turned to me and then to Cody. We both nodded.

"Yes, you will," Brad said softly.

Casey jerked her head up. "What do you mean?"

"We want you to live with us," Cody blurted out. "Mom and Dad and I talked it over, and we want you to stay."

Casey didn't seem to believe him. "I can stay here as your foster kid?"

"No, Casey. We want you to be our *daughter,* part of our family," I said, my voice cracking with emotion. "Brad and I want to adopt you."

"And I want you for my big sister," Cody added, refusing to be left out. "I didn't like you when you came here. *I* was supposed to be the oldest when they adopted 'nother kid." He grinned. "But, you know, it wouldn't be so bad to have a big sister."

Casey just stared at us.

"Would adopting you be all right?" I asked.

"You mean it?" she asked, her voice barely above a whisper, as though testing us to see if this was some cruel hoax.

Brad and Cody nodded vigorously.

"This isn't a trick, is it?" Her eyes implored me and then Brad before she swiveled around to look at Cody.

"No, Casey, we mean it," I said. "We love you and want you to be with us."

"Forever and ever," Cody chimed in.

I saw tears form in Casey's eyes. In all the weeks she'd been with us, I'd never seen her cry. Not once. She'd been terribly upset the day she'd heard from her brother but if she'd cried, she hadn't let anyone see. Emotion came to her so tentatively that when I saw how affected she was, my own eyes filled with tears. I gave her a watery smile.

"*That's* why we got the ice cream cake," Cody explained happily. "That's why Aunt Margaret and Uncle Matt are coming over tonight with Hailey and Julia."

Casey gulped back a sob and covered her mouth with both hands.

I reached for her, almost fearing she'd push me away as she so often had in the past. But Casey moved willingly into my arms and leaned her head against me, her shoulders shaking with sobs.

"We love you, Casey," I whispered through the tightness in my own throat.

"I . . . love you, too—all of you," she choked out.

I murmured quiet endearments as she clung to me and I to her.

"I hoped . . . I didn't want to leave you and . . ." She gulped between sobs.

"This is your home now," Brad told her, placing his arms around the two of us. Cody joined in, and I felt his small arm curl around my waist.

"We want to be your family," Cody said sweetly, "okay?"

"Okay." She hiccuped.

Family.

Casey might have come to us as an unexpected surprise, but she was in our hearts now and there she would stay.

EPILOGUE

There is no life without knitting; every pattern on my needles presents an exotic challenge. My love for knitting is similar to my mother-in-law's infatuation with her soap operas. On her deathbed, she said to me, "I don't mind dying, but could you put a TV in my coffin so I could see how my stories turn out?" That's how I feel about knitting. Could I please have needles and lots of yarn in my coffin so I can see how my patterns turn out?

—Rita Weiss, www.creativepartnersllc.com

The adoption went through rapidly and with ease, thanks to Evelyn Boyle, who smoothed the process for us. Only a month had passed, and now Brad, Cody, Casey and I stood before a judge to make legal what had begun from almost the moment Casey had arrived in our home.

Evelyn was with us as the judge asked a few simple questions, then declared Casey Marie Goetz to be our daughter.

The courtroom was respectfully quiet except for

my sister, Margaret, who sat in the front row and wept like a baby. I was emotional myself, but managed to hold back the tears until the judge made his declaration. Then I sniffled and turned to throw my arms around Casey.

She remained dry-eyed. But what I read in my daughter was joy—pure, profound joy. She hugged me back, squeezing hard in her enthusiasm. Then she hugged Brad and Cody and finally, to everyone's astonishment, she spoke to the judge.

"Would it be all right if I hugged you, too?" Casey asked, ready to bound up the steps.

At first the judge seemed taken aback. "I've never received such a request," he said formally. Then he grinned and added, "I do believe I'd like that very much."

Casey bolted up the steps and the judge stood and accepted her embrace.

"You're a very fortunate girl," he told her.

"I know," she said, locking eyes with me.

Margaret continued to wail in the background and I couldn't help it, I burst out laughing. So did Cody and Brad. You'd think my sister was at a funeral instead of a celebration.

I suddenly saw that Alix and Jordan were in the courtroom. I was touched that they'd come, along with some of our other friends. Susannah from the flower shop sat next to Alix, and of course Anne Marie and Ellen were there, too.

As Brad, Cody, Casey and I paraded out of the

courtroom, Margaret and Matt followed, with our friends trailing behind them.

"We're treating everyone to lunch," Brad called out. "It isn't every day a man gains a daughter."

"Especially one who can order off the adult menu," Casey told him smugly.

"I want to order off the adult menu, too," Cody insisted.

Someone suggested we go to Chinatown and as it happened, Brad knew a good restaurant that was on his UPS route. We'd eaten there once, and I'd found it delicious. And that way, *everyone* got to order from the adult menu.

As we left the courthouse, we ran into Hutch and Phoebe. To be honest, I'd forgotten the "Candy Man Trial," as it was being called in the media, was still going on.

"We won!" Phoebe cried jubilantly. "The jury came back with their decision less than half an hour ago."

"Was there ever any doubt?" Hutch asked, raising his eyebrows.

"You're joking, aren't you?" Phoebe said to Hutch. She turned to me. "I wish you could've seen Clark's face when I walked into the courtroom this afternoon. He assumed I was there for *him*."

I'd been following the case in the news and getting updates from the local TV station. In my view, Clark Snowden, the plaintiff's attorney, was exceedingly full of himself. He seemed to pose for the camera and struck me as both overconfident and egotistical. Even if the case itself hadn't been so ridiculous, his attitude alone would have swayed my opinion. I knew from talk around the shop that others shared my feelings.

I'd recently learned how Phoebe was linked to Clark, so of course I'd studied him on TV with avid interest.

"Phoebe's presence shocked him," Hutch was saying.

Her eyes gleamed with exhilaration. "When I walked over and sat behind Hutch, Clark didn't know *what* to think."

"He did once I told him you'd agreed to marry me."

"Congratulations!" I said, but I could see they were bursting with news from the trial and I was anxious to hear what had happened.

"It's a good thing you waited to show Clark your engagement ring until the recess—otherwise I'm betting the judge would've expelled him."

Phoebe agreed with an exaggerated shudder. "I thought he'd start frothing at the mouth." She went from jubilation to a moment's sadness. "I do feel bad for his father, though. This was yet another humiliation for Max. Clark's performance in the courtroom today was nothing to be proud of."

"Yeah, his closing argument was as weak as any I've ever heard," Hutch said. "It's no wonder the jury decided in my favor."

"I'd like to see anyone try and take *my* chocolates away," Margaret said, stepping up to join us.

I would, too. Clark Snowden was a fool if he expected to come between a woman and her chocolate. Having seen both men in action during the trial snippets on TV, I was firmly convinced that Phoebe had made a wise choice in Hutch. I loved seeing them together. They seemed a good match in so many ways, and I was thrilled to discover I'd been right in my assumptions of a romance between them.

"We came over to tell you the news and congratulate you, too," Hutch said. "This seems to be a day for celebrating."

"It is." Brad invited Hutch and Phoebe to join us for a celebratory lunch.

Unfortunately, Susannah had to get back to the shop. When the rest of us entered the restaurant, Brad explained to Mr. Wong, the proprietor, why we were there. In short order we were ushered into a private room.

Mr. Wong said we wouldn't need menus, and before long, plates and chopsticks were distributed and tea was poured.

"To family." Brad offered a toast, lifting his teacup.

Everyone around us raised theirs.

"We have an announcement," Jordan said, smiling fondly at Alix, who actually blushed.

"I'm pregnant," she said. "Jordan and I are having a baby."

"Congratulations!" everyone yelled.

"To enlarging families," Brad offered next.

"We have an announcement, too," Hutch said, taking Phoebe's right hand in his.

"You're pregnant, too?" Margaret asked, sounding shocked.

"Not yet," Phoebe said with a laugh. "But I hope to be soon after Hutch and I are married. The wedding's in October." She held up her left hand to show off her diamond engagement ring.

"Can I be the ring-bearer?" Cody asked.

"Cody," I whispered, "you should wait to be asked."

"Oh! If Cody's the ring-bearer, can I be the flower girl?" Ellen squealed.

"Ellen!" Anne Marie said, obviously embarrassed.

"It's okay if I'm not," the nine-year-old assured Phoebe. "I want to be in another wedding, but if I'm not in yours I'll be in Mom's."

Anne Marie's face reddened. "Ellen!"

"Is your mother getting married?" Brad asked in a teasing voice.

Ellen blew on her tea and sipped it carefully. Then she nodded. "Only we don't know who she's going to marry yet. There's my dad and then there's Mel. But I like my dad better."

"I think it would be a great idea for both of you to be in the wedding," Phoebe told the children. She spread out her arms to include everyone at the table. "I want you all there."

"Guess what? Our wedding cake's going to be chocolate," Hutch said.

The group laughed.

The food started to arrive then, platter after platter brought by an entire staff of waiters. As the dishes were set on the table, I saw that Casey had gone very still. She sat next to me and I reached for her hand.

"Is something wrong?" I leaned close to ask her.

"No." She shook her head. "I was just wondering if I'd always feel this way."

"What way?"

She pressed her free hand over her heart. "Happy," she whispered. "Really, really happy."

"I hope that happiness never leaves you," I whispered back.

"I belong," she said with such emotion that it was hard for me to swallow. "I belong."

"Yes," I said, slipping my arm around her shoulders. "You belong with us."

I shared my daughter's feeling. I'd found belonging, too—a husband, a home, a family. A whole world with all my friends on Blossom Street.

KNITTING PATTERN
CABLE SAMPLER SCARF

© 2009 Bev Galeskas/Fiber Trends, Inc.
www.Fibertrends.com

Size: About 8" wide by 60" long, relaxed after blocking.

Materials and Supplies: 5 skeins Harmony 8 ply 100% merino wool (50gr–130 yds per skein) or other DK weight yarn to equal gauge.

U.S. size 6 needles; cable needle.

Gauge: 21 sts = 4" (10 cm) in garter stitch.

Stitches and Abbreviations:

Sl-1 (Slip 1): All slip stitches on this pattern should be slipped purlwise with yarn in front of work.

k2tog: Knit 2 sts together as one.

Inc (increase): Lift the stitch below the stitch on left needle and place the loop on the point of left needle. Knit this loop, then knit the stitch. (1 st increased)

Brackets: Work all stitches within the brackets the specified number of times (x).

Asterisks: Repeat stitches between the asterisks, including any repeats within.

C6B (Cable 6 back): Slip 3 sts to the cable needle and hold in back of work. Knit next 3 sts from left needle, then k3 from cable needle.

C6F (Cable 6 front): Slip 3 sts to the cable needle and hold in front of work. Knit next 3 sts from left needle, then k3 from cable needle.

C4B (Cable 4 back): Slip 2 sts to the cable needle and hold in back of work. Knit next 2 sts from left needle, then k2 from cable needle.

C4F (Cable 4 front): Slip 2 sts to the cable needle and hold in front of work. Knit next 2 sts from left needle, then k2 from cable needle.

Notes: Scarf is bordered in garter stitch. These stitches are included in the directions, so there should not be a need to use markers.

Slip the first stitch of every row as if to purl with the yarn held in front of work.

Instructions:

Loosely cast on 43 sts.

Knit 10 rows (5 ridges of garter stitch).

Cable Pattern 1:

Set Up Row 1: (WS) Sl-1, k7, [p3, k3] 5x, k5.

Set Up Row 2: (RS) Sl-1, k4, p3, [inc in next 3 sts (see above for method),p3] 5x, k5. (58 sts)

Begin Cable Pattern:

Row 1 and all WS rows: Sl-1, k7, [p6, k3] 5x, k5.

Row 2: Sl-1, k4, p3, [k6, p3] 5x, k5.

Row 4: Sl-1, k4, p3, [C6B, p3] 5x, k5.

Rows 6 & 8: Repeat Row 2.

Work Rows 1 through 8 a total of 6 times, then Rows 1 through 5 once more.

Final Row: (RS) Sl-1, k7, *[k2tog] 3x, k3,* repeat to last 5 sts, k5. (43 sts)

Knit 10 rows (5 ridges of garter stitch), ending ready to begin a WS row.

Cable Pattern 2:

Set Up Row 1: (WS) Sl-1, k4, p33, k5.

Set Up Row 2: (RS) Sl-1, k4, p6, [k1, inc in next st, k1, p6] 3x, k5. (46 sts)

Begin Cable Pattern:

Rows 1, 3, 5 & 7: (WS) Sl-1, k10, [p4, k6] 3x, k5.

Row 2: (RS) Sl-1, [k4, p6] 4x, k5.

Row 4: Sl-1, k4, [p6, C4F] 3x, p6, k5.

Row 6: Repeat Row 2.

Rows 8 & 10: Sl-1, k4, p1, [k4, p6] 3x, k4, p1, k5.

Rows 9, 11, 13 & 15: Sl-1, k5, [p4, k6] 4x.

Row 12: Sl-1, k4, p1, [C4F, p6] 3x, C4F, p1, k5.

Row 14: Repeat Row 10.

Row 16: Repeat Row 2.

Work Rows 1 through 16 a total of 3 times, then Rows 1 through 7 once more.

Final Row: (RS) Sl-1, k11, k2tog, [k8, k2tog] 2x, k12. (43 sts)

Knit 10 rows (5 ridges of garter stitch), ending ready to begin a WS row.

Cable Pattern 3:

Set Up Rows 1 & 2: Work as for Cable Pattern 1. (58 sts)

Begin Cable Pattern:

Row 1 and all WS rows: Sl-1, k7, [p6, k3] 5x, k5.

Row 2: Sl-1, k4, p3, [k6, p3] 5x, k5.

Row 4: Sl-1, k4, p3, [C6B, p3] 5x, k5.

Rows 6, 8 & 10: Repeat Row 2.

Row 12: Sl-1, k4, p3, [C6F, p3] 5x, k5.

Rows 14 & 16: Repeat Row 2.

Work Rows 1 through 16 a total of 3 times, then Rows 1 through 5 once more.

Final Row: (RS) Sl-1, k7, *[k2tog] 3x, k3,* repeat to last 5 sts, k5. (43 sts)

Knit 10 rows (5 ridges of garter stitch), ending ready to begin a WS row.

Cable Pattern 4:

Set Up Row 1: Purl.

Set Up Row 2: Sl-1, k5, inc in next st, k3, [inc in next 2 sts, k2] 7x, k5. (58 sts)

Begin Cable Pattern:

Row 1 and all WS rows: Sl-1, k4, purl to last 5 sts, k5.

Row 2: Sl-1, k4, *C4F, k2,* repeat to last 5 sts, k5.

Row 4: Knit.

Row 6: Sl-1, k6, *C4B, k2,* repeat to last 9 sts, C4B, k5.

Row 8: Knit.

Work Rows 1 through 8 a total of 6 times, then Rows 1 through 7 once more.

Final Row: (RS) Sl-1, k5, k2tog, k4, *[k2tog] 2x, k2,* repeat to last 10 sts, [k2tog] 2x, k6. (43 sts)

Knit 10 rows (5 ridges of garter stitch), ending ready to begin a WS row.

Cable Pattern 5:

Work Set Up Rows 1 & 2 as for Cable Pattern 1. (58 sts)

Begin Cable Pattern:

Row 1 and all WS Rows: Sl-1, k7, [p6, k3] 5x, k5.

Row 2: Sl-1, k4, [p3, C4B, k2] 5x, p3, k5.

Row 4: Sl-1, k4, [p3, k2, C4F] 5x, p3, k5.

Work Rows 1 through 4 a total of 13 times, then work Row 1 once more.

Final Row: (RS) Sl-1, k7, *[k2tog] 3x, k3,* repeat to last 5 sts, k5. (43 sts)

Knit 10 rows (5 ridges of garter stitch), ending ready to begin a WS row.

Cable Pattern 6:

Set Up Row 1: (WS) Sl-1, k4, p33, k5.

Set Up Row 2: (RS) Sl-1, k8, inc in next st, k5, [inc in next 2 sts, k4] 4x, k4. (52 sts)

Begin Cable Pattern:

Row 1 and all WS rows: Sl-1, k4, p42, k5.

Row 2: Sl-1, k7, C4B, [k4, C4B] 4x, k8.

Row 4: Sl-1, k5, C4B, C4F, [k8, C4B, C4F] 2x, k6.

Row 6: Sl-1, knit to end.

Row 8: Sl-1, k5, C4F, C4B, [k8, C4F, C4B] 2x, k6.

Row 10: Repeat Row 2.

Row 12: Sl-1, k13, C4B, C4F, k8, C4B, C4F, k14.

Row 14: Repeat Row 6.

Row 16: Sl-1, k13, C4F, C4B, k8, C4F, C4B, k14.

Work Rows 1 through 16 a total of 3 times, then Rows 1 through 9 once more.

Final Row: (RS) Sl-1, k6, *[k2tog] 2x, k5, k2tog, k5,* repeat once, [k2tog] 2x, k9. (44 sts)

Knit 10 rows (5 ridges of garter stitch), ending ready to begin a WS row.

Cable Pattern 7:

Set Up Row 1: (WS) Sl-1, k7, [p4, k3, p2, k3] 2x, p4, k8.

Set Up Row 2: (RS) Sl-1, k4, p3, [inc in next 4 sts, p3, inc in next 2 sts, p3] 2x, inc in next 4 sts, p3, k5. (60 sts)

Begin Cable Pattern:

Row 1 and all WS rows: Sl-1, k7, [p8, k3, p4, k3] 2x, p8, k8.

Row 2: (RS) Sl-1, k4, p3, C4F, C4B, p3, C4F, p3, C4F, C4B, p3, C4B, p3, C4F, C4B, p3, k5.

Row 4: Sl-1, k4, p3, [k8, p3, k4, p3] 2x, k8, p3, k5.

Row 6: Sl-1, k4, p3, C4B, C4F, p3, C4F, p3, C4B, C4F, p3, C4B, p3, C4B, C4F, p3, k5.

Row 8: Repeat Row 4.

Row 10: Repeat Row 6.

Row 12: Repeat Row 4.

Row 14: Repeat Row 2.

Row 16: Repeat Row 4.

Work Rows 1 through 16 a total of 3 times, then Rows 1 through 7 once more.

Final Row: (RS) Sl-1, k4, k2tog, k1, *[k2tog] 4x, k3, [k2tog] 2x, k3,* repeat once, [k2tog] 4x, k8. (43 sts)

Knit 10 rows (5 ridges of garter stitch), ending ready to begin a WS row.

Cast off loosely, knitwise.

Work in yarn ends neatly. Rinse in cool water and roll in a towel to remove excess water. Lay scarf out on a flat surface and pull into shape. Blocking wires are helpful for nice straight edges.

Pin as needed and leave until completely dry. Note that while the scarf may pull out to about 9" wide while wet, it will relax back to about 8" wide afterward.

Enjoy!